The Truth *Be*
DAMNED

The Truth *Be* DAMNED

Janet Uhlar

ARCHWAY
PUBLISHING

Archway Publishing books may be ordered through booksellers or by contacting:

Archway Publishing
1663 Liberty Drive
Bloomington, IN 47403
www.archwaypublishing.com
1 (888) 242-5904

ISBN: 978-1-4808-5592-2 (sc)
ISBN: 978-1-4808-5593-9 (hc)
ISBN: 978-1-4808-5594-6 (e)

Library of Congress Control Number: 2018900546

Print information available on the last page.

Archway Publishing rev. date: 1/30/2018

Dedicated to the memory of my beloved son,

Josiah G. Tinney

June 6, 1988–December 6, 2014

and to my best friend,

Robert W. McCarthy

May 4, 1934--June 18, 2010

In Remembrance Of

Douglas Barrett
Seventeen years old; murdered by John Martorano on January 6, 1968. Doug existed; his life mattered.

Elizabeth F. Dickson
Nineteen years old; murdered by John Martorano on January 6, 1968. Liz existed; her life mattered.

Deborah Hussey
Twenty-six years old; murdered in January of 1985 by Steve Flemmi. From the innocent age of two, when Flemmi became her stepfather, Debbie didn't stand a chance.

Author's Note

The Truth Be Damned is a work of fiction, based on my experience as a juror in the 2013 federal trial *United States of America vs. James J. Bulger*. I seemed to be the perfect juror with no preconceived idea of the defendant's guilt or innocence. Going into the trial, only the name of "Whitey" Bulger was familiar to me. Who from Massachusetts hadn't heard of the notorious Irish mob boss? And, though I was from Massachusetts, I had lived outside the state for thirty years. During that time, I'd wanted nothing to do with tales of organized crime.

Going into the trial, I expected to be disturbed by the criminality of Bulger. What I certainly did not expect was for his attorney to declare in his opening statement that his client was guilty of many of the crimes with which he'd been charged. And I had no expectation of learning of the abyss of abuse and corruption that was revealed within the Boston US Attorney's Office and the FBI.

"Everyone knew it!" declared those who had stayed abreast of the story through the numerous newspaper articles on the subject and the many books published by Boston journalists and law enforcement officers. But I'm not talking only about what was purported in these writings. I'm referring to more, so much more, which, following the trial, I was shocked to discover the media did not mention. I needed to know why. And, I needed to know the story behind the "story."

My research has put me in contact with various individuals and has revealed facts that are quite alarming. I have communicated with Bulger since the end of the trial, through letters and also face-to-face. I have been in contact with Bulger's girlfriend Catherine Greig, former

FBI agent John Connolly, and witnesses for both the prosecution and the defense. I spoke to one of Bulger's attorneys as well as to former law enforcement officials who were involved in investigations pertaining to Bulger.

In Bulger's vast correspondence with me, he casually mentioned chronic insomnia and frequent hallucinations since the MKULTRA experimentation fifty years before. I sought to learn more on the subject, and obtained the Senate hearing dated August 3, 1977.

Though I present a fictional account of my experience, the reader should determine through his or her own investigation where the fiction ends and the truth begins.

In September of 2016, I was told, after waiting for over two hours in the visitation room of the US penitentiary where Jim Bulger is presently imprisoned, that I was no longer allowed to visit (I had visited him at this same prison previously). Jim Bulger waited on the other side of the doors of the visitation room for that same period of time as guards waited upon the official word of whether he would be allowed my visit.

Janet Uhlar
November 7, 2017

Chapter 1

Justice is but Truth in Action.
—Louis Brandeis (1856–1941), US
Supreme Court Associate Justice

"GET UP, DEVANEY!" THE CELL DOOR RATTLED OPEN
as the startled prisoner awoke. Before he had time to comprehend the
hostile order, a guard grabbed his shirt and dragged him off the flimsy
metal bed. The thin mattress and skimp bedding slid onto the dank
concrete floor alongside him.

Dressed only in a T-shirt, boxers, and socks, the elderly prisoner
shivered as a second guard yanked him to his feet. There were three
guards crowded into the small cell. These were the special guards assigned to Devaney by the Department of Justice. Each was young, buff,
and cocky as hell. Devaney had dubbed them the "goon squad" and
suspected that they were under orders of the assistant United States
attorney prosecuting the case to provide singularly ill treatment for
Devaney, treatment that no one within the walls of this prison had
before experienced; treatment that would shock even the ACLU, were
they concerned enough to respond to Devaney's pleas for help; treatment equivalent to that experienced by prisoners of war—probably
worse than that experienced at Guantánamo Bay.

"Get him out of here!" one guard yelled, as another pulled Devaney
out of the cell by the collar of his already overly stretched T-shirt.

"Search him."

The few items of clothing Devaney had on were yanked from his body for the ritualistic strip search. It happened at least eight times a day. The guards didn't care that this eighty-year-old prisoner was in solitary confinement with a sentry sitting outside the cell, watching over him 24/7. And they had a camera on the ceiling of the cell track-ing his every move—a camera they now planned to avoid.

The purpose of the strip searches, so it seemed to Devaney, was not only to humiliate the former mob boss but also to break him. The guards, like a pack of hyenas in heat, made the most of it each time, eight times a day. Crude remarks accompanied the violation of his genitals and the penetration of his orifices. This wasn't a standard procedure being carried out by trained professionals. These special guards seemed to take pleasure in degrading the elderly man. Devaney shuddered, as he always did, wondering if they were getting a personal thrill at his expense.

When they were done, the goon squad grabbed the naked Devaney, shoving him back into the cell and tossing his clothes after him. The heavy barred door slammed shut. The cell had been ransacked, as it always was during the strip search. The little that Devaney claimed as his own—his letters and books—was scattered on the floor, tossed into the sink with the faucet set at a steady drip, or draped across the toilet bowl, absorbing the water from within.

"We'll be back, Tommy!" one guard jeered at Devaney as he boast-fully sauntered past Assistant United States Attorney Carla Chavere, who had observed the entire scene from a distance—distant enough that Devaney didn't see her, distant enough to be out of any camera's range. Chavere was pleased with the performance of her goon squad.

~

Seventy of the original six hundred seventy-five citizens remained. We were the survivors. "The ignorant" would be a more accurate description. We were the last of the jury pool, sitting in a rather small federal courtroom on the final day of jury selection. It had been a long, arduous process, during which we'd been herded about like sheep being led to the slaughter.

2

That's exactly how I feel, like a penned animal awaiting my doom, I thought, as I sat shivering in the overly air-conditioned room on a hard wooden bench seemingly designed to be uncomfortable.

We had started the selection process exactly a week before. On that day, all 675 of us had been ushered into a large assembly hall with hundreds of folding chairs in neat rows facing a wooden podium flanked by two small tables. The walls in the hall were impressively inscribed with lengthy inspirational passages by renowned US justices Oliver Wendell Holmes and Louis D. Brandeis.

The jury administrator and his staff handed out packets of paperwork that included various instructions, phone numbers, a pen, and a page to fill out regarding the mode of transportation we would use to get to the courthouse, what parking lot we would use if we chose to drive, and how far we had to travel. Also within my packet was a small brooch with the insignia of the US federal court on it, as well as a small piece of paper upon which the number 104 had been handwritten. I looked at the brooch, wondering if I was supposed to put it on. Uncertain, I placed it back in the envelope and began to fill out the form. Name: *Alexandra Fisher;* Address: *26 Chatham Rd., Manchester-by-the-Sea, Massachusetts …*

After turning in our transportation sheets, we all watched a short film on federal jury duty. When that was over, all was silent for about ten minutes. It seemed that none of the potential jurors dared talk. Some had books to read.

Why didn't I bring one? was my frustrated thought.

I occupied my mind by reading the passages on the walls, in which Justices Holmes and Brandeis encouraged broad and open-minded discussion as a right and duty of American citizens. Somehow, I felt a distant sense of comfort in reading the words.

These passages are meant to inspire potential jurors for the deliberation process, reminding us that we have the responsibility and the power to think outside the box.

From the entrance to the hall, the voice of the jury administrator bellowed out, "All rise!" The shuffle of 675 bodies standing filled the room. An older man adorned in a judge's robe entered the hall with an entourage of five. Each took his or her respective place behind the podium or at one of the tables.

The judge introduced himself as Peter Blake.

Judge Blake introduced those assembled at the tables. To his left was the prosecution team, which consisted of two well-dressed assistant US attorneys. The senior of the attorneys prosecuting the case was Carla Chavere. She was clearly nearing retirement age. A bit overweight, she presented herself with an air of dignity. Her face was perfectly made up and her nails neatly polished. Her snow-white hair, styled in a cropped bob, seemed to attest to wisdom. Chavere sat with her head tilted back just enough to point her nose upward.

Does she have a problem with her neck, or is her arrogance that obvious?

Her body language—hand on the hip when she stood to say her obligatory hello, and seemingly exaggerated hand gestures and facial expressions—led me to believe the latter was true.

Beside Chavere was Dick Altier. Although younger, Altier was introduced as the lead prosecutor. Middle-aged with a full head of neatly groomed light brown hair, he offered an immediate attraction with his purchased professionalism. Tall in stature, with a trim body and perfect posture, Altier commanded respect from innocent onlookers.

I bet he served in the Marine Corps. He carries himself with such composure; he must be a veteran officer.

The defense team was seated at the table to the right of Judge Blake. Curt Jordan was an older man of African American descent with a neatly trimmed salt-and-pepper beard that complemented a full head of matching hair. Jordan was tall, slim, and smartly dressed. His was a quiet, polite, and stoic presence.

Emotionless; almost robotic. Perfect for a defense attorney, I figured.

Then there was Defense Attorney Rob Willis, a younger man, Scandinavian in appearance with his light blond hair and pure blue eyes. He was of average height with a firmly toned form.

Expensive suit. Looks timid for a high-end attorney. Must just be starting out. He seems more afraid of the entire process than I am.

Between Jordan and Willis sat the defendant, Thomas D. Devaney.

He was referred to as "Sly" by his enemies, of which he seemed to have many. Though I knew little about the man, I was aware that he was said to have wreaked havoc in the streets of Boston for three decades as the leader of the Irish mob, referred to as the Old Harbor Gang. The crimes he was said to have committed? You name it and he did it—allegedly.

He was quite aged, thin, and frail. He seemed weak, perhaps ill. His attorneys assisted him into the assembly hall and then into the chair between them at the table. Barely able to stand on his own, he struggled to get to his feet when allowed to offer a short greeting to those assembled. His voice was faint and barely audible.

This is the scary Sly Devaney? I don't think he's gonna make it through this trial!

Devaney was of average height with short gray hair. He was clean-shaven and neatly dressed in a light blue Henley shirt, dungarees, and white sneakers. Except for the greeting, Devaney was silent and still, his eyes cast downward.

Before jury selection even began, the media was referring to this trial as the "trial of the decade." It was expected to last at least four months: the *United States of America vs. Thomas D. Devaney*. Upon learning that the US Attorney's Office had issued an indictment against him, Devaney had vanished. He remained on the FBI's Ten Most Wanted list for eighteen years. It turned out that all the while he was hiding in plain sight. He'd rented an apartment in McLean, Virginia, only twenty miles from FBI Headquarters in Washington, DC.

That was all I knew of the sickly old man seated between his attorneys at the table to my left. I was seated in the front row, no more than twenty feet from the notorious Sly Devaney. It was hard to believe that this aged man could have inflicted such horror. Also hard to believe was that he was a cold-blooded murderer. In my mind, he wasn't.

Innocent until proven guilty, the right to legal counsel and representation, and the right to a trial by a jury of one's peers are foundational principles in the United States. As a US history teacher, I was keenly aware that those who had fought in the American Revolution had understood, firsthand, the horror of what not being granted these civil liberties meant. They were willing to die to obtain these basic rights. *How can I, no matter the inconvenience or fear, evade this sacred duty? How can I evade this sacred right of the defendant, no matter how vile he's said to be?* Regardless of the noble argument within my head, I was still afraid, and hoped to be set free.

After introducing the key players, Judge Blake read the long list of indictments against Devaney, which fell under the complex Racketeer Influenced and Corrupt Organizations Act. This act, referred to as RICO, was enacted in 1970 by the federal court as a means of controlling organized crime. The charges against Devaney consisted of twenty-five counts and twenty-eight predicate acts, which included racketeering, money laundering, extortion, weapons violations, and numerous murders. It was overwhelming.

As soon as he completed reading the indictments, the judge instructed us to stand and raise our right hands. He began to read an oath, which we didn't have the opportunity to review or refuse. In the controlled chaos, before I knew what was happening, I, along with the others, completed the oath.

My thoughts were chaotic. *What happened? I'm not even sure what I just swore to!*

The judge, attorneys, and defendant then left the room, and we potential jurors began the vetting process. For this we were instructed to fill out a lengthy questionnaire. I answered honestly, even made certain to mention that I had a book under contract, thinking they might not want a juror who they suspected might turn around and write about the case. As for the possibility of my writing about this trial, as a high school teacher with a book to be published on forgotten heroes of the American Revolution, I had no desire whatsoever to write about *United States vs. Devaney.* Organized crime just wasn't my thing.

We all turned in our questionnaires and were told that we could leave for the weekend. That evening we were to call a particular phone number contained in the packet of paperwork, for further instructions.

I fought the rush hour traffic out of the city as I headed to my home in Manchester-by-the-Sea, located thirty miles north of Boston. During the off-season, this quaint coastal town, located on a rocky promontory known as Cape Ann, is serene. It offers few attractions for tourists, so even throughout the summer months it is spared a full influx of vacationers. The small New England town's natural beauty with its picturesque harbor, unique beach, and historic homes is calming to the soul. A walk along the half-mile stretch of the town's shoreline known as Singing Beach was an almost daily routine I'd started when we first moved here ten years ago. My children would often join me, and we'd enjoy the almost musical squeak of the sand beneath our feet. On those rare occasions when my husband was home on leave, he would too.

I had grown up in neighboring Salem, where my mother and siblings still lived. When the older of our two children neared high school age, my husband, Paul, a career army officer, insisted we purchase a home close to my family. He felt the children needed stability in their teen years. Though I grieved the fact that in doing so we would all see less of him, I understood. Except for the frequent and often lengthy separations from Paul, I never regretted the move.

On my way home, I drove by the beach, hoping to find a parking space in the small lot. There were none. Disappointed, I went straight home.

I parked the car and walked to the house. The summer sun felt good on my body, which was still chilled by the frigid temperature of the courtroom. Once inside, I used the bathroom, poured myself a glass of merlot, grabbed my laptop, and went out on the deck to soak up the rays of the June sun. Still shaken by the vow I'd sworn to earlier, I was determined to pull up the Juror's Oath on the computer. I discovered that the oath was usually given when jury selection was complete, but subject to the individual judge's discretion, it could be administered at the start of jury selection. The oath itself could not be found, which frustrated me.

My initial thought was to call an attorney friend and ask him what exactly I had sworn. I picked up my cell phone, found his number, and pressed Call. As my finger pushed the button, I realized that I, along with the other potential jurors, had been cautioned by the judge not to discuss anything with anybody. Quickly, I moved my finger to End, canceling the call. Apparently, it was too late. My phone instantly rang, and caller ID displayed the number I had just canceled. I answered.

"Alex! You hung up on me!" Bob's voice called out.

"Dialed accidently," I lied.

"I've got someone on call waiting. I'll see you at the board meeting Tuesday."

"Don't think I'll make it," I shot back, having totally forgotten about the meeting.

"You okay?"

"Yeah. Committed to something else." That certainly wasn't a lie.

"Free for dinner that night?"

"Sure."

"I'll pick you up at seven." Bob hung up.

Sighing, I stared at the phone for a moment. "Damn! Why did I commit to having dinner? I have no idea what to expect next week," I said to no one, disgusted at myself for being so easily pulled into situations. First the oath, now dinner with Bob. I needed to figure out a way to cancel. That thought added to my frustration. Not only had I allowed myself to be easily manipulated, but also I was searching for lies to correct my inability to obtain control.

After making a sandwich, I sat down to watch the news. Every station was talking about the Devaney case. I turned off the television, ate my sandwich in silence, and then took a shower. When I got out of the shower, there was a message from a friend. "Alexandra! It's Nancy! You never answer the phone anymore. I'm having a pool party next Friday. Just us girls. Give me a call!"

I erased the message. Next Friday? My life was on hold. I couldn't make plans, or explain why.

Pouring myself another glass of merlot, I considered that it wasn't good to drink alone. "But I am alone, so who gives a damn?" I mumbled, toasting the air. After taking a sip, I dutifully dialed the number to the courthouse. As anticipated, I was instructed to report back on Monday morning. I took a gulp from the wineglass.

I determined to put jury selection out of my mind and to enjoy the weekend as much as possible. The weather promised to be warm and sunny. My son was to arrive home from West Point tomorrow. Ilona had already told me that she would come down from New Hampshire with little Paul to visit her brother. It promised to be a perfect weekend, with my children home and my grandbaby to spoil.

~

Monday came all too quickly. Our numbers had significantly dwindled. My estimation was that there were only about two hundred potential jurors present. On that day of jury selection, the attorneys would eliminate certain members of the jury pool through a process known as "removal for cause." We were herded into a large courtroom. Every twenty minutes or so, the jury administrator entered the room and called out assigned numbers of particular jurors. These jurors were escorted to a different room, where Judge Blake and the attorneys would ask specific questions to clarify answers on the questionnaire. Depending on the responses, the juror would be dismissed or instructed to return to the courtroom. In all, about forty potential jurors were singled out of the group. Few returned. I likened undergoing the private questioning to entering a star chamber. Except for the opportunity to personally meet the attractive attorney Dick Altier, I dreaded the thought of being summoned.

The hours passed slowly. I remembered to bring a book and a warm sweater, but I wished I had a cushion for the hard bench. My number was never called, which meant they had no problem with my answers in the questionnaire—not even the fact that I was an author. *Not a good sign,* I realized. Finally, when I felt certain that I could no longer sit on the bench, those of us who remained were dismissed for the day, and again told to call that evening to learn our status.

I called, and was told to return the following day. *Dammit!*

~

Here I was among the 70 remaining out of a jury pool of 675. We assembled in the jury hall and were escorted to the elevators. An assistant to the jury administrator ushered us into the elevator on the second floor, and another greeted us as we exited the elevator on the fifth. We were then led to the open foyer, which accommodated five courtrooms. Up until now, we had entered courtrooms through side doors. This was the first time we were taken to the main entrance. The marble floors and oak-paneled inner wall gave the foyer a majestic feel. Each courtroom had large, heavy oak doors. The outer wall was of glass, offering a stunning view of Boston Harbor. The water glistened under the brilliant sun; boats sailed softly upon the shimmering water.

Here, we were lined up according to our jury pool number. Today I felt like a prisoner, ordered about and watched over by guards. A young woman was behind me. We struck up a conversation. She shared her concern about being put on the jury. With three young children at home, she felt it would be a great hardship. Thus far, the judge and attorneys hadn't agreed. The young mother was emotionally distraught. We were abruptly ordered to be silent.

How many have a similar story? I wondered.

In silence, we were led into a small courtroom. Judge Blake was at his bench before us, and the attorneys and Mr. Devaney at their respective tables. Two well-dressed men hovered near Devaney and his attorneys.

Probably US marshals, I surmised.

They all were standing and staring at us as we entered. The benches in the gallery to our right were already filled.

Reporters? I wondered.

A sketch artist stood in the front row, her back resting against the wall as she balanced her large pad in her left hand and busily worked at capturing the moment with the pencil in her right. Another sketch artist was positioned similarly in the front corner of the gallery to our left. We were ushered into specific rows.

Again, we waited, but this time, we were subjected to the irritating scratching sound of a noise machine utilized to cover the conversations between the judge and the attorneys as they worked to eliminate members of the jury pool through strike for cause and peremptory challenges. It was obvious that the stakes were high; the stress and emotion of the attorneys came through loud and clear in their body language.

My purposeful ignorance of anything to do with organized crime, a decision I'd made years before, not wanting to fill my mind with stories of thugs, might now prove to immerse me into this dark world. *Ignorance is supposed to be bliss, but not in this case. But there's still a chance. I'll probably be dismissed.* I knew that only 1 percent of the state's population is called for federal jury duty. From this, 675 were plunged into the jury pool of the Devaney case. Now, 18 from the 70 remaining would be seated. *The odds are in my favor,* I told myself. *But it's not looking good.*

I'd stopped buying lottery tickets long before, as my Irish blood was less than pure and, therefore, never seemed to bring me any luck. Now, somehow, I knew my number—Juror 104—would play out. Somehow, I knew I wouldn't be released from my civic obligation this day. A shiver ran through my body. From the frigid temperature of the courtroom or from fear? I couldn't tell. Probably a bit of both.

Whatever happens today, Alex, you're a part of history in the making. These constant worries are keeping you from living in the moment. I determined to clear my thoughts and to watch, learn from, and experience this event as it unfolded before me, shivering all the while. I once heard a yoga instructor say that a lengthy exhalation encouraged calmness. I took a short breath in and released it slowly. It seemed to work. *Yoga classes might be a good idea,* I told myself.

The four attorneys involved in the case gathered at the judge's bench like merchants at market buying and selling their wares. Their animated squabble, though silent to us, was interesting to observe. Each carried a legal pad to which they frequently referred. After a few minutes of what appeared to be quarrelling in unison, they went to their assigned seats at the tables before the judge's bench. The prosecution was to the right of the judge; the defense, to the left.

Of course, I was drawn to Dick Altier. *I wonder if he's married?* The thought immediately prompted guilt. It had only been three years since my husband died. Every time I found myself attracted to a man, I felt I was betraying Paul.

It was only strong, powerful men who caught my attention, and Altier was certainly that. Though even he would not hold a candle to Paul. A retired army colonel, Paul had proudly served in the Green Berets for twenty-eight years. It was difficult, given the lengthy separations and secrecy his position demanded. Paul's retirement began for us a second honeymoon that promised to last forever. The kids would soon be out of the house, and we would have all the time in the world to ourselves. But "happily ever after" was just in fairy tales, and my life was no fairy tale. Less than a year after Paul retired, he was killed when his car plummeted off the road into a deep ravine during an ice storm. Paul's death was instant. He didn't suffer. We who loved him did.

My gaze remained on Altier as my thoughts wandered. He, along with the other attorneys, was writing hurriedly on a legal pad. Suddenly he stood, distracting me from my morbid thoughts. The four attorneys marched to the side of the judge's bench again. Once more the noise machine came on, and the quarrelling in unison began.

What if I am seated? Financially I'm good, between my pay and Paul's pension, but I'd be out for the remainder of this school year. Will I be able to return to class by the end of August for the next school year? The questions weren't new; they were ever present, and silently screaming to be answered once more. *So much for clearing your thoughts and living in the moment, Alex.*

Will I be in danger? Will my family be in danger? What if we're sequestered? Being on a jury that might declare a head mobster guilty could be a problem, to say the least. If we're sequestered, I'd have no time with my son on summer break. And little Paul is growing by leaps and bounds each day. I'd miss so much! Family and friends want me to lie and get out of this jury pool. I understand their concerns; I have them too. But how can I lie?

How can I shirk this duty, and teach my students about the sacrifices made to obtain it? The rights of an American citizen throughout the judicial process are the backbone of the United States. If that were to be broken, then we'd become powerless as a nation.

The judge's voice addressing the jury pool startled me. It was done. "The clerk will call out the numbers you have been assigned. Upon hearing your number, you are free to leave. You are released from jury duty. If your number is not called, remain sitting where you are."

I glanced at the paperwork in my hand to double check the number I had been answering to for days. *One hundred four. Yes, one hundred four,* I nervously assured myself.

The clerk began. Perspiration beaded on my body, even though I was cold. I pulled my sweater closed, with my arms folded tight. My heart began to pound. *Please, Jesus, be close to me,* was my silent prayer. The numbers continued to be called; men and women scurried toward the courtroom door in their escape. How I wished I were among them. I closed my eyes and listened to the numbers as they neared mine. I took a short breath and exhaled slowly.

"Eighty-six, ninety-nine, one hundred two, one hundred sixteen—"

One hundred four, she didn't say one hundred four! In a panic, I took a deep breath, keeping my eyes closed until all the numbers had been read. Upon opening my eyes, I looked about me at the seventeen remaining souls. Each of them was looking about the room too, and like me, appeared stunned. Each was pale, wide-eyed, and in shock.

"When your number is called," the judge began, "you will move to the jury box, where you will be assigned a seat."

How can this be? All too fast! This isn't really happening. … I don't want this.

Our jury pool numbers were called out one last time. Robotically, I responded to my number and was guided to the jury box and seated in the twelfth chair—juror number 12. The eyes of the attorneys were fixed upon us. Thomas Devaney scanned our faces, seemingly avoiding eye contact. The media and sketch artists, in their own little corner of the courtroom, seemed to stare us down as they somehow simultaneously tweeted, scribbled notes, and outlined our forms. Indeed, we were like animals, now boxed in our small cage for all present to study, analyze, and poke fun at.

In this state of shock, we were given jury instructions. In this state of shock, I barely heard them—nor did my fellow jurors, I was sure. We now viewed the courtroom from a different perspective. The jury box was raised slightly, and was situated to the far right, just forward of the judge's bench. His bench was raised significantly above the level of the jury box. Directly in front of the judge, also raised, though to a lesser degree, was the area for the judge's clerk and court reporter. To their left was a space for the court stenographer. This area was known as the Well, and no one was to approach or walk past it without permission from the judge. Opposite the jury box was the boxed-in witness stand, raised to the same level. A microphone sat on the small table built into the stand. Behind the witness stand was a large lattice panel with a door to the left. Set back a bit, in the center of the room, were the tables where the attorneys and Thomas Devaney sat. The defense team and defendant occupied the table to the judge's left, and the prosecution occupied the table to his right. Between the table for the prosecution and the jury box, facing the witness stand, was a lectern. Behind the attorneys' tables was a wooden railing, sometimes referred to as the Bar. Only the attorneys, their clients, and witnesses could go past the railing into this appointed area. Behind the railing was the gallery, where the reporters, sketch artists, and spectators sat. The gallery was divided into three sections of hard oak benches.

The interior design of the courtroom was pleasant. Oak paneling ran throughout, coordinating with the furnishings. A motif of three large arches enclosed the judge's bench, the witness stand, and the jury box. Each was defined by oak molding, with a graceful stencil design above. A similar stencil on the ceiling was centered above the theater of the courtroom, forming a perfect circle.

We were shown the jury room, given our jury badges, and escorted to the back exit of the courthouse. Here, we were dismissed, after being instructed to report back the next day by 9:00 a.m.

Not sequestered, thank God!

Once outside, we were approached by the media. "Have you been seated on the jury?" they called out incessantly. We each went off in a different direction, keeping silent as instructed.

Even though the judge implied that we should not tell anyone we were involved with the Devaney trial, the reality was that family, close friends, and our employers already knew. The media had announced when jury selection was to begin. Those close to me knew I had been summoned to jury duty on that same date. They would also know I was seated by my daily treks to Boston.

My mom was worried. I determined that it would be best if I went to visit and tell her in person. From the courthouse parking lot, I drove directly to Salem, stopping downtown at a favorite flower shop to pick up a pretty summer bouquet for her. I remembered that Bob Costa's law office was around the corner.

I wonder if he's back from the board meeting? Probably best to cancel dinner in person.

I left the florist and walked toward Bob's office. As I turned the corner, he was approaching from the opposite end. We met at the entrance to the building.

"Alex! The meeting adjourned about an hour ago. You were missed," the former district attorney and US congressman said, giving me a hug and a kiss on the cheek, ever the politician. "You're as beautiful as ever," he stated, looking me up and down.

I was flattered. Bob was attractive both in appearance and personality. Though in his midsixties, his hair, as dark as mine, didn't show a hint of gray. And though slightly overweight, he carried his six-foot frame well. He preferred to dress casually but always looked sharp. He had lost his wife to cancer many years before. As one of the most eligible bachelors in town, he had quite a following of female admirers. He enjoyed the company of the fairer sex, and, I learned, he had been in a couple of long-term relationships.

Twenty years my senior, Bob flirted but never came on to me. In fact, he often referred to me as "kiddo," giving the distinct impression that I was too young. I knew better. Some of the women I had seen him with were younger than I. All of them were blonde.

Most from a box, I bet. Perhaps that's it: the congressman prefers blondes. Or maybe it's because I'm a widow. I found myself questioning his seeming lack of interest and wondering why it bothered me.

Bob and I had become friends through my support in his campaigns, my son's internship, and our joint involvement on the board of trustees of the Wounded Soldiers' Trust.

"A bit early for dinner," he joked, looking at his watch. "How's Charlie?"

"Just back from the Point."

"That kid has enormous potential. I'm ready to prep him."

Bob had envisioned Charlie as a politician from the day my son approached him with a challenging question on the steps of the Capitol during his high school field trip.

"All in due time, Mr. Congressman." I laughed.

"Thought you were tied up today."

"Just got back from Boston."

"Hope you avoided the federal courthouse. I hear the media influx has traffic all tied up. The jury was seated today. Trial's supposed to start tomorrow."

"What trial?" I asked sheepishly, and then looked downward.

"Devaney's trial," he stated. I didn't look up. "You're not on that jury …" It was more a statement than a question.

I looked at him with a weak smile.

"Dammit, Alex! Tell me you're not."

I said nothing.

A car passed slowly. The driver called out to the former congressman. Bob returned the greeting, addressing the driver by name. After the car had passed, he looked about, as though concerned someone might be watching.

"I can't talk to you. I'm too close. We can't be seen together or we'll both be dragged into federal court to swear under oath that we didn't discuss Devaney."

"We haven't," I protested.

"Alex, you don't understand. When I was district attorney"—he hesitated and looked around again—"I was too involved. I know too much. We can't talk." He leaned in and kissed my cheek. "I'll call you when the verdict's in, I promise."

"I guess this means dinner's off?" Determined for days to get out of it, I was surprised that I suddenly felt disappointed.

He smiled sadly while squeezing my upper arm. "I'll make it up to you, kiddo." He moved away from me toward the door.

I turned my head to look at him. "Am I in any danger?"

His eyes reflected concern as they met mine. "Not from Devaney. We'll talk when it's over." Bob turned his head away, and disappeared into the building.

I stood there feeling like a fool. In my naïveté regarding the Thomas "Sly" Devaney story, I'd never considered that Bob, as district attorney for a county neighboring Boston during the years Devaney was active, might be involved in trying to prosecute him. It was something that had never come up in conversation. If I hadn't already fully understood the gravity of the situation I had been plunged into, I did now.

I continued to stand there as people passed, the bouquet of flowers resting on my arm. I was in the world but secluded from it. There would be no one to talk to about the horror and confusion I was to witness in the months to come, not even my fellow jurors. I was surrounded by people but utterly alone.

~

How does one prepare for a trial? I tossed and turned the night before opening statements. Questions from the trivial and mundane to the pertinent and uncommon filled my mind. Though the week had seemed to drag out, in truth, it all had happened so quickly. My world was now inside out. Plans and commitments still had to be addressed. I needed to contact the headmaster of the private school where I taught to inform him of the uncertainty of my schedule.

In regard to the trial itself, I had minimal experience, only having served on a jury in a district court. That trial had lasted a few hours. This trial would be very different!

Will I recall enough throughout the weeks of testimony? We can take notes, but will my notes capture the words and emotions of the witnesses and attorneys? Or will I, in the drama of the moment, fail to take accurate and descriptive notes? Am I worthy of making decisions that will affect the life of the defendant—and the lives of so many others involved in this trial? The questions continued to race through my mind as I drifted off to sleep.

Chapter 2

There is no such thing as half justice. You either have
justice or you don't. You either have a democracy
in which everyone—including the powerful—
is subject to the rule of law or you don't.
—John Joseph Moakley (1927–
2001), US Congressman

DEVANEY HIT THE FLOOR WITH A HARD THUD.
Disoriented, he scanned the unfamiliar surroundings. "What's goin'
on?" he whispered breathlessly. He was still in a cage, but it was exactly
that—a cage. Moldy straw scattered the floor. The pungent stench of
animal dung permeated the wood. A faint deep growl came from
the shadows. Was the creature within or beyond the cage? Devaney
couldn't tell. Carefully, as though in slow motion, he turned his head
to assess his surroundings. Would the cage prove to protect him from
harm or make him easy prey? The roar of Devaney's pounding heart
drowned out the predator's snarl.

Footsteps of an approaching figure went unnoticed on account
of Devaney's internal pounding. The sudden appearance of Carla
Chavere forced a visible jerk of Devaney's body as a gasp emitted from
his lips. Chavere's laugh was a ghastly cackle echoing off the unseen
walls beyond. Placing her hands on the bars of the cage, she began to
shake them.

In response to the rocking motion, Devaney lay flat, hugging the
filth of the floor. He heard the growl grow louder, spurred on by the

rattling of the cage. Devaney realized that the animal was above him. On top of the cage? Or within it, upon a ledge? The uncertainty was maddening. He heard the animal move about as though positioning itself to pounce.

Scrambling to the closest corner, Devaney curled his body into a ball, letting out a muffled cry as the animal swooped upon him with a fierce roar.

Chavere's laughter intensified.

~

The eighteen jurors wandered in around the same time. We were greeted by a friendly court bailiff, an older man who introduced himself as Smitty. Smitty explained that he would usher us to and from the courtroom, and stand watch whenever we were in the jury room.

"Standard procedure in any trial," he assured us. He used a key to open the jury room door. "Whenever you're assembled in this room, the door will be locked so that no one can enter. Again, standard procedure." Though Smitty sounded convincing, I couldn't help but wonder if it truly was "standard procedure."

As we entered the room, we looked upon twelve damnably heavy chairs neatly tucked in around the matching polished rectangular table. Six identical chairs stood like sentinels against the wall to the front of the building. Large windows adorned this wall, looking out upon the bustling city of Boston, and the courthouse parking lot six stories below. The opposite wall had a large TV-like screen hanging upon it, with the impressive insignia of the United States of America Federal Court as the screensaver. In the back of the room was a large old-style black chalkboard on wheels, pushed against the wall between two bathrooms. In the front was a small kitchenette and closet.

A fresh pot of coffee awaited us in the kitchenette. Shortly after our arrival, two large trays containing muffins, bagels, and sliced fruit were brought in by members of the cafeteria staff and set upon the table.

"If there's a dietary need required, or a specific item desired, let us know," one of the uniformed women offered. We thanked her, almost in unison, and laughed at ourselves.

"Looking good," I said. "We're united!"

Each of us gravitated to the food and caffeine, a common ground that started small talk between us. As each claimed a chair, we shared our first names. The jury consisted of six women and twelve men. There was some racial diversity with four of Asian, African, and Hispanic descent. The age range was wide, with one young man who appeared barely old enough to vote and three senior citizens.

Upon finishing our therapeutic cup of coffee, there was a knock on the door followed by Smitty's entrance. "It's time," he announced. Silence filled the room, along with a distinct sense of apprehension. Smitty ushered us into the foyer in front of the elevators and leading to the top of the stairs. "I want you to line up by your jury number," he instructed. We did. Smitty then asked if any of us needed to use the elevator. No one responded. He led us down a flight of stairs, where we were greeted by Judge Blake's clerk, Amy. We stood before a closed wooden door facing Amy; her hand was on the knob.

"Are you ready?" she asked. Some nodded in response. I couldn't help but wonder what would happen if one of us said no. No time to think about it, as Amy quickly pulled the door open and called out to a courtroom filled with people, "All rise for the jury." I followed the elderly male juror in front of me, who was named George. Behind me was a middle-aged man named Richard.

As the door opened, we saw that the faces immediately before us were those of Assistant US Attorneys Chavere and Altier. Their expressions were intense. Seated behind their table was a woman and two men, each with laptops before them and boxes surrounding them on the floor. Each one stared at us as we walked into the courtroom.

I met their eyes, lingering a bit longer on Altier, and then glanced to their right at the defense attorneys and their client. The tension was apparent on their faces as well. Behind them sat two women, also with laptops and boxes of files.

They must be paralegals, I assumed.

All eyes were upon us. A pen and a spiral notebook with our jury number written on it sat upon each of our seats. Once we were seated, Judge Blake greeted us and gave opening instructions explaining what we were there to judge and what we were not to judge. I was surprised and relieved to hear that we were each to determine in our own mind the credibility of a witness. The fact that the witnesses were under oath did not mean they were telling the truth, regardless of who they were, the judge explained. Also, we were encouraged to bring our life experiences into our personal decision-making process Again, he instructed us not to speak about the trial among ourselves until deliberations. And again, he read the long list of charges in the indictment, this time with a bit of explanation.

With this completed, Assistant US Attorney Dick Altier was invited to give his opening statement. And so it began.

Altier's presentation was impressive. He was blunt, rattling through crimes, dates, and names, all of which had my head spinning.

"Devaney was the mastermind behind numerous violent criminal acts. He is a cold-blooded murderer who was protected by law enforcement," Altier professed. Then he boldly declared to us that the prosecution would certainly prove Devaney to be guilty of all charges, beyond a reasonable doubt. When Altier finished, he received an approving nod from fellow prosecutor Carla Chavere as he sat down beside her at their table.

Defense Attorney Curt Jordan was given permission to speak to the jury. He began by comparing the prosecution's case against the defendant to a fine meal served in a restaurant.

"It will be thoroughly thought out and prepared to seeming perfection. The presentation will appear attractive, appealing, and complete. But such a presentation can be deceiving," he warned.

Jordan went on to discuss the corruption in all branches of law enforcement in Boston in the 1960s through the '80s. He spoke of Thomas Devaney's criminal partners—Tony Diavolo, Vinnie Giuda, and Ben James—and how they had become key informants for the assistant US attorneys. They accused Devaney of masterminding various murders and crimes of that they themselves had carried out. By implicating Devaney, these men were spared the death sentence and given minimal prison time for their confessed horrific crimes. Some also received substantial monetary compensation for their questionable information.

"By implicating Thomas Devaney, these men were offered freedom. Therefore, how much of their testimony can you believe?" Defense Attorney Jordan paused, scanning each juror's face. "Make no mistake. My client is indeed guilty of certain crimes, but the purchased testimony of these witnesses cannot prove beyond a reasonable doubt which crimes he committed."

I was stunned! *If Devaney is willing to acknowledge through his attorney that he is guilty, then why are we here?* I glanced over at Thomas Devaney and Defense Attorney Rob Willis to see if they were upset by Jordan's statement. Devaney had been writing on a legal pad on the table before him and seemed totally engrossed. Willis was looking through paperwork. Neither seemed at all disturbed by Curt Jordan's words.

My eyes darted to Chavere and Altier. They shared a glance, indicating to me that they *were* surprised by Jordan's statement. I then quickly scanned the members of the media I could see to the right of the jury box. They were busily sending out messages on their cell phones, again an indication that Curt Jordan's statement was unexpected.

What is this all about? I questioned, as Jordan finished his opening statement and sat down. There was no search for an approving nod from his partner or client. In fact, neither stopped what they were doing to look at him.

We were dismissed early by the judge. All within the courtroom stood as we were marched out the rear door and up the staircase to the jury room. A few dared to murmur what I was wondering: *If Devaney's own attorney is acknowledging his guilt, why are we here?* No one answered—we had no answers. And we weren't even supposed to voice such questions. But one juror surprised us all as he loudly blurted, "This trial is gonna be over in two weeks, tops. Devaney is as guilty as hell!"

"Larry! You can't talk about it yet," Irene, an older juror, immediately called out.

"Why not? It's obvious he's guilty! His own attorney said so!"

"We're supposed to consider him innocent until *proven* guilty," I interjected, but I was grateful that Larry didn't respond. Under the circumstances of the defense admitting Devaney's guilt, I too was confused and really wouldn't know what to say if my statement were challenged.

"Did you go through the witness list we were all shown on day one of jury selection? Did you see how many witnesses they're gonna call? Did you hear the judge say it would take three to four months?" Dan, a young juror, exclaimed.

"That's nonsense," Larry argued.

"Are you saying the judge is wrong?" Chris, another young juror, asked incredulously.

Larry fell silent. We all gathered our belongings and left.

The ride home offered me the opportunity to churn the opening statements over in my mind, as well as Larry's disturbing remarks. I felt sick inside, sensing that my life was to be forever changed, and not for the good. This was only day one. I had four months ahead with no one to talk to, nowhere to vent. Of all the family and friends I might seek out to find comfort, it was Bob Costa's company I found myself wanting. Was it his knowledge, not only of the intricacies of this case but also of the ins and outs of the court system, that drew me? Or was it the strength he offered in having such knowledge? Regardless, he was now forbidden fruit, and that alone made him most desirable.

Day two began bright and early. Awake at 6:00, in the car by 7:00, and stopping at Dunkin' Donuts for a cup of coffee shortly thereafter. This was to be my routine for a long, long time.

I picked up the newspaper while waiting to order the coffee. The Devaney trial was plastered over the front page. Quickly, I put the paper down, looking around to see if anyone was watching. Somehow, I felt guilty for even seeing the headline.

Purposefully arriving early at the courthouse, I parked the car and strolled along Boston's Harborwalk. At the Boston Children's Museum, I stopped and looked at the waterway. Directly across was the Boston Tea Party Ships & Museum, with replicas of the ships flanking each side of the museum building. The Harborwalk led to Fan Pier, where the courthouse is located. At the back of the courthouse, a glimmering glass wall rose almost one hundred feet in the air, with an unobstructed view of historic Boston Harbor. A pristine harbor park adorned the back and one side of the building, with tasteful displays explaining the history of Fan Pier. It is here that Boston meets the open sea; one has a panoramic view of the impressive architecture of the Financial District, East Boston, and the Harbor Islands.

Walking on the path surrounding the courthouse, I stopped to read the various engravings on the building. They were excerpts from various state constitutions discussing justice, and notable quotes from wise and distinguished US attorneys.

Though the security guards within the courthouse greeted me with warm smiles and friendly hellos, I felt awkward as I stumbled through the routine of checking in. My cell phone was not allowed in the courthouse. The guard kept it, placing a sticky tab with a number on it, and giving me another tab with the same number so I could claim my phone at the end of the day. My purse and belongings were x-rayed. I walked through the scanner, grabbing the jury badge from my purse on the other side and attaching it to my sweater. I then had to sign in on the sheet marked for Judge Blake's case. The guards were patient, and assured me that this process would become second nature in no time at all.

Coming off the elevator, I was greeted by Smitty. He was seated at a small table just outside the closed jury room, already dutifully attending his post. I noticed that he picked up a pen, looked down, and marked a paper on the table before him.

Attendance, I surmised. *And he already knows who we are.*

There were already seven jurors in the room. Each smiled and said hello. I struggled to recall their names as I prepared my second cup of coffee. I sat down, choosing the empty chair at the far head of the table, where two jurors were already seated on both sides.

"I put my name on the chalkboard," Richard announced, as he brought his coffee to the table. I had no trouble remembering his name, as he was the juror who sat to my left in the jury box. "Maybe if one of us puts our name up each day, we'll have an easier time associating the name with a face."

"Good idea," I agreed. Then I stumbled over the names of the other six present, getting only one right. That one was Dan, who was now seated to my immediate right. He was a younger man with a kind face. The others reintroduced themselves to me. Maureen, seated at the opposite head of the table, seemed to be an energetic woman, younger than I. She, it was announced by Richard, had made the coffee. Sam was an older man, reserved in a professional manner. Brad had his own business, and voiced his concern that he might lose clients over the summer. Pam was seated to my immediate left—about my age, seemingly somewhat timid. Katie was the youngest woman on the jury. She appeared comfortable in her own skin, conversing easily with those gathered, a rarity in a young adult.

One by one, the others made their way into the jury room. Larry came in. Though middle-aged, he immediately and purposefully drew attention to himself in an immature and boisterous manner. He was followed by Irene, Chris, Jake, Elizabeth, George, Ed, Steve, Dave, and Kim.

Ushered into the hall at the appointed time, we again did the lineup, and followed Smitty one flight down to the hall outside the back of the courtroom. Amy awaited us, again with her hand on the doorknob, again asking if we were ready to enter. No sooner had she asked the question than the door was thrust open.

"All rise for the jury."

I looked at Chavere and Altier as I walked toward the jury box. Then, turning my head a bit to the left, I looked at Willis, Devaney, and Jordan. When all were seated, the judge greeted us and awaited our return greeting. I scanned the room. The reporters and one sketch artist were again to the right of the jury box, almost close enough for the jurors on that end to touch. A well-dressed young man sat between the jury box and the railing in front of the reporters.

He must be there to keep the reporters from trying to talk to the jurors, I assumed.

The courtroom was packed. Eager faces stared at us from the

middle section of the gallery. Some were contorted with anger; some revealed agony deep in their souls. These were the same faces that had been seated in the same places for opening arguments. By the intensity of their expressions, I surmised that they were victims, or family of the victims, to the crimes Devaney was said to have committed. The right section of the gallery was more difficult to see from my vantage point without leaning forward. But I could see the second sketch artist there, standing against the wall in the front row, already busy at work.

I pulled my sweater closed in an attempt to stay warm. My bare legs under the summer skirt were covered with goose bumps. Dressing for this trial was already a challenge. I wanted to dress properly, out of respect for the court. The outside temperature called for summer attire, whereas the inside temperature made me wish I had on a wool suit and heavy nylon stockings.

The first witness, a former Massachusetts State Police detective, was called to the stand and sworn in. Altier walked over to the attorney's lectern and placed his paperwork down. He waited patiently as the witness took the oath, his posture erect and his focus intent. I imagined him in the dress uniform of a marine officer and enjoyed the image conjured. Altier turned his head to look at the jury, as though he sensed my constant stare. Embarrassed, I picked up my notebook and pen. He began the presentation of evidence with the direct examination.

Numerous surveillance pictures, which were displayed on our monitors, showed Thomas Devaney with several unsavory characters, including members of the Boston Mafia.

No doubt about it, I thought, bored by the overkill of the pictures, *Devaney hung out with bad guys.*

Then, under direct examination, the witness related the animosity between the state police, local police forces, and the FBI. He accused the FBI of sabotaging wiretaps the state police had placed in an investigation of Sly Devaney. The line of questioning then moved onto a summary of the murders associated with Devaney.

"Objection, Your Honor." Defense Attorney Willis stood up in response to one of Altier's questions. His objection was so timid that it was barely audible. It took a moment for anyone, including the judge, to know he was objecting.

I actually snickered, thinking, *Devaney doesn't stand a chance with this frightened young man defending him.* I remembered hearing, before jury selection, that Devaney had been appointed attorneys by the court. Though Willis's appearance was that of a successful high-end attorney, he behaved as though he had little experience. *What a cruel thing to put such a high-profile trial on an inexperienced attorney,* I thought, feeling bad for Rob Willis, given the task ahead.

Altier completed his direct. My sense was that this first witness's testimony revealed little more than mistrust and animosity between different branches of law enforcement. I was not impressed with the testimony, and found the animosity between these authorities to be pride-based and sophomoric. It certainly wasn't conducive to fighting crime!

And what does any of it have to do with Devaney's innocence or guilt? I was confused.

Willis walked over to the lectern and softly introduced himself to the detective. I found myself feeling embarrassed for the attorney.

"Sir," Willis began. Though addressing the witness, he was looking at the jury. "In your position with the Massachusetts State Police during the time previously discussed with Mr. Altier, it wasn't just the local police forces and FBI you sensed hostilities from, was it?"

"I don't understand the question," the detective responded.

Willis was still looking at the jury. "Didn't you report, sir, that the US Attorney's Office and the Drug Enforcement Administration were interfering with your investigation of Thomas Devaney?" Willis directed his attention to the detective. "Sir, didn't you accuse a large portion of the Department of Justice of wrongdoing?"

Altier objected loudly.

"Sustained," Judge Blake responded.

"Sir, during this time in question, did you bring the confessions made and evidence obtained pertaining to murders committed by members of the Mafia and Old Harbor Gang to the attention of the district attorneys who presided over the counties represented?"

"Objection, Your Honor! Relevance?" Altier whined.

"Overruled," Judge Blake responded.

"Sir, shall I repeat the question?" Willis was anything but timid.

"No. No, I did not bring it to their attention. I—"

"Wasn't it your duty to inform the local district attorneys of the confessions and evidence pertaining to the murders committed in their counties?"

"My focus at the time was to obtain evidence against the Old Harbor Gang for racketeering."

"And, therefore, you chose not to assist the local DAs in forming a case to prosecute these murders?" Willis asked suspiciously.

"The statute of limitations for racketeering is only five years. Murder doesn't have a statute. Prosecuting the murders could wait."

Attorney Willis was clearly not pleased with the detective's response.

Was Bob one of those DAs? I wondered.

"At this time," Rob Willis began, "most of the leaders in the Mafia and Old Harbor Gang had already been indicted for racketeering—"

"Not Devaney!" the detective offered.

"So, it was Thomas Devaney you were focused on?"

"Yes."

"What about the families of the murder victims who were seeking justice and closure?" Willis asked.

The detective didn't respond.

"Wasn't it important to see to that?" Willis asked.

Still no answer.

"Objection." Altier stood.

"Withdrawn," Willis responded. "I'm done with this witness." Rob Willis gathered his notes and walked away from the lectern.

How could the detective have neglected to bring evidence and confessions to the DAs? What else did he neglect in his attempt to gain fame through Devaney's arrest? I considered.

Altier's redirect feebly attempted to reestablish the detective's integrity. Yet when Attorney Willis went to the lectern for recross, I was amazed, as he quickly and thoroughly, in my opinion, smashed to pieces whatever was left of this witness's credibility.

Five witnesses were called that day. There were numerous objections by both sides—and four sidebars.

Day two of the battle ended. I felt the defense held the higher ground.

~

Day three was a Friday. The weather forecast was predicting a warm and sunny weekend. This meant one thing: everyone would be eager to leave Boston for weekend getaways. They would head south to Cape Cod, or north to Cape Ann or New Hampshire. Because of this, I decided to avoid the traffic and take the train into the city that day. The ten-minute walk from Boston's South Station to the Moakley Courthouse was pleasant. The city streets were already bustling as people hurried to their workplaces. I took my time, enjoying the warmth of the sun. The stroll along the Harborwalk was relaxing. The sun glistened upon the open harbor, where a ferry slowly glided toward the Financial District pier, across from Fan Pier and the courthouse.

Thank God I was called to jury duty in the summer, I thought, shuddering at the thought of the fierce gale winds that would blow in the winter.

Richard took the elevator up to the jury room with me. He talked about the security guards by name, as though they were personal friends. Exiting the elevator, he immediately walked over to Smitty and struck up a conversation. I was surprised, because we had been told by the judge that the guards and staff would be polite to us but could say very little. Richard, it seemed, was making lasting friendships.

Oh well, I thought, pulling open the heavy jury room door, *he's just extremely social.*

Most of the jurors were already present. I had barely crossed the threshold when Larry called out, "Hey, Alex, being a history teacher, you must have gone to the Tea Party Museum."

I nodded. "Yeah."

"That Sam Adams was really something! And John Adams was

his cousin." He looked around the room as though offering a tidbit of information of which none of us was aware. "Sam and John Adams were fearless during the Boston Tea Party."

Larry was staring at me, waiting for a response, as I prepared my coffee. I took my cup and walked toward a seat at the table. "Actually, John Adams had little to do with the Tea Party."

"That's not true!" Larry bellowed. "They have all kinds of quotes by him and his wife—and their pictures hanging on a wall. Even the tea room is named after them! You don't know what you're talking about."

I looked at him with a slight smile, fascinated by his oddness. *If he were a student, he'd be on his way to the headmaster's office.*

"Well, Larry," I began calmly, "it seems to me that the museum displays John and Abigail Adams because their names are known to tourists who visit. And though they use their names and display their portraits freely there, it doesn't mean they took part in the Tea Party. John Adams was at home the night of the Tea Party, and Abigail was right by his side."

"You're nuts!" Obviously, Larry didn't believe me.

"Really?" Brad asked, ignoring Larry. "And the museum says they were there?"

"No, but they don't make it clear that they weren't. No doubt most visitors walk away thinking they were. It's a shame. Accurate history is fascinating, but we often settle for the abbreviated version, or out-and-out fiction. There were two remarkable men who were deeply involved in the Tea Party, and neither is recognized—but John Adams is."

"Who?"

"Josiah Quincy Jr. and Joseph Warren. You probably don't recognize their names. Few do. They died young, casualties of the war. History, or should I say historians, has forgotten them. Yet, had Quincy and Warren not met the challenges presented to them, our history would be altered."

Amy's entrance put an end to the history lesson. She was checking to make sure we were comfortable in the room and that everything we needed was being provided. Richard took it upon himself to answer for the group.

He seems to have already developed that chummy relationship with her as well. Probably talked her up out in the hall before coming in. He certainly has a gift.

~

Today, the jury's education on the corruption within the US Attorney's Office began. The first witness called by Prosecutor Chavere was Maurice Becker, a former career bookie who claimed he'd paid tribute to the Old Harbor Gang to operate. Tribute, we were told, is a form of extortion where the person in question pays money to a gang in order to stay in business without being physically threatened. It also guarantees protection from other gangs. Chavere's direct exam presented this man as a seasoned criminal with deep ties to the Old Harbor Gang. It was Defense Attorney Jordan's cross-examination that gave the rest of the story.

"Mr. Becker, you were eventually indicted, tried, and imprisoned?" Jordan asked.

"Yes."

"What was your sentence?"

"Four years in prison and one million dollars in fines."

"And who, sir, was the prosecuting attorney?" Curt Jordan was confidently looking down at his notes when he asked the question.

"Assistant US Attorney Carla Chavere."

"And, sir, did Ms. Chavere encourage you to implicate members of the Old Harbor Gang, namely, Thomas Devaney?"

"She did."

Chavere jumped up to object, to no avail.

"Did you implicate Thomas Devaney?" Jordan asked.

"No. Not initially."

"Did Assistant US Attorney Chavere approach you more than once?"

"Yes."

"How many times?"

"Objection!" Chavere shouted. The judge shut her down.

"Three," Maurice Becker said, with what seemed to be an anxious look at Chavere.

"What was Assistant US Attorney Chavere looking for?"

"Objection! Sidebar, Your Honor!" Chavere demanded. As the attorneys walked to the side of the judge's bench, along with the stenographer, the static from the noise machine filled the courtroom.

When the sidebar ended, Curt Jordan put the question to Maurice Becker again.

"Chavere was seeking truthful, substantial information that would help the US Attorney's Office indict members of the Old Harbor Gang."

"Was there mention of a reduction in your sentence if you cooperated?" Jordan asked.

"Objection!" Chavere was red in the face.

"Overruled."

"Yes, there was," Becker answered. He appeared uneasy as he shifted position.

"Did you cooperate when Ms. Chavere asked the third time?"

"No."

Curt Jordan brought out through questioning, despite many objections from Chavere, how Chavere had put Becker before a grand jury, where he was ordered to offer information or else be found in contempt. Here, Becker claimed that he'd been afraid to "talk" because one member of the Old Harbor Gang, a thug named Tony Diavolo, had threatened to kill him if he did. Becker claimed that he and the defendant, Thomas Devaney, had never spoken. Once Devaney rode in the backseat of a car Becker was driving, but no words were shared. That, according to Becker's testimony, was the only contact he'd ever had with Devaney.

The grand jury's determination was that Becker was not telling the truth. He was held in contempt, and his sentence was increased by eighteen months. The eighteen months were to be served before his original sentence of four years, now increasing his sentence to five and a half years behind bars.

Becker then discovered that his home, where his wife and four young children lived, was to be confiscated by the US government and sold. The proceeds would go toward the one million dollars in fines. His wife and children would be out on the streets.

"After you were made aware of this, did Assistant US Attorney Chavere contact you again?" Curt Jordan asked.

"Yes."

"With another offer?"

"Yes."

"What was it, Mr. Becker?"

I looked at Chavere, expecting her to jump up with an objection. Surprisingly, she didn't.

Becker hesitated. Curt Jordan waited.

"If I gave truthful, substantial information that would indict Thomas Devaney, my sentence would be reduced and my home would not be confiscated."

"Did you offer information to Assistant US Attorney Chavere?"

Becker cast his eyes downward. "I did," he admitted.

"And was your sentence reduced or the house released?"

"No. Ms. Chavere dismissed the information as not being substantial enough."

Curt Jordan continued to question the witness, bringing out the details of his release. After a year of imprisonment, with continued threats of contempt, and faced with the destitution of his family, Becker had succumbed to the pressure. He requested to speak with Chavere. This time, the information given proved acceptable to the assistant US attorney. That same day, Becker was released from prison and put on probation. His house was safe and his fines dismissed.

I couldn't believe what I was hearing. *Chavere threatened the well-being of Becker's family to get the information she wanted? What Chavere did was no better than Becker being forced to pay tribute to the Old Harbor Gang—in fact, it's far worse! And why would we believe that the information Chavere finally accepted was true? Probably Becker made it up in a desperate attempt to satisfy Chavere. Perhaps everything Becker said about Thomas Devaney and the Old Harbor Gang was a lie perpetrated to save his family.*

As Maurice Becker completed his testimony, I couldn't help but focus on Chavere. I expected to see some sign of emotion in reaction to the awful picture Becker's answers had painted of her character. Chavere remained stoic, as though the actions Becker had just discussed were a common and ethical practice she bore no guilt or shame from engaging in.

My hand was shaking as I made my final notes. Becker was dismissed. I looked up and watched as he stepped out of the witness box. I was aware that my face was flushed. My skin was burning. Incredulous, I gazed at Chavere. She was busy preparing for whatever was to come next.

The second witness on this day was a colorful character named George O'Malley. He was a bookie. O'Malley informed us, under Chavere's direct, that he had inherited the family business from his dad and that he intended to pass it on to his son Henry.

The long and short of this odd man's convoluted story, as far as I could gather, was that O'Malley, like Becker, was paying tribute to the Old Harbor Gang to operate. O'Malley moved to Arizona in the mid-1990s, where he met up with a member of the Old Harbor Gang by the name of Vinnie Giuda, who was on the lam. O'Malley shared that he and Giuda had previously spent time together "in the can," where they'd developed a close friendship.

While in Arizona, O'Malley discovered through his son that vicious rumors were spreading, claiming that he and Henry were going to give information to the feds about the Old Harbor Gang. This rumor would bring retribution from Thomas Devaney and the Old Harbor Gang, putting the O'Malleys' lives in danger.

Terrified, O'Malley went to Vinnie Giuda and assured him that the rumor was unfounded. Giuda, it seems, stood up for his friend O'Malley, calming the agitation of Devaney and the gang members.

At one point during direct examination, O'Malley accused Devaney of making a profane death threat to one of his associates.

Devaney let out a full unnatural laugh.

The courtroom was immediately filled with murmuring. Judge Blake swiftly restored order, and instructed the defense attorneys to speak to their client.

I felt uneasy, even disgusted, instantly assuming that Devaney's laughter was in response to his fondly remembering the threat he'd made. I stared at Devaney, who seemed calm, as were his attorneys.

What else might cause such a reaction? I wondered, now questioning the seemingly obvious and immediate conclusion of my thoughts. *He might have laughed because the statement was utterly ridiculous.* Neither defense attorney showed any reaction to their client's brief laughter, though the full focus of the prosecuting attorneys was now on Devaney. Chavere stared at Devaney from the lectern. Altier leaned forward over the table to catch a glimpse of him. I looked over at the reporters seated to the right of the jury box. Each seemed mesmerized by their cell phones, their fingers moving rapidly over the minute keypads. *Texting? Tweeting? Emailing?* I wondered. *Whichever it is, and whatever their message, it's getting out in real time. Amazing!*

Defense Attorney Jordan was now on cross. His questions seemed to make Mr. O'Malley uneasy from the start. Jordan pointed out that court documents proved that O'Malley had lied three times to a grand jury. If he had no problem lying then, why wouldn't he lie now?

"Could your testimony claiming Devaney made such a death threat be a lie as well? Wasn't it Tony Diavolo, and not Thomas Devaney, who made the threat?" Jordan asked.

Tony Diavolo, Vinnie Giuda—they keep mentioning them as if we're aware of what they did. There are so many characters in this convoluted story of crime spanning thirty years. The reason I'm on this jury is because I don't know anything. They're throwing names around as if we've been following the story for years! I was frustrated, trying desperately to follow the chain of events. I wondered if my fellow jurors felt the same.

"Mr. O'Malley, were you and your son Henry indicted for book-making?" Curt Jordan asked.

"Yes."

"And was Assistant US Attorney Chavere involved in that indictment and trial?"

"Yes."

"Court documents show that your sentence and that of your son was greatly reduced. Could you explain to the jury how that came about?"

Chavere objected and asked for a sidebar. The familiar static sounded as the attorneys met with the judge. A few jurors used the break to stand and stretch.

"Mr. O'Malley, do you remember my question?" Jordan asked after the sidebar.

O'Malley shook his head.

"Sir, you must answer yes or no for the stenographer," Judge Blake stated.

"Sorry, Your Honor," O'Malley offered, as though he were a young child being scolded.

"Let me repeat the question," Curt Jordan began. "Could you please explain to the jury why your sentence and that of your son Henry was reduced?"

O'Malley related how he'd offered information to Chavere implicating Devaney in crimes.

"Was this a proffer agreement?" Curt Jordan asked.

"Yes."

With permission from the judge, Defense Attorney Jordan explained to the jury that this is an agreement written between the federal prosecutor and the person being investigated. It offers certain protection from prosecution for information given.

There were many objections by the prosecution during Jordan's cross, and another sidebar. I realized that, unlike the defense attorneys, the assistant US attorneys did not possess the skills to hide their emotions, not even the seasoned Carla Chavere. As Jordan continued his cross-examination, Chavere's expression was filled with arrogant rage. And while Altier's body language appeared relaxed, fire blazed from his eyes.

"Mr. O'Malley, was your son's health affected by his involvement in the family business?" Jordan asked.

"I don't know what you mean."

"Objection. Relevance?" Chavere shouted.

"Overruled."

"Didn't your son suffer physical ailments in response to the indictment?" Jordan was determined.

"Yes, but I love my son. I wouldn't do anything to hurt him," was O'Malley's twisted response.

"You love him!" Curt Jordan exclaimed. "Yet you pulled Henry into this illegal and dangerous business, corrupting him and putting him in grave jeopardy! Isn't it so, Mr. O'Malley?"

"Objection," Chavere whined, with minimal attempt to get out of her seat.

"Sustained," was Judge Blake's immediate response.

O'Malley answered the question anyway, "I'm sorry he was hurt—" Though he failed to verbalize personal responsibility for his son's illness, he did appear sorrowful. But then he offered a comment that was totally off point: "I want the court to know that my friend Vinnie Giuda was good to me. Vinnie's intercession saved Henry and me. He—"

Curt Jordan cut him off in midsentence, telling the judge, with noted loathing, that he had no further questions for this witness.

Vinnie Giuda. Tony Diavolo. Who are they? What part did they play in Thomas Devaney's life? Shouldn't we have been given a synopsis of the complexities of Devaney's alleged crimes, rather than be thrown into this maze of unattached events and inconsistent dates? I felt like my brain was on overload.

Judge Blake mercifully ended the day early. With its being Friday, he was sympathetic to the traffic being heavy.

On day three of the battle, though confused by the way the story was being presented, the defense, in my opinion, fortified their position.

Friday was "payday." We jurors gathered our belongings in the jury room, waited for our checks, and then filed out once we'd received them. I walked with Pam to the train station. Our conversation was light—about the weather, our destinations, and some details of our family life—with *no* talk of the trial. It was strange not to discuss what we were hearing. Once we reached the subway station, we went our separate ways. Walking into South Station, I saw Elizabeth, Dan, and Chris in the crowd. We entered the same train, oddly pretending we didn't know one another.

Chapter 3

Justice consists not in being neutral between
right and wrong, but in finding out the right and
upholding it, wherever found, against the wrong.
—Theodore Roosevelt (1858–1919), twenty-
sixth president of the United States

"DEVANEY! FOR CHRIST'S SAKE! GET YOUR ASS BACK
on the bed!" the guard yelled, banging the cell bars with his baton.

Disoriented, the prisoner remained crouched in the corner as he
briefly glanced at the guard. He then turned his full attention back to
the camera hanging from the ceiling in the opposite corner of the cell,
which recorded his every move.

After a few moments, Devaney struggled to his feet. Perspiration
soaked his body. The elderly man stumbled to the small rusty metal
table attached to the far wall. Clumsily, he fell into the ice-cold matching chair. His hand was trembling as he picked up a pen.

"Fell out of bed," he wrote in a spiral notebook. "Pain in left hip
intensified by the frequent falls. Hallucinations continue, heightened
by stress of trial. Camera morphs into the form of an animal. Not
always the same: a tiger, wolf, or eagle. Trapped in the same cage.
Chavere always present, always taunting."

~

As I pulled into the parking lot in front of the courthouse on day four, a procession of three security vehicles, their lights flashing, came down the road. All other cars moved out of their way. I quickly realized it was the defendant, Thomas Devaney, being escorted by the US marshals from a prison south of Boston, where he was incarcerated. I wondered why it took three vehicles to transport him.

What are they afraid of, his escape or his assassination? Doesn't seem likely that a handcuffed, ankle-chained, sickly eighty-year-old can get away from armed US marshals. They must be concerned that he might be assassinated. By whom? I wondered. Former gang members? Hardly likely, as they're almost as old as he. Why would they murder Devaney only to risk ending up in prison themselves? Maybe it's his victims, or family members of victims. There's certainly enough rage on the faces of a few to suspect they might be capable.

I pulled my car into an empty space and turned off the engine. The security vehicles, with Devaney, had disappeared around the right side of courthouse. I got out of the car, still considering the size of the security detail needed to transport the prisoner.

The FBI and the state police are being exposed as corrupt and incompetent. Could Devaney be in danger from within one of these institutions? If he takes the stand in his own defense, might he reveal truths that certain government officials don't want revealed? "Alexandra!" I whispered to myself. "Your imagination is running wild!"

The check-in to the courthouse had already become routine, as the security guards had promised me it would. They were a friendly bunch of gentlemen, older in age. I couldn't help but wonder how well they would handle a couple of belligerent individuals trying to sneak in weapons. My gut told me that, given their age and physical condition, they couldn't. It was a scary thought.

I greeted Smitty upon exiting the elevator, and he checked off my name. The smiling faces of the early-arriving jurors welcomed me as I entered the room: Richard, Dan, Katie, Sam, Brad, Maureen, and Chris. I looked at the chalkboard. Katie had written her name for today. "Hi, Katie," I said, looking right at her.

Maureen had the coffee ready, and was comfortably seated at the head of the table nearest the kitchenette. I was relieved that she had volunteered for that duty, as I made a lousy pot of coffee. I moved to "my seat" at the opposite end of the table, with Pam on my left and Dan on my right. The conversation was light, mostly about our weekend activities, which for most of us involved catching up on work. Poor Brad, with his own business, had worked right through the weekend. Richard, having been laid off from his job, had become a stay-at-home dad with a young child. Sam, who was retired, had a relaxing weekend. The conversation was easy and balanced. When others wandered in, we stopped to greet them and then continued.

Then Larry entered. He appeared friendly and was always dressed nicely, often in a dress shirt and tie. But from the moment he walked into the room, he dominated the conversation. He didn't bring up history again but this time wanted to talk about engines. It didn't seem to matter what kind, just as long as the discussion was about engines, from trucks to boats to Jet Skis. The friendly back-and-forth group conversation ended as the men gravitated to Larry's dominating influence.

Strange, I thought. *He's not charismatic or intellectual—not a leader by any means. But everyone goes along with him. He's like a child wanting attention.*

The last to arrive, just in the nick of time, was Kim. Though hurried, she didn't appear so. Her slim figure and beautiful face were enough to draw attention from men and women alike. She was always professionally dressed in a tailored suit with a tantalizing hint of seduction. Her makeup was perfectly applied, and her posture was straight as an arrow. The men, no doubt, delighted in the view. As for the women—Kim oozed beauty, and therefore was the type all women secretly "hated." But, unlike many so wonderfully endowed, Kim was a genuinely sweet, likable, and intelligent young woman. We enjoyed her company. Her arrival always indicated that it was time to line up.

It was obvious that the next witness the prosecution called was important. When the tall bulky figure entered the courtroom, one could feel the silence. It was as though the pope himself had walked into a local Mass unannounced. All eyes were fixated upon him.

Judging from the eerie silence, it was obvious that all those within the courtroom knew who this man was except me.

He identified himself as Vincent Giuda. His friends called him Vinnie. At seventy-two, this hulk of a man was still a scary-looking figure. His face seemed chiseled from stone, with no ability to smile. His eyes were dull—not quite lifeless, but not alive either. He looked like a stereotypical Mafia hit man—though he denied being a hit man, or at least objected to the term.

The jury had to struggle through three days of testimony from this vile creature. Giuda, by his own admission, was a cold-blooded killer. He gave detailed testimony of the many lives he'd ended as though each was like swatting a fly. There was no indication of emotion or genuine remorse for the twenty senseless murders he confessed to committing. And of course he had a gamut of reasons for doing what he did, depending on how the particular attorney put the question to him.

Under Chavere's lead, Giuda educated us about his background, from growing up under the influence of a corrupt father to his early involvement in gangs, and the subsequent vigilante murders of those who dared to hurt his kid brother. From that point, Giuda's thirst for blood seemed to escalate.

"Were all the murders you confessed to the result of a personal affront to you or your brother?" Chavere asked rather methodically as she shuffled through her notes on the lectern.

"No. Sometimes I would help out a friend. If a friend was hurt or insulted, I'd offer to intercede." Giuda shrugged, appearing as if he were simply talking about mediating an argument. "I never took money. I wasn't a hit man." He showed more emotion when denying the title than when discussing killing the people.

"If you didn't see yourself as a hit man—" Chavere began.

"No, I didn't ask for money—" Giuda interrupted.

"Then how did you view yourself in carrying out these murders?" Chavere asked, with no inflection to her voice.

"I was helping friends get rid of the Judases in their lives," Giuda stated.

"The Judases in their lives? Could you explain?"

"I went to Catholic school; the nuns and priests taught me that the Judases of the world are bad and need to be punished. Just like Judas, these people betray a trust and hurt people by doing it."

"So, you felt justified in the murders?" Chavere asked.

"Yes."

Chavere seemed quite at ease with Giuda's explanation.

I, on the other hand, was sickened. *Giuda is fully aware of his brutality to his victims and he shows no shame or remorse. He took no money? Highly unlikely. Maybe he didn't ask for it, but I bet it was just given. And, somehow Chavere expects the jury to buy into this fiction? I went to parochial school too. Giuda has the story wrong. Judas didn't need an executioner; he took care of the job himself!*

Gruesome murder after gruesome murder was revealed through Giuda's testimony, culminating in the murder of his best friend of more than twenty years.

Who exactly was the Judas in this murder? I scoffed.

Giuda's earliest murders occurred before he'd even met Thomas Devaney. According to Giuda's testimony, once the two had met, Giuda cowered to Devaney's authority. In fact, from the picture that Giuda painted, he was so subservient to Devaney that it took only twenty minutes for Devaney to convince Giuda to murder his best friend, Paul Scalise.

As Chavere continued to draw out the details of the ghastly murders Giuda had committed, I wondered if her strategy was to convince the jury that Vinnie Giuda's absolute honesty was somehow proof that this former mass killer had turned over a new leaf, and therefore was now a new man.

Bewildered sarcasm filled my mind. *Hallelujah! Giuda confessed to Chavere that he committed these murders—murders that would never be proven otherwise. And therefore, at least as far as Chavere wants us to believe, anything that sweet Vinnie tells us must indeed be the truth, the whole truth, and nothing but the truth.* I was disgusted, and felt certain the other jurors must be as well.

I noticed that one of the paralegals sitting behind the defense attorneys' table was intently staring at each of us, one by one, and then scribbling notes. *Looking for our reaction,* I surmised. *I'm sure she'll have plenty to write as we listen to this monster.*

The long and short of Giuda's one and a half day of testimony for the prosecution was that after his arrest almost twenty years before, Chavere had informed him that his dear friend Thomas Devaney was an FBI informant. At this point, Giuda, who was already in prison and facing the electric chair, had decided to confess his own gruesome crimes to the feds, being sure to implicate Devaney.

Defense Attorney Willis's cross-examination initiated my exposure to the seeming bottomless pit of corruption that existed in the Boston office of the US attorney and the FBI. The reward from the US Attorney's Office for Vinnie's "honesty and good citizenship" was basically a get-out-of-jail-free card with a ticket to pass go and claim an outrageous amount of money.

Giuda's information on Devaney, which had a way of changing from court document to court document presented by Willis, had proved so pleasing to the US Attorney's Office that Giuda served less than six months for every cold-blooded murder he'd committed. There were also devastating injuries to individuals who happened to be with his target at the time of the hit. It didn't matter that many killed were innocent bystanders, or taken out because of mistaken identity. Giuda was a serial killer. He callously slaughtered people, one being a child and another being a teenage girl. And that was not all; while Vinnie was incarcerated, money was provided to him by the federal government. Upon his release, he was awarded $20,000.

Taxpayers' money! I realized. *This monster has been given money from us!*

Willis continued the disturbing story through questioning. Giuda had been on the lam for sixteen years. He left Massachusetts in 1979 with his seventeen-year-old girlfriend. At the time, Vinnie was forty. When she matured to adulthood, or perhaps even before, she became involved in blatant acts of money laundering. Then, when Giuda was arrested, she boldly lied to a grand jury. She was never indicted. She never spent a minute in a prison cell.

"Mr. Giuda, didn't the last two of your confessed twenty murders take place while you were on the lam?" Defense Attorney Willis asked.

"Are you implying that there were more than twenty murders?" Giuda shot back.

Rob Willis silently held him under a steady gaze for a moment. "Were there?" he finally asked.

Chavere jumped out of her seat. "Objection. Beyond the scope."

"Sustained."

"Did you commit the last two murders on record while on the lam?" Willis asked.

Chavere attempted to stand, but Giuda answered.

"Yes."

"The first of these murders was a businessman named David Walton?"

"Yes."

"Mr. Walton owned a popular chain of sports clubs. To your knowledge, did he have a connection to crime, either through his business or on a personal level?" Willis asked.

"No, not to my knowledge."

"Isn't it true, Mr. Giuda, that your good friend Paul Scalise worked for Mr. Walton?"

"Yes."

"Wasn't Paul Scalise embezzling funds from Mr. Walton's business?"

"Objection. Beyond scope of direct, Your Honor." Chavere stood.

"Your Honor, in Ms. Chavere's direct examination, she introduced the jury to the Walton murder. The jury should be informed of the known facts surrounding that murder."

"Sidebar, Your Honor!" Chavere called out.

Obviously, Rob Willis had prevailed. When the sidebar ended, he continued to relate the known facts of the Walton murder through his questions to Giuda. The many objections by Chavere were immediately silenced by Judge Blake.

Scalise, a businessman and wannabe thug, was secretly embezzling funds from the coffers of the sports clubs. An investigation into the missing funds was being conducted by Mr. Walton. Scalise knew it was only a matter of time before he would be discovered. His plan was to buy the clubs before Mr. Walton discovered his treachery. Scalise made a generous offer to Mr. Walton, which was turned down. Scalise knew he had to act fast to stop the investigation or he would soon be in jail, so he went to Giuda.

"Paul was my best friend. I had to help him," Giuda stated.

"How did you help him?" Willis asked. He succeeded against Chavere's expected objection.

"I went to Tommy and Tony and assured them that once Paul owned the sports clubs, they would get a cut of the profits."

"Tommy is the defendant Thomas Devaney, and Tony is Anthony Diavolo?" Willis attempted to clarify.

"Yeah, Devaney and Diavolo."

"But Mr. Scalise's offer was turned down by Mr. Walton. How was he to gain ownership of the sports clubs?"

"Tommy and Tony agreed that I should take out Walton."

I found it interesting that Giuda continued to refer to the defendant as Tommy. *Does he still consider Devaney a friend? Or are old habits just hard to break?*

"How was this accomplished?" Willis asked.

"Tommy had Tony ship a duffle bag filled with weapons on a Greyhound bus to a specific destination in Kentucky, where Walton lived. The man in charge of security at the sports clubs was a friend of Paul and me. He knew Walton's daily routine. A plan was made to kill Walton after he finished playing his weekly match of tennis."

"This friend in charge of security, wasn't he Andrew Ricardo, a former FBI agent?"

"Yes."

"You knew him well?"

"Fairly well."

"You were introduced to him by your mentor, Emilio 'the Beast' Maldade. Ricardo was Maldade's FBI handler?"

"Sidebar!" Chavere yelled. Both she and Altier were standing, obviously enraged. Judge Blake immediately called all attorneys to his side.

What's happening here? I wondered, as the noise machine was turned on to hide the sound of Chavere and Altier's obvious fury. *A former FBI agent an accessory to murder? And who is this Maldade character, the Beast?*

Thomas Devaney looked over at Giuda. Giuda looked away.

The sidebar ended, and inexplicably there was no more mention of Emilio "the Beast" Maldade or his homicidal FBI handler Andrew Ricardo.

Giuda went on to explain how he picked up the duffle bag at the Greyhound station and then waited for Mr. Walton in the parking lot behind the tennis courts. When Mr. Walton got into his car, Giuda approached, leaned in, and shot the unsuspecting victim in the face.

"Tony sent me a bad gun. The damn thing backfired."

"Tony Diavolo sent you a bad gun?" Rob Willis probed.

"I could've been hurt because of his damn carelessness!"

I heard myself gasp. *No remorse for the fact that poor Mr. Walton is slouched in the front seat dead, only that you might have been hurt? If only the gun had blown up in your goddamned face!*

"Following Mr. Walton's murder, did Paul Scalise purchase the sports clubs?" Willis asked.

"No. Walton's wife turned down Paul's offer."

"Did she end the embezzlement investigation?"

"No."

"How did your good friend Paul Scalise become your next target?" Willis asked, turning to look at the jury.

"Tommy and Tony had me meet them in New York. They insisted it was only a matter of time before Paul's part in the embezzlement was discovered. Tommy said Paul was weak and would squeal about our involvement in Walton's murder to save himself."

"And so you agreed to kill your best friend?" Willis turned his full attention back to Giuda.

"No. I told Tommy he was wrong, and that Paul wouldn't squeal. I suggested we send him away instead," Giuda argued.

"How long was this meeting with Mr. Devaney and Diavolo?"

"Don't know. About twenty minutes." Giuda was staring into space, almost as if trying to distance himself.

"And was it decided to send Paul Scalise away?"

"No. Tommy wouldn't go along with that plan."

"Did you agree to kill your best friend?" Willis persisted.

"Tommy convinced me."

"You're telling this court that within twenty minutes, Thomas Devaney convinced you to murder your best friend of twenty-five years?" Again, Rob Willis turned to face the jury.

"Tommy was right. We had no choice—"

Giuda went on to explain how he had convinced Scalise to visit him in Arizona. He picked his friend up at the airport, gave him a warm embrace, and offered to put his suitcase in the back of the van while Scalise got into the front passenger seat. Unbeknownst to Scalise, Giuda had a gun waiting. The front passenger's-seat area was lined with plastic. Before Scalise had a chance to ask about the plastic, Giuda shot him in the back of the head. Scalise's body was thrown into the trunk of another car. This car went unnoticed until the body, quickly melting under the relentless Arizona sun, leached the horrific odor of decomposition, revealing the van's secret cargo.

Sweet Jesus! His best friend! My thoughts were screaming. *He hugged him before he shot him? He is Judas!*

The jury was then enlightened, through Rob Willis's questions, as to how, upon Vinnie Giuda's release from his short stay in prison, he was offered $250,000 for movie rights to his story. Of course, he accepted the money. Then came Nick Mudd, a so-called journalist for the *Boston Post*. Unbeknownst to the public, Mudd offered Vinnie partnership for his story in a book titled *Memoirs of a Serial Killer*. Vinnie Giuda stated in his testimony that he had already received $70,000 in royalties from his agreement with Nick Mudd.

I was sickened. *How many people bought that book unaware that they were supporting Giuda? Even die-hard readers of anything to do with organized crime would be disgusted!* I thought—I hoped.

The worst part about it, Vinnie Giuda had been allowed by the court to make money off his story. And, per the court, all proceeds made were his to squander however he pleased. No restitution was to be made to the victims of his crimes, those severely injured, or the grieving family members of the many he had put in the grave. The money from the book he partnered on with Nick Mudd was his and his alone. Those who bought it became accomplices of a sort to the murders he'd committed. If Giuda hadn't committed the gruesome murders, there would be no story. The book was purchased, it seemed to me, because the reader was fascinated by Giuda and the demon he is. They, in fact, ended up aiding him with their financial support.

Blood money! The story of Judas does play a part in Giuda's life. And Nick Mudd made a conscious choice to become a cohort to the murders Giuda committed, not caring what the book would do to those injured or the grieving families. And it seems as if Chavere and the federal court were somehow in on it. It's as if the twenty people Giuda murdered, and those harmed, never existed. The decisions of the court in effect declared that those individuals had no value, and therefore no justice had been offered them or their families. It feels as though the rally cry of Chavere and the federal court is "Giuda lives! Long live Giuda!" My skin was crawling.

Vinnie Giuda now lives a normal life, and in addition to his money from movie rights and book royalties, he receives a regular check from Social Security. He's happily living in a normal neighborhood with normal, hardworking neighbors, hardworking neighbors doing the best they can to protect and raise their families. If he were a sex offender, it would be known within the neighborhood—but a mass murderer doesn't have to be identified? The thought took my breath away. *Alex, do you really know who your neighbors are? Does anyone?*

As Giuda was dismissed, I could not take my eyes off him. I watched as he walked toward the door in the back of the courtroom. People were swarming out after him.

Bodyguards? Reporters? Lawyers? Fans? As I watched, it sordidly occurred to me, *Vinnie Giuda is living the new American dream, enjoying a comfortable life while getting away with murder—all with the blessing of the federal government! God have mercy on the United States!*

The defense team won days four through six of Giuda's testimony hands down.

Day seven brought another testimony, which impacted me greatly. The witness for the prosecution was an older man who had difficulty walking. He needed help up into the witness box, and then he struggled to sit after being sworn in.

"Hello, sir. I'm Assistant United States Attorney Altier. Could you please state your name?"

The witness tried to speak into the microphone, but he couldn't be heard. The judge asked a bailiff to check the microphone.

"My name is Stanley Onesta," he meekly stated after the microphone was fixed. "And I want it to be known that I'm here under duress."

Jordan stood and asked if he and Chavere could speak with the judge. The judge's response was to send the jury out.

Interesting, I thought.

We went back to the jury room and had a second cup of coffee.

"What's up with that paralegal?" Maureen asked.

"The one staring us down? She's a hoot!" Chris stated with a laugh.

"She's trying to read our expressions," Brad offered.

We finished our coffee, and had time for a bathroom break before being called back down. Mr. Onesta was still seated in the witness box. Altier was at the attorney's lectern, again ready to begin his direct.

"Mr. Onesta, have you ever spoken to me or Assistant US Attorney Chavere?" Altier asked.

"No."

"Why are you here?"

"I was sent a subpoena ordering me to appear. I'm here under duress," he repeated.

"That's understood, sir."

"I intended to invoke my right under the Fifth Amendment but was informed by your office that I'd be found in contempt and imprisoned for eighteen months."

Denied his constitutional right? And threatened with imprisonment if he attempted to invoke it? I couldn't believe what I was hearing!

Altier then asked Mr. Onesta questions about his background. Onesta had just been released from prison after serving twenty-two years for conspiracy to commit a robbery.

Though he appeared frail and sounded meek, Stanley Onesta was anything but. "I spent the maximum time in prison because I refused to implicate others in crimes. If I did, I was told that my sentence could be greatly reduced. Through the years, I watched many make these deals and leave prison. I wouldn't. I never was involved in murder. Nor did I commit the robbery I was imprisoned for."

Twenty-two years for conspiracy to commit a robbery—yet no robbery was committed? And Giuda served only six months for murder? This can't be! My mind was protesting.

"Please, sir, just answer the questions put to you," Altier commanded.

Certainly, the defense attorneys have no problem with anything this witness has said thus far. Why would they? And why would the prosecution want him as a witness in the first place? I wondered.

Altier continued questioning Mr. Onesta. The gist of his testimony was that he and his wife had been introduced to a young man named Pete McFarland at a friend's home many years before. McFarland was the father of their friend's small daughter. He had come by to celebrate her birthday. The mother of the girl, having told Mr. Onesta that she was being harassed by neighbors, asked if he could help her with this problem. He told her he would try, and then he made a phone call. Mr. Onesta made plans to meet a man named Marty Hill later that day at a nearby bakery to discuss what might be done to stop the harassment. McFarland needed to pick up a birthday cake at the same bakery, so he asked Onesta if he wanted to ride over with him.

Pete McFarland bought the cake while Mr. Onesta spoke to Marty Hill. Both men completed their tasks and left the bakery.

"When we pulled out of the parking lot, I noticed in the side mirror that Marty Hill had come out of the bakery and was getting into a car with two other men. That car began to follow ours. I couldn't identify the men with Marty Hill, but something wasn't right. I told McFarland to hit the gas. He laughed. I yelled that I was serious, as the other car pulled up alongside and opened fire—" Mr. Onesta stopped, obviously disturbed.

"Then what happened?" Altier asked methodically as he shuffled through his notes, not even looking at the witness.

"I slumped down on the floor. When the shooting stopped, I pulled myself up and reached for McFarland—"

"Continue, Mr. Onesta," Altier ordered mercilessly, still playing with his papers.

Stanley Onesta's voice was shaking. "His head was gone. Somehow, I managed to get out of the car. I fell to the ground. I'd taken nine bullets."

"Sir, are you aware that Vincent Giuda confessed to the murder of Peter McFarland?" Altier asked, finally looking at the witness.

"I am."

"Vincent Giuda alleges that Thomas Devaney was in the car with him. Did you see Thomas Devaney in the car with Marty Hill and Vincent Giuda?"

"I couldn't identify anyone in the car except Marty Hill."

"Do you believe that Vincent Giuda was in the car?"

"I don't know why he would say he was and implicate himself if it wasn't true," Onesta answered with a shrug of his shoulders.

"And Thomas Devaney was there as well," Altier stated.

As Rob Willis stood, seemingly prepared to object to the statement, Onesta answered:

"I cannot identify the third person in the car."

"I have no more questions." Altier gathered his prized notes and left the lectern.

"Mr. Onesta, that was a traumatic experience," Rob Willis said as he positioned himself behind the lectern. "Do you need a break before continuing?"

"No. But thank you," was the soft reply.

Willis responded with a slight smile. "Sir, as Mr. Altier stated, Vincent Giuda confessed to the murder of Peter McFarland. And, as stated, Vincent Giuda alleges that Thomas Devaney was in the car with him. I will ask you again, for further clarity: did you see Thomas Devaney in the car with Marty Hill and Vincent Giuda?"

"I couldn't identify anyone in the car except Marty Hill."

"Have you ever seen Thomas Devaney, spoken to him, or communicated with him in any way before today?"

"No, sir. I have not."

"Thank you, Mr. Onesta. Do you have anything more to say?"

"I do." Stanley Onesta, in an act of pure courage, as far as I was concerned, raised his voice. "I'm disgusted by the fact that a serial killer who murdered twenty people in cold blood was released from prison upon implicating others in equal and lesser crimes. Such deals are made on a regular basis. I'm outraged by what I witnessed time and again in the extraordinary deals given to heinous criminals. Where's the justice in this? Where's the justice for the victims of serial killer Vincent Giuda?"

I was astounded both by his words and the passion revealed as he spoke them. I gazed at Chavere and Altier. I felt a deep sense of revulsion for the games they played with the lives of the victims and their families, whose pain and grief was ignored as the US Attorney's Office bought information.

How is it determined that the crimes of one outweigh the crimes of another? Could Thomas Devaney be more evil than Vinnie Giuda? And was Stanley Onesta such a danger to society that he deserved twenty-two years behind bars for planning a robbery but not carrying it through, while Vinnie Giuda lives a normal life in a normal neighborhood—his dark soul hidden to all? I pictured the image of Lady Justice, the honored symbol of the US judicial system. Like a marionette, she was attached to strings that were connected to a control bar above. Her every move was manipulated by a master puppeteer.

To further my revolt, I watched as Altier went out of his way to help Stanley Onesta exit the witness box. As far as I was concerned, it was a scene meant to impact the jury. This same man who had threatened Onesta with eighteen more months in prison if he dared to invoke his constitutional right was now playing the Good Samaritan in helping poor Mr. Onesta as he struggled to get out of the witness box. *Altier is disgusting, absolutely disgusting!*

Chapter 4

It is essential to the preservation of the rights of every individual, his life, liberty, property and character, that there be an impartial interpretation of the laws, and administration of justice. It is the right of every citizen to be tried by judges as free, impartial and independent as the lot of humanity will admit.
—Constitution of Massachusetts, 1780 (drafted by John Adams)

THIRTY PRISONERS FILED INTO THE MESS HALL UNder heavy guard. Each was assigned a seat, all distant from one another. Young Tom Devaney scanned the faces of the other prisoners, faces he saw every day at the Atlanta penitentiary. Two men, strangers in suit coats, introduced themselves. Devaney didn't follow their drawn-out presentation filled with medical terminology that he didn't understand or necessarily want to be bothered with. At twenty-six, he was facing almost two decades in prison for armed robbery. All he really cared about was the opportunity to shorten his sentence. He, and the others, were told by the warden that these doctors were looking for prisoners to take part in testing an experimental drug to cure schizophrenia.

"The drug is safe," one of the doctors assured them. "The court has agreed to significantly reduce the sentence of those prisoners willing to be part of the testing."

"It will only take a couple of weeks," the second doctor added.

"You'll be kept in the prison hospital the entire time, with good food and extended time in the sunshine and fresh air. All you are required to do is journal what you experience each day after receiving the drug."

That sounds easy enough, Devaney thought, eager to sign his name on the dotted line.

~

The cast of characters presented to the jury throughout days eight and nine were varied. We heard the emotional testimony of families whose loved ones had been killed or maimed, and then the detached testimony of police officers and firearm specialists. When the firearm specialists took the stand, a display of about twenty guns was placed on a table before the judge's bench. The firearms consisted of everything from tiny pistols to submachine guns, the barrel of each facing the jury.

Richard, to my left in the jury box, seemed bored as he played with the buttons on the monitor we shared. I glanced at him. He whispered something, which I couldn't make out.

ADHD? I wondered. *Lord knows I've seen it enough in the classroom. It would fit given his chattering personality and restlessness.* I had quickly glimpsed a page in his notebook. Large print covered it, his penmanship ignoring the printed lines completely. *Poor guy,* I thought, *if he's ADHD, sitting through this trial must be brutal. I hope he doesn't break the monitor.*

Chavere handled each weapon for the jury to see. Every time she picked one up, she had the barrel pointed toward us. Though no bullets were supposed to be in any of them, the way the guns were presented was unnerving.

What if there is a bullet? What if she accidently fires? Why isn't she holding the guns downward, as we're all taught to do—even with toy guns?! Why doesn't the judge say something to her about her improper handling of the guns? Just as I'd finished that last thought, Chavere somehow managed, after fiddling with one of the firearms, to have it fall apart in her hands. *We aren't safe!* my thoughts screamed. *Is this a show? Is this meant to upset the jury? What the hell is going on?*

After what seemed like an eternity, Chavere finished her childish antics and boring direct examination of identifying the model of each gun, noting that the serial numbers had been scratched off, and determining if each was fire-ready. Defense Attorney Jordan then came to the lectern and politely greeted the firearms specialist.

"Sir, please tell the jury, can any of these guns can be tied to Thomas Devaney?"

"No."

"Thank you, sir. I have no more questions," Jordan announced. He sat down.

I wanted to laugh as I envisioned a scene from the first *Indiana Jones* movie. A larger-than-life swordsman was attempting to frighten Indiana Jones with a stunning show of his ability to handle a scimitar. Indiana Jones took out a small pistol and shot him dead. Such was Chavere's ridiculous display—and Curt Jordan had taken her down with one quick question.

Restlessly, I shifted position in my chair, pulling my sweater tight against the cold air. The judge offered the jury an opportunity to stand and stretch. I took him up on it. A few others joined me.

Then a couple of outlandish characters were called to the stand by the prosecution. Both had been involved in illegal gambling. The first man claimed he was a friend of Vinnie Giuda. He seemed proud of that fact, explaining how he had made housing arrangements for Giuda when the latter was on the lam. Chavere was on direct, and was throwing so many names of criminals and dates of particular crimes spanning thirty years into her questioning that my head was spinning.

Too damn confusing. Is she trying to confuse us?

This witness seemed to have excellent recall as he rattled off details for Chavere. He related how Thomas Sacchetti, a member of the Boston Mafia, decided that he wanted to take over as boss. This, of course, didn't sit well with the present Mafia boss. A meeting was called by the boss, and plans were made to take out Sacchetti. Giuda was said to have been present at the meeting—and years later, as part of his proffer, he confessed to killing five others in his sick attempt to get Sacchetti.

The witness was delighting in reliving his life of crime. Suddenly, his countenance changed dramatically as he furiously yelled out, "Stop staring at me! Why are you staring at me?"

Even Chavere seemed dumbstruck by the outburst.

"What is the problem, sir?" Judge Blake asked calmly.

"That attorney with the blonde hair keeps staring at me!" he bellowed, rising to his feet and pointing at Rob Willis.

"Sir, you need to sit down!" the judge called out. A well-dressed man seated to the right of the witness stand immediately stood, his hand positioned on his hip as though prepared to pull out a firearm.

Must be a federal marshal, I realized.

The witness sat down. "Focus on Ms. Chavere's questions," Judge Blake instructed.

But it seemed that Chavere had no more questions, as she surprisingly announced that she was done.

Is she done? I wondered. *Or did this crazy man manage to shake her up? Maybe Chavere decided to get him off the witness stand as quickly as possible.*

Rob Willis moved to the lectern to begin his cross-examination. Almost every one of Willis's questions was answered with, "I do not recall."

"Sir, it's very interesting that you gave detailed answers to Ms. Chavere's questions but now, suddenly, you have no recollection," Willis stated with controlled frustration.

The witness became belligerent as Willis pointed out the many lies in his testimony when compared to transcripts of his other court appearances. In restrained disgust, Willis ended his cross-examination.

The second colorful fellow called was an old guy with a shaved head and a long, bushy white beard. He claimed to have a neurological problem that caused his brain to immediately translate conversations spoken in English into French, and therefore asked the attorneys to be patient with his condition and need for clarification.

What? I've never heard of such a thing. And even if it's so, if he understands French, as he claims he does, what's the problem? I had to keep from laughing when I heard a few of the jurors near me snicker.

The man with the shaved head had no problem understanding the questions put to him under direct examination. Yet when Jordan began his cross, suddenly this witness began to experience his "neurological impairment." He couldn't understand the questions or had no recollection of anything put to him. His tone became obnoxious and his expressions and mannerisms exaggerated. Finally, when it seemed that he'd realized his foolishness wasn't stopping Jordan from digging deeper for answers, this strange man with the shaved head called out to Judge Blake, "I want to invoke … I want to invoke—" He never finished the statement, seeming unable to come up with the phrase "my Fifth Amendment right." The judge sent the jury out of the courtroom. When we returned a few minutes later, the strange man with the shaved head was gone.

It was Friday—payday. We all waited in the hall outside the jury administration office for our big jury pay of $50 per day, taxed. Even the office staff had successfully begun to associate our names with our faces I realized as they passed out the checks.

Over the weekend, I wandered into a local bookstore to browse. Upon entering, I was blasted with a huge display of Nick Mudd and Vinnie Giuda's book, *Memoirs of a Serial Killer.* There was no warning or notice stating that Giuda was monetarily rewarded with each sale, and no mention of his concealed partnership with Mudd whatsoever. But there was a colorful poster announcing Mudd's book-signing event, which was to take place the following weekend in this small bookstore on Cape Ann. I felt sick inside as I walked beyond the display, tempted to knock the entire thing over as I passed.

"Obviously, I need to stay clear of this place next week," I whispered to myself.

That night, I had a nightmare of being chased by three men with submachine guns.

~

Monday was a hot, humid day. The ride into Boston was more than unpleasant, but the stroll along the Harborwalk and Fan Pier made up for it. The harbor was glistening under the summer sun. A tall ship was anchored, bobbing with the gentle flow of the sea. My intent, from the start of the trial, was to spend time in Boston after court was dismissed, to further my research on John Hancock, the subject of my next book. And though court was often dismissed early, I found myself emotionally exhausted and unable to focus. As I looked out upon Boston's historic harbor, I imagined the horizon being lined with the towering masts of frigates, sloops, schooners, and brigantines as they transported their wares across the open water. It was a scene the wealthy merchant John Hancock would have been very familiar with.

I'd rather lose myself in that world, I thought, *where right was right and wrong was wrong, rather than in this world of deals, schemes, and deceit. In this world, it's hard to identify the "good guys." There's only corruption and disgraceful excuses for justification.*

I gazed once more upon the glistening harbor, before taking a deep breath and going into the courthouse. "Good morning," the guard greeted me with a friendly smile.

"A warm one," I replied, handing him my cell phone and placing my purse on the scanner belt.

I caught the guard beyond the scanner staring at my legs as I walked through. *A pair of heels will do it all the time,* I thought, realizing it was the first time I'd worn anything higher than two inches. The alarm sounded. I looked at him, anticipating being sent through again, or having to be checked by the wand.

"You're okay. It's your shoes," he said knowingly.

I looked down at my heels and back up at him. "Really?"

He nodded with a smile.

Embarrassed by my obvious vanity, and disappointed in not having drawn attention to my legs, I gathered my purse, put on my juror badge, and walked toward the ascending marble staircase.

"Just getting too old, Alex," I whispered to myself. Glancing back, I saw both guards looking toward me—at my legs. I grinned. *Heels will do it all the time!* I thought, feeling better about myself.

"Busy weekend?" Pam called out to me as I prepared my cup of coffee.

"Went up to my daughter's in New Hampshire," I replied. "And you?"

"With my grandkids."

"I'm uncomfortable doing much of anything," Katie commented. "Afraid I'll be exposed to information I'm not supposed to hear."

"That's why I stay around my family. They know to keep quiet," Pam agreed.

"As much as I hate the thought of it, we should've been sequestered," I heard myself saying. They were looking at me. "Consider it. We've made ourselves prisoners. Our free time isn't free. We're all afraid to socialize because of what we might overhear. We're cut off from work and society." I hadn't socialized beyond family since the trial began.

My good friend's upcoming wedding came to mind. It was only a couple of weeks away. Thank God, the bride's family insisted on running the show, so I had nothing to do with preparation. I had no intention of not being there. *But it might prove awkward,* I realized, not only because my participation on the jury couldn't be discussed and I'd have to dodge any conversations about the trial, but also because the groom was friendly with Bob Costa. *Bob will be there.* I suddenly realized that might be a problem. *I'm sure he'll have a date, so I'll be able to avoid him without raising suspicion.*

Larry entered the room and disrupted my thoughts and every conversation, as usual. "It's stifling out there! The air-conditioning feels good."

At the moment, I agreed, but I knew I'd be wishing for the heat once in the courtroom.

"Every window was open last night and I couldn't get a breeze," he complained.

"I wouldn't be able to sleep without air-conditioning in the bedroom," Ed interjected. Others nodded in agreement.

"The bedroom has air. My girlfriend sleeps there. I sleep on the couch in the living room."

Unbeknownst to Larry, every juror in the room shared a questioning glance. No words were needed between us. *If he lives with this girlfriend, why does he sleep on the couch? And why in the world would he announce that he sleeps on the couch?*

No one asked the obvious questions.

~

A special agent from the Department of Justice's Office of the Inspector General by the name of Michael Biscione took the stand on day ten. I had seen Biscione in the gallery from day one. He was an odd-looking man, tall and gangly. His features were grossly exaggerated, with a permanent scowl chiseled into his face. His was a long, drawn-out, mostly boring account of corruption within the Boston FBI that was to last four torturous days. According to Biscione, he had been assigned to investigate reports of corruption within the Boston FBI, with the focus on one particular agent named Skip Goot.

FBI document after document was presented to the jury via the monitors before us. Ours wouldn't turn on initially, no doubt because of Richard's insistence in playing with the buttons. Once he fidgeted with it, the monitor began to work correctly.

The documents, presented by Chavere and verified by Biscione as official, were supposed to prove that Thomas Devaney was an FBI informant. They were also supposed to prove that the corrupt special agent Skip Goot was his handler. Document after document after document. It was difficult to stay alert. For the first time, I was grateful for the overly air-conditioned courtroom; at least the cold would keep me from dozing.

When Chavere ended her first round of direct examination, Willis stepped up to the lectern. We had all learned that Willis's method of cross-examination would liven things up. I noticed that many of the jurors, like me, straightened up in their chairs, taking hold of their pens and ready to take notes. Willis did not disappoint.

His questions set Biscione squirming from the get-go, with Chavere jumping up in objection to each one. She never even uttered her reason for the objection, I noted, nor did the judge seem to care, as he shut her down on most.

"Could these documents be fabricated?"

"Objection."

"Overruled."

"Would be very difficult, but I suppose—" Biscione hesitantly replied.

"How easy was it to gain access to other files within the FBI?" Willis's questions were as rapid-fire as the objection interruptions would allow.

"Objection."

"Overruled."

"At the time in question it was fairly easy for agents to gain access to the files of other agents—"

"Can you explain why it was that Mr. Devaney's supposed information, mirrored—often verbatim—statements already on file of other informants?"

"Objection."

"Overruled."

"No."

"In examining the FBI file of Mr. Devaney, practically all initials or signatures of those collecting the supposed information were found to be corrupt agents. Isn't that so, Mr. Biscione?"

"Objection."

"Overruled."

"Yes."

"Where is the pink cover sheet, which was standard for all such files?"

"Objection."

"Overruled."

"I don't know. It wasn't with the file when I reviewed it."

"That strikes me as odd, Mr. Biscione. The missing cover sheet would have had a current mug shot of Mr. Devaney, along with his fingerprints, voluntarily placed on that sheet. Why is it that the only picture in the file is a mug shot of a very youthful Thomas Devaney and there are no fingerprints at all?"

"I have no knowledge of why the cover sheet is missing—"

"Did you ask?"

Chavere remained silent. It seemed that she realized her objections weren't getting her anywhere.

Biscione's countenance reflected abandonment as he fixed his gaze on Chavere.

"Mr. Biscione, did you ask where the cover sheet was?" Willis demanded.

"Yes. No one knew what happened to it." Biscione's eyes stayed on Chavere as though searching for a response.

"Perhaps there never was a cover sheet because Thomas Devaney was never an informant and the file is a fabrication of corrupt agents," Willis stated matter-of-factly.

Now Chavere jumped up. "Your Honor!"

"Mr. Willis, you will contain such comments," Judge Blake scolded.

"Of course, Your Honor. I'm sorry, Your Honor." He didn't sound sorry.

"Sir, did you read all FBI files pertaining to Thomas Devaney?" Willis asked, looking at his papers on the lectern.

"Yes."

"Even the document in the safe of the FBI special agent in charge?"

"I wasn't aware of a safe—" Again, Biscione's eyes fell on Chavere as if searching for direction.

Chavere, appearing taken aback by the question, offered no facial expression in response to her witness.

Biscione's attention turned back to Rob Willis. "All files pertaining to Thomas Devaney were ordered to be made available to me."

Willis picked up a paper from the lectern. "If that was the case, Mr. Biscione, then you must have read this one. May I approach the witness, Your Honor?"

"Objection!" Chavere was vehement. "This document hasn't been properly introduced!"

Judge Blake quickly excused the jury.

We were delighted to have the break, as it was an opportunity to have a cup of coffee to wake us up. Different jurors moaned and groaned about how boring the testimony was, but no one said any-thing specific pertaining to it.

When we were summoned back to the courtroom, Biscione was on the witness stand, looking as though he were sitting on a pile of hot coals. Willis laid in to him again.

"No, I have never seen that document," Biscione admitted after reviewing the paper. Willis entered it into evidence.

The focus turned to Special Agent Skip Goot. Willis informed the jury through questioning Biscione that upon his arrest, Goot had accused the Department of Justice of being knowledgeable of and con-senting to the corruption found in the Boston FBI. Goot's claim was that this knowledge and consent went all the way to the US attorney general. Of the many corrupt Boston FBI agents indicted, Goot was the only one who had verbalized such an accusation. And, as it turned out, of the many corrupt Boston FBI agents indicted, Goot became the primary focus of the US Attorney's Office. As for the punishment of the other FBI agents found to be corrupt? There was none. Yet Skip Goot had been sent to prison for a long, long time.

Thomas Devaney, too, had been vocal about the corruption within the Department of Justice. And, like Goot was, I realized that he was the primary focus of the US Attorney's Office. *Monsters like Vinnie Giuda can go free, but not Devaney. Why?*

Richard began squirming in the seat next to me. It was constant and distracting. He leaned toward me, telling me he had to use the bathroom.

"Raise your hand," I whispered. *It works in the classroom. Why not here?*

He didn't raise his hand, but he did continue to squirm, adding quiet moans to indicate his distress. I imagined him soiling himself right then and there, and considered raising my hand for him.

Upon Chavere's redirect, she accused Willis of making up his claim that files had been kept locked in the safe of the FBI special agent in charge.

Willis was smiling as he stood up to object. "Your Honor, I would ask that Ms. Chavere be admonished for that comment."

Judge Blake did not admonish Chavere, but simply stated to the stenographer that the statement be stricken.

Biscione was let go. *Praise be to God!* I shouted in silence, not only because his testimony was so ridiculously boring, but also because poor Richard obviously needed to get to the bathroom. As soon as we were dismissed, Richard bolted up the stairs to the jury room. As the rest of us gathered our things to leave for the day, he came up beside me.

"Sorry about the distraction. My bladder was ready to burst."

Your bladder? I thought. *With all that squirming, I figured your bowels were ready to let loose. It was because of your bladder?* "Maybe you should ask Amy what to do if it happens again," I suggested. He said he would.

It was pouring out as the jury left the courthouse. Unfortunately, my car was being worked on at a garage that day, so I had taken the train. A few of us waded through the puddles together as we briskly walked to South Station. Water could be wringed from our clothing by the time we reached shelter.

The train to Manchester-by-the-Sea arrived. Dripping, I stepped into the car. I immediately spotted a familiar middle-aged woman and young man enter through another door. I recognized them as daily spectators at the trial. They always sat with family members of murdered victims but were never called to the stand to testify as many of the other family members had been. We sat opposite one another on the train, pretending not to notice. There was something exceptional about them, though I couldn't define what. The quiet manner in which they carried themselves? The gentle way in which they seemed to relate to one another? I just didn't know. As I was watching them, I heard the young man refer to the woman as "Mom."

Why are they present every day? Which victim do they grieve? My questions would have to wait.

~

By day thirteen, the jury members were familiar and comfortable with one another—except Larry. He just wasn't fitting in—with anyone.

His know-it-all attitude and need to dominate every conversation was wearing on everyone.

Other than that, we were bonding. Irene twisted her knee and as a result was forced to take the elevator up and down to the courtroom. We all watched out for her. Kim was planning a weekend getaway to Las Vegas; we were all jealous. She continued to arrive each day just as we were ready to line up. That was just the way it was. Brad's grandmother had become very ill, and his son was taking it hard. Sam's daughter was getting married in just a few weeks. Poor Sam, father of the bride while in the midst of this trial. Elizabeth had had a car accident. She was fine, but the car needed help. The men gave her pointers on what to do. Pam wasn't sure if she had a job to go back to after the trial; we were all pulling for her. We had bonded, yet none of us knew what the other was thinking with regard to this trial, except for Larry, of course, because he was determined to let it be known whenever possible: "Hang him now and hang him high!"

The routine was the same. Line up, go down a flight, wait for Irene to get off the elevator, line up again. Except now Smitty would pretend to lead us in some jumping jacks or stretching exercises. We were now comfortable enough with one another to push down a tag on the back of the shirt or straighten the collar of the juror in front of us as we waited for Amy to open the door. On more than one occasion, Richard, standing behind me, was kind enough to attend to a mishap on the back of my blouse or sweater.

"Amy, I need another notebook. I go through them fast," Richard said. Amy nodded and asked if anyone else needed one. No one did.

No surprise you need one, I thought, remembering the size of his penmanship.

"I spoke to Amy," Richard whispered to me. "She said we should raise our hand if we need to use the bathroom."

"Good to know," was my response. "Just like in a classroom."

"All rise for the jury." The words rang out once Amy opened the door. As I walked toward the jury box, I continued to glance at the prosecution and defense teams, as well as at Thomas Devaney. The difference now was the growing contempt I felt for the assistant US attorneys.

Day thirteen introduced Ken Arnold, the retired supervisory special agent of the Organized Crime Squad of the Boston FBI. Chavere was on direct, and from the start, she treated Special Agent Arnold with noted respect. We soon discovered that Arnold had been in that supervisory position with Skip Goot as his direct subordinate. Goot, we were told, had introduced Arnold to Thomas Devaney and to Devaney's apparent sidekick, Tony Diavolo—a name that continued to come up frequently in various testimonies. According to Arnold, both Devaney and Diavolo had been informants handled by Goot. And, per Arnold, Devaney became somewhat of a social associate as well, dining at Arnold's home, where the latter's poor wife felt threatened, or dining at the home of Arnold's mistress, who was his personal secretary at the FBI office. She, apparently, didn't have a problem with having high-echelon organized crime figures at her dinner table.

Quickly, the relationship between Arnold and Devaney had become tainted, as Arnold began to accept gifts of expensive wine and large sums of cash. Devaney, we were told, even made arrangements, at his expense, to have Arnold's mistress fly to meet him and enjoy the luxury and leisure at an official FBI function.

In a word, Arnold was crooked. That was determined quickly. But it did not stop Chavere from tormenting the jury again with FBI document after document. They were all the same documents we had seen when Michael Biscione, the scowling agent from the Inspector General's Office, was on the stand.

Except for one …

This document had been filed in 1985. It stated that Devaney had informed Special Agent Goot that then district attorney Bob Costa was seen at a political fund-raiser at a Boston restaurant. According to the document, DA Costa was taking "toots" of cocaine in the men's lounge, along with some other notable figures who were not identified.

I was stunned, and grateful that the defense's paralegal wasn't looking at me. *This doesn't make any sense!* my thoughts screamed. *It has nothing at all to do with tipping off the FBI on members involved in organized crime. It's nothing like the other documents we viewed. Why wasn't it shown when Biscione was on the stand? Why now? What worthy insight does it reveal, even if true?* I glanced at those journalists visible to my right. As I feared, they were tweeting and texting.

Bob has no idea that the media is making this accusation public! Agitated, I suddenly felt sick to my stomach. There was absolutely nothing I could do, but I desperately wanted to warn him, to protect him.

As quickly as the document came onto the screen, it came off.

"I suppose Mr. Devaney didn't care much for DA Costa," Chavere smugly stated as she moved on to another document.

"No. He didn't," came Arnold's short reply.

The questioning went on as my body trembled. *Deep breaths, Alexandra; take deep breaths,* I told myself.

As with Biscione's testimony, Chavere attempted to prove that Devaney was an informant. I didn't buy it then, and I certainly wasn't buying it now. Arnold began giving details of his relationship with Devaney. The defense made an objection on some point, and a sidebar was called. The annoying static of the noise machine came on.

Normally, Devaney would stay focused by writing on a legal pad in front of him. On the rare occasion, he would look up at the attorneys during a sidebar. I noticed that whenever he did this, Chavere would fix a stern gaze on him, and keep it fixed until the defendant looked away. During this sidebar, Devaney looked straight at Ken Arnold and said, in a barely audible voice, "You fucking liar."

Of course, this set the journalists into a silent frenzy. Their fingers moved frantically over the keyboards of their cell phones, each wanting to be the first to get this "news" out!

Judge Blake apparently didn't hear the statement, but Altier did, and made certain that the judge was immediately informed. The judge admonished Devaney, instructing him to speak through his attorneys. Softly, Devaney apologized.

When Chavere returned to the lectern, she had Arnold describe how the FBI had asked Devaney and his cohort Diavolo to draw a detailed map of the office where the Mafia met in Boston. Because of the map, the FBI was able to successfully conceal wiretaps in the building. Shortly thereafter, the FBI took down the hierarchy of the local Mafia.

Rob Willis was on cross; he was magnificently brutal. Under fire with firm and relentless questions, Arnold admitted to having lied again and again. He lied to superiors, FBI headquarters, judges, and of course his poor wife. Rules that applied to others didn't seem to apply to Arnold. He had a history of unethical behavior from the start of his FBI career. It was apparent to me that this man was not a reliable witness.

He claimed to have received a total of $5,000 in cash from Devaney, and admitted that he had taken bribes of money and gifts of costly trips from other informants.

Judge Blake, stopping Willis, suggested it was a good time to end for the day. Willis reluctantly agreed. As Arnold moved away from the witness box and toward the doors at the back of the courtroom, Michael Biscione, the scowling agent from the Inspector General's Office, walked alongside him, placing his arm over Arnold's shoulders in what appeared to be an act of comfort. For the first time, Biscione wore a smile.

There's something very wrong with this picture. My thoughts were disrupted as Judge Blake began to give us his standard weekend warning to remember the oath we took and behave ourselves.

Though it was Friday and I knew I had to beat the weekend traffic heading north, I drove straight to Salem. I pulled into Bob Costa's parking lot. His car was there. I tore a piece of paper out of the notebook I had in my car. "You were mentioned in a derogatory manner in court today. The media might try to have a field day with what was said." I didn't sign the note. Timidly, I got out and placed it under the windshield wiper of his car, praying that no one would see me. Nervously looking around, I got back into my car and headed home. "Damn! I should have asked if he was going to the wedding."

It occurred to me that Nick Mudd was to appear at the local bookstore this very weekend. As I drove, I imagined what I would do if I went to hear him speak. *I'd just stand in the back of the room and glare at him. Then, after he was done with his presentation, I'd ask him outright, in front of his mesmerized audience, "Isn't it true, Mr. Mudd, that half of the money these good people give you for the book will be placed in the hands of Vinnie Giuda? Isn't it true, Mr. Mudd, that he has made $70,000 off this book, and counting, because he murdered twenty people? There's no story if there are no gruesome murders. And Vinnie is being rewarded monetarily because he is a murderer. Isn't it true, Mr. Mudd?"*

I knew that because I was a juror, I couldn't do it, but somehow I found pleasure in thinking about it.

I stopped by to see my mom, and then I headed home. Charlie and I took a ride up to New Hampshire to have dinner with Ilona; her husband, Steve; and the baby. My phone rang a few times. I let it go to voice mail. When I arrived home later that night, I listened to the messages. One was from Bob.

My heart raced as I listened to his voice. He laughed at me for being so worried about his being mentioned in court, informing me that he had been made aware of it through a journalist friend as soon as it happened. He then went on to gently scold me for leaving the note, and teasingly pointed out that, as an officer of the court, he would now be forced to properly discipline me when we next met. Again, he assured me that when the verdict was in, he would call.

I played the message three times. Tears welled in my eyes and a smile came to my lips as I listened to his calm and reassuring voice. My skin tingled at the thought of his properly disciplining me, with the hope that, at the very least, it would result in a passionate embrace. With the thought came the guilt. I thought of Paul as I twisted the diamond ring and wedding band on my left hand.

Chapter 5

Justice, sir, is the great interest of man on earth. It is the ligament which holds civilized beings and civilized nations together. Wherever her temple stands, and so long as it is duly honored, there is a foundation for general security, general happiness, and the improvement and progress of our race.
—Daniel Webster (1782–1852), US Congressman, US Senator, US Secretary of State

"TELL ME ABOUT IT, DEVANEY! WHAT DO YOU SEE? What do you hear?" the doctor shouted at the frightened prisoner, who was huddled in an upright fetal position in the corner of the hospital bed. Tommy Devaney attempted to cover his head with his arms.

A prison guard moved from his station near the door, yanked the young man's arms away, and smacked him on the side of the head. "Goddamn it! Do what you're told!"

Tommy slowly looked up, struggling to hold back sobs of terror. Hesitantly, he looked around the small white room, his moist blue eyes defensively squinting, his brow creased with apprehension. "Your voice is sending flames into the ceiling! It's catching fire! Green fire—" Again, he attempted to cover his head with his arms.

The guard hauled him off the bed and forcefully dumped him on the floor. Tommy quickly sat up, rapidly flapping his arms and blowing as though trying to put out the hallucinated fire. "It's working!" Tommy yelled breathlessly, and then he blew harder.

"What's working?" the doctor demanded, looking from Tommy to the bulky tape recorder on the table near to him.

Tommy frantically blew again, his arms still flapping. "The wind, frigid, blue. Deep, purple. Frigid blue."

"November 20, 1960, 0930," the doctor spoke to the tape recorder. "Twenty-six-year-old healthy Caucasian subject ingested five hundred micrograms of liquid lysergic acid diethylamide. Fifth dose in five days, titrated from fifty micrograms on day one." The doctor moved near to Tommy and squatted next to him, grabbing hold of one eyelid with one of his hands, while placing the other on his neck. "Pupils dilated. Rapid, bounding carotid pulse. Copious perspiration. Subject complained of nausea, vertigo, xerostomia, and insomnia prior to ingestion. Prior ingestion of five hundred micrograms has presented episodes of euphoria, instantaneously shifting to despair and confusion. Synesthesia was present, with subject describing the visualization of colors, odors, and sounds."

"Don't kill me!" Tommy desperately cried out, grabbing the doctor's neck. The guard lunged forward, hitting Tommy hard on the side of his head with the butt of his pistol.

Bleeding, Tommy fell to the floor and hurriedly slithered his body across the floor through his own dripping blood and under the small bed, hissing like a snake from beneath the metal frame.

~

Day fourteen began with a continuation of retired FBI supervisory special agent Ken Arnold's testimony. As I gazed at Arnold sitting in the witness box, I was taken aback by the likeness he bore to an elderly Adolf Hitler. He had the same beady eyes, toothbrush mustache, and spasmodic mannerisms. The realization sent a shiver up my spine.

Willis continued his cross-examination in true Willis style. I could see that we the jury were prepared, sitting with our pens against our papers, ready to feverishly attempt to catch as much as we could of the fast-paced, emotionally charged interrogation.

God, I would definitely want him if I were accused of a crime! I thought with admiration. *And I'd be terrified if called in to testify against one of his clients!* This timid young man turned into a tiger whenever he stood in front of the lectern. Frequent comments from the jury members indicated that others felt the same as I did.

Today, Willis would direct Arnold to tell us of his failing marriage. *No surprise,* I thought, *given the fact that his secretary was his mistress for ten years, and that he scared his wife and kids to death by bringing mob bosses home. "Guess who's coming to dinner?" took on a new meaning in that household!*

But as the line of questioning went on, we quickly discovered that Arnold's was not a normal divorce. Hardly!

The divorce was occurring at the same time pressure was being brought down on the Boston office of the FBI for possible corruption within. Arnold's wife was aware of some of the bribes he took, and she had proof of these large sums of cash being deposited into a savings account. This did not sit well with Arnold. She could reveal his corruption. Then what? Willis brought Arnold to this point and then asked a question that shook me to the core.

"Isn't it true, Mr. Arnold, that you asked the defendant Thomas Devaney to 'take care of' your wife?"

Devaney had stopped writing and was staring straight at Arnold.

"No!" Arnold called out. He appeared stunned. The color of his face turned ashen.

"Isn't it true, Mr. Arnold, that Thomas Devaney's response to your request to kill your wife was, 'Absolutely not!'?"

"Objection!" Chavere jumped up. "Asked and answered, Your Honor!"

This is insane! I thought. *The good guy is plotting a murder, and the bad guy is saving the victim's life!* With my immediate thought in response to Willis's question, I realized that I had no doubt that Arnold was capable of doing such a thing. The next line of questioning only solidified that belief.

"Mr. Arnold, who is Edward O'Leary?" Willis asked.

"O'Leary was involved in organized crime. Murdered a drug dealer working for the Mafia. This made O'Leary a marked man. He came to the FBI seeking protection for himself and his family. He wanted to get into the witness protection program in exchange for information."

"What information?"

"O'Leary informed the assistant special agent in charge of the Boston FBI office that Devaney had contacted him to ask if he would make a hit on a wealthy private businessman in Kentucky by the name of David Walton."

"Who was the assistant special agent in charge at this time?"

"Joseph Wallace."

"And ASAC Wallace was your superior?"

"Yes," Arnold answered.

I scanned my notes and found Vinnie Giuda's confession to the Walton murder. He had murdered Walton in an attempt to force the sale of his sports clubs to his best friend, Paul Scalise.

"O'Leary told ASAC Wallace that he turned down the offer to carry out the murder. Someone else killed Walton a few weeks later."

"Were you involved, in any capacity, with the handling of Edward O'Leary as an informant?"

"No."

"Did ASAC Wallace agree to place O'Leary in the witness protection program?"

"He tried."

"He tried? Wasn't he successful?"

"No."

"Why not?"

"I spoke to the special agents working directly with O'Leary. I convinced them that he wasn't a credible witness."

"Why did you do this?"

"The information O'Leary was claiming, and willing to testify to about Devaney, Giuda, and Diavolo, would be enough for indictments. My accepting bribes from Devaney would be found out."

"So, let me see if I have this straight, Mr. Arnold. You convinced Edward O'Leary's handlers that O'Leary shouldn't be in the witness protection program in an attempt to keep Thomas Devaney from being indicted?"

"Yes."

"And was Thomas Devaney made aware that Edward O'Leary would not enter the witness protection program?"

"Yes."

"How?"

"I told him," Arnold confessed, with no visible sign of shame.

"Did ASAC Wallace give up in his attempt to protect O'Leary?"

"No."

"Did he try to keep O'Leary in the program?"

"Yes."

"To your knowledge, was ASAC Wallace concerned that information about Edward O'Leary had been leaked and that O'Leary would be murdered if he weren't in the witness protection program?"

"Objection. Calls for speculation," Chavere called out.

"Overruled," Judge Blake responded.

"Yes," Arnold answered.

"What did he do in an attempt to keep O'Leary safe?"

"Wallace went to his superior in the Boston office. He was told that the request for protection was denied higher up and that nothing could be done. Wallace contacted FBI Headquarters in Washington, DC, directly, with no success."

I was amazed that this scummy former FBI agent was seemingly praising the attempts of his superior Joseph Wallace as Wallace struggled to protect the man Arnold was setting up to be murdered. *Guilt?* I wondered. *Is that why he's telling us of Wallace's determination to do the right thing?*

"Did ASAC Wallace give up?" Willis pressed.

"No. Wallace then went to the Massachusetts US attorney Floyd Nichols."

"Did the Massachusetts US attorney offer protection to Edward O'Leary?"

"No. US Attorney Nichols denied O'Leary protection."

"At this point, ASAC Wallace had nowhere else to turn, did he, Mr. Arnold? Edward O'Leary was on his own." Willis looked at the jury as he waited for the answer.

"No. He had exhausted his options and O'Leary had no protection."

Floyd Nichols? The same Floyd Nichols who became the governor of Massachusetts? I wondered, instantly remembering that this former governor's name was on the sheet listing the witnesses to be called. My thoughts were interrupted as I caught the stare of the defense attorneys' paralegal. She wrote something down and moved her gaze to Richard. She was studying us again.

Rob Willis dragged out of Ken Arnold what had become of Edward O'Leary. A few days after O'Leary was thrown out of the witness protection program, he and a friend named Donald Monahan were murdered. They had just gotten into a car after having a drink at a South Boston restaurant. A second car drove up; a man got out, firing a semiautomatic machine gun at O'Leary and Monahan.

"Donald Monahan was just in the wrong place at the wrong time?" Willis asked.

"Unfortunately," was Arnold's emotionless response.

"Mr. Monahan had a wife and three young daughters at the time. Do you realize, Mr. Arnold, that they are sitting in the gallery?"

Arnold had no response.

"Did you ever apologize to the Monahan family, or the O'Leary family, for taking part in the murder of their loved ones?" Willis boldly asked.

"No," Arnold mumbled.

"Objection. Irrelevant!" Chavere awkwardly blurted.

"Don't you think you owe them an apology?" Willis persisted.

Judge Blake banged his gavel and mumbled something. Chavere sat down.

Arnold's face turned a vibrant red. "I am so very sorry for the grief I have brought—" he began, with tears rolling down his cheeks.

He's not crying because he's sorry for setting these men up to be murdered. He's crying because he's embarrassed that Willis has him by the balls and is forcing him to acknowledge the families of his dead victims. How very strange that the attorney defending Devaney, the man accused of murdering O'Leary and Monahan, is more sympathetic to the grief of these families than the prosecuting attorneys seem to be. What's happening here?

This moment of high drama was not the close of Willis's cross, as I'd assumed it might be. He went on to draw out more information from Ken Arnold. My thoughts protested, realizing that this sleazy man's testimony had me emotionally drained. It was as though Judge Blake could read my mind. He'd probably observed that we were all pretty wasted in the jury box, and perhaps he was too. He called for a twenty-minute break.

We jurors drank our coffee in silence. Most of us stood, enjoying the opportunity to stretch our legs. Some, like me, gazed out the window, lost in our thoughts. Everyone seemed shaken by Arnold, all except Larry, who was sitting at the table trying to get one of the men to talk about motorcycle engines. None of them would. All too soon, we were lining up to go back in.

Arnold was back on the witness stand. He stared at the jury as we filed in.

Willis took us back to the time when Arnold was seeking a divorce from his wife. At that time, the corruption within the Boston office of the FBI was being uncovered by ASAC Wallace. Arnold was afraid it would be discovered that he was taking bribes from informants.

But Arnold's corruption wouldn't be known unless others involved came forward. Who could have accused him? Special Agent Skip Goot? Devaney and Diavolo? Arnold's wife? Is this the reason he asked Devaney to kill her? I considered, determined in my mind that this last option was true.

"So, Mr. Arnold, you had to divert attention away from yourself. You had to silence Thomas Devaney. How did you attempt to do this?" Willis asked, unintentionally indicating that I was on the right track.

"I told a Boston reporter that Devaney was a top-echelon FBI informant," Arnold stated.

"It was a particular reporter you asked for, wasn't it?"

"Yes."

"A reporter who would later write a book called *Devil's Town*, which is partially based on your version of the relationship you had with Thomas Devaney?"

"Objection. Irrelevant." Chavere barely tried to stand.

"Sustained," Judge Blake agreed.

"This reporter was a journalist for the *Boston Times*, wasn't he?"

"Yes."

"And this journalist knew it was sacrosanct within the FBI to keep the identity of an informant—especially a top-echelon informant—secret, didn't he?"

"I don't know," Arnold lied.

Willis laughed. "Of course he did, Mr. Arnold. Just as you knew that revealing the identity of an informant was a severe violation within the FBI, a violation you were publicly willing to commit." Rob Willis turned and faced the jury as he continued. "Please, Mr. Arnold, tell the jury why you were willing to commit such a public violation."

Arnold looked toward Chavere. Chavere offered nothing but a blank stare.

"By stating that Devaney was an informant, I felt certain that he would be murdered by one of his own men, or members of the Mafia."

"And if that were to happen, Devaney would never have the opportunity to tell about your corruption or silence you." Willis was still looking at the jury.

"No. He wouldn't." Arnold was noticeably trembling as he squirmed to avoid Devaney's stare.

Willis turned back to face Arnold. "But things didn't work out as you'd planned. The fact is, Mr. Arnold, no one within organized crime believed Devaney was an informant."

"No."

"But now, sir, you had backed yourself into a corner. You revealed the identity of a so-called informant and were found to have taken bribes from him?"

"Yes."

"You were concerned that your estranged wife might have financial documents attesting to the fact that you accepted bribes from three criminals?"

"Yes."

"You were facing certain indictment, weren't you, Mr. Arnold?"

"Yes."

"But you never were indicted. Why don't you tell the jury what occurred that kept you out of prison."

"Objection. Inflammatory!" Chavere bounced up.

"Overruled."

"I made a proffer with the US Attorney's Office."

"Yes. Quickly! You quickly made a proffer. In fact, you gave up the names of a few in the brotherhood of the FBI, didn't you?"

"I identified corrupt agents, yes."

"During Assistant US Attorney Chavere's direct-examination, didn't you describe your colleague Special Agent Skip Goot as a very close friend?"

"Yes."

"He was among those you declared corrupt as part of your proffer, wasn't he?"

"Yes."

"And you continued to insist that Thomas Devaney was a top-echelon informant, which somehow gained you great favor from both the FBI and US Attorney's Office."

Chavere began to rise from her chair to object. Willis glanced at her and kept talking.

"Mr. Arnold, following your proffer to the US Attorney's Office, were you caught, on more than one occasion, lying to a grand jury?"

"Yes."

"Mr. Arnold, let me see if I have this straight. You revealed the so-called identity of a top-echelon informant to a newspaper in the hopes of having Mr. Devaney murdered; you lied numerous times to a grand jury; you were found to have taken bribes while in a supervisory role within the FBI; and you were an accessory to the murders of Edward O'Leary and Donald Monahan by knowingly leaking information. Did you spend any time in prison?"

"No."

"Were you discharged from the FBI?"

"No."

"Were you punished at all, sir?"

"Yes."

"Please, enlighten the jury as to what your punishment was."

"I was docked a month's pay and put on probation for one year," Arnold stated.

"And, Mr. Arnold, after that year's probation, weren't you praised within the FBI for your superior performance as an agent and promoted?"

"Yes, I was," Arnold's proud response came.

"You were sent to head up the Los Angeles office, and continued to be promoted as the years passed, teaching recruits at the FBI Academy in Quantico, Virginia, and serving at FBI Headquarters in Washington, DC, when you finally retired with a full pension?"

"Yes. I realized my error and worked tirelessly to make up for it."

"Your error—" Willis tried in vain to conceal a scoff. "You were forced into retirement because of a heart condition?"

"Yes."

"Why don't you tell the jury about your last day at work, sir. You were in your Washington, DC, office. Did Thomas Devaney call you on the phone?"

Devaney was intently staring at Arnold.

"Yes. Somehow he tracked down my number."

"When you received this phone call, how long had it been since you'd had any contact with Thomas Devaney?" Willis asked.

"Seven, maybe eight years."

"I imagine you were taken aback when you heard Mr. Devaney's voice on the other end of the phone?"

"Yes."

"Please tell the jury about the request Thomas Devaney made on the phone that day."

"He asked me to recant the story of him being a top-echelon informant for the FBI—"

"Did he make a comment that he bought information from the FBI, that he didn't sell it to them?"

"He did."

"He asked you to recant the story. Did he say any more in reference to this request?"

"He told me that he would never talk about our relationship. If I recanted the story, he wouldn't rat on me."

"Was that all he said?" Willis pressed.

"He said if I didn't recant the story and he went down, he'd take me with him." Arnold seemed shaken.

"And the conversation ended? Tell the jury why it ended."

"I suffered a heart attack and dropped the phone. I was forced into retirement because of it." Arnold tried to sound like a victim.

"So, Mr. Arnold, are you telling the jury that Mr. Devaney's threat to take you down with him if you did not retract the story of him being an FBI informant was the cause of your heart attack?"

"Objection! Incompetent! Calls for speculation!" The veins in Chavere's face were bulging. Her bases for the objection were so loud that Willis's response could not be heard by the judge.

Curt Jordan, coming to the aid of his partner, stood. He shouted above Chavere's disorderliness, declaring, "I object to her objection!"

"Objections sustained," Judge Blake called out.

"All objections, Your Honor?" Rob Willis timidly asked.

"Ms. Chavere's objections!" The judge seemed almost as confused as me.

"Following this sudden heart attack," Rob Willis began without missing a beat, "you retired with your former secretary, who was also your mistress—"

"She's my wife," Arnold interrupted.

"Ah, yes, Mr. Arnold. You divorced your first wife and married your secretary. So, following this sudden heart attack, you and the new Mrs. Arnold moved immediately to the West Coast?"

"Yes."

"With a full pension?"

"Yes."

"That's quite an amazing story. You're an accessory to two murders, and a federal judge determined that you employed a willing Boston journalist to help you get Thomas Devaney killed by the underworld in publishing the article about his supposed informant status. Add to that your acknowledged corruption while working for the FBI—"

"Is there a question in this monologue, Your Honor?" Chavere objected, not even attempting to stand.

"Mr. Arnold, you collect a full pension from American taxpayers. Do you also have a monetary agreement with the authors of *Devil's Town* regarding a percentage of book sales?"

"Objection! Irrelevant."

"Your Honor, Ms. Chavere had no problem revealing the income of Vincent Giuda for his movie rights and book royalties with Nicholas Mudd. Why shouldn't Mr. Arnold be able to reveal what proceeds he may be receiving for his confessed crimes?"

"Answer the question, Mr. Arnold," the judge instructed.

"Minimal."

"How minimal, Mr. Arnold?"

"I would have to consult with my accountant to get a figure."

"And, Mr. Arnold, isn't it true that this book, the story of which you set in motion, is in the process of becoming a feature film?"

"That's what I'm told."

"And with the production of this movie, the book sales for *Devil's Town* will increase, won't they?"

"I suppose."

"Yeah, I suppose," Rob Willis agreed, gathering his notes from the lectern. "It seems crime does pay, doesn't it, Mr. Arnold? How do you sleep at night?"

"Objection! Inflammatory!"

"I have no more questions."

I was aware that I was leaning forward at this point, shaking my head in disbelief. I didn't give a damn who saw me. I was also aware that Thomas Devaney was shaking his head, ever so slightly. *Well, isn't that a storybook ending! Arnold and his adulterous secretary can live happily ever after at the taxpayers' expense! And a so-called professional journalist takes part in a conspiracy of murder yet never gets punished—never even loses his job. Yet Stanley Onesta spent twenty-two freaking years in jail for a robbery he didn't commit?* I was so disgusted that I wanted to spit!

Chavere eagerly came to the lectern determined, so it seemed, to set things straight with her redirect. She accomplished nothing, as far as I was concerned. Willis then returned for one last jab. With a few questions, he dug the knife in deeper and deeper. Finally, when the damage to Arnold's character was complete, Willis stopped. And again Michael Biscione walked out with his buddy Arnold.

I was able to hold myself together on the drive home. Then, in the safety of my house, I sobbed as the emotions of the horrific day poured out. The absolute cunning, deceit, and murderous treachery of a man who had taken an oath to uphold the US Constitution and protect the citizens who claimed it as their own was almost too much to bear. The Department of Justice went on to reward him with praise and promotions. And the scandalous attempt he made with a willing journalist to have Devaney murdered was turned into a profitable book. Now it would be a movie and perhaps Hollywood would reward him as well. The rage within threatened to push me over the edge.

Charlie came into the house, and followed the sound of my sobs. I was sitting on the ottoman in the living room, my head down, my arms folded tightly across my chest, attempting to soothe myself by rocking back and forth. I looked up at his innocent young face; mine was stained with tears and swollen with grief. His expression was one of love and concern. He walked toward me, kneeled, and held me in his arms. Our roles were completely reversed. The fearless son was comforting his distraught mother. With the reassurance of his strength, my body began to tremble as I fought to keep the oath sworn.

~

When we arrived in the jury room on day sixteen, there was a floral plant in the center of the table. "Where'd that come from?" Kim asked as she came in—the last one, as usual.

"Don't know. It was just here," Maureen responded.

"A nice bit of décor," Irene added.

"I hate to complain, but I wish they'd add a little protein to the food they bring for break. I'm getting tired of muffins and bagels. I need something with more substance," Pam said. She prepared her coffee and sat down.

"Like what?" I asked.

"I don't know, maybe cheese and crackers."

"That'd be nice," Katie agreed.

A knock on the door, followed by Smitty's appearance, meant that it was time to line up.

Day sixteen proved more merciful, with a couple of flamboyant thugs. One was a sleazy drug dealer. His testimony was more of a comedy act. He even had Judge Blake laughing at one point. And his friendship with the defendant, who years before had saved his brother's life, was apparent.

"Hi, Tommy! It's been a long time," came the cheerful salutation from the witness in the middle of his testimony.

Devaney had been observing since the moment this witness had taken the stand, and laughing out loud at times. He returned the greeting with a warm smile, saying, "Hi! Wish it had been longer."

"That's right, Tommy. Wish we never had to meet again, at least not like this."

There were no objections. This was the prosecution's witness, and their team seemed momentarily taken aback by the situation. The defense seemed content to let the conversation continue.

This is too strange, I thought with a grin. *Kind of sweet, but in a sick sort of way!*

Judge Blake gave both men a stern look, and then instructed the jury to take an early break.

Walking into the jury room, we were surprised to see that the food had already been delivered: muffins, bagels, fruit, and a tray of cubed cheese and crackers. Pam was visibly stunned. "How'd they know?" she asked, referring to her stated desire for cheese and crackers only an hour or so earlier. "Is that plant bugged?"

We all laughed—except for Pam.

Court ended early that day. I took the opportunity to wander over to the Boston Public Library to do some research on John Hancock. As I waited in line to speak to the reference librarian, I overheard the young man in front of me ask where he would find the books on Thomas Devaney and the Old Harbor Gang. I wanted to say something, but obviously I couldn't. I took a deep breath as the librarian directed him to a particular section of the massive library.

I don't think the kid's gonna get a true account of anything from those books, I thought, sighing. *What is the truth?* It was already apparent to me that we in the courtroom weren't hearing it, and probably never would.

Chapter 6

Injustice anywhere is a threat to justice everywhere.
—Martin Luther King Jr. (1929–1968), American
Baptist minister, activist, humanitarian

THE SMALL BLACK-AND-WHITE PICTURE, NO MORE
than three inches by two inches, was Tom's most valued possession.
He would stare at it several times a day. Each aspect was memorized,
every shade known. This faded picture of Tom, Kathleen, and their
two pups, Luna and Bella, flooded his mind with pleasant memories. "She achieved in me what prison and law enforcement couldn't:
eighteen years crime-free." He smiled as he recalled the many stray
animals they would attempt to rescue. It became their life's work while
on the lam.

Tom had felt affection for Kathleen years before he went into hiding. She was a beautiful and accomplished woman, fifteen years his ju-
nior, who valued her family and friends above all else. Kathleen knew
little about his dark side, and it was Tom's intent to keep it that way.

He came to love her when she agreed to share his life on the run.
It turned out to be a honeymoon that lasted almost two decades. Now
she was gone.

He tucked the picture safely within a pad of paper. Though he wrote
many letters to many people from his solitary prison cell, this writing
pad was used only for letters to Kathleen. Daily he wrote her, expressing his love and greatest concerns—mostly for her. The letters, dozens
of them, were placed in neat piles under his mattress. They'd never be

sent. They couldn't be sent; Kathleen's sentencing demanded that she not be allowed to communicate in any way with Tom Devaney. It had been almost two years since he'd heard her soft voice, gazed upon her delicate face, or felt the gentle stroke of her hand. This punishment proved to be the harshest of anything Chavere had inflicted—worse than solitary confinement, worse than the strip searches, worse than the goon squad's frequent destruction of his belongings. "Yet they never touch these letters," Tom whispered. "Another form of torture, keeping me aware of all I can't tell her. The letters will pile up, week after week. month after month, year after year."

~

On day seventeen, the guns were back on the table, pointed at the jury. I noted that the witness called did not enter the stand to take the oath, but stopped well to the left of it, out of Devaney's view. When Devaney heard the man's voice in response to the oath, he turned quickly, straining to look. I was immediately curious.

This witness was a middle-aged man. He was quite attractive—stocky and formidable, with a military-style haircut. He wore a black T-shirt under a powder-gray suit coat. The look was reminiscent of the old cop show *Miami Vice*—very sexy. And, by the way he conducted himself, one might assume he was in law enforcement. A bad assumption.

He identified himself as Ben James. The name was instantly recognized. He had been spoken of in various testimonies as having been like a son to Devaney—his trusted aide-de-camp.

No wonder Devaney was straining to look at him. It's the first time he's laid eyes on him in eighteen years. I observed that Ben James had Devaney's full attention.

Ben came across as a gentleman. He was rather soft-spoken and mellow under the careful guidance of Altier. He explained how he had gotten involved with the Old Harbor Gang straight out of high school. He was Devaney's chauffeur. They quickly bonded, and Devaney took the teen under his wing.

Within no time, Ben was quite involved with the crimes of the gang: extortion, racketeering, money laundering, and murder. Document after document was presented to the jury regarding these crimes. Also introduced was picture after picture of Devaney with Ben, eagerly pulled from the piles of documents and handed to Altier by his ever-willing female assistant. Altier saturated the jury with "proof," through pictures, that Ben James was indeed close to Devaney.

It became so obnoxious that I wanted to cry out, "What, do you think we're stupid? We get the point! They were friends!" I remained silent, but angrily imprinted my frustration in my notebook.

Upon the request of Altier, James was given permission by Judge Blake to approach the gun table and identify the pieces. He picked up each piece, carefully pointing the barrel downward.

A criminal handling submachine guns? Isn't this special! Well, at least he knows the proper way to hold them! I thought, recalling Chavere's prior clumsy and potentially dangerous display.

Ben James narrated for us the supposed details of five murders to which he was an accessory. The first two were Ed O'Leary, the informant whom the FBI removed from witness protection, and his friend Donald Monahan. Ben claimed he had notified Devaney over a walkie-talkie when O'Leary came out of the restaurant. Devaney was allegedly waiting in a nearby car, submachine gun in hand.

"Unfortunate for Monahan. He was in the wrong place at the wrong time." Ben's emotionless statement came with a slight shrug of his shoulders.

Hearing a gasp from the gallery, I turned to see an older woman in the center section who was obviously distraught over the callousness of Ben James's remark.

Again, the paralegal for the defense attorneys had her radar fixed on us. Scanning each of our faces, she jotted down notes.

The third, fourth, and fifth murders Ben James confessed to having taken part in took place in a house owned by the brother of an Old Harbor Gang member, Alan Hand. According to Ben James, each of the three victims was lured to this house under false pretenses on separate occasions. Once in the house, they were killed by Diavolo and Devaney. Ben James did nothing to bring about their deaths—and nothing to prevent them. He was simply part of the cleanup and burial detail. It was on-the-job training of sorts. Tony Diavolo taught him how to strip the bodies, pull out the teeth, clean up the blood, and dig the graves in the dirt floor of the cellar. Alan Hand would provide the lime to aid in the decomposition of the bodies.

"You have confessed to being present when Buddy Bartlett was murdered. Why was he brought to the house?" Altier asked.

"Bartlett robbed banks. He gave a percentage to the Old Harbor Gang to safely stay in business. Tommy discovered that Bartlett was holding out on payment from a recent robbery."

"What happened when Mr. Bartlett arrived at the house?"

"He was chained to a chair and questioned about where the money was hidden."

"How long did this go on?"

"Five, six hours. Brutal interrogations, threats to his life. They wore him down."

"He gave up the hiding place?"

"Yeah."

"Then what happened."

"Tommy and Tony told me to stay with Bartlett while they went to retrieve the money."

"Did it occur to you to let him go while they were gone?"

"No. I figured they'd come back and let him go."

"But they didn't?"

"No. When they got back, Bartlett was unchained and told to go down the cellar. He asked if he could have a picture from his wallet. Tommy had me get it out for him and then pushed him toward the cellar door. Before we reached the bottom step, Tommy pulled out his revolver and shot Bartlett in the back of the head."

"Where were you and Anthony Diavolo when the gun was fired?"

"I was behind Tommy. Tony was in front of Bartlett."

"And then what happened?"

"Tommy said he was going upstairs to take a nap and told Tony and me to take care of the body."

"You said earlier that Alan Hand assisted with this?"

"Yeah. He came by later with the lime."

"Who was in the photo that Mr. Bartlett wanted from his wallet?" Altier asked.

"A little girl. He held the picture to his chest and was whispering a prayer when he walked down to the cellar. I was later told that it was a picture of his daughter." Ben James looked toward the gallery while answering.

Is the daughter here? I wondered, a tear escaping my eye.

"Please, give the jury the details of the second murder you witnessed in this house," Altier instructed.

Ben James went on to give his account of Will McCarthy's death. McCarthy was suspected of leaking information that had led to a botched attempt to smuggle guns to the Irish Republican Army, as well as information on a shipment of marijuana. Once McCarthy was lured to the house, he was taken to the kitchen, chained to a chair, and interrogated. About six hours later, he was taken to the cellar, where Devaney allegedly attempted to strangle him. It wasn't working. Devaney then asked McCarthy if he wanted it fast.

"Yes, please," McCarthy was purported to have answered. Ben James claimed that Devaney shot McCarthy in the head, but the bullet didn't kill him. Devaney shot him four more times in the face, and then declared, "Now he's dead." Again, Ben James claimed, Devaney went upstairs to take a nap while he, Diavolo, and Alan Hand took care of the body.

Devaney takes a nap? What's that about? I wondered. It seemed a strange fact to throw in. And though the first two murders described were disturbing, the third, for me, was exceptionally so.

Tony Diavolo had a stepdaughter named Sandy Ford who, as a young adult, had been caught up in drugs and prostitution. According to Ben James, she became a problem for Diavolo and Devaney. She often spoke about them in public, drawing unwanted attention. Diavolo brought her to the house one cold January afternoon. Diavolo lied to Sandy, telling her that he was taking her out to buy a winter coat, but saying that he had to make a quick stop at the house first.

"Were you at the house when Sandra Ford arrived?" Altier asked.

"Yes. I was upstairs in the bathroom. I opened the bathroom door and heard a thud downstairs. When I came down, I saw Sandy on the floor with Tommy standing over her."

"Did you know that Thomas Devaney and Anthony Diavolo intended to kill her?"

"A woman? No."

"Sandra Ford was on the floor with Thomas Devaney standing over her. Then what happened?"

"Tony dragged her down to the cellar and mumbled that her heart was still beating. He grabbed a rope and strangled her." Ben James showed no emotion.

"What happened next?"

"Tony took her clothes off and pulled out her teeth. We dug a hole and buried her beside the two other bodies."

Defense Attorney Curt Jordan was on cross. As he began laying the groundwork that Ben James, not Devaney, turned out to be the informant, the witness's personality changed drastically. Suddenly, Ben James was quick with wiseacre remarks.

Poof! I thought. *Just like magic. A complete gentleman one moment and an absolute ass the next!* I found myself thinking.

Chavere quickly became flustered by Jordan's questions, and was aggressively whispering to Altier, who hesitantly responded with objections. Two sidebars were quickly called.

Jordan went on to develop the story. Ben James had been Devaney's closest associate. James claimed that FBI Special Agent Skip Goot met him on an exceptionally warm December day and instructed James to tell Devaney that an indictment was coming down. Upon hearing James's warning, Devaney left Massachusetts. Throughout the first year that Devaney was on the lam, Jamesz was in contact with him.

James, it seemed, knew many of Devaney's secrets. He was aware of all the gifts of money and expensive items that Devaney passed out to all branches and levels of local law enforcement—especially at Christmastime. Ben James claimed that he delivered many of the items himself.

"What was it that my client Thomas Devaney said about Christmas?" Jordan asked.

"Tommy told me that Christmas was for kids and cops," James stated, with Jordan uttering the words in unison.

"And, Mr. James, what was the last instruction that Thomas Devaney gave you?"

James hesitated, and then he looked straight at Devaney when he quoted the words: "If you're ever indicted, put it all on me."

Again, Jordan uttered the last part of his statement in unison. "And isn't that what you did, Mr. James? When you were indicted, didn't you implicate Thomas Devaney in all these crimes so that you could get a deal with Assistant US Attorneys Chavere and Altier?"

"No!" the witness protested.

"But of course, Mr. James, you never anticipated that Mr. Devaney would be caught. Now you have to stick to your story or you go back to prison."

"That's not true!" James continued to protest. Altier jumped up to object. Regardless of Altier's objection, Ben James continued to talk. Altier finally gave him a hand signal, which obviously meant "Shut up now!", because that's exactly what the witness did.

"How long were you prepped by the assistant US attorneys for today's testimony, Mr. James?"

"About ten hours. They're good attorneys, very thorough," he replied, attempting to praise the character and dedication of Chavere and Altier.

"Very thorough, I'm sure," Jordan said sarcastically, glancing at Chavere and Altier. He then quickly turned his focus back on Ben James and his problem of being a habitual liar. Jordan's questions were relentless.

"I'm telling the truth!" James furiously yelled to Jordan.

"Mr. James, you have been lying for a very long time. Are you capable of differentiating between truth and a falsehood?" Jordan chided.

"You goddamn ... Why don't you meet me in an alley after we're done here?" Ben James roared.

"Excuse me?" Jordan asked, and then he looked at the judge, who seemed engrossed in whatever was on his computer screen.

"I'm not lying!" James yelled as he attempted to get up. The US marshal sitting next to the witness stand rose to his feet, gesturing for James to sit.

Attorney Jordan went silent, his gaze fixed on Judge Blake. The dramatic hush of the courtroom sent a chill up my spine.

"Your Honor, in my many years serving before the bench, I have never witnessed such behavior be allowed in a courtroom."

Judge Blake appeared to me like a child being shamed into doing what was right. He quietly—hesitantly—warned Ben James to comport himself.

Jordan continued, pulling from Ben James's own mouth the summation of his life.

"Yes, I'm a liar!" the witness finally declared under oath. "I've spent my life as a criminal, and I'm a good liar. I lied to my wife about my girlfriends, and to my girlfriends about my other girlfriends! I lied to my parents. For Christ's sake, I shouldn't play poker if I can't lie!" Rather than appearing embarrassed, Ben James, I noted, seemed to be proud of his candid outburst.

"Mr. James, during Mr. Altier's direct examination, he questioned you about the O'Leary and Monahan murders. Witnesses at the scene of the murders said there was a second gunman in the car. Who was this gunman?"

"Don't know. I was never told. He had on a ski mask. I couldn't see who it was."

"Really? Would it surprise you, Mr. James, if I told you that my client identified the other gunman as Alan Hand?"

Ben James looked uneasy. "I have no idea who it was," he mumbled, as Altier stood to object.

"Withdrawn," Jordan said.

As the questions continued, the jury was told how indictments came down on Giuda, Diavolo, Ben James, and Devaney. Of course, Devaney was already on the lam and nowhere to be found. The others had been arrested. Giuda had been the first to cut a deal with Chavere.

Upon hearing of Vinnie Giuda's deal, and having been convinced by Chavere that Devaney was an FBI informant, Ben James was ready to spill his guts to get out of prison.

"Mr. James, if you were not bound by your immunity agreement with the US Attorney's Office, would you change anything in regard to your testimony?" Jordan asked.

Altier and Chavere shot to their feet, yelling, "Objection!"

"Why would I change my testimony? I'm telling the truth!" James shot back above the roar of the prosecuting attorneys' objection.

Curt Jordan smiled at Ben James.

"Why should I change a word of my testimony when the one person I trusted the most turned out to be an informant?" He stopped, looking straight at Thomas Devaney. "You can't rat on a rat!"

"Fuck you!" Devaney shouted to Ben James.

"Fuck you!" James yelled back.

"Order!" the judge shouted.

The US marshals were immediately on their feet, hands resting on their firearms.

Seven of them, I counted in my head. *Two with Devaney, one near the witness stand, one near the judge, one near the jury, and two at the doors.* From day one, the members of the jury wondered how many US marshals were present. No one would give us an answer. *Now we know!*

The actual outburst didn't shake me in the least. *No surprise with such tension between these two! It's amazing there hasn't been more,* I thought. But of course the journalists were busy relating the outburst in real time, I noted. *Drama sells!*

"Mr. James, your deal with the assistant US attorneys came immediately after you learned that Vinnie Giuda had talked, and just one day before Tony Diavolo did. You gave information about Mr. Devaney to Ms. Chavere. It was your version of the truth. But you just admitted under oath that you're a liar."

"Objection ... Your ... Honor." Standing, Altier dragged out the words as though Curt Jordan's offense was apparent to all.

"Overruled," the immediate response came from the bench.

I couldn't help but smile. The arrogant Altier plopped down in unanticipated defeat. The look of incredulity upon his face was priceless.

Curt Jordan continued. "You gave your version of the truth to assure yourself of a lighter sentence for your part in five murders. For that information, you got five years for five murders. Not a bad deal; not a bad deal at all." Jordan paused, scanning his eyes over Chavere, Altier, and then Thomas Devaney. His gaze settled on Ben James. "Mr. James, you became the informer rat—" Turning to the judge, Jordan stated, "I have no more questions for this witness."

In the jury room, a few remarks were made about the outburst in court and the immediate response from the US marshals.

"I just wish that paralegal would stop staring at us!" Katie said as we gathered our things to leave.

"I stare right back. She turns away," Brad stated.

"She's just doing her job," Irene offered.

Pam was talking to the plant. "What?" she asked in response to our laughter. "I thanked them for the cheese and crackers. I'm telling you, it's bugged!"

"You're probably right," I agreed.

Irene and Pam waited for me after we'd picked up our phones. I had a voice message from my sister. I listened. Irene and Pam could tell by my expression that something was wrong.

"What's happened, Alex?" Pam asked.

"My mom fell and broke her hip. You go on ahead; I need to make some phone calls."

My mom's surgery went well, though at eighty, her road to recovery promised to be long and difficult. I decided to stay at her apartment during the week, both to keep an eye on her and be closer to the hospital. The only problem was that I'd have to drive by Bob Costa's office twice a day. *That might be a temptation,* I thought. *He works late. What if I pass him while driving by? Certainly, I can stop and say hi. It would be rude not to. Wouldn't it?*

~

Days eighteen through twenty-three presented a gamut of witnesses, some fascinating, some emotionally stirring, some boring, and some just plain strange.

We listened to forensic scientists who for days explained the identification procedures of human remains that were found. The science lesson itself was absorbing, but the length of time spent in explaining the methods used to determine the cause of death and identify the skeletal remains discovered seemed unnecessarily drawn out.

I fought back an urge to vomit while watching a video of the medical examiner scooping out what was left of brain matter from one of the skulls. I turned my head away from the monitor, wishing for once that Richard had screwed it up so it wouldn't work. I took a deep breath, exhaling slowly, and then scowled at Chavere, who was displaying the gruesome images.

We heard the process of identification on each set of remains. Certainly, no one on this jury questions who these people were. Bullet holes are in most of the skulls. The bodies were all thrown in plastic bags and dumped in a hole. No question about it, they were murdered. So why do we need ghastly detail after ghastly detail on the condition of the remains? What does that have to do with us determining whether or not it was Devaney who killed them? The families shouldn't be subjected to this. I scanned the horrified faces in the center gallery, some crying, others enraged. *What's Chavere trying to prove with these needless facts? This bitch is victimizing the families all over again.*

Now glaring at Chavere, I silently shouted, *We get it! These poor souls were brutally murdered! But what we're here to determine is if Thomas Devaney took part in their murders! And this disrespectful dragged-out process is doing nothing to help us make that decision!*

When that was finally over, we heard from former FBI and law enforcement personnel. Many family members of those murdered were also called to testify. Their stories were deeply disturbing and terribly sad. The one that impacted me the most was that of Mrs. Monahan, the widow of Donald Monahan. Tragically, Donald Monahan had been with his friend Ed O'Leary on the night O'Leary was scheduled to be murdered.

Mrs. Monahan was an attractive and composed middle-aged woman with three adult daughters. They were always by her side in court. She was forced to relive the night of her husband's murder as she shared her dreadful experience with us.

"Don's wallet was with him and his identity known, yet no one in law enforcement called to tell me he was shot. No one from the hospital called to tell me he was dying. He suffered for hours surrounded by strangers. No one ever tried to contact me—"

She was visibly upset. Carla Chavere gave her a moment to regain her composure.

"How did you discover that your husband had been killed?"

"On the nightly news. They reported the shooting, saying that both men had died. I saw the car and knew it was Don's."

"Edward O'Leary was the target of the shooting?"

"That's what I was told, yes."

"How was it that your husband was with Mr. O'Leary?"

"They worked together. I was told that they met in a restaurant and Ed asked for a ride home."

"Thank you, Mrs. Monahan."

Chavere was gentle, thank God, and the poor woman is done, I thought. The defense had mercifully announced after every family member's direct examination that they had no questions for the witness. I fully expected they would show such mercy to Mrs. Monahan. As my body began to relax in the knowledge that the excruciating testimony of this poor woman was over, Curt Jordan stood, but he didn't announce to the judge that he had no questions. He walked toward the lectern.

My body stiffened. With a feeling of dread and concern, I looked at the vulnerable witness. *Why torment this widow any more?* I screamed in silence.

That was never the defense attorney's intent. Instead, Curt Jordan led Mrs. Monahan through a series of questions, the answers to which informed the jury of the cruelty shown her by the US Attorney's Office. She explained, with passion, that FBI Supervisory Special Agent Ken Arnold had targeted her husband for murder by leaking information about Ed O'Leary's whereabouts.

"Had Agent Arnold not leaked that information, my husband would still be alive. My life and the lives of my daughters would be vastly different. We loved him so very much." Mrs. Monahan wiped a tear from her eye.

She went on to share her disgust over the fact that Arnold had never been punished for his part in taking the life of her husband. And, though Mrs. Monahan was a witness for the prosecution, she had nothing but contempt for them.

Calls for sidebars and frequent objections from Chavere frequently interrupted Mrs. Monahan's testimony, but none of these were granted. The jury was engrossed by what Mrs. Monahan was saying as we tried to capture her words on paper.

I was stunned, wiping tears from my own eyes. *She hates the assistant US attorneys who are bringing the man claimed to be the actual murderer to justice—and her respect for the man who's defending this so-called murderer is obvious. Everything is inside out and upside down! And we're supposed to make sense of it all in deliberations?*

Following Mrs. Monahan's gut-wrenching testimony, a man by the name of Herman Pander was called to the stand. He had been present each day in the gallery, sitting among family members of victims. Pander was a tall, bulky middle-aged man, neatly dressed and clean-shaven. His blond hair seemed professionally styled. *Perhaps colored too,* I thought, because it didn't seem appropriate for his apparent age. He was attractive, but what appeared to be an occasional nervous twitch of his mouth took attention away from his facial features.

Under Chavere's lead, Mr. Pander told the story of his sister Carol. They were very close in age and practically "joined at the hip," according to Pander. Carol was an exceptionally attractive girl who had drawn the attention of Tony Diavolo. She was about fifteen when they met, and he was more than twenty years her senior. They began dating shortly thereafter, and were living together by the time Carol was seventeen. Pander told the story as if it were the most normal thing in the world for a seventeen-year-old to be with a man more than twice her age.

Where the hell was her mother? the mother in me screamed out in my mind. *What kind of family is this?*

The family story got stranger still. Pander's father had been murdered. His brother, a drug dealer, had been killed in prison. A second, younger sister had died, and it was clear the prosecution didn't want us to know how.

"Did your parents approve of your sister Carol dating Tony Diavolo?" Chavere asked.

"Not my father. When they began dating, Diavolo bought Carol a sports car. The old man was furious and ordered him to take it back. Diavolo wouldn't. My father smashed the windshield."

"Did your father come to accept Diavolo's involvement with Carol?"

"No. About a week later the old man was found dead—a bullet in his chest."

"Was anyone charged with the murder?"

"No."

Herman Pander went on to tell us how Diavolo had showered Carol—and their mother—with money, expensive gifts, and exotic vacations. When Carol and her mother were away on one of these vacations, Carol met, and subsequently fell in love with, a man closer to her age. Before she returned home, Carol arranged with her new lover to have him call her at a set time each day on her mother's phone. Together, they made plans for her to sneak out of the country.

"But she never left the country?"

"No. She disappeared. Her remains were found nineteen years later. She was murdered."

"By whom?" Chavere asked.

"Objection. Hearsay," Rob Willis stated.

A sidebar was called.

Against my will, my mind displayed for me the image of Carol's skull, only a clump of her beautiful long blonde hair remaining intact.

It was hard to believe that the gruesome image was once a beautiful, vivacious young woman.

"Did Tony Diavolo confess to being present when your sister was murdered?" Chavere asked after the sidebar ended.

"Yes."

"Who did he say murdered Carol?"

"Sly Devaney." Pander's mouth twitched as he pointed at Thomas Devaney.

"Why, according to Mr. Diavolo, did Mr. Devaney murder your sister?"

"Because Tony let it slip that he and Devaney were FBI informants. Devaney said that Carol knew too much and needed to be silenced. He had Tony lure Carol to a house he was planning to buy for them. Devaney was waiting, and he strangled my sister." Pander began to cry. "I loved my sister. She was a good girl—a gorgeous girl!" he uttered between deep sobs.

With that, Carla Chavere ended her direct.

I found myself gasping as Attorney Rob Willis moved to the lectern for cross. *Oh my God! I hope he's gentle with this guy.*

"Do you need a break, Mr. Pander?" Willis asked.

"No. … I'm okay—" And just as quickly as the sobs had begun, they ended.

Strange, I thought.

"If you're certain, sir."

"I am."

"Was Tony Diavolo aware of the phone calls made to your sister Carol by the man she was planning to run away with?"

"Yeah."

"How did he become aware?"

"He suspected something was up and tapped the phone line."

"Did the members of your family know of Carol's phone calls and plans?"

"Yeah." Pander fidgeted in his seat. As his mouth twitched, he raised his hand, wiping his mouth as if to make it stop.

"Did anyone in the family inform Tony Diavolo?"

"Objection! Calls for speculation!" Chavere shouted.

"Sustained."

"Did your mother go to the FBI for help after Carol disappeared?"

"Not right away."

"Was Tony Diavolo welcome in your mother's home after Carol disappeared?"

Herman Pander was hesitant to answer. His mouth twitched. "I wouldn't say that he was welcome—"

"But he still came by?"

"Yeah. He acted like he was concerned about where Carol was—like he didn't know."

"Did your mother continue to receive gifts and money from him?"

"Yeah." Another twitch.

"And shortly after Carol's disappearance, wasn't Tony Diavolo dating another sister?"

"Yeah, Cindy."

"What happened to Cindy?"

"She died." The twitching was constant.

"While dating Tony Diavolo?"

"Yeah—"

"Cindy took her own life, didn't she?"

"Objection. No relevance, Your Honor," Chavere whined.

"Sustained."

Did she really commit suicide, or did it just appear like she did? I wondered.

"Was it after Cindy's death that your mother met with the FBI?"

"Yeah. She met with two agents a few times."

"Did she share with them what she thought became of Carol?"

"Objection. Hearsay." Chavere jumped up.

"Your Honor, Ms. Chavere knows that the FBI interviews with Mrs. Pander are in evidence," Willis said, countering the objection.

"Overruled. Answer the question, Mr. Pander," Judge Blake stated. I couldn't help but notice that his attention went to his computer screen.

"Yeah. She told them that she thought Tony Diavolo killed Carol and hid her body."

"Did she tell the FBI agents that Thomas Devaney was involved in Carol's murder?"

"No." The twitching was painful to watch.

"Mr. Pander, didn't your mother believe that Tony Diavolo, alone, killed your sister Carol?" Willis pushed.

"Yeah. That's what she thought, but—"

Willis didn't let him finish. "Did your mother say anything to the FBI agents about your father's death?"

"Objection. Relevance?" Chavere stated.

"Ms. Chavere brought up Mr. Pander's murder in her direct examination."

"You opened the door, Ms. Chavere. Overruled," the judge stated.

"What did your mother tell the FBI agents in regard to your father's death, Mr. Pander?"

"That she believed Tony Diavolo killed him."

"Did the FBI agents stop meeting with your mother?"

"Yeah."

"Did she say why the meetings stopped?"

"She told them she didn't think they'd ever find Carol, and asked if they could at least find her white fur coat," Pander said matter-of-factly.

Willis was obviously stunned. "Excuse me? Carol's white fur coat?" he asked incredulously, and then looked at the jury.

"It was a beautiful coat, very expensive," Pander added.

"A gift from Tony Diavolo?" Willis was still looking at the jury.

"Yeah. He has good taste."

"Thank you, Mr. Pander. Your Honor, I have no more questions for this witness."

I watched Herman Pander as he walked over to the gallery. The twitching had stopped. He now had a wide grin on his face. The people who sat with him were patting him on the back, as if congratulating him for a job well done. I was aghast! *Is this the epitome of white trash?* I wondered. *He has no idea that his testimony was revolting—his sister being with Diavolo at such a young age; his father's, brother's, and two sisters' violent deaths; the fact that his mother seemed to care more about Carol's white fur coat than she did about her daughter's fate. I would never believe such families exist if I weren't staring at one right now!*

Judge Blake had new instructions for us jurors at the close of day twenty-three. We were not to visit the house, river, or beach site where bodies had been buried. Problem was, Chris, Dan, and I passed the river and beach site twice every day we took the train; the exact spots of the exhumations were in plain view. As we approached the areas on this particular day, each of us made eye contact with the other from across the train, trying to distract ourselves, so it seemed, from looking.

~

I stopped by the hospital to visit Mom. A couple of my siblings were there, as well as a priest, who was standing by her bed.

"Father, this is my daughter Alexandra. She's the one on the jury of the Sly Devaney trial," my mother blurted.

"Mom!" I exclaimed.

"Your secret's safe with me." The priest smiled.

"Father, when Alexandra was in the jury pool, I told her to tell a white lie. That wasn't wrong, was it?"

I looked at my sister Terry, who stood at the foot of the bed and mouthed, "Oh my God!"

Terry moved to my side. "It's the pain med. No filter," she whispered. My brother sat in a chair in the corner, offering me a shrug as he shook his head.

"What was the white lie?" the priest asked, taking hold of my mother's hand.

"I told her to say she was biased against Devaney so she wouldn't be picked for the jury. That wasn't wrong, was it?"

I took hold of Mom's other hand, looking at the priest and then at her. "I wouldn't be so sure, Mom. Your encouragement to get me to lie may have put you in this hospital bed," I said. Then I smiled at the priest and gave Mom a kiss on the forehead. She laughed along with the others.

Mom was to be moved to a rehab facility after spending more than a week in the hospital, with half of that stay in ICU. Though the meds had a peculiar effect, her condition was quite stable. I finally felt it was safe to return home.

It promised to be a relaxing weekend. I was elated. Back in my own home, I was delighted to spend the evening watching a stupid movie with Charlie and a couple of his old high school buddies. It was a comedy that only males could truly appreciate. I laughed more at their hilarity than at the show.

After the movie, I climbed into bed, feeling restful and safe back in my own home. My last thoughts were about tomorrow's wedding. *Bob will be there. It will be awkward not to talk. He'll be preoccupied with his date and stay clear of me. Oh God, I hope he doesn't have a date.*

That night, I was haunted with a nightmare of being chased by a man with a submachine gun. I had on a white fur coat. My screams brought Charlie running from his room. I lied, assuring my son that I was all right.

Chapter 7

The most sacred of the duties of a government is to
do equal and impartial justice to all citizens.
—Thomas Jefferson (1743–1826), principal
author of the Declaration of Independence;
second vice president; third president
of the United States of America

WHEN TOMMY DEVANEY ENTERED THE FEDERAL
prison system at age twenty-six, he didn't realize that it was standard procedure to disrupt prisoners by moving them from one facility to another. It's referred to as "diesel torture"—an appropriate term, as the prisoner is forced to breathe fumes from diesel engine buses that transport them from prison to prison. Devaney was subjected to this torture four times in nine years: Atlanta, Alcatraz, Leavenworth, and Lewisburg.

For him, release wasn't as difficult as it was for most long-term prisoners. He had a home to go to back in South Boston, and a mother whose love was unconditional. Even so, he found himself missing those he'd befriended, especially at Alcatraz. As he reminisced, his thoughts wandered to the friends who hadn't made it, choosing to take their own lives rather than stay another day longer in the cold, often rancid conditions of the island prison. His mind would often wander to the kindness of a prison guard who sought to offer comfort when word of Devaney's father's death arrived. Tommy would never forget his kindness, or understand why a man whom he'd shown nothing but contempt would even care.

Tommy discovered that some *did* care. Was it because of the frequent nightmares and hallucinations he suffered because of his participation in the schizophrenia drug testing? The guards did respect prisoners who took such risks. Or perhaps it was because they had children who were Devaney's age. Most were God-fearing men who understood *There but for the grace of God goes my son.*

Shortly after returning home, Tommy took a night job as a janitor. A local diner became a regular stop for breakfast after his shift ended, not so much for the food but for the attention of the young woman who served it. Her name, he quickly discovered, was Karen.

Tommy had no intention of ever settling down, and he'd made that clear to Karen from the start. She didn't believe him. The announcement of her pregnancy came as a shock to Tommy. Though he kept his word about not settling down, he accepted financial responsibility—and fell in love with his newborn son, whom Karen named Danny.

~

Weddings for second marriages usually proved less formal and pretentious. I knew this would be the case for Nancy and Don's celebration. From the entrance of the not so young bride to the seal of the kiss, all was lighthearted and mirthful. While I was giving Nancy a big hug in the receiving line, she held on to me. "Don said Bob's been asking if you'd be attending. He says Bob's really stuck on you."

"No, that's not it," I whispered back with certainty.

"Really? Then why is he staring at you while holding two glasses of wine?"

"The second glass, I'm sure, is for his date. And if he's staring, it's because he's trying to figure out a way to avoid me all evening."

Don took my hand and pulled me away from Nancy. "He didn't bring a date. And I'm guessing that wine's for you. He's walking this way."

Startled, I turned my head. Don was right.

"You look beautiful, Alex," Don said as he squeezed my hands.

"In this dim light, he won't notice that your cheeks match the color of that sexy dress."

"Very funny," I said, reclaiming my hands and feeling to see if my necklace was hanging properly. I was confident that Don was right. The embroidered lace sheath dress of deep rose flattered my figure. Between the tasteful snug fit, the flirty scalloped V-neck, and the four-inch heels, I had no doubt that I would hold Bob's attention.

Turning away from Don's grin, I walked toward Bob. "For me?" I asked with a confident smile, taking the glass of red wine from his hand and leaving him with the white. "You're alone?"

"No. I'm with you."

"I'm flattered. But I didn't think we could be seen together."

"I've been giving that some thought," he began, slowly scanning the room.

"And?"

"We're good friends of the bride and groom, and well acquainted with many in this room. It would appear awkward if we avoided one another."

"We don't want to appear awkward," I agreed, taking a sip of the wine.

"Absolutely not. This is Don and Nancy's night. I think we can manage to stay clear of things we can't discuss."

"The last thing I want to think about is the things we can't discuss." I laughed.

Dinner was delicious, or perhaps it was the fact that I was relaxed and, for the first time in weeks, actually tasted the food. The conversation at the table was light and humorous. Beneath the table, Bob positioned his leg to rest against mine. I smiled at him, and though he continued to converse, he threw a glance at me, acknowledging my pleasure. Without missing a spoken syllable, his hand slowly moved off the table and down to my leg, gently massaging my thigh. My heart was racing as I felt my face flush. The conversation and faces at the table became distant as my mind and body yielded to the carnal thrall his touch invoked.

He moved his hand and leaned toward me, placing his arm around my shoulders. His breath was warm, his eyes seductive. "Let's dance," he whispered.

He knew he had me under his spell as he led me onto the dance floor. As though in a trance, my body melted into his as he pulled me tight. I felt the rapid beat of our hearts. No words were spoken. Never had I felt such yearning. I longed to feel his bare skin against my naked body. My imagination whisked us away, his mouth and tongue frantically seeking mine and then eagerly racing to the plumpness of my taut nipple. My longing was turning to agony just as the music ended. Bob continued to hold me close as he lifted my hand, turning it to kiss my palm.

For me, the intensity of the enchantment lingered, but not, or so it seemed, for Bob. The passion had dissipated. He remained attentive and kind, but his touch became familial. Our next dance was one between friends, not potential lovers.

A gentle breeze danced across the parking lot as a small group of us stepped outside, preparing to leave. Our parting was filled with warm embraces and promises to get together.

"Come on, I'll walk you to your car," Bob said, placing his hand upon my back.

"Beautiful night." I gazed into the star-filled sky.

"Perfect night," he replied, taking hold of my hand and squeezing it gently as we walked.

Maybe he realized the intensity was too much, I thought, glancing at him. *Maybe he was concerned about what others might think and thought that he needed to tone it down.*

Bob let go of my hand and continued to walk toward the car without a word.

"Here it is," I said, turning to face him as I stood to the left of the car.

"We managed to stay clear of the trial," he said with a smile.

"We did."

"Maybe we'll bump into each other again before it's over."

"Maybe," I offered in response.

"If not, I'll call you when the verdict's in." He placed his hands on my shoulders as he leaned in to kiss my cheek, and then opened the car door for me. "Take care, kiddo."

"You too." Stunned, I climbed into the driver's seat. He closed the door and walked away.

I sat for a moment, watching him in the rearview mirror. He stopped to talk to a couple in the parking lot.

My mind was numb as I turned on the ignition, backed up, and made my way out of the parking lot. Once I was on the road, the anger hit.

"Was that a game? He knew he had me, so the excitement of the chase was over? Is that the thrill?" I audibly asked myself in frustrated confusion.

"Damn him!" I yelled, wiping a single tear that had managed to escape my eye.

~

Ilona brought little Paul by on Sunday. We had a nice visit, though she knew I was troubled, thinking it was solely from the trial. More than once I caught her dark eyes searching my expression as she struggled not to ask any questions. The baby, now a toddling one-year-old, brought comfort as his smiles and laughter filled the room. He was so innocent, a light in my present world of darkness and despair.

By evening, my morale was depleted. With dread, I laid out my clothes for court, wondering what purpose, or perhaps *whose* purpose, this trial served. It certainly wasn't the defendant's. The trial had been a sham thus far, and I had no hope of any change.

"Paul, my life would be so different if you were here," I whispered to my dead husband. Such "dialogue" was not unusual, but it happened less and less as time went on.

How so? I anticipated his response. *You'd still be serving on this jury.*

"But I wouldn't be so conflicted," I argued.

By the trial? My presence wouldn't do a thing to change that. You're feeling outrage for losing faith in a belief you once held.

I nodded. "Yeah, I believed our system of law was still sacrosanct, our Constitution intact." Frustrated, I picked up a decorative pillow and threw it across the room. "So, why do I insist on blaming you for my misery?" I sat down on the bed feeling dejected.

"Loneliness," I whispered to myself, wiping a tear from my cheek. "Ilona has her own family, and Charlie belongs to the army. I anticipated a full and happy future with you, Paul. The army was your first love. I always came second. I grieve the relationship we never had. What I held onto all those lonely nights, for all those miserably lonely years, was anticipation of your retirement, and the dream of being one. I've lied to myself, wanting to believe that our marriage was happy. But lengthy and stressful separation doesn't make for a good marriage. I grieve that I never had the opportunity to be your first love or to feel your full attention as a husband—"

Standing, I walked over to the dresser, removed my wedding band and diamond, and placed them in the jewelry box. Exhausted, I climbed into bed, turning off my thoughts along with the light.

~

On day twenty-four, the parade of witnesses continued. We heard from a couple of sketchy characters who claimed that Devaney extorted them. Upon cross, it was learned that these guys were best buddies with Vinnie Giuda. I couldn't help but wonder, with their being as close to Giuda as they were, if he had put them up to making their claims against Devaney.

Then there was the odd guy whose story said one thing and whose body language said quite another. His name was Jackie Holmes. He was a "former" heroin and coke dealer, and appeared to be flying high as a kite while on the stand. He seemed afraid to look at Devaney. The man pushed his body into the right side of the chair within the witness stand as though trying to get as far from the defendant as he could. Then, Holmes awkwardly positioned his head so that he couldn't see Devaney.

Funny thing is, Devaney isn't the least bit interested in looking at this guy, I thought. Devaney focused on whatever he was writing on a legal pad before him, as he almost always did.

The long and short of Holmes's story was that he was allegedly extorted by Devaney with high drama—rifles pointed at his groin, and Russian roulette being played with a silenced revolver. Upon hearing these stories, Devaney did look at Holmes. His expression seemed to reveal curious surprise.

Can a revolver even be silenced? I wondered, thinking that might have been why Devaney reacted to the testimony.

Though Holmes had been indicted for being a major dealer on the East Coast, his arrangement with the US Attorney's Office for providing information against several criminals was marvelous. He walked; they went to prison.

Something's just not right about this piece of garbage, I thought. *And something's certainly wrong with the US Attorney's Office.*

My thoughts flew to the recent funeral of a friend's daughter—a talented young woman addicted to opiates she took for a difficult-to-diagnose medical condition. Once she had been properly diagnosed and fixed, the prescriptions suddenly stopped. With no adequate plan for detoxing from the prescribed narcotics, her daily struggle didn't end. The constant craving pushed her to secretly turn to heroin. The heroin killed her, and as far as I was concerned, the dealers involved were guilty of murder.

This bum has destroyed the lives of so many while making millions, and yet he walks free. No punishment for the lives he is responsible for taking, or the families destroyed because he pushes heroin. Doesn't this somehow make the US Attorney's Office an accessory to this man's crimes? Their total disregard for the horror Holmes has visited on so many is unacceptable—and it is absolutely revolting that there is no punishment!

The last witness of special interest during this seven-day stretch was the former girlfriend of serial killer Vinnie Giuda. She was a pretty woman who seemed young compared to the aging Giuda. I turned back the pages in my notebook to what had been said about this woman in Giuda's testimony. *If my memory's correct, he's much older than she.* I found what I was searching for. This woman was seventeen when she ran away with Giuda. He was forty. *These bastards certainly have a thing for young girls. I guess if they have no qualms about killing, they have no qualms about statutory rape!*

It was obvious that this witness was frightened. Her name was Roberta Little, but she went by the nickname Bobbie. Just as Giuda was the epitome of a hit man, Bobbie was the epitome of a hit man's woman. She had lived with Giuda in Arizona for sixteen years. Not only had she entertained Vinnie and his friends, but also she'd aided in his financial support. Bobbie, we were informed, made several trips to her mother's house in Boston, where envelopes filled with large sums of cash were left. She also admitted to lying to a grand jury, "because Vinnie told me to." When asked why she had harbored a fugitive, Bobbie exclaimed, "I had no idea what Vinnie did!"

"And his friends whom you entertained?" Attorney Jordan asked.

"Oh, you mean Tommy and Tony?"

"Yes, Thomas Devaney and Anthony Diavolo."

"I thought Tommy and Tony were just friends. I never knew they worked with Vinnie!"

I could barely contain myself. *Is she for real? This woman must be about fifty years old! Could she really be that ignorant?*

Whether or not Bobbie was truly ignorant, she continued to appear so. Though she had harbored a fugitive, had been actively involved in many counts of money laundering, and had perjured herself before a grand jury, Bobbie had never set foot in a prison cell. Lovely Bobbie, no doubt thanks to Vinnie's sweet deal with the federal government, had never been charged with anything!

~

That night, I received phone calls from my daughter and siblings. They voiced their concerns that a witness for the prosecution had been found dead. Reports indicated that he had been murdered.

Chapter 8

Justice is the end of government. It is the end of civil society. It ever has been and ever will be pursued until it be obtained, or until liberty be lost in the pursuit.
—James Madison (1751–1836), "Father of the Constitution" and fourth president of the United States of America

DEVANEY FILED INTO LINE AND WAITED FOR THE guard. A young man came and stood behind him. Devaney had seen him talking to an older woman.

"Was that your mother?" Devaney asked.

"Yeah."

"She's concerned about you," Devaney said knowingly.

"Yeah. Pretty upset."

"Listen to me, kid. You're young. You have time to straighten up. Get outta here. Get a job. Get an education. Have a family. Stop tormenting your mother."

The guard opened the heavy metal door and directed the prisoners from the visiting area.

"I broke my mother's heart. She went to her grave worrying about me. Spare your mom that agony. Smarten up."

~

Day twenty-five revealed that each one of us had been informed of the murder by concerned family members. And we all knew that the murdered man was scheduled to testify for the prosecution. Our expectation was that the jury would be staying in Boston that night, and for the remainder of the trial.

That day we were introduced to Anthony "Tony" Diavolo. When we entered the courtroom, he was already on the witness stand. I remembered prior testimony that Diavolo hadn't fed the feds the information they wanted soon enough. Because of this, he'd ended up serving a much longer sentence than the chirping Vinnie Giuda and Ben James.

We were informed by the judge that he had been sworn in prior to our arrival. Two well-dressed men, not seen before, sat on each side of the witness stand.

His personal US marshals? I wondered. *Already seated and sworn in? They didn't want us to see that. Why? Handcuffs and shackles? The cuffs are off, but I bet he's still shackled.*

Diavolo had on a khaki uniform. *Must be a prison uniform.*

I was taken aback by Diavolo's appearance. Even though I knew he would be in his early seventies, I expected to see a formidable man. He was not. In fact, he was anything but. He looked more like a scarecrow, tall and paper-thin. The crows could pick him up and carry him off. I wondered if he had cancer, or maybe AIDS. It was hard to believe that he had ever held power or effected terror in the streets of Boston.

I saw that all the guns had been put on display again, and of course, the barrel of each gun was aimed at the jury. Then, looking around, I observed that one of the family members of the victims had moved from the center of the gallery to sit in the front row of the media's section in the courtroom. It was the woman I saw on occasion with her son on the train. She was now just to the right of the jury, paper and pen in hand.

Who is she? Maybe she isn't family. Maybe she's writing a book. She's situated herself so that she can get a clear view of Diavolo. Why?

Chavere stood and made her way to the lectern. I settled in for what promised to be a long, gruesome testimony.

Chavere started her cross by taking a gun off the table and walking toward Diavolo. Judge Blake immediately called for a sidebar. Chavere returned the gun to the table.

The sidebar was short. Once it was over, Chavere again picked up the gun and walked toward the witness stand.

What was that about? Was the judge making certain that Chavere wasn't gonna hand the gun to Diavolo? It was bad enough that Ben James had gotten to hold the guns. Would Chavere be stupid enough to hand a gun to a man presently incarcerated for murder? Probably!

Every one of the guns was paraded before Diavolo. Then, finally, the subject changed, and Chavere spent a ridiculous amount of time trying to convince the jury of Diavolo's close relationship to Devaney. Once she had satisfied her seeming need to force the point, she moved on.

"Mr. Diavolo, did you know that Carol Pander had been planning to leave the country to be with another man?"

"Yeah. We discussed it. She was upset with me because she wanted to get married and have kids."

"And you didn't want to marry?"

"Thought it would complicate her life. My line of business was risky. I didn't want her to be stuck raising kids alone."

"So, did you come to an understanding about her desire to run off with someone else?"

"Yeah. I gave in and agreed to marry her and start a family. We were looking for a house to buy. I couldn't lose Carol. I loved her; in fact, I probably loved her too much."

No one is buying this! Certainly no one is buying this. I looked at the media. They were busy getting the testimony out as it happened. The paralegal with the defense attorneys was again staring at us jurors, but now she was staring down anyone who offered a challenge. *Just doing her job,* I thought, wondering what exactly it was that she jotted on the paper.

"You loved her, yet you went along with killing her. Why?"

"I indulged her with gifts, but she didn't have enough sense to keep quiet about it. She told everyone I gave them to her. Tommy kept warning me that I needed to keep a low profile and that Carol needed to be more discreet. Then, I screwed up and mentioned to her that me and Tommy were FBI informants. When Tommy found out, he said there was no choice but to silence her."

"And you agreed?"

"Tommy had a way of persuading, and I figured he'd kill both me and Carol if I didn't."

"How was she killed?"

"I had her meet me at a house we might wanna buy. I had the key. Tommy was with me, hid in another room. When Carol got there, Tommy came from behind and began to strangle her. I still have nightmares—the panic in her eyes, her arms reaching for me—"

"Did you attempt to stop Mr. Devaney?"

"Why bother at this point? She'd go straight to the police. I felt awful. Tried to comfort her. Told her she was going to a better place. Tommy saw I was shaken up and told me he'd get rid of the body."

He just stood there and watched Devaney kill the woman he loved? He's totally detached from the memory, telling it as though he's reading from a car manual!

"Earlier testimony from a medical examiner said Carol's teeth were pulled. Did Mr. Devaney do this?"

"No. Tommy didn't like to. I took off her clothes and pulled her teeth before Tommy took the body." Diavolo's gruesome answer didn't offer a hint of emotion.

God! Her body was still warm; her gums would bleed.

My heart was suddenly pounding and perspiration instantly covered my body as I imagined this young woman's last moments of sheer terror, and then the mutilation by the monster in the witness box. My stomach felt sick.

I need to get out of here! I looked at the door to the left of the jury box. *I'll force myself out of this damned jury box, through the door, and run*, I thought in my panic. I took a deep breath and exhaled slowly, desperate to calm myself. *If I do it, I'll end up in jail. Most of these demons aren't in jail, but if one of us has an emotional breakdown and does something out of line, or doesn't show up for jury duty, we'll be thrown in jail, no questions asked! After all, the federal court must make it known to potential jurors that their absolute adherence to the law is fully expected. Murderers can run free, but not unruly jurors! What hellhole have I fallen into?*

Perhaps Judge Blake sensed my anxiety. Probably all of us looked like we were on the edge. He mercifully called it a day, and told us that we were free to return home.

We aren't going to be sequestered? I was confused. *A man involved in this trial has been murdered, and we aren't going to be sequestered? For our own safety? To keep us from hearing about the investigation into his death, which is sure to be plastered all over the news?*

Not much was said about anything in the jury room as we prepared to leave, although some of us did mention our surprise that the judge was allowing us to go home. Pam and I silently walked out of the courthouse together. She looked like she had been crying—because of the testimony or because she was afraid to make the trip home? Probably both, I surmised.

All the way home, my thoughts replayed Diavolo's grisly details. I put in a CD as a distraction, having learned that the radio couldn't be used. News announcements always included the Devaney trial.

"Why would Chavere want us to know that it was Diavolo and not Devaney who stripped Carol and yanked out her teeth?" I asked out loud. "If she'd let it go, I would have assumed Devaney did it. After all, Diavolo claimed Devaney was getting rid of the body."

I turned off the distraction. "Chavere is carefully choosing her questions. Why ask that? Because the defense is bound to, so she just got it out of the way?" That conclusion didn't satisfy, as my thoughts kept rolling. "Or was it to make the jury believe that Diavolo was being thoroughly honest with his testimony? After all, if he confessed to mutilating the woman he loved, why would he hold anything else back?"

I pulled into my driveway, turned off the engine, and sat there. "It's all a mind game, Alex. Guilt or innocence doesn't really matter."

Charlie pulled in beside me. I returned his smile and got out of the car.

"Home to pack?" he asked.

"Huh?"

"Aren't you being sequestered?" he asked, opening the door to the house.

"No."

"What the fuck?"

"Watch your mouth." I pretended to slap his face as I walked past him.

"It's all over the news. Some creep already confessed. Supposedly had nothing to do with the trial—"

"Stop talking, Charlie."

"But they're saying that this witness's testimony would have contradicted Ben James's. Probably a —"

"I'm not supposed to hear this," I interrupted, kicking my shoes off and putting my purse down on the foyer table.

"Come on, Ma. This is serious," he called after me as I walked toward the kitchen.

I turned to face him. "You don't think I know this? You don't think I'm frightened?"

"What the hell are they thinking?" Charlie asked.

"It's part of the game. Scare us to death. Let us believe Devaney had this guy killed. ... All part of the fucking game," I heard myself say.

~

I awakened to every noise that night, as did almost everyone else on the jury, I learned later. Exhausted, we were paraded into the courtroom the next morning. Again, Diavolo was already in the witness stand.

They don't want us to see the shackles. But why? We know he's in prison. I pondered the question for a moment while staring at Diavolo. He momentarily caught my gaze and quickly averted his eyes.

The game is to make us believe he's now an honest man. Subconsciously, the shackles might hinder us from believing the lie. I was satisfied with my conclusion.

Chavere's first question that morning took me by surprise.

"Mr. Diavolo, which of Carol Pander's brothers was a drug dealer and police informant? Wasn't it Herman?"

"Yes, Herman," Diavolo agreed.

There was instant disruption in the gallery as Herman Pander jumped to his feet screaming, "You piece of shit! You fucking piece of lying shit!" Those near to Pander had to hold him back as he tried to get out of the bench. "You're a piece of fucking shit!"

Judge Blake began to pound his gavel. "Order! I'll have order!"

Pander stopped shouting once Diavolo calmly said, "I'm sorry, Herman. I was wrong. It was your brother."

The judge gave a warning to Pander, who apologized for his outburst. The cunning Chavere continued with her direct examination. Oddly, she made no mention of the brother who did deal drugs or of the Pander family at all. The subject was completely changed.

What was that about? I wondered, staring at Chavere, and then watching a shaken Herman Pander leave the courtroom. *Was Pander set up? Did Chavere purposely pose that question, having prepped Diavolo with the answer, just to anger Pander? Does Chavere have a reason for wanting Pander removed from the courtroom?* I certainly had no answers, but I felt in my gut that the entire scene was a planned one. It seemed a cruel act against Herman Pander.

The questioning moved on to educate us about Diavolo's stepdaughter, Sandy Ford. There was no emotion from Diavolo as he narrated the story of Sandy's murder. She'd gotten messed up with drugs and kept running off her mouth. Diavolo supposedly tried to help her again and again.

"How did you help her?" Chavere asked.

"Put her in drug rehab. Put the money up to relocate her. She kept coming back, and running off her mouth in public about Tommy and me. Tommy decided she had to be taken out."

"By taken out, you mean killed?"

"Yeah."

"And this occurred at the same house where Mr. Bartlett and Mr. McCarthy were murdered and buried in the cellar?"

"Yeah. Same place."

"Did Devaney kill Sandy Ford?"

"Yeah, strangled her. Me and Ben James took her to the cellar and buried her."

"Did you pull her teeth?"

"Yeah, had to. And took her clothes."

No emotion! Absolutely no emotion! My mind railed against his lack of any sentiment.

The gruesome questions and emotionless responses continued throughout the day.

On day twenty-seven, Defense Attorney Jordan began his cross. Jordan's mannerisms and voice appeared calm at first, but his face was flushed. I sensed there was a fire within, and that Diavolo might be in trouble.

Jordan brought out the details of Diavolo's failed attempt to make the deal he wanted with the US Attorney's Office. Diavolo had stalled for too long; Vinnie Giuda and Ben James beat him to the finish and claimed the prize. Diavolo was only a runner-up. But, still, he received compensation for his information. He avoided the electric chair, and all his assets and cash were returned. This amounted to millions of dollars, all of it tainted. No restitution was ordered to the victims of his crimes. He got it all. And he was transferred to a secret federal home where the menu read more like that of a resort hotel and the accommodations came close.

"I found Jehovah in prison," Diavolo blurted.

Curt Jordan, who was busy with the paperwork before him, seemingly ignored Diavolo's claim to having found religion.

Jehovah? Jehovah's Witness? I wondered. *That would make sense. They're big on letting people know they don't refer to God as God. He probably wanted Chavere to bring it up. Chavere wouldn't, so he's taking the opportunity to let us all know.*

Jordan looked up at Diavolo. "Are you hoping Jehovah will help you get out of prison?"

Diavolo seemed taken aback by the question. "I can hope."

"Yes, you can, Mr. Diavolo. But isn't it more likely that it will be the assistant US attorneys that get you out of prison through the Rule 35 motion?"

"Objection!" Chavere was quick to jump up.

"Sidebar!" Judge Blake seemed concerned. The sound machine came on as the attorneys argued before the judge.

Rule 35 motion? Whatever it is, it's causing a stir. I had the feeling we weren't going to find out.

I was wrong. When the sidebar ended, Curt Jordan continued where he'd left off.

"Have Assistant US Attorneys Chavere and Altier spoken to you about the Rule 35 motion?"

"Yeah, they mentioned it."

"And what is your understanding of the motion?"

Diavolo looked at Chavere, who nodded.

"If my testimony offers additional information that assists them in getting a conviction of Devaney, then they can request the court to reduce my prison sentence," Diavolo stated proudly.

"Greatly reduce your prison sentence. And what is your current sentence?"

"Life."

"Did the assistant US attorneys make it clear that this motion can request that time already served be taken into consideration?"

"Yes."

"Did they explain to you that if a conviction is made, you could be let out of prison shortly thereafter?"

"Objection, Your Honor!"

"Sustained."

"Of course they did," Jordan mumbled.

Am I hearing this correctly? If Diavolo does his part, and the Rule 35 motion is requested, he walks out of prison a free man? He already testified that he got all his property and money back. He'll be free with plenty of money to spend!

Sweet mother of God! Obviously Giuda and Ben James said whatever they needed to say to get out of prison—the truth be damned! And now, if Diavolo can come up with enough "good stuff" to convince us of

Devaney's guilt, he too will be back on the streets. Again, the truth be damned! I was in a silent rage.

Curt Jordan spent hours pulling from the witness more information relating to Carol Pander's death. Diavolo stayed true to form, insisting that he had not wanted Carol to die. The day finished with his sick attempt to convince the jury that Thomas Devaney was solely responsible for the murder of Carol. Diavolo, the loving boyfriend, was an innocent bystander. In fact, he wanted us to believe that he, too, was a victim of the crime.

Day twenty-seven seemed to last forever. Day twenty-eight came too quickly.

"How old was Sandra Ford when you moved in with her mother?"

"Two."

"Were there other children?"

"I had a couple more with Sandy's mom."

"You were a family?" Jordan asked.

"Yeah."

"And Sandy considered you her father?"

"I guess."

"Were you the only father she knew?"

"Yeah."

"Did you take her on your lap and read stories to her at bedtime?"

"Objection. Relevance," Chavere stated.

"Your Honor, I'm trying to establish the relationship between this father and his small stepdaughter," Curt Jordan argued.

"Overruled."

"Yeah, I read her stories."

"Sandy trusted you. She loved you. She called you Daddy, isn't that right, Mr. Diavolo?"

"Yeah."

"Of course she did. You were the daddy to her brother and sister. As far as she knew, you were her daddy too. But at some point during her childhood, Mr. Diavolo, you crossed a line. Tucking her into bed at night turned into sex play, didn't it?"

"Objection! Inflammatory!" Chavere shouted.

"Overruled."

"Didn't it, Mr. Diavolo?" Jordan waited for the witness to answer.

"It wasn't like that—" Diavolo tried to protest

"Before long, Mr. Diavolo, you were forcing your stepdaughter to perform oral sex, and in time you began to rape this girl who called you Daddy?"

"It wasn't like that!" Diavolo protested again.

Jordan's gaze remained fixed on Diavolo for a moment. "Tell the jury what it was like."

"She was only my stepdaughter, and she wasn't a kid anymore. She wanted it as much as I did."

Jordan took a deep breath. "How old was your stepdaughter when your sexual relationship began?"

"I don't know, eighteen—?"

"Eighteen? According to the sworn statement of her mother, Sandra Ford was fourteen when she discovered that you were forcing her daughter to perform oral sex—"

Chavere objected, as Diavolo screamed, "I didn't force anything!"

I fought back the flashback of my own molestation: nine years old, abandoned by my best friend's mother with a photographer who happened to like snapping pictures of naked children. Boys, girls? He didn't seem to have a preference. He plastered both genders upon the walls of his studio. Much of what happened at the hands of this pedophile, my mind had mercifully blocked. But Sandy Ford' tragic story was threatening to rip open the curtain and reveal the darkness beyond. My body began to tremble.

Curt Jordan looked toward Chavere's standing form, and then held a steady gaze on Judge Blake, who seemingly refused to respond.

"Your Honor," Jordan began, "Mrs. Ford's sworn statement is in evidence."

"Objection overruled," Judge Blake declared, causing Chavere to sit down.

"Did Sandra tell her mother that you had molested her for years?"

"I didn't molest her!" Diavolo protested.

"Did Sandra tell her mother that you had been having sexual relations since she was a child?" Jordan demanded.

"She wasn't a child," Diavolo scoffed.

"Fourteen is a child." Curt Jordan's repulsion was evident. "Did she tell her mother?" he demanded.

"Yeah."

"Did her mother believe her?"

"Yes."

"And did Sandra's mother tell you to leave?"

"Yeah."

"Sandra Ford became a problem when she began to speak up for herself, when she informed her mother of what you had done to her?"

"That wasn't a problem. I moved back into the house," Diavolo boasted.

"And when Mrs. Ford let you back in, Sandra moved out?"

"Yeah. Then the foolish girl started talking on the streets, talking about my involvement with Devaney."

"How old was she when she was forced out of the only home she had known? Was she even sixteen?"

"She wasn't forced out."

"Her choice, it seems, was to be molested again or to leave—"

"Objection. Speculation," Chavere whined without standing.

"Sustained."

"When Sandra left, Mrs. Ford told you to leave again, didn't she?"

"Yeah."

"Did Sandra move back home?"

"No."

"How did Sandra survive on the streets?" Curt Jordan asked.

"I tried to help her," Diavolo stated.

"Tried to help her? How?"

"I sent her to rehab. I relocated her. She kept coming back!"

"Rehab? Did Sandra become addicted to drugs, Mr. Diavolo?"

"Yeah. Whored herself out to supply her damn habit. I sent her to rehab a few times. Moved her away. She always came back."

"And that became a problem, didn't it?"

"She'd go back to the drugs, back to the street. She talked too much. Devaney said she needed to shut up. I tried to tell her. She didn't listen. Devaney said we needed to stop her."

"And you agreed?" Jordan asked.

"Yeah." There was no hesitation, no sign of sorrow, nothing.

"How did you kill her?"

"I didn't kill her; Devaney did." Diavolo looked straight at Devaney. The defendant met and held his gaze.

"What happened?"

"It was winter. She didn't have a coat. I told her I'd take her to buy one, but first I had to stop by the house to get something."

"The same house in which Buddy Bartlett and Will McCarthy were buried in the cellar?"

"Yeah. Same house. I had her come in with me. Tommy was waiting. He grabbed her from behind and strangled her." Diavolo's voice remained monotone.

"Did he kill her?"

What an odd question, I thought. *If he strangled her, then didn't he kill her?*

"Yeah. Devaney killed her."

As Curt Jordan pulled out of Diavolo his gruesome obsession with stripping the body, yanking out the teeth, and performing the burial process, my thoughts turned to Ben James's testimony. I flipped the pages back in my notebook to see what I had written about his version of Sandra Ford's murder. *James claimed he didn't see who initially strangled Sandra. He testified that the girl was lying on the floor when he came down from the bathroom. Diavolo dragged her down the cellar. Diavolo then told James that Sandra's heart was still beating, and he strangled the poor girl with a rope until it stopped. Now Diavolo's claiming he had nothing to do with the physical murder; Devaney did it all. Something's not right.*

"Ben James claimed that when he was upstairs, he heard a thud," I quickly jotted in my notebook. "When he came down, Sandra was on the floor, apparently unconscious. How she got this way, he doesn't know. Assumed she was dead. Said she was strangled. Why did he think she was strangled?"

I looked up. Curt Jordan was searching for a document to display on the monitor. My thoughts continued. *James heard a thud and all he saw was Devaney standing near Sandra's unconscious body. Diavolo was there too. Truth is, no one saw Devaney put a hand on Sandra Ford. All we have is this miserable pedophile's testimony saying Devaney killed her. Sandra Ford ruined Diavolo's relationship with her mother. Diavolo wanted revenge. The girl wasn't a problem for Devaney. She was a problem for Diavolo and him alone.*

The monitor was now working. Jordan directed our attention to a crudely drawn map. "Do you recognize this map, Mr. Diavolo?"

"Yeah."

"Did you draw it?"

"Me and Tommy Devaney did."

"Please tell the jury what it is."

The scarecrow-like Diavolo lifted a scrawny finger and pointed it at Devaney. Devaney didn't flinch. "Tommy and me were informants for the FBI. They wanted to put a wire at Mafia headquarters and asked Tommy and me to draw a detailed map of the room."

"Did the FBI succeed in placing the wiretap?"

"Yeah."

"Did any arrests come from it?"

"Took down the Boston Mafia."

"Mr. Diavolo, didn't you become a top-echelon informant for the FBI in 1965, four years before you ever met Thomas Devaney?"

"Objec—" Chavere didn't even finish the word before Judge Blake overruled.

"Yes."

"And, Mr. Diavolo, weren't you an associate of La Costa Nostra before getting involved with the Old Harbor Gang?"

"What's La Costa Nostra?" I whispered to George, seated to my right.

"Mafia," he whispered back.

Why don't they just say "Mafia"? I wondered.

"Yeah. I was an associate."

"Was Thomas Devaney ever inducted into La Costa Nostra?"

Diavolo hesitated. He glanced at Chavere. "No."

"It's my understanding, Mr. Diavolo, that only initiates and made men of La Costa Nostra are allowed in the room where the induction ceremony takes place. Is this true?"

"I don't know."

"But you were an associate?"

"Yeah."

"And Mr. Devaney was not?"

Diavolo didn't answer.

"Thomas Devaney had never been in this room and therefore had no knowledge of its layout. Mr. Devaney had no part in drawing this map, did he, Mr. Diavolo?"

"Yes, he did," was Diavolo's edgy response.

"You drew the map, Mr. Diavolo. You betrayed your oath to the Boston Mafia and gave the FBI the information they needed to take them down."

"Objection. Badgering the witness." Chavere was standing.

"Withdrawn."

The day wore on, and the following day was filled with Diavolo's testimony as well. Finally, the witness was dismissed. *Was it enough?* I wondered. *Did it please Chavere and Altier enough to release him from prison?* My body shuddered as I considered the question.

Chapter 9

Justice commands us to have mercy upon
all men, to consult the interests of the whole
human race, to give to everyone his due.
—Marcus Tullius Cicero (106 BC–43
BC), political theorist, politician,
lawyer, Roman philosopher

"I DIDN'T SELL INFORMATION; I BOUGHT IT!" TOM
Devaney brought his palms down hard on the table.

"Counselor?" a guard called through the closed door. It was the
first time Devaney was meeting with his court-appointed attorneys,
and the guards weren't at all sure what might happen.

"We're okay," Curt Jordan called out as the guard pushed the door
open. The guard quickly shut it again.

"You didn't know about this file?" Jordan asked.

"I wasn't an informant. Tony was the rat, not me." Tom was
shocked to discover that his former friend Tony Diavolo had been an
FBI informant for many years, giving them significant information
about the Boston Mafia. Tom never suspected.

"There are a couple of thousand pages in that file," Rob Willis
stated, pointing to the large bound document on the table in front of
Devaney. "Skip Goot claims to be your handler. Documents throughout of statements you were supposed to have given are signed by different FBI agents. How do you explain it, Tom?"

Devaney pushed the file away in disgust. "They created it to protect themselves. Every one of them was corrupt. There's not an agent's name in that file that didn't take large sums of cash from me: Goot, Arnold, Carson, Palmer, and a few others. Money is more addictive than narcotics, and there wasn't a man I couldn't manipulate."

Jordan and Willis looked at Tom.

"Arnold realized he had to silence me or risk being caught. He ran to the reporter at the *Boston Times* and told him I was an informant, fully expecting that the Mafia would take me out."

"And why didn't they?" Willis boldly asked.

"They didn't believe it because it wasn't true."

~

On day thirty, we assembled in the jury room as usual. Conversations were lively as we drank our coffee and shared events from our lives. The mention of nightmares was brought up; obviously, I was not the only one experiencing them.

"Hey, guys, look at this," Chris called out. We went over to the window and focused on the area of the parking lot he was pointing to. Below, a herd of journalists and cameramen were racing toward Curt Jordan. Jordan had just gotten out of his car, and was approached and warmly greeted by Herman Pander. The media seemed determined to catch that moment as they tripped over one another in their attempt to be the first.

No one remarked, though all of us, I'm sure, thought it odd. Why would a family member of a murder victim want to shake the hand of the attorney defending the man on trial for the murder?

"Jordan left his window open. It's supposed to rain," Irene said.

"I'll tell Smitty," Richard responded.

Assistant US Attorney Dick Altier started the day by announcing that the prosecution was bringing an IRS agent to the stand. The agent's testimony was short and dull, as one might expect the testimony of an IRS agent to be. She reviewed canceled checks and copies of mortgages that connected Thomas Devaney to money-laundering schemes.

Curt Jordan didn't have too much to say in his cross-examination. But he did make it clear, through questioning the agent, that even though Tony Diavolo was supposedly equally involved in the money-laundering schemes as his client was said to be, more than two million dollars was returned to Diavolo by the Department of Justice as part of Diavolo's proffer deal. And none of it, Jordan pointed out, had to be used to reimburse the victims—not one penny.

The second witness was a guard from the prison where Thomas Devaney was being held. His name was Stewart Simpson. Altier was on direct examination, and reviewed with Simpson, for the jury, some audiotapes of visits Devaney had from family members. They were short clips, with talk of machine guns and perhaps even the imitation of the sound of a machine gun from Devaney.

Short excerpts taken from an entire conversation—can't base any-thing on that. How many times have I read a summation of a historical event, only to find that the full context of the actual documents sur-rounding the event revealed a totally different conclusion?

Altier didn't take long for his direct examination. He seemed proud of his performance, looking at Chavere for approval.

Curt Jordan was on cross. Devaney seemed intrigued by this wit-ness's testimony. He stopped writing on the legal pad and directed his full attention to the prison guard as Jordan tore at the audiotapes, expressing that nothing could be determined from them.

Exactly. Stop playing us for fools, Altier! I agreed.

"Mr. Simpson, would you please describe for the jury the condi-tions of Mr. Devaney's imprisonment."

We were told that Devaney was in solitary confinement. In his cell was a camera that caught his every move. A guard sat outside the cell, viewing him at all times. He was allowed out for only thirty minutes each day. He spent this time walking back and forth in the hall. The cell was thoroughly searched twice a day, as was his body. He was stripped naked, and a cavity search was conducted.

"Five," Devaney said softly, holding up his hand to display four fingers and a thumb to the guard.

"Mr. Simpson, isn't it five times a day that this strip search is conducted?" Jordan asked.

"I only know about two. I don't know what the other shifts do." He stumbled over his words.

"So, you admit that two are done on your shift? And are there three shifts at the prison?"

"Yes."

"And you have no idea what the other shifts are doing?"

"If they don't document it, I don't know."

"But isn't it filmed by the camera?" Jordan pursued.

"Yes. It would be on the camera footage."

"Unless, of course, the camera was turned off, or Mr. Devaney was taken out of the cell?"

"Well, yeah. Then it wouldn't be filmed."

"Isn't it true, Mr. Simpson, that before the court assigned Attorney Willis and me to Mr. Devaney's case, strip searches were being conducted at least eight times a day?"

"I don't know."

Jordan smiled. "Well, Mr. Simpson, the superintendent of the prison does know, because I confronted him with the fact that this was cruel and unusual punishment—as are the five searches a day. In fact, the two searches on your shift that you just testified to are a serious concern, given the fact that Mr. Devaney is constantly being watched."

Simpson's face turned white. Curt Jordan announced that he had no more questions.

Instantly, I recalled a fellow teacher's story of being arrested following a fatal car accident. He was instantly charged with manslaughter, even though the dynamics of the accident were still unknown. Though he had no criminal record, and a stellar driving record, he was imprisoned, strip-searched, and thrown into what's known as a "turtle suit" to keep him from attempting to take his own life. Several months—and $30,000—later, the charges were dropped. He had not caused the accident. *Innocent until proven guilty? Another foundational principle long gone.*

I looked at Dick Altier, so proud of his witness's testimony a few minutes before, now visibly disappointed. Altier was staring at the palm of his right hand. As I watched, he put his left hand to his mouth and licked his index finger. Moving the saliva-covered finger down to his right hand, he rubbed the saliva on his skin and then returned the finger to his mouth. He repeated the action again, and again, and again.

A disgusting nervous tic? I wondered. *Or is he subconsciously trying to clean the filth of dirty deals and the stench of corruption from his hands? Ah, Mr. Altier,* I thought as I continued to watch his bizarre behavior, *the only way to do that is to cut them off.*

The third witness on day thirty was a man named Tom Donovan. He was brought in, in a wheelchair and helped to the witness box. His general appearance indicated that he had been beaten up by life. This man was clearly in very poor health. It was also clear that he was on edge, not so much frightened as disgusted.

Donovan had been the owner of a South Boston tavern that Devaney, Diavolo, and Ben James had frequented. Donovan was well acquainted with the three, admitting that he'd been deeply involved in some of their gambling and money-laundering schemes.

Again, Altier was on direct. He revealed to us, through Donovan's abrupt answers, that Devaney allegedly had Donovan arrange two meetings for him on the upper floor of the tavern with a man Devaney said he needed to talk to. Donovan claimed that both times this man had left the tavern, he appeared visibly shaken, although Donavan said he had no knowledge of what had transpired. Donovan also stated that Devaney had him pick up envelopes from this man.

"Extortion money?" Altier asked.

"I never looked in the envelopes."

Altier's direct ended quickly.

Under cross-examination by Curt Jordan, Tom Donovan, we discovered, had been arrested on federal charges of extortion, money laundering, and racketeering—and murder.

"Tell us about the murder charge, Mr. Donovan."

"There's really not much I can tell. A young woman was killed and I was charged."

"Did you know the woman?"

"No."

"Did you have any connection to her or to the circumstances or scene of the murder?"

"None whatsoever."

"So, you are claiming that you're innocent of this charge?"

"Absolutely."

"Did you hire an attorney?"

"I did."

"Did your attorney, as any defense attorney would, attempt to have you released on bail with specific conditions?"

"He did."

"Were you released?"

"No."

This guy's determined not to give more than what he's asked. He's constantly looking at Altier and Chavere. What power do they have over him? I wondered.

"Mr. Donovan, who was the prosecuting attorney?"

"Objection. Irrelevant." Altier stood.

"Overruled." Judge Blake was quick with his response.

"Assistant US Attorney Altier."

"The same prosecuting attorney here with us now?" Curt Jordan gestured toward Altier.

"Yes, sir."

"Isn't it true, Mr. Donovan, that your attorney submitted evidence to the judge at the bail hearing documenting that you had a number of long-established and successful businesses in Boston; had been married for twenty-five years; had a stable family life; and rarely traveled outside of Massachusetts?"

"Yes."

"Did you realize that normally a judge would set bail if such proof was submitted and conditions were established?"

"Yes."

"But this presiding judge did not. Do you know why?" Jordan asked, looking at Altier.

"My understanding is that Assistant US Attorney Altier convinced the judge that I was a very dangerous man, and a high flight risk."

"Because of the gruesome circumstances of the murder you were being charged with?"

"Yes."

"So, you were denied bail, and sat in prison anticipating that you would be tried for a murder that you did not commit?"

"Yes."

"Did Assistant US Attorney Altier meet with you while you were in prison?"

"Sidebar, Your Honor!" Altier said, making a demand more than asking.

It was a lengthy sidebar, which didn't seem to change a thing. The judge told Mr. Donovan to answer Jordan's last question. Altier was obviously displeased, licking his finger and rubbing his hand again.

"Yes, Assistant US Attorney Altier met with me on several occasions."

"Isn't it true, Mr. Donovan, that Mr. Altier told you that if you offered him substantial information that would help the US Attorney's Office prosecute and convict former FBI special agent Skip Goot, and possibly Thomas Devaney upon his capture, then you might be released on bail?"

"Yes."

"What was the specific information that Mr. Altier wanted in regard to Thomas Devaney?"

"Information about the alleged claim of extortion mentioned earlier."

"The gentleman you claimed met with Mr. Devaney on the second floor of your tavern?"

"Yes."

"And did you give Assistant US Attorney Altier the information he sought?"

"Not at first."

"How long did it take?"

"For almost a year, I told Mr. Altier that I had no information to give, and that I was innocent of the murder."

"And during this time, any attempt to seek bail with conditions applied was denied?"

"Yes."

"What was the condition of your health, and the state of your businesses, while you were in prison?"

"My health was deteriorating. My businesses were going under."

"And what of your family, Mr. Donovan?"

Donovan hesitated. After taking a deep breath, he replied. "My wife and kids were scared. They were threatened with losing the businesses and our home. And, as far as we knew, I'd be tried and sentenced for a murder I didn't commit."

"Did Mr. Altier offer you an Alford plea?"

"Yes."

"Did you accept?"

"No."

What's an Alford plea? I wondered.

As if reading my mind, Curt Jordan looked toward the jury. "Is it your understanding, Mr. Donovan, that an Alford plea allows a defendant to maintain his or her innocence when accepting a plea bargain?"

"Yes."

"With the threat of your family becoming homeless, with no source of income, what did you decide to do, Mr. Donovan?"

"I gave Mr. Altier the information he wanted."

"And isn't it true, Mr. Donovan, that three days later, all federal charges were dropped?"

"Yes."

"As for the murder, the court suddenly realized, with the help of Assistant US Attorney Altier, that you were indeed innocent and had somehow been mistakenly accused?"

As Mr. Donovan said yes, Dick Altier flew to his feet with an objection.

Too late, Altier! The truth is out. I was horrified! *Imprisoned on a false charge of murder. Could Altier have concocted the charge himself?*

Held indefinitely, Donovan had no hope of getting out until he gave Altier what he wanted to hear, true or false. Did Altier even care? What of Tom Donovan's rights? What of his basic constitutional rights? If they could do this to him, they could do it to anyone! My mind was racing.

The final witness that day was FBI Special Agent Joseph Lawson, who'd made the arrest of Thomas Devaney. He told us the story of tips that led to the knowledge of Devaney's whereabouts, the plan to arrest him, and the actual arrest.

Devaney had been living with his longtime girlfriend Kathleen Mercer in an apartment complex near Washington, DC.

Right under the nose of FBI Headquarters? I was astonished.

Two witnesses who had come to know the couple personally gave their location to the FBI after seeing a newscast about them on television. The FBI felt it was best to lure Devaney out of his apartment to make the arrest. They devised a plan to have Devaney come to the basement of the apartment complex by making him think someone had broken into his storage area. The plan worked. When Devaney appeared in the basement, the FBI and local police SWAT team came from the shadows, all guns pointed at Devaney.

At this point in the testimony, Devaney put down the pen he'd been holding, propped his left arm on the table, and rested his jaw in the palm of his left hand. He sat there, making eye contact with the FBI agent on the stand, patiently waiting for him to continue.

FBI Special Agent Lawson was looking straight at Devaney as he continued. There was nothing threatening, and no anger noted in the countenance of either man. They held one another's gaze as though there was an unspoken bond or agreement between them.

Lawson told us that as soon as Devaney realized what was happening, he calmly told the armed law enforcement officers that he would cooperate fully, and even aid them in the search of his apartment. Devaney's only concern was for Kathleen. He would cooperate, not wanting special treatment for himself but desiring consideration for Kathleen.

After the arrest of both Devaney and Kathleen Mercer, the FBI located in the apartment, with the help of Devaney, thirty guns, ammunition, scopes, silencers, and knives. Devaney even warned the FBI agents about particular guns that were loaded. There was also close to a million dollars in cash.

When Lawson finished with this portion of his testimony, Thomas Devaney picked up his pen and went back to writing.

The direct examination went on, with information about the process that followed. Then, Curt Jordan came to the lectern.

"Special Agent Lawson, didn't Mr. Devaney offer more than his cooperation?"

"Objection!" Altier shouted. "Mr. Jordan knows that this has been discussed with Your Honor!"

Judge Blake called for a sidebar. On went the familiar noise machine. I saw that Chavere was staring at Devaney.

Devaney offered the FBI more than his cooperation? What's that about? I wondered.

With the sidebar over, Curt Jordan returned to the lectern. "Special Agent Lawson, did you give Kathleen Mercer consideration as Mr. Devaney requested?"

"There was not much that I could do personally, but I filed a report with my superiors stating that Mr. Devaney was cooperative, and asked that his request be considered."

"And why did Mr. Devaney warn you of the loaded guns?"

"He said he was concerned that we know which guns were loaded so that one didn't discharge accidently."

"And, Special Agent Lawson, did you find it odd that Mr. Devaney had the arsenal that he did?"

"Yes, sir, I certainly did. I asked him if he intended to shoot it out."

"His response?"

"That he wouldn't do that, because a stray bullet might hit a bystander."

"Thank you, sir. I have no more questions for this witness, Your Honor."

"Special Agent Lawson, you may step down," Judge Blake instructed him.

Before he stepped down, I noticed that Thomas Devaney made eye contact with him again. Devaney nodded ever so slightly, and Lawson responded with a rather sad smile.

No more mention of Devaney offering the FBI more than his cooperation? I thought as I watched the interaction between the two men.

"Your Honor, the federal government rests," Dick Altier announced.

~

The ride home seemed to take an eternity as my thoughts fixated on the testimony of Thomas Donovan. I turned on the radio, going from station to station, hoping to find something that would occupy my thoughts and take me into a state of mindlessness. It wasn't working. I popped in a CD, then another, and then another. Nothing seemed to calm the alarming fury I felt within. I desperately needed someone to talk to, somewhere to vent. Raw emotions were coming to a boil as my body began shaking uncontrollably. I pulled the car into the empty section of a large parking lot. Putting the transmission into park, I left the windows closed, the air-conditioning on, and the radio blaring as I screamed in my rage.

"They have utter disregard for the rights of individuals! Did they make up that murder charge? If so, how can they keep a man they know has been falsely charged in prison indefinitely? For Christ's sake! I believe they made up the charge! And they show no concern, no regret for their actions, openly displaying it in this court of law with no shame!"

Tears began to stream down my cheeks. My heart was pounding. Taking deep breaths, I exhaled slowly and rested my head against the headrest. "Court of law?" I was no longer screaming. "A federal judicial system where anything seems acceptable as the means to an end. Where serial killers are free to walk the streets if their testimony is a means to an end. Where a child and a teenage girl can be gunned down and the confessed killer set free. Where a girl can be raped and murdered by her stepfather and no one seems to care. After all, she was 'only an addict and prostitute.' Where FBI agents, sworn to protect fellow citizens and uphold the Constitution, are involved in murders, found out, and rewarded."

The tears stopped. I used my hand to wipe my wet cheeks. "Court of law? Whose law? The legal system that this country was founded on is gone. If the legal system is gone, no one is safe from false prosecution. If the legal system is gone, the nation is gone."

I was moving through the stages of grief: denial, anger, bargaining, depression, and acceptance. I knew from personal experience that they didn't always come in order, and they often repeated. But here I was, mourning alone.

Chapter 10

The administration of justice is the
firmest pillar of government.
—George Washington (1732–1799), commander
in chief of the Continental Army; first
president of the United States of America

IT CAME EASILY. TOO EASILY, TOM REALIZED, AS HE
had so many times before. He lay upon the metal-frame cot in the jail
cell. The thin mattress offered little protection against the springs of
the cheap mesh frame, which poked into his back, buttocks, and legs.
The memory of taking Brian Caffey's life—his first kill—frequently
played out in Tom's mind.

It was a spur-of-the-moment decision, simple and quick. Tom
saw Caffey in a car opposite his at the intersection. He hated Caffey.
Caffey hated him. An effortless solution to an annoying problem: pull
alongside Caffey, call out his name, point the revolver, and boom—
problem gone.

Tom felt no emotion in recounting the memory, just as there was
none when he decided to do it. It was so easy, so very easy.

The cars were alongside one another. Caffey was close enough to
touch.

"Hey, Caffey!" Tom remembered calling out.

Caffey looked at Tom. It all happened quickly. Caffey's expression
never registered recognition.

With a steady hand, Tom pointed his piece at Caffey. He aimed the barrel of the revolver right between Caffey's eyes and squeezed the trigger. The noise of the blast from the gun was muffled by the passing traffic.

It was done. Simple and quick. Easy. The only problem was, Tom immediately realized as he calmly drove off, that he had put a bullet between the eyes of Brian Caffey.

"Damn," he said, as he methodically leaned forward and placed the revolver under the seat. "They could pass as twins." Tom had no issues with Brian Caffey; it was his brother Paul he wanted dead.

"Damn," he repeated as a smile took form, instantaneously followed by a searing pain pulsating in his temples. Never had he felt such agony. He could barely breathe as he struggled to drive to the nearby apartment of a friend.

Tom looked at the gray ceiling above the cot as he remembered the shocked reaction of his friend upon seeing him at the door, clasping his head in agony.

"I gotta lay down. Let me lay down." Tom stumbled to the sofa.

With each murder, the searing pain returned. Sleep was the only cure.

~

As we gathered on day thirty-one, there was a noticeable sense of anticipation. Today, the defense would begin calling witnesses—and it was possible that Thomas Devaney would take the stand himself.

Days thirty-one through thirty-three introduced us to former FBI agents and a former officer from the Massachusetts State Police. Their testimonies differed from those of FBI special agents and Massachusetts State Police officers who were called in as witnesses for the prosecution. The FBI agents for the defense added to my conviction that Thomas Devaney was not an FBI informant. These agents shared their knowledge and concerns about the Boston FBI files having been accessible to all agents. They told the jury that any agent could take information from a particular informant's file and superimpose it into another. Because of this lack of security in the filing system, a false file could be created, drawing information solely from other files.

So much for the boring days of testimony Chavere and Altier put us through to prove that Delaney's informant file was legitimate. What a freaking waste of time all that testimony was. I shook my head slowly in disgust.

The state police officer informed us that he'd interviewed both Vinnie Giuda and Tony Diavolo before they'd made their proffers with the assistant US attorneys. Their accounts of certain crimes differed significantly at that time. Shortly after that interview, the officer told us, both Giuda and Diavolo had been given improper access to Ben James's statements. Who gave them access to this file was never determined. After reading Ben James's statements, Giuda and Diavolo changed their testimonies to reflect his.

No kidding! What a surprise! I was seething at this point. *And, of course, no one thinks it important enough to find out who violated the law in giving them the file.* My eyes, with daggers flying, settled on Chavere. I couldn't help but wonder if she had played a part.

There were numerous objections and sidebars called by the prosecution during these testimonies. In fact, there were so many that it became difficult to stay connected and follow the story lines of these witnesses.

Probably exactly what Chavere and Altier are attempting to do, I thought. *Their buttocks barely touch the seat and they jump up again to object. They remind me of little Paul's jack-in-the-box. What a couple of sick clowns.*

We also heard from a real estate attorney who gave an account of the various properties still owned by Tony Diavolo. Combined, they were worth close to seven million dollars—much more than the prosecution had indicated in prior testimony. Chavere's attempts to trip up this intelligent and disciplined woman in her cross-examination boomeranged. The real estate attorney's direct, knowledgeable answers made Chavere appear ignorant of anything pertaining to the subject.

Is Chavere trying to defend the federal court's decision to give Diavolo access to all of his property? She obviously knows nothing about real estate law, but she's determined to make this woman look bad. Why has Diavolo been rewarded with the ownership of his property? He has a life sentence. If he'd been ordered to pay restitution to the victims, it would make sense, but the court didn't order restitution. It's all his.

On day thirty-four, direct examination began with another former FBI agent. His story proved quite different from that of other agents.

This man introduced himself as Joseph Wallace, the assistant special agent in charge about whom Ken Arnold had spoken respectfully in his testimony. Attractive and trim, Wallace's physique displayed robust health. His countenance revealed the opposite. This witness appeared exhausted; his ashen face and slow movement hinted that he might be ill or in physical pain.

Joseph Wallace had served more than twenty years with the FBI before being assigned to the Boston office as assistant special agent in charge. In this position, he was second in command. His accomplishments prior to coming to Boston were astounding; he'd played a major role in notable historical cases. When ASAC Wallace first began in Boston, he was immediately taken aback, not only by the conflict between the Boston FBI, Massachusetts State Police, and local police, but also by the conflict within the FBI office itself. There was a strong sense of distrust between agents, beyond anything ASAC Wallace had experienced in the many FBI offices he'd been assigned to through the years.

Part of his responsibility was overseeing the work of the Crime Squad, headed by Special Agent Ken Arnold. After reviewing the handling of top-echelon informants, Wallace asked Arnold to set up a meeting with Thomas Devaney. Arnold did so, and accompanied ASAC Wallace to Devaney's apartment. ASAC Wallace told the jury that he quickly determined Devaney was not an informant.

"What transpired to bring you to that conclusion?" Rob Willis asked.

"Mr. Devaney's response to direct questions. He stated that he had not given information to the FBI; he'd bought it. He admitted his active and ongoing leadership in the Old Harbor Gang, and was adamant that he would not, under any circumstances, testify for the bureau."

"You stated earlier that you attended this meeting with Special Agent Ken Arnold, whom the jury heard from already. Were any other agents present?"

"Special Agent Goot was already at Mr. Devaney's apartment when Arnold and I arrived."

"You knew he would be there?"

"Absolutely not. I had no knowledge of his presence throughout most of the interview. Goot came out of a back room shortly before I was ready to leave." Wallace's tone changed, revealing his upset over the situation.

"This alarmed you?"

"Greatly. No one was supposed to be present for that interview except me, Devaney, and Arnold. For an agent to be present without my knowledge or consent was out of line."

"Did Special Agent Arnold know that Agent Goot would be present?"

"Yes. And it was obvious to me upon being introduced to Mr. Devaney that he and Arnold had a social connection. Goot's casual presence clearly indicated that he was part of this social relationship."

"Was there any conversation between you and Special Agent Arnold on the ride back to headquarters?"

"Yes. I told Arnold that based on the interview, Devaney needed to be closed as an informant and pursued as a targeted criminal. Arnold objected."

"Were your concerns about the interview shared with your superior?"

"Yes. I gave a verbal and a written report of the interview to the special agent in charge. In the report, I clearly stated that Thomas Devaney did not meet the criteria for an informant and should be a target for investigation. In my presence, the SAC read the report, assured me that he would send it to headquarters in Washington, and placed it in his office safe."

"There was a safe in the special agent in charge's office?"

"Yes."

"Who had access to this safe?"

"Only the SAC."

"And, sir, what was the response from Washington?"

"There was none. I sent another report directly to headquarters. Again, there was no response. I then set up a meeting with the head of the New England Organized Crime Strike Task Force."

"This task force was part of the Department of Justice?"

"Yes. The federal attorney heading it up at the time was Joshua O'Toole."

Joseph Wallace barely had the name out of his mouth when Dick Altier was up and shouting, "Objection! Sidebar, Your Honor!"

Without hesitation, Judge Blake agreed. The sound machine was turned on and the judge heard the arguments of the attorneys. Filled with emotion, this highly animated sidebar was observed by all present. Former ASAC Wallace waited patiently. He gave no indication of alarm or concern over the volatile sidebar.

Devaney periodically looked up from his writing during Wallace's testimony. With the mention of Joshua O'Toole, Devaney's attention remained fixed on what was being said.

The safe in the SAC's office? It was mentioned before, I recalled, quickly scanning my notes. *Michael Biscione, the weird guy from the Inspector General's Office—the defense asked him about reading the papers in the safe. He said there wasn't a safe.*

My thoughts were distracted when the attorneys returned to their assigned tables. I noticed that Chavere and Altier seemed pleased.

Rob Willis returned to the lectern. Whatever reprimand he'd been given didn't seem to have an effect. "But, Mr. Wallace, Mr. Devaney was not closed as an informant, nor targeted as a criminal. Why?"

"FBI Headquarters and Joshua O'Toole—"

Again, Altier jumped up.

Before Altier had a chance to object, Judge Blake said, "Mr. Willis, please remember what we discussed at sidebar."

"Of course, Your Honor," Willis said robotically. "Mr. Wallace, in answer to my question as to why Mr. Devaney was never closed as an informant or targeted as a criminal, you were saying that FBI Headquarters and the New England Organized Crime Strike Task Force did what?"

"They stated that Devaney was to remain open as an informant. There was no reason given."

Obviously, there can be no mention of Joshua O'Toole. Why? And why would they insist that Devaney is an informant, when Devaney told Wallace he wasn't, nor would he ever be? If Sly Devaney is as evil as they want us to believe, why wouldn't he be targeted by the FBI and by this man who can't be mentioned—Joshua O'Toole?

Rob Willis now directed questions to ASAC Wallace about his involvement in trying to protect Ed O'Leary, the man who was thrown out of the witness protection program and subsequently murdered. The fact that O'Leary was giving the FBI information against Devaney was yet another reason to close Devaney as an informant, ASAC Wallace explained. "You can't have two informants informing on each other."

And, though Wallace was determined that O'Leary needed protection, no one with higher authority allowed him that protection. Not those in command at FBI Headquarters, not this Joshua O'Toole of the New England Organized Crime Strike Task Force— who could not be named—and not US Attorney Floyd Nichols of the Boston US Attorney's Office, who would later become the governor of Massachusetts. Because of their united denial of protection for O'Leary, both he and his friend Donald Monahan had been gunned down.

You can't have two informants informing on each other. I mulled over ASAC Wallace's statement. Of course you can't. One of them has to go. But according to Devaney's statement to Wallace, he wasn't an informant. And after seeing the shoddy informant file purported to be his, I believe Devaney. So why was he protected by the FBI? O'Leary needed to die because he was informing on Devaney. Ken Arnold made certain that happened—and it seems to me that many played a part in that decision, perhaps even this Joshua O'Toole and Governor Floyd Nichols in their denial of protection. And the fact that FBI Headquarters was ignoring Wallace's concerns suggests that perhaps they were part of this seeming conspiracy to have O'Leary murdered. O'Leary was killed in 1982. J. Edgar Hoover was long dead. Who was heading up the FBI then?

Wallace went on to tell us that the former special agent in charge retired and was replaced by a man named Brown. ASAC Wallace later discovered that Special Agent in Charge Brown was, along with Ken Arnold, leaking information about a drug investigation. According to protocol, ASAC Wallace was duty bound to report to FBI Headquarters what he had discovered. The response from Washington, DC was to "keep quiet about it."

"And did you keep it quiet?" Willis asked.

"No, and retribution was dealt out in the Boston office and from headquarters. It culminated in a sudden notification of a transfer to the Midwest. At the time, my wife was confined to bed with a complicated pregnancy. I couldn't risk moving her."

"Is it unusual to get notification of an immediate transfer?"

"Yes."

"What did you do?"

"There was an opening in Rhode Island for a lower grade level, but from there I could be close to home. I requested assignment in Providence."

"A lower grade level. Does this mean you took a cut in salary?"

"Yes. A significant cut."

"Did you stay there long, Mr. Wallace?"

"About a year."

"And then you were transferred elsewhere?"

"No. Unfortunately, Providence was no better than Boston in regard to corruption within the bureau. I reported it through the chain of command, as protocol dictated. The response from headquarters again was, 'Keep it quiet.' I couldn't accept corruption from within as the norm, and I knew that if I persisted in reporting it, I'd face worse retribution than I did in Boston. So, I turned in my resignation, expecting to receive a reduced pension."

"Yes, for early retirement it would be reduced." Rob Willis turned to face the jury before he continued. "So, Mr. Wallace, you continue to receive this pension for your many years of service?"

"No, sir, I don't."

Willis was slowly scanning the faces of the jurors. "Why not?"

"Accusations were made against my service and character immediately following my resignation. I never received my pension."

"Did you appeal this decision?"

"I certainly did—all the way to the top."

"And?" Willis asked, still watching us.

"I have yet to receive a single penny due."

"Thank you, Mr. Wallace," Rob Willis said, gathering his notes. "And thank you for your service."

"Objection." Dick Altier jumped up.

"Withdrawn," Willis muttered as he walked away from the lectern.

I was dazed by ASAC Wallace's testimony, and remembered prior testimony regarding him that supported what he'd just told us. *He's punished for seeking truth. Punished, but not silenced. Determined still to bring accountability to the FBI.*

As Altier took his place behind the lectern, I felt my body relax. *This won't take long,* I thought, looking at the clock on the wall above the doors to the courtroom. *Every FBI agent the prosecution called had respect for Wallace.*

"Mr. Wallace, did you write a book about your service with the FBI?"

Altier held up a book with many colorful sticky tabs, as he called out the title. "Isn't it true that you claim to have had a leading role in the investigation of the Birmingham, Alabama, bombing, Abscam, and the assassination of Martin Luther King Jr., to name a few?"

"Yes, I did."

"But, Mr. Wallace, let's be honest: didn't you fabricate these stories to sell your book?" Altier's tone became haughty.

"Fabricate?"

"Mr. Wallace, why is it that the FBI makes no acknowledgement of your part in these cases?"

"You'd have to ask the FBI."

"But of course. You were run out of the FBI for trying to do the right thing. Isn't that your testimony, Mr. Wallace?"

"Objection. Badgering the witness," Rob Willis said softly.

"Sustained."

"Why is it, Mr. Wallace, that those FBI agents who are acknowledged to have been present during these investigations denied that you were involved?"

"You would have to ask them." ASAC Wallace didn't seem the least bit shaken.

"Objection, Your Honor. This is speculation and hearsay. If Mr. Altier wants to discuss the reports of the FBI, or those of former agents, then let him bring these individuals in for questioning," Willis stated.

"Let's move on, Mr. Altier," the judge said, not even looking up from his computer.

Is he bored? He doesn't seem to be paying attention to what's being said. What's with Altier? His own witnesses had nothing bad to say about Wallace, but now he's going to support alleged accusations from nameless agents? This bastard is determined to discredit Wallace. And the judge doesn't seem to give a damn. Why?

Accusation after accusation was thrown at ASAC Wallace in the form of questions. The assistant US attorney even crossed a line, tapping into Wallace's medical records and questioning if his medication might cause him to be delusional and forgetful.

Isn't that a federal crime? What about HIPAA? But I suppose the federal government can violate any law it wants. I looked at Judge Blake. He was still engrossed in his computer screen.

Altier's fangs and claws were exposed in a most brutal manner as he tried to convince the jury that this former ASAC, with a long career, was nothing but a liar.

Objection after objection was voiced, the judge barely acknowledging the argument. Even the few times the judge agreed with Rob Willis's concerns, Altier seemingly ignored the decision and continued with no reprimand. *It's as if the judge anticipated this vicious attack on Wallace. It almost seems that he's compliant.*

"And isn't it true, Mr. Wallace, that you invented the story of reporting that Thomas Devaney needed to be closed as an informant and made a target?" Altier shouted, "In fact, isn't it true, Mr. Wallace, that no safe existed in the SAC's office? This safe, like the report, is fictitious!"

Rob Willis was standing, and practically screaming to be heard over Altier's loud and vicious verbal attack. Willis's flushed cheeks and bold tone revealed his frustration. Judge Blake failed to acknowledge Willis's loud repeated objections. Curt Jordan, his face as crimson as Willis's, rose to his feet and yelled in unison with his partner, finally getting Judge Blake to look up from the computer.

"Sustained," Judge Blake uttered, immediately turning his attention to the computer screen.

What the hell is going on? I leaned forward in my seat, frustrated and somehow frightened by what I was witnessing. Altier's hostility toward the witness was intensifying, and the judge didn't seem to care.

"I turned in a report stating that after my interview with Thomas Devaney, I felt he should be removed from informant status and made a target," ASAC Wallace calmly responded, though his countenance hinted that he was shaken. "I gave the report to the special agent in charge. He placed it into the safe in his office. I also sent a report to those in command in Washington, DC. That is my testimony, and it is the truth."

We are to believe that Giuda, Ben James, Diavolo, and Arnold were telling the truth but that this man is a liar? I was aghast. *How can this be happening? Ken Arnold was treated with such respect by the assistant US attorneys, and this man, a man who risked his career to do the right thing, is vilified? Arnold has his pension after being caught and confessing to the crimes he committed, including accessory to murders. Yet Wallace's career is destroyed and his pension stolen by the United States government! For God's sake, the taxpayers are responsible for paying these pensions. Shouldn't we have a say in whether Arnold gets his and whether Wallace doesn't?*

By the time Altier was finished, he had emotionally drawn and quartered ASAC Wallace. Even so, Wallace walked out with a sense of strength and dignity.

Strength, in knowing the truth. Dignity, in not being sucked into the slime pit that the hierarchy of the FBI has seemingly created, and perhaps the hierarchy of the Department of Justice as a whole. I realized, as I watched Joseph Wallace leave the room, that the image of him being attacked by Altier would be seared forever in my mind. Then looking at Dick Altier, I whispered, "*You goddamn son of a bitch!*" and silently prayed that he would one day pay for this outrage.

The next witness was a petite very old woman by the name of Lucy. She had served as secretary to the Boston FBI special agent in charge for many, many years, under many, many SACs. She was in that position when ASAC Wallace was there. She had Thomas Devaney's full attention, I noted.

"Were you aware of a report from ASAC Wallace regarding the informant status of Thomas Devaney being given to the special agent in charge?" Rob Willis asked.

"Yes. I transcribed a copy of this report per order of the special agent in charge."

"Where was the original report kept?"

"In the safe within the office of the special agent in charge. It was kept there for years."

Chavere tried to object but was silenced by the judge.

"Were you given any instructions by the special agent in charge in regard to this report in the safe?"

"Yes. Shortly before he retired, he instructed me to inform the next SAC to carefully read the report in my presence, and then have me return the report to the safe."

"Was ASAC Wallace still at the Boston office when this happened?"

"No."

"And were your duties fulfilled after doing this?"

"No. For as long as I remained secretary to the special agent in charge of the Boston office, I was to repeat this ritual with each newly assigned SAC."

"How many times did you carry out this order?"

"Three times. The first and second special agents in charge read the report and had me return it to the safe. The third SAC read the report and then instructed me to immediately destroy it."

"Did he say why he wanted the report destroyed?" Again, Rob Willis turned to face the jury.

"Yes. He said, 'Destroy this immediately, or we'll all lose our jobs.'"

"Did you destroy it?"

"Yes. The original was destroyed as ordered. But the transcribed copy was overlooked."

Willis turned his attention back to the lectern and picked up a piece of paper. "Your Honor, may I approach the witness?"

"Yes," Judge Blake said.

Willis walked to Lucy and placed the paper on the witness stand before her. "Is this the transcribed copy of the report we are discussing?"

"Yes, it is."

"Did you transcribe this from the original report that remained in the safe for many years and that was later destroyed by you?"

"Yes."

"Please read this report, and tell me if it has been altered in any way."

Lucy took her time in reading the report. "No. It has not been altered."

"Thank you," Willis said to Lucy. He walked back to the lectern and asked his paralegal to put the report up on the monitors through his laptop.

Chavere stood. "Your Honor, is this report documented in evidence?"

"Mr. Willis?" Judge Blake asked.

"It was entered into evidence when Mr. Biscione was on the stand, Your Honor. When he denied any knowledge of a safe within the special agent in charge's office, it was shown to him and entered. There was no objection by the prosecution at that time."

Amy, seated in front of the judge, stood and handed the judge a piece of paper. The judge read it, typed something on his keyboard, and looked at his computer screen.

"The document is in evidence, Ms. Chavere."

Chavere asked Rob Willis if she could look at the report before it was put on the monitors. Willis handed it to her, and waited patiently as Chavere and Altier reviewed it.

The report, which ASAC Wallace had written, and which Lucy had transcribed many years before, was viewed by the jury.

"I have no more questions for this witness, Your Honor," Rob Willis announced.

Carla Chavere was on cross. She had very little to ask. Nothing was said about the report or the safe. She seemingly wanted to get Lucy off the stand as quickly as possible.

After Lucy stepped out of the witness box, Defense Attorney Curt Jordan stood and announced, "The defense rests."

What? I was entirely taken by surprise. *They had so many witnesses on the list we were given during jury selection. What about the governor? What about the federal judge that was listed? What about the different reporters from the Boston newspapers? What about Nick Mudd? How can the defense be done with so many witnesses left? What about Devaney? He's not taking the stand? We need to hear what these witnesses have to say. There's no logical conclusion to anything right now! Where's the truth? Where are the facts? Nothing has been proven or disproven! Nothing has been accomplished at all, except the realization that the Department of Justice is far less than just! Maybe when they give closing arguments we'll be told why these witnesses didn't appear. Yes, that's it; closing arguments will pull it all together and make sense of the confusion.*

We were dismissed for the weekend. Closing arguments would begin on Monday.

~

Each side had ninety minutes to present their closing arguments to the jury. Curt Jordan and Rob Willis divided the time. Jordan reviewed the many forms of government corruption revealed throughout the trial. He pointed out that there was no remorse, not even embarrassment, in the face of the exposure of such corruption, or for the unthinkable deals given to vicious criminals in return for testimony that aided the assistant US attorneys in their determination to convict Thomas Devaney.

"Thomas Devaney has been accused of taking part in murders that were confessed to and committed by star witnesses for the US

Attorney's Office. How can the testimony of Giuda, Diavolo, James, or Arnold be trusted? They cut outrageous deals with the assistant US attorneys to get out of prison. The testimony of these witnesses, and others, was for sale; the government made the purchase. The currency used was freedom from prison. For Tony Diavolo, it was escape from a lethal injection"—Curt Jordan paused and looked at Chavere and Altier before continuing—"and possible release from a life sentence for his testimony through a Rule 35 motion. For Vinnie Giuda, less than six months for every cold-blooded murder he committed—including the slayings of two youths who were in the wrong place at the wrong time. For Ken Arnold, a slap on the hand for accessory to two murders while serving under oath to protect the men he set up to be killed. Was any of their testimony true?"

Rob Willis's closing argument was an impassioned plea for us to consider all that had been presented, and to be willing to reject the testimony of the many vile witnesses. "As citizens, you now have a unique opportunity to stand against corruption within the Department of Justice," Willis stated. His eyes went from juror to juror, finally locking with mine. "Your verdict can punish the Department of Justice for its immoral dealings with criminals. This is the time for us to say, 'There has to be accountability!'"

Carla Chavere gave the ninety-minute closing argument for the prosecution. She reviewed the "facts" that had been presented. When she went over the informant files, I quietly but audibly moaned, "Holy mother of God! Not the files again."

I found myself watching the clock, praying for the minute hand to turn quickly. Eighty-five minutes into Chavere's closing argument, she said, "Thomas Devaney is one of the most sadistic, brutal, calculating criminals to walk the streets of this city. The defense team's attempt to manipulate this jury by trying to make this trial about government corruption is wrong. They're asking you to make a statement, through your verdict, about how the bad federal government needs to be punished." Chavere paused. Her eyes visibly filled with tears. "To do so would be a violation of your oath. You must find Thomas Devaney guilty as charged."

A violation of our oath? I thought, considering Chavere's tears. My eyes followed her as she sat down. *Either she truly believes what she's saying or she has so much invested in this case, perhaps even her reputation and job, that she's terrified we won't come back with a verdict of guilt.*

We were dismissed for the day. Still none of us knew who the twelve were who would be sent into deliberations.

Chapter 11

The best and only safe road to honor,
glory, and true dignity is justice.
—George Washington

TOM DEVANEY'S RACING THOUGHTS RUMINATED over the prior weeks of testimony: the fierce betrayal of men he'd once considered friends, the shock of discovering an informant file existed, the lies Chavere and Altier purported. Yet what tormented him the most was the damage done to those he loved. Kathleen's lengthy imprisonment—her first year had been spent in solitary confinement—besieged his every waking moment. Any word he received of her came through family members.

Tom was haunted by the pain he had caused his parents in choosing a life of crime. His brothers and their children had suffered because of him as well. To bear the name Devaney was an instant judgment of guilt by association. Each of his brothers' careers had been ruined by the determined obsession of Carla Chavere to destroy him. Each of his brothers' characters was libeled and slandered by Boston's media, seemingly forgetting their responsibility to unbiasedly report the facts, and instead taking on the characteristics of tabloid journalists.

Kathleen was now forever taken from Devaney.

Darkness surrounded and permeated him. There was no escape.

~

The next morning, we jurors assembled in the courtroom. Judge Blake's instructions to the jury lasted almost two hours. It was a recitation of statute after statute, law after law. Each seemed to contradict the one before. My mind was on overload, as I'm sure was true of my fellow jurors. Finally, the judge finished.

"Copies of the indictment and all physical evidence, except the firearms and cash, have already been placed in the jury room. The firearms and cash will be brought to you upon request. Any questions you may have can be submitted to me in writing. I will send back a written response. Jurors one through twelve, please take your notebooks. You will now begin deliberations. Jurors thirteen through eighteen are the alternates, and will be instructed where to go."

He deceived us, I thought, disturbed at the realization. *When we were seated, he told us not to assume that the first twelve would make up the jury. He purposefully deceived us, but deceit seems to be par for the course in this courtroom.*

The order came, "All rise for the jury." We filed out. As the deliberating jurors were guided up the stairs, many of us looked down at the alternates, who were being ushered toward the elevator.

Where are they taking them? I wondered. Kim, Elizabeth, Irene, Chris, Dave, and George held us in their gazes for as long as they could. The same look of shock that we'd shared when jury selection was completed was upon many of our faces. Kim and Irene were visibly fighting back tears.

They're needed in deliberations, I realized. *Each has more to offer than some assigned to this jury.* Larry quickly came to mind.

We, the deliberating jury, quietly finished our ascent of the stairs we had all climbed together at least twice a day since the trial had begun ten weeks before.

What will they be doing while we deliberate? Will we see them at all during this process? I can't imagine the frustration of being pulled out at this point! Each, I realized, was a unique and pleasant presence among the group, Chris's dry humor, Elizabeth's gentle soul, Kim's joy of life, Dave's vast knowledge, Irene's calming effect, and George's fatherly presence. *The dynamics of the "family" have changed. Will it alter our ability to work effectively together?*

My body trembled as I walked into the jury room. I stepped behind the chair to the left of the table, closest to the door, and placed my notebook down. A folder marked for the foreperson and twelve copies of the indictment were piled in the middle of the table, along with a container filled with pens. Toward the back of the room, I noticed a large metal cart loaded with large manila envelopes and brown paper bags. *Must be the physical evidence from the trial,* I surmised as I remained standing. My hands were placed firmly against the back of the chair.

We've heard the testimony of almost eighty witnesses. We sat in the courtroom for thirty-five days, subject to hearing testimony of crimes that spanned thirty years. Now the burden is on us to determine the guilt or innocence of Thomas Devaney. My knuckles were white against the chair.

Larry came out of the restroom and bellowed, "Well, we all know he's guilty, so this won't take long!"

Richard, who claimed the seat at the head of the table closest to the restrooms, firmly told Larry to be quiet.

Larry ignored him. "What? It's obvious! If anyone in the room thinks he's not guilty, then they're nuts!"

"We'll go through the charges one by one," Sam stated.

"The man's innocent until proven guilty, and we have to determine whether or not he was proven guilty beyond a reasonable doubt," I added.

Larry went to say something, but he was distracted by the metal cart in the back of the room. He walked to it and randomly began rummaging through the envelopes and bags. "I wish we had the guns! Look!" he called out, sounding like a schoolboy rather than a responsible adult. "The boot!" He laughed as he pulled out what was left of a deteriorated boot that had been found on one of the murder victims.

"Put it back!" Katie yelled. Many of us, aghast, voiced our disbelief of what he had done.

"What? It's here for us to look at—"

"Show some respect for the dead," Pam scolded, obviously upset by Larry's disregard.

Finally, we were all seated at the table. Unfortunate for me, Larry took the seat to my left. Each of us had our notebooks. Richard, I noticed, had two to every one of ours.

"We need to pick a foreperson," Richard began, eyeing the folder on the table. "Perhaps those willing to be in that position should let us know and we can draw names. I'll start by saying that I'm willing. Anyone else?"

"Yeah, I'd like to be foreman," Larry blurted. A few of us made eye contact with each other, horrified at the thought.

"I'd do it," Katie offered.

"Anyone else?" Richard and a few others looked at me.

I shook my head, concerned that the revulsion I had developed for Chavere and Altier would be an impediment.

"Okay, then let's vote," Richard suggested.

"Remove my name," Katie offered, looking straight at Richard. "You've got my vote."

The vote was taken. Richard received eleven. Larry received one—obviously his own.

"Okay," Sam agreed. "It's done. Richard is the foreman."

Richard took a deep breath and picked up the folder containing the instructions. As he tried to make sense of it, the rest of us pored over the indictment. There were a dozen pages listing twenty-five counts, with twenty-eight predicate acts under the racketeering charge. These acts included sixteen murders. We were to make a determination of "proven" or "not proven" on each and every one. Only two counts, committed within a ten-year period, needed to be proven to put Thomas Devaney in prison for the remainder of his life. As I read the counts, I knew that two of them were indeed proven. Guns were found in his apartment, and the money-laundering argument seemed solid. But those crimes hadn't occurred within ten years of each another. The money laundering took place in the 1980s. The guns were not found until 2011. Perhaps we would agree on finding Devaney guilty of counts that fulfilled the qualification of being committed within the ten-year time frame, but in my mind, there were many that were far from proven beyond a reasonable doubt. My thoughts were rushing.

"Okay. The determination is 'proven,' 'not proven,' or 'no finding,'" Richard began. "The proven and not proven need to be unanimous. Judge Blake made it clear that he doesn't want us coming back with no finding."

Whether or not he wants that, it's bound to happen, I thought.

"Let's start at the beginning with count one," Richard suggested.

We were instructed in the paperwork that even though Devaney might not have been present during a crime, he could be found guilty by association with the members of the Old Harbor Gang who had carried out the act. I was taken aback by this particular instruction.

What does that mean? I wondered. *How far do you take this? If Devaney had no knowledge of the crime, is he automatically guilty just because someone in his scary circle of friends carried it out? I think Giuda and Diavolo probably committed murders that Devaney had no part in. Something isn't right here. Take Devaney out of the equation, Alex,* I told myself. *If Joe Smith's friend robs a bank, should Joe Smith be charged with the crime as well, simply because they're friends?*

We muddled through the first few hours. It was evident that none of us knew what we were doing as we struggled to locate notes that were scattered because of the mishmash of chronology throughout the trial. Pages upon pages of our notes were devoted to ten days of testimony concerning Devaney's supposed FBI informant file.

"Why was there so much testimony on Devaney's informant file when there's no mention of it in the indictment?" Dan asked incredulously.

"Yeah, we should tear all those notes out. They're just in our way," Katie agreed.

I'm not the only one questioning the informant file testimony, thank God, I thought, nodding as I looked from Dan to Katie.

We moved through counts one and two fairly quickly, but we hit a glitch when we reached count three. Now we were faced with the sixteen murders. It was evident from the start that our views varied widely. And other than the evidence that bodies had been found and identified to be the individuals in question, the only testimony we had to connect Thomas Devaney to the murders was that of Vinnie Giuda, Tony Diavolo, Ben James, and Ken Arnold. As for me, I wasn't going to base the determination of guilt on anything they'd said, and I let it be known.

"Nothing?" Richard asked.

"You're just going to take every bit of their testimony and ignore it?" my friend Pam asked incredulously.

"Yeah. They had every reason to lie."

"Why would they lie?" Larry exclaimed, twisting his body to look at me. "They're witnesses for the prosecution."

"Because they're witnesses for the prosecution," Katie called out.

"Alex, how can we possibly proceed if you won't accept the testimony of any of the key witnesses?" Sam asked, obviously annoyed.

"Perhaps we can't proceed. There was no physical evidence, and only tainted testimony to connect Devaney to some of these murders. I can't, in good conscience, state that Devaney's involvement was proven beyond a reasonable doubt."

"You're nuts!" Larry snarled, as Sam threw himself back in the chair. Ed mumbled something about us not getting anywhere. Richard, void of expression, was staring at me.

"Alexandra, you can't be serious." Pam, who was sitting to Richard's right at the head of the table, leaned forward, straining to get me in her view.

"I am."

"It's almost time to leave," Richard announced, looking at his watch. "We agreed on the first two counts. That's a good start. Why don't we skip over the murders for now, and move to count four when we return tomorrow?" he suggested. Quickly, we all agreed.

At 4:30 we were ushered into the courtroom. All of the regular spectators were in attendance. The alternates were already seated in the jury box. Chavere and Altier looked as cocky as ever. Jordan, Willis, and Devaney appeared tense. The families scanned the members of the jury, their facial expressions a mixture of terror and hope. The media fixed their eyes on us, following our every gesture like heat-seeking missiles. If one of us changed position, they altered their own. It was as if they had become mesmerized by our every movement. I felt certain that if a juror stood up, they, as a group, would do the same.

We were dismissed for the day. As I waited to file out, I whispered to George, "Where are the alternates staying?"

"The other end of the courthouse," he whispered back as we began to move out of the jury box.

When we exited the courtroom door, Chris was close to me. "What do you do all day?"

"We can bring in our laptops or books," he whispered, and quickly moved past me.

"We were told not to talk to any of you," Dave whispered as he came up behind Chris.

Pam and I walked out of the courthouse together. "Looks like we might have opposite views," she said with a smile.

"Looks like," I agreed, smiling back.

"Kim told me this is the second time she's been an alternate. Irene said they're not supposed to talk to us."

"I heard. Rough day for them."

"Rough day for us."

We finished our walk in silence.

~

Wednesday morning began the second day of deliberations. The morning ritual continued. We did the lineup with Smitty, and waited for Amy to open the door to the courtroom. "All rise for the jury" rang out, and the rustle of more than one hundred bodies was heard as they got to their feet. Judge Blake welcomed us, gave a few instructions, and sent us back to lockup in the jury room.

"Hey, Richard, you gonna call up the guns?" Larry persisted as we moved to our chairs.

"We don't need the guns."

"Well, what if we do?"

"Then I'll ask for them."

Larry had a gaping smile upon hearing the answer.

"I keep wondering about the statute of limitations," I said.

"The statute of limitations? Yeah, me too. I was thinking about it all weekend," Richard added.

"What do you mean?" Dan asked. Richard only offered Dan a blank stare.

"Remember when Judge Blake instructed us about the Massachusetts statute of limitation being up for a particular charge of conspiracy?" I asked Dan and the rest of the jurors. "That same charge is in the indictment. Does a federal charge have a statute of limitations?" I asked.

"The exact thing I wondered," Richard stated hesitantly. "Maybe we should ask the judge." We all agreed. Katie offered to write the request, and Richard sent it through Smitty to Amy, the judge's clerk.

"Well, until we get an answer, we should probably skip over conspiracy charges," Brad suggested.

We flipped through the pages of the indictment until we found a charge that didn't pertain to conspiracy.

As we considered the next count and discussed the testimony and evidence before us, I quickly discovered that Larry was opposed to anything I had to say. His support of the assistant US attorneys was astounding. It seemed to me that he considered them infallible simply because of their position. His ongoing attacks against anything I had to offer quickly became personal. I was growing weary of him as he continued to assault my motives. When he digressed to attacking my character in regard to a sensitive situation I had shared, I couldn't take it any longer.

"She hates the government because her sister lost that malpractice suit about her kid! You think because your sister had a kid die, you know how the families of Sly Devaney's murder victims feel? That kid dying comes nowhere close to what those families feel—nowhere close. You have no idea what you're talking about!"

"Larry, shut up!" Brad shouted from across the table.

"What, you're gonna let her make us think the government's wrong? This ain't about the government. It's about Sly Devaney!"

Hours went by with Larry's raving every time I voiced an opinion. Very little was accomplished throughout the day.

Exhausted, I went home. Charlie was back at the academy. Pulling the blinds and locking the doors, I shut out the world. The only ones I spoke to were Paul and Jesus.

~

The third day of deliberations was a Thursday. When we all assembled at the table, Richard announced that Judge Blake had sent a lengthy handwritten response to our question about the federal statute of limitations concerning conspiracy. The response told us there was none. We decided to go through the entire list of crimes, and tackle the murders last.

There were three firearm charges. The first was dealt with quickly, because according to the testimony of the firearms specialists, there was no physical evidence linking Thomas Devaney to those particular guns. We had a unanimous "not proven." The second charge was also a slam dunk, because these particular guns were found in Devaney's Virginia apartment. His fingerprints were all over them. We all agreed this was proven. The final charge concerning the guns, the last charge on the indictment, was that each gun's serial number was made illegible. We were all in agreement that they were—all except Larry.

"I can't say that the serial numbers were scratched out," Larry stated as we went around the table for a vote.

"What?" Dan asked. "We had two firearm specialists tell us they were. We had pictures on the monitor to show it."

"The pictures weren't clear. How can I know the firearms specialists were telling the truth?"

"You can't be serious!" Ed bellowed.

"Why?"

"Larry, you believe the testimony of Giuda, Diavolo, James, and Arnold, but you don't believe the firearm specialists?"

"I don't know for a fact that the serial numbers can't be read."

"He just wants the guns up here. He's been whining to see the guns since day one, and now he's gonna pull this stunt to get them," Ed commented in disbelief, and then mumbled something under his breath.

"Will you be satisfied seeing one gun, or do I need to ask for the entire arsenal?" Richard calmly asked.

"I don't believe this," Pam uttered.

"One of the submachine guns," Larry answered with a smile.

A few of the jurors voiced their disgust.

"If he has a doubt, he has the right to see the gun," Richard said, in an attempt to stop the mumbling around the table.

"Problem is, he doesn't doubt it. He's like a kid wanting a toy," Steve said with a sigh.

Richard gave Smitty the written request.

Good, I thought. *Maybe his delight in getting his way will keep him pacified.* Unfortunately, it didn't take long before I realized it wasn't to be.

"The government this, the government that!" he screamed at me after I'd stated, while deliberating a charge, that in my opinion, the deals many of the government witnesses got seemed like a form of bribery. "She's obsessed with hating the government!"

I couldn't believe, or even follow, his lack of logic.

Larry leaned toward me, his face so close I could feel the spittle as he yelled, "You get excited learning about people who hated the government. You brought books here to read about those people!"

"Those people?" Dan asked incredulously. "You mean George Washington and John Hancock?"

"I need a break," I said, looking at Richard.

"Okay, let's take a short break."

I stood to leave. Larry attempted to grab my arm. "Don't you dare!" I snarled.

I could hear Larry hurling insults at me, and the other jurors admonishing him, as I walked out of the jury room. I pushed the door with force, desperate to block out the noise. The heavy door closed with a thud. Smitty, sitting dutifully at his post, looked concerned.

"I just need to stretch," I lied with a forced smile. He nodded. I proceeded to walk into an empty jury room across the hall, where our lunch was already laid out.

Within a minute, Richard and Katie came into the room and shut the door.

"That guy is such jerk. They're all over him in there," Katie offered as reassurance.

A weak smile was my response. Defensively, my arms were folded across my chest as I gazed out the window. "He won't let us deliberate, Richard. His personal vendetta against me will prevent him from focusing on what needs to be done. These disruptions won't end."

"I'm sending a note to Judge Blake asking that he remove a juror who continues to make personal attacks against a fellow juror. We'll see what he has to say."

"I'll get a pen and paper," Katie offered, quickly leaving the room.

"What he's doing to you is wrong, Alex. We all know that he wants a guilty verdict and won't consider anything else. You're blocking his means to get that, so he resorts to attack. I wonder if he has a screw loose."

Katie came back. "He's still arguing with all of them. I told the other jurors what we're doing, without letting Larry know. They're all in agreement."

"Good," Richard said. Dictating the words, Katie wrote the note. After reviewing it out loud, they both looked at me as though searching for a response.

I nodded as I pulled my arms tighter around my chest and turned back to the window.

Richard immediately took the note out to Smitty.

I was uneasy with the scene, uneasy with the note. *None of this should be happening,* I thought. *Is it me? Am I provoking Larry? Obviously, the other jurors don't think so, or they wouldn't agree that the note should be sent.* My stomach was sick.

"Let's go back in," Richard suggested when he returned.

"I need to use the bathroom. I'll be in shortly."

Richard and Katie left.

When I returned to the jury room, Larry had moved to another seat at the table, one out of my view. Young Jake, always silent and attentive, took Larry's seat. I thanked him.

Emotionally exhausted, I said very little for the rest of the day. Whenever I did offer a thought, Larry strained to look at me from where he sat. His face appeared contorted, like a rabid animal ready to pounce.

The gun was delivered to the jury room at the end of the day. Like a giddy child, Larry picked it up, practically drooling as he turned it over. He didn't seem interested in the serial number.

"Serial number legible?" Dan asked.

Finally, Larry looked, and with a grin called out, "It's scratched out!"

"What a surprise," Dan said with noted contempt.

Young Jake was staring intently at Larry as he fondled the gun. "You should take a look," I suggested.

"Can I?"

"Sure. Hopefully you'll never get another chance to see one," I said with a smile.

Larry shared nicely. In fact, he was excited to show off his toy. No one else cared to look.

Finally, we were summoned by Smitty to go down to the court-room. Anxious expressions studied our faces as Judge Blake gave us permission to leave for the day.

Richard approached and stood in front of me as I was waiting to get my cell phone from the security guard. "Judge Blake's response was that you need to work through the difficulty with Larry."

Though the letter to the judge was not my idea, I was hoping for resolution. Disappointed, I shrugged my shoulders and mumbled, "Okay." What else could I say? "Probably best. I imagine Larry would've run straight to the media. We'd end up with a mistrial."

Richard placed his hands on my shoulders. "I have your back, Alex."

I offered him a weak, though grateful, smile and began to walk toward the door. *When did Judge Blake contact him? We just left the jury room. Smitty didn't deliver a response. Did the judge speak to Richard?*

~

It's Friday. Halleluiah! I thought as I rode the train to Boston on day four of jury deliberations. I was exhausted, desperate to shut down for a couple of days. *God, I hope they don't make us deliberate through the weekend!* With the thought, I felt a tightness in my chest as my body tensed.

Walking alongside the harbor's edge, I thought about what lay before us this day—the deliberation of the murders. As I watched the ferry glide into the dock across the harbor, I imagined boarding it, sailing away to wherever, and disappearing. It was a pleasant momentary escape.

As was their custom, Brad, Ed, Dan, and Chris were sitting on a bench outside the courthouse. Most mornings I would see them gathered, getting every bit of fresh air they could before being cooped up all day. Usually as I walked past, I teasingly admonished them for talking to one another. Today I stopped in front of them.

"Chris, we miss you. We need your humor," I said to the alternate.

"Yeah, I'm sure things are rough."

"What are you guys doing all day?" Dan asked him.

"Reading. Sleeping. Playing games on our laptops. Looking at the walls. Loads of laughs," Chris said sarcastically.

"You'd get plenty of new material for jokes in deliberations," Ed offered.

"You can't discuss that with me," Chris said with a definite hint of resentment. Then he took a puff of his cigarette.

I felt for him, and the other alternates. I'd be resentful too, sitting through the trial and then being whisked off to what seemed like the equivalent of a holding cell. And here we deliberators were, stuck with Larry hindering our progress, when any of the alternates would be an asset.

"Not saying a thing about what we discuss," Ed clarified. "Just saying that Larry's more bizarre than any of us had imagined. He's a piece of work."

"No surprise," Chris responded, taking another drag on the cigarette.

"I'm tellin' ya, Alex," Brad began, looking straight at me. "We think he's a plant."

Ed and Dan were nodding.

"Wouldn't surprise me a bit," Chris added.

"You guys serious?" I asked.

"Considering the possibility," Ed replied.

"There's been so much wheeling and dealing by the feds in this trial. Probably anything's possible," Chris said.

Dave, another alternate, joined us.

"Maybe we should all meet after the verdict's in," I suggested. "I think you guys should know what's been going on," I said, looking at Dave and Chris.

"And we'll be more than ready for a drink," Ed interjected.

They all agreed.

"Okay. You guys tell the other alternates. We can walk to the Palm Restaurant from here," I said, pointing in the direction.

Chris put out his cigarette and glanced at his cell phone. "Time to report to the prison guard."

In silence, we walked toward the courthouse door. The alternates left us after checking in.

Larry was at it from the get-go. Walking into the jury room together, Brad, Dan, Ed, and I heard him ranting about me bringing up the United States government all the time.

"What's the United States government got to do with any of this?"

"My God!" I said, looking at the guys with an incredulous snicker. I walked to where Larry was seated and pounded my hand down on his copy of the indictment.

"Read it!" I shouted, pointing at the paper. "*The United States of America vs. Thomas D. Devaney!*"

Larry began ranting as I walked away. The dumbfounded expressions on the faces of Brad, Dan, and Ed were priceless. "He's not a plant. Not smart enough to be a plant," I said as I got in line behind them to get coffee. "For God's sake, I'd sooner believe Pam's theory that the centerpiece on the table is bugged before I'd believe that Larry's capable of being a government spy."

"You've got a point," Ed agreed.

We made our ritualistic visit to the courtroom, and then went back upstairs.

When we were all assembled, we prepared ourselves to tackle the sixteen murders. Steve suggested we pull the chalkboard out from the back of the room and use it to keep track of our votes.

The first murders listed occurred in the late 1960s. Giuda confessed to the killings and claimed that Devaney was involved.

"Do we have anything more than Giuda's testimony?" I asked.

"No," Maureen responded.

"Giuda's testimony isn't enough for me."

"Alex, I can't believe you're just gonna disregard everything he said." Pam's voice was calm; her countenance was not.

"I can't believe you won't. And it's not just Giuda. Diavolo, James, and Arnold as well. They had every reason to accuse Devaney. The better the story, the better the deal. In my opinion, they're no more than puppets on a string. Chavere and Altier are the puppeteers."

"Are you serious?" Maureen asked with a laugh.

"Absolutely. To put it in stronger, more vulgar terms, again in my opinion, Chavere and Altier have the four of them by the balls."

"You're saying the assistant US attorneys are purposefully getting them to lie?" Richard asked. "That's a serious charge."

"I'm saying that, in my opinion, whatever testimony Chavere and Altier finally accepted from these diabolical creatures was, in all likelihood, fabricated."

"She's insane! She needs to be taken off this jury because of her mental problems. She's a nutcase!" Larry's tirade went on and on.

"For some of the murders, their testimony is all we have!" Sam yelled above Larry's ranting.

"Exactly."

"Come on, Alex, you can't believe that Devaney didn't commit these murders." Richard was frustrated. "Shut up, Larry!" he screamed in Larry's face.

Larry's face was crimson with rage, but he finally shut up, looking like a puppy that had been scolded.

"Did he commit some of them? Probably. All of them? Doubtful. If there's corroborating evidence, or even testimony from someone other than the fraudulent four, then I'll consider his possible guilt."

"Possible guilt?" Larry practically threw his body on the table to look at me. "He's guilty as hell. Those guys were there! What, are you one of those crazies that has the hots for criminals?"

No one responded to Larry's remark. He continued his attempt to take control again. We tried to ignore him as he went on.

"Fraudulent four? It suits them," Steve said loudly, and with a smile.

"We don't have to be unanimous with proven or not proven," Katie offered, trying to be heard above Larry.

"Yes, we do," Richard shot back at her, his eyes cast on me.

"Why do we have the option of undecided?" Dan asked, pointing at the paperwork in front of him.

"For Christ's sake, Larry, shut the fuck up!" Brad yelled.

The room became quiet.

"We should get clarification from the judge," Katie suggested.

"No! I'm not sending a note to him," Richard shot back rudely.

Katie's face flushed. She pushed her chair away from the table. Without uttering a word, she walked out of the room. Once she was gone, all eyes fell on Richard.

"What the hell? What's wrong with her?" Larry began. "You're the foreman. Whatever you say should be how it is. She's beginning to sound like Alex." He leaned over the table to look at me. "What, are you talking to her outside? Maybe calling her on the phone to fill her with your shit?"

"Knock it off, Larry!" Maureen scolded. Larry ignored her.

"I never heard the judge say that. Did he tell you that?" Brad asked Richard.

Richard didn't answer the question. He stood and left the room.

"Did he have a private conversation with the judge?" Ed asked.

I immediately remembered Richard telling me that the judge had instructed him to tell me to work through the difficulty with Larry. Had he had a conversation with Judge Blake?

"It's her!" Larry said, standing and pointing at me. He began to move. Pam grabbed his arm. It was enough to stop him. "She's filling everyone's head with this crap. And I know why!"

No one cared to know. Larry stood in silence for a moment, still pointing.

"She's gonna write a book about how she was the juror that held out, the juror that caused a hung jury!"

Richard and Katie returned. Richard immediately told Larry to sit down. Katie had obviously been crying.

"I'll ask the judge to clarify," Richard said. He sat down and began dictating the note to Katie.

"Good idea," Ed mumbled sarcastically.

I caught Dan's and Brad's glances from across the table. Their eyes revealed confused concern.

Richard delivered the note to Smitty and suggested that we begin deliberating the murders while waiting for the judge's response.

Vinnie Giuda had testified to committing the first three murders in his attempt to kill the Mafia boss wannabe Thomas Sacchetti. His claim was that Devaney was present. My position held firm: if Giuda's testimony was all that connected Devaney, then I couldn't, without reasonable doubt, determine Devaney's guilt.

"How can you have reasonable doubt? Giuda was part of the leadership of the Old Harbor Gang!" Larry screamed.

"Even if you can't put him there, Alex, it's guilt by association," Pam stated.

"The Old Harbor Gang wasn't well organized then. And Giuda admits that he was making hits for the Mafia at that time," I pointed out.

"Pull up the charts on the formation of the Old Harbor Gang," Richard instructed. Though we did have access to a monitor to pull up all evidence, we chose to look at the actual poster.

"The gang was in its earliest stages at this point," Dan remarked as we studied the poster.

"Giuda actually testified that he met with the Mafia when they discussed Sacchetti's declaration of wanting to become boss," Katie reminded us.

"Exactly," I said. "And we do have a creditable testimony in regard to the murder of Sacchetti."

"Who?" Brad asked.

"Sacchetti's son's testimony."

"That's right. When did he testify?" Richard asked.

I gave the date. Everyone flipped through their notebooks.

"Yeah, look at this," Steve began. "He was a kid at the time, but he remembers the family being rushed out of the house in the early hours of the morning and whisked off to the airport. They were taken to Oregon. The next day his father was killed."

"And, according to his testimony, the family didn't return to Massachusetts, not even for the funeral," Sam added.

"Sounds more like a Mafia hit," I said. "Aren't they known to take out entire families?"

"Yeah, that's what they do," Larry responded with a snicker. I couldn't tell if he was making fun of me or agreeing. If agreeing, his finding humor in it was sick.

Many nodded in agreement. Pam, Richard, Larry, Jake, and Sam held their ground, feeling that Devaney was involved in every murder. After hours of deliberation, with many disruptions by Larry, it was unanimously agreed that the murders pertaining to Giuda's attempt to kill Thomas Sacchetti carried reasonable doubt as to Devaney's involvement.

The next murders were those of Billy Manning and his close friend Marty Hill. Manning's body was found in Marty Hill's car. Hill's body wasn't discovered until twenty years later. Looking through our notes, we discovered that the prosecution brought up Manning's name only twice during Giuda's testimony. Giuda claimed that Devaney was involved. That was it: two fleeting references, no evidence, no corroborating testimony. We had absolutely nothing to declare this murder proven beyond a reasonable doubt.

"This is disgusting!" I exclaimed. "Chavere and Altier didn't even have the decency to attempt to prove this man's murder. I guess, as far as they are concerned, Billy Manning wasn't worth putting any time into."

It seemed that the assistant US attorneys had no regard for the family of Billy Manning, leaving them no possibility of closure from this trial. Given the lack of anything to link Devaney to the murder, other than Giuda's brief mention, we were forced to declare it not proven.

Marty Hill's murder did have evidence, along with the testimony of Giuda, Diavolo, and Ben James.

"What's going on, Alex?" Richard shot at me with intense sarcasm. "Now, because you say so, we can believe the testimony of three members of the fraudulent four?"

That's all it took for Larry to go into what seemed like a manic state, hurling insult after insult at me. Absolute chaos filled the room.

Finally, I stood up and shouted, "From the first day I said that if there was corroborating evidence or testimony other than theirs, then I would consider what they said. In this situation, we have evidence, along with Chavere's puppets, that puts Devaney at the scene."

As I spoke, Larry continued with the verbal assault. He, not Richard, had control of the room. As long as Larry retained control, we could not deliberate.

Larry stood and moved toward me, spit spewing from his mouth as he screamed.

Defensively, I put out my hands toward him, yelling, "Stop!"

Pam, Brad, Dan, and Ed were already on their feet.

Richard didn't move or say a word. It was clear he didn't have my back as promised. Larry returned to his seat, and continued ranting.

"Richard, it's time to have an alternate called to replace me." I turned, opened the heavy door, and pulled it shut. I heard it thud. Again, I was greeted by Smitty's anxious stare.

I intended to walk up and down the hall for a few minutes to blow off steam. Richard quickly appeared, and ushered me into the lunchroom.

"My remark was rude. I'm sorry, Alex."

"The remark isn't the problem, Richard. I don't care what you think. Can't you see it?" Tears began to pool in my eyes. "This sham trial isn't what our founding fathers spilled their blood for." I turned to face the window. The replica ships of those from the Boston Tea Party were in plain view. Boston, *the Cradle of Liberty*, was sprawled out beyond. "This is the type of trial the Brits were forcing on them.

Truth? Where is it? In the testimony of those puppets? In the FBI files? Where is it? It's obvious that with the determined objections and sidebars by the prosecution whenever certain names were mentioned, we don't have the entire story. And what we did get is tainted with deals so immoral it makes your skin crawl."

Richard had nothing to say.

"Larry's constant disruption is detrimental to the process. If we can't complete a statement without his commotion, then we can't get thoughts out to properly deliberate. I feel myself shutting down at times because of his attacks."

I turned to look at Richard. My tears were gone. "I think the only way to solve the problem is for me to be replaced by an alternate. If the judge won't remove Larry, then the solution is for me to leave."

"No, Alex." Richard put his hands on my shoulders. "Can't you see how much you're needed? You're the one who convinced us to look deeper into the Sacchetti murders. You made us realize that the prosecution failed in their responsibility to present anything in regard to the Manning murder. We're not done yet; your insight is still needed."

Richard hugged me as my eyes again filled with tears. I didn't want to leave, nor did I want to face Larry's abuse.

"But, Richard, regardless of what the jury does, this trial was a sham and the judicial system has been compromised."

"Maybe so. But we need to finish the job we started. And it seems that the jurors need your sense of patriotism to get things back on track."

We broke for lunch, and then went back into deliberations.

Moving through the murders, there was much discussion and argument. Most of the murders we came to an agreement on; however, I struggled with my vote. Though most of our decisions were based on the testimony of the fraudulent four, the guilt by association instruction we were being forced to abide by was impossible to get around. This particular instruction continued to eat at me.

"Guilt by association! My God, each and every one of us could be in prison for something a friend or family member might do!"

"I told ya! She has a thing for Devaney!" Larry blurted.

"I have a thing for keeping the judicial system honest and intact. If the tables were turned and it was Giuda on trial, I'd have a problem with this guilt by association mandate."

"Regardless of how you feel, Alex, it is what it is," Richard stated with annoyance.

Smitty knocked on the door and entered. He had a note from the judge, and informed us that it was almost time to call it a day. Judge Blake stated in the note that we could declare a charge undecided, although he implored us to dutifully attempt to reach a unanimous decision.

Two murders remained. Both promised to be extremely difficult to deliberate. With the day at an end, they would have to wait. The question was, would we be deliberating over the weekend?

We entered the courtroom and felt the anxious stares of all present. I chanced a glance at the widow Monahan. Her agony was heavy as she slouched under its weight. One daughter seemed emotionally crippled by a lifetime of rage. Her face was contorted. The fire blazing from her eyes was directed at the jury.

I wanted to comfort them, to shout, "You will have closure. Your loved one's murder was proven." But that was impossible.

As the judge announced that we had the weekend off, I winced. Though I longed for the downtime, this announcement meant at least three more days of torture for these families.

~

The trial and indictment filled my mind throughout the weekend. Reluctantly, I attended a party for my friend's birthday, hoping it would be a distraction from my churning thoughts. Yet I found myself deaf to the conversations around me as I mentally reviewed the testimonies, indictment, and lack of evidence for most of the murders. Guilt by association was the flimsy connection to declare culpability. I couldn't shake the feeling that this simply wasn't right.

When Bob Costa entered the room, I knew I had made a mistake in being at the party. I went over to the wine table and poured myself a glass. My hand was visibly shaking. Turning from the table, I almost bumped into a casual friend.

"Can't believe it's taking this long to declare this monster guilty," he said, addressing me.

How does he know I'm on the jury? My heart was racing as others, hearing his remark, began to congregate.

"You are gonna find him guilty?" another added. It was more a statement than a question.

"Excuse me, I need to go." Almost in a state of panic, I put my wineglass on the table, my trembling hand causing some wine to spill out.

"There better not be a hung jury—" The statement sounded like a threat.

I felt paralyzed as more and more people gathered. Perspiring profusely, I felt my legs begin to wobble. I leaned on the table.

"Can you imagine? There'd be riots in Boston," another added.

"That juror would be lynched, and rightfully so." They all began to laugh.

"Get away from her!"

The laughter ceased as Bob pushed his way through the throng.

"What the hell are you doing? She's under enough pressure without this bullshit!"

They moved away, apologizing as they left.

"You okay, kiddo?"

"No." Embarrassed, I couldn't look at him.

"I'll get you a ride home."

"I can drive." Pushing past him, I headed straight out the door and ran to my car. I heard him call my name as I drove away.

Twenty minutes later, Bob sent a text message: "Did you get home safely?"

"Yes. Thanks," I responded, and turned the phone off.

I tossed and turned all night as I struggled with the mockery of the trial and the ignorance of those who were basing their knowledge of it on snippets from the media. "Or is it your ignorance, Alex?" I whispered. "Could Devaney be so evil that Chavere and Altier are justified in doing whatever it takes to take him down?"

~

Monday didn't come soon enough, and yet it came too quickly. A great ambivalence consumed me. I wanted to be on this jury. I wanted to run from it. I wanted to see justice done. There was no justice.

We jurors went through our ritualistic assembly in the courtroom. Before we separated, Dave informed us that all the alternates would be at the Palm following the verdict.

"Should happen today," Richard let him know.

Taking our seats at the table, we wasted no time in getting down to business.

"The murders left are Diavolo's stepdaughter, Sandra Ford, and his girlfriend Carol Pander," Richard announced.

As I suspected, these were tough. Of all the murder victims in this case, Sandra Ford's story affected me the most. An innocent child, she was victimized, disabled, tossed aside, and then murdered by the hellish Tony Diavolo. From the tender age of two, this precious child didn't stand a chance.

Half of us held our ground in putting Sandra's actual murder on her damnable stepfather. The other half believed the testimony of Diavolo claiming that it was Devaney who had killed the girl.

"Why would he?" I asked.

"To shut her up. She was blabbing about them in public!" Pam shot back.

"The only one who says it was Devaney is Diavolo. How convenient," Brad said.

"Yeah. Even Ben James claims he doesn't know who actually killed her," Katie added.

"Yes, he did," Maureen began. "He said Devaney tried to kill her, but didn't, so Diavolo finished the job."

"What difference does it make which one strangled the life out of her?" Richard shouted. "Devaney was there!"

"We can't even be sure of that," I said.

Larry started, this time joined by Richard and Pam.

"Two other murders took place in the house where Sandra was killed. Two other bodies buried in the cellar. Are you forgetting that?" Sam asked above the voices of the others.

"No."

"You said the other two were proven. Why not this?" Steve asked.

"I don't know for a fact that Devaney was present for the other murders. None of us do. We were forced to make the decisions about those murders on guilt by association."

"Yeah, and what's different with this one, Alex?" Pam asked above Larry's continued ranting.

"The opening statement by his attorney" was my weak reply. I reached for my notebook.

"What are you talking about?" Richard's annoyance was evident.

"He said that Devaney was guilty of many of the charges," I replied, reading from my notes. "Prior to saying that, he stated that Devaney determinedly claimed innocence for the murders of Sandra Ford and Carol Pander."

Sam started to interrupt.

"And the fact that Sandra's murder was personal for Diavolo. The girl told her mother that Diavolo had been raping her for years."

"Whether Devaney actually killed her or not, and whether you like it or not, it boils down to the fact that she was killed in the same house as the other two. If it was guilt by association in those murders, then how can you say it isn't for hers?" Sam demanded.

"Same MO, Alex! They were killed and Devaney took a nap!" Pam pointed out.

"According to Diavolo and James!" I shouted back.

"For Christ's sake, Alex!" Pam held me under a fierce gaze for what seemed like an eternity.

Same site as two other murders that I gave my assent to. Guilt by association. Goddamn this guilt by association! My thoughts were raging. *Should I change my assent to the other two murders committed in this same house? Should I dig my heels in and force a hung jury? But his own attorney said he was guilty of many of the charges! I don't believe he killed this girl, but what can I do?*

"Alex?" Richard shouted.

"I guess—" I rested my head on my hands.

"You guess?" Richard demanded.

I lifted my head and looked at those sitting around the table. Each face was anxious, each tormented by the toil of this entire experience.

"Guilt by association," I heard myself say.

"Proven!" Steve jumped up and marked it on the chalkboard.

"One more to go!" Richard exclaimed, as though we were participating in a sports event. "Carol Pander. I'm sure we all agree on Devaney's guilt." He looked at me, as did the others.

Slowly, I shook my head.

"Here we go again!" Larry began. It troubled me that I had adapted to his raves and could now turn them off in my mind.

"What's the difference here?" Pam demanded.

"Everything."

"Everything? Diavolo lured her in and Devaney killed her. That's the testimony," Pam stated.

"To hell with the testimony!" I shot back. "Carol Pander was killed in a house Diavolo lied to her about, telling her he wanted to buy it! The lying Diavolo's testimony is all we have."

"You don't know he's lying!" Larry shouted.

"Devaney knew where her body was buried," Sam added.

"You sure about that? Is that a fact? Who told you that? Tony Diavolo? Ben James? Anyone else declare that to be true?" I was livid. "We're supposed to be dealing with facts. There are none! Her own mother told the FBI she believed Diavolo killed her husband and Carol. She said nothing about Devaney being involved!"

"Guilt by association. For Christ's sake, Alex, Devaney and Diavolo did everything together!" Richard shouted back.

"They lived together? No! They took a shit together? No! That statement is ridiculous!"

"She has something here," Dan interjected. "Diavolo found out Carol was seeing another guy. It may very well have been a crime of passion."

"Yeah, Devaney might not have known," Katie added.

"Then how did Devaney know where she was buried?" Pam insisted.

"Like Alex said, who says he knew? Diavolo told Ben James. They both claimed Devaney did it as part of their 'get out of jail package,'" Brad interjected.

"No, he did it," Pam stated adamantly.

"I'm with Pam on this," Richard said.

"Then it's gonna have to be undecided." Steve stood to mark the chalkboard.

"No, I won't accept undecided!" Richard demanded, pounding his fist on the table.

"I won't budge," I stated, staring at Richard.

"You're not a judge, Richard; you're a goddamn foreman," Brad said with controlled restraint.

"Let's go around the table," Richard suggested rather meekly.

We were evenly divided, six "not proven," six "proven."

"Undecided." Richard looked at Steve, who marked the board.

"We're done. Let's send a note to the judge." Katie wrote the note. Richard signed it and gave it to Smitty.

About twenty minutes later, we were summoned by Judge Blake to appear.

For the last time, Smitty instructed us to line up and led us down the familiar flight of stairs. For the last time, we waited outside the closed door that led into the courtroom, Amy's hand resting on the knob. No words were spoken. The gravity of the situation weighed heavily on all.

Amy opened the door, and one last time announced, "All rise for the jury." Anxious stares from each attorney met ours. I could empathize with the likely stirring in their bowels as the twisting and turning began in mine. The families of the victims mirrored the same trepidation reflected on the face of Thomas Devaney, his, no doubt, brought on by dread of the inevitable—life in prison. Yet as his eyes anxiously scanned each member of the jury, I questioned my former thought. He knew from day one that he would spend the rest of his life in prison. His attorney told us he was guilty. So why the anxious anticipation? For the first time, our eyes met, and his anxiety became clear. So many facts were kept from the jury, and much of the testimony presented under oath was far less than truth. Did anyone realize that? Did anyone care?

The anxiety of the families was transparent. Our decision would continue their imprisonment within the emotional horror each carried, or else offer closure and help them break free from the shackles they bore. The tension in their bodies was evident. The agony of their countenance was almost too much to bear.

The judge had us remain standing, and asked if we had completed our decisions. Richard answered yes, and was asked to give the completed verdict sheet to Amy.

We continued to stand. Devaney and his attorneys were instructed to do the same. Chavere and Altier sat, with what I presumed to be a copy of the verdict sheet in front of them. Their pens were ready to mark down whatever was read.

Amy started announcing the charges one by one, followed by our verdict.

My body began to tremble. I felt like I was going to be sick as perspiration beaded. I looked straight ahead at Devaney. So far, he was taking the blows with resigned passivity.

When the murder charges were read individually, I closed my eyes. The first three were the Sacchetti murders. All of these, I knew, were not proven. Murmuring began in the gallery as the first was announced. The widow Monahan's tormented cry echoed in my head when the second was declared not proven. I didn't dare open my eyes. I was afraid I would vomit. Judge Blake asked for silence. Mrs. Monahan couldn't stop.

Forcing my eyes open, I looked at her, desperately wanting to yell, "Wait! Wait, dear lady! You'll find some closure today!" I could do nothing but witness her grief as Amy continued to go through the first three murders. With the next declaration of not proven, Mrs. Monahan's panic intensified.

My heart threatened to violently leap from my chest. My legs began to wobble. I focused on breathing. *Inhale, Alex. Exhale slowly.*

Next on the list was the brutal death of Donald Monahan.
Amy began to read the charge.

Inhale. Exhale.

Mrs. Monahan seemed to stop breathing. Two sobbing daughters
supported her body on each side. The third daughter, her face contorted with rage, fixed a threatening glare on the jury.

The courtroom became blurry, and Amy's words became like
those on a warped tape recording, dragging slowly.

Just say it, Amy! Dammit, say it! I realized that I, too, had stopped
breathing. *Inhale, inhale.*

"Proven," Amy finally announced.

Cries of sorrowful joy came from Mrs. Monahan and two of the
daughters. The third sprung from the bench, climbing over those in
the way, and quickly left the courtroom.

The O'Leary murder was announced as proven.

The next murders were those of Marty Hill and his friend Billy
Manning. Amy announced the proven verdict for Hill. For Manning,
it was not proven.

A cry came from the gallery as the family of Billy Manning released their shock. Tears began to run down my cheeks. My gaze fell
on Chavere and Altier. Their only concern was to mark the verdict
sheet like gamblers at a racetrack.

God damn your souls to hell! I screamed within. *This family has
no closure because you didn't care enough to give us more than two
mentions of his name! God damn you both!*

The next murder was that of Carol Pander. "Undecided," Amy
announced.

Herman Pander stood, disrupting the court, and forced his way
out of the bench. He fell over the woman seated on the end. Without a
word to the stunned woman, he bounded toward the courtroom door.

Amy continued. Of the twenty-five counts, Devaney was found
guilty of twenty-three. Of the sixteen murders, nine were proven.

It was done. Judge Blake thanked us for our service and released
us from jury duty. For the last time, all stood as we left the courtroom.

Silently, we found our seats in the jury room. Everyone was

emotionally drained, though a sense of relief was apparent upon the faces of most. Pam's face reflected torment, tears slowly dripping from her eyes. Mine, no doubt, reflected the same, but not for the same reasons.

We were told that our cell phones would be brought to us and that Judge Blake would be up to see us. We waited. The only subject discussed was our desire to avoid the media. We began to plan our joint escape to the Palm. The alternates, we already knew, were waiting for us downstairs. Smitty informed us that he would lead us to a secret exit out. From there, we would pretend to be tourists, walking two by two and pointing to the ships in the harbor and the skyscape beyond.

The phones arrived, as did Judge Blake. Again, he thanked us for our service, and informed us that he would hold our names back from the media for a few days. If we wanted to speak to the media beforehand, that was our right. He then asked us if we had any suggestions to improve his courtroom. I bit my tongue, almost to the point of drawing blood.

Pam spoke up. "I have a suggestion." She looked around the table at all of us. "We've talked, and we agree that it seems inappropriate for the media to be able to gawk at the jury each and every day. We feel certain they were reporting our reactions."

"The jury should be hidden from the media," Maureen added.

Though the judge nodded, it was apparent that he wasn't taking the suggestion seriously. Maybe he couldn't.

With that, we were finally released. We followed Smitty six floors down on a metal staircase. Saying goodbye, he opened the door and ushered us out. After getting our bearings, we began to walk toward the restaurant, picking up the alternates on the way.

We proceeded with our plan of escape, passing numerous reporters on the way. None suspected that we were the ones they wanted to assault with their microphones and cameras.

Within a few minutes, we safely entered the Palm Restaurant. It was midafternoon; the place appeared empty.

"May I help you?" a well-dressed, attractive manager asked.

"Do you have a private area where we can sit?" I queried.

He led us to the back of the restaurant, where French doors could be used to ensure privacy.

"This is perfect," Richard said.

"Anything else?"

"Could you close the blinds on the windows?" I asked, looking at the throng of pedestrians passing by.

He was hesitant.

"We'll let you in on a secret," Richard said. "We're the Devaney jury, and we don't want the media to know we're here."

Without hesitation, he closed the blinds.

Each of us ordered a drink. With the drinks came five trays of appetizers. The manager announced that they were on the house. We thanked him. He quickly escorted the waitresses out, ensuring our privacy.

The alternates were briefed on the reasons for our decisions. Everyone voiced their desire to avoid the media. We exchanged email addresses and phone numbers. Steve and Jake announced that they didn't want to participate in the exchange. They intended to walk away from the trial and never look back. Steve was the first to say goodbye. We later discovered that he had picked up the tab for the drinks.

"Larry's missing," Maureen announced. "He said he was going to the men's room about a half hour ago, and never came back."

Certainly, I wasn't concerned.

After hugs and promises to stay connected, we went our separate ways.

Chapter 12

If individuals be not influenced by moral principles;
it is in vain to look for public virtue; it is, therefore,
the duty of legislators to enforce both by precept
and example, the utility, as well as the necessity of a
strict adherence to the rules of distributive justice.
—James Madison

"WOO-HOO! LISTEN UP, BOYS! GUILTY! GUILTY! Guilty!" Steward Simpson, the officer in charge of the goon squad, shouted, parading the shackled Tom Devaney past the prison cells. He ran his baton over the cell bars lining the narrow walkway. Behind him, four guards surrounded the shackled Devaney. Hampered by the ankle constraints, Tom struggled to keep pace.

"No release for the infamous Sly Devaney!" Simpson yelled. "He'll rot behind bars. This bastard's headed to Colorado! That's right, boys! Sly is headed to the depths of the supermax."

The mention of the Administrative Maximum Facility in Colorado caused the most hardened of prisoners to wince. The facility was rumored to be a tomb for the living, descending ten stories below the ground. One never saw the light of day—or so it was rumored.

~

I went straight to Mom's, to assure her that I was okay. When I arrived home, I left Ilona and Charlie a voice message, then immediately turned on the television. As I'd anticipated, the Devaney verdict was all over the news. The Massachusetts US attorney, Feng Yan, was taking questions from the media. Behind him stood Chavere and Altier.

A reporter began questioning US Attorney Yan. "The three not proven decisions on the murders connected with Thomas Sacchetti seem to indicate that the jury didn't believe the prosecution's key witness Vincent Giuda. His testimony against Devaney is what gained him his freedom. It didn't work. How do you justify his release?"

"Without the plea agreement with Mr. Giuda, the US Attorney's Office would not have convinced Anthony Diavolo, Ben James, and others to plead," Yan responded. "Without their valuable information, the corruption of former FBI special agent Goot would not have been revealed. Neither would the remains of many murder victims have been recovered. The plea agreements with these men helped bring closure to many family members."

"And the circus continues." I shook my head. "The corruption of Goot? What about the other corrupt agents in the Boston office of the FBI who got away with it? Bringing closure to the families? What about closure for the families of Giuda's and Diavolo's victims?"

I turned the volume down on the TV with the remote.

"Lady Justice has the combined crimes of the fraudulent four in one scale and the crimes of Devaney and Goot in the other. Somehow, Devaney's and Goot's criminality outweighs theirs?" I booted up my computer. It was time to research Thomas D. Devaney.

That evening, Katie texted, and then Pam called with the same message.

"Alex, did you see Larry's interview on TV?"

"No."

"He's talking about you. You need to watch. You should call the reporter and clarify," Pam suggested.

"That bad?"

"Pretty bad. That son of a bitch knew at the restaurant he was going to the media. He said he talked with them to arrange an interview before we got to the Palm. The bastard said we went to the Palm to celebrate. Jesus! Celebrate what? He makes it sound like this was some sort of game. And he makes you sound like an idiot!" She was starting to cry.

"What channel, Pam? I'll watch it at eleven."

~

I took a sleeping pill that night, knowing that otherwise I would toss and turn. In the morning, I was awakened by the phone. I looked at caller ID. It was Bob Costa.

"Hi." I tried to sound like I had been awake for hours.

"I want to congratulate you on a job well done."

"I'm not so sure. I have so many questions—"

"Are you free?"

"No, I have an interview with CNN this afternoon in Boston."

"You sure you want to do that?"

"I have to."

There was a brief silence.

"Why do you think you have to?" Bob asked.

"I want to." I couldn't tell him that it had been scheduled in response to Larry's bizarre interview.

"It might be best to let a week pass."

I didn't respond.

"Okay. Be careful. Say only what you want to say. Think before you speak."

I know he was trying to help, but somehow it annoyed me.

"Do you have plans after the interview?"

"Maybe. I don't know —"

"Why don't you meet me for dinner? Marble Head Harbor, the Landing, at eight o'clock."

I knew the popular waterfront restaurant. "The Landing will be too crowded on an August night."

"Okay. What would you like? We'll have dinner at my place."

"Surprise me. I'm not picky."

"Wine?"

"Please."

He laughed. "Come to my place at eight. You'll have a shoulder to cry on."

"You have no idea," I stammered. He didn't respond. "What's the address?"

~

Bob greeted me with a long, warm embrace that felt genuine and healing. Two tall glasses of wine were already poured, and the meal laid out on the table.

"Sit down." He walked to the table and pulled out a chair for me.

"Thank you."

"The interview?"

"It went well."

"Good. When will it air?" he asked, sitting down at the head of the table to my left.

"Tomorrow."

He nodded, and then studied me for a moment, taking a sip of wine. "How much did you know going into the trial?"

"Nothing … absolutely nothing."

"The perfect juror." He smiled.

"I'm not sure the prosecuting attorneys are going to feel that way after the interview airs." I took a gulp of wine.

He smiled again. Picking up a roll, he began to butter it. "Good for you."

I was taken aback by his response. "I'm confused."

"I have no love for the FBI." He handed me the buttered roll.

"But, Bob, it goes much deeper than the FBI."

He nodded. "I know." He buttered another roll and took a bite. Then watching me take another gulp of wine, he said, "Eat something or that'll go right to your head."

I took a bite of the roll and looked down at my plate filled with seafood risotto. I didn't have much of an appetite, but I forced myself to eat. With the first bite, I realized I was ravenous.

"Why were you brought up in testimony?" I asked after a few forkfuls.

He wiped his mouth with a napkin, took a sip of wine, and looked at me in silence for a moment. "Did you believe what was said?" he finally asked.

"About you using cocaine? I don't want to believe it. But I don't know what to believe anymore."

Bob reached his open hand along the table in search of mine. Reluctantly, I placed my hand in his.

"You were thrown into a dark and ugly side of life that most never experience. It's one thing to read about it in a book or watch it for entertainment, and quite another to be immersed. You walk away with the taste and smell—with memories you'll never escape."

I felt a tear trickle down my cheek and turned my head in a vain attempt to hide my utter vulnerability.

"The only truth to what was said about me was that I attended a fund-raiser at Anthony's Pier 4." He squeezed my hand and let go. "When I was DA, Devaney and his wiseguys were trying to start up some bookmaking in my county. I had a court order to wire the place. Goot and Arnold found out and confronted me, saying I was interfering with their investigation. I stood my ground. Someone told Devaney the place was wired. I suspect it was Goot and Arnold. They attempted to harass me. I ended up being called in before a federal judge to answer questions. Nothing came of it."

Bob reached for another roll before continuing. "One of my former assistant DAs was attending the trial. He called me the day I was mentioned. We had a good laugh. Obviously, Devaney still hates me. I wear it as a badge of honor."

"Devaney had nothing to do with you being mentioned, Bob. And the entire reference was totally out of context," I stated, shaking my head.

"Why do you say that?"

"Chavere had Arnold on the stand under direct. It was Chavere who brought up the information about you. Supposedly Devaney gave Arnold the tip. And I'm telling you, Bob, from all I witnessed, I don't believe Devaney was an informant."

"Really?" Bob actually appeared to be considering my statement.

"I believe the informant files were created by Goot and Arnold in an attempt to save their asses. And, if what I believe is true, it wasn't Devaney trying to destroy your reputation; it was Goot and Arnold. And with Chavere making it part of testimony, I suspect she wanted the media to pick up on it and run with it."

"I've never had a problem with Carla Chavere—"

"But you did with the FBI, which casts a shadow on the Department of Justice. Chavere, I believe, has been given the task of damage control."

Bob was staring at me but not seeing me. I could almost hear the neurons in his brain passing from one synapse to the next as he pulled up detailed information from years gone by.

"The congressional hearing on the FBI," he muttered.

I looked at him questioningly.

"I was part of a congressional hearing before the Committee on Government Reform in regard to the FBI's controversial handling of organized crime investigations in Boston."

"What came of it?" I asked.

Bob shook his head. "Not much. Phil Dauger was awarded a substantial amount of money from the federal government. But certainly that didn't negate having thirty years of his life ripped away. The initial focus of the hearings was Dauger's false imprisonment." Bob paused. "You look confused."

I nodded.

"Sorry." He smiled. "You really don't know any of the stories surrounding the case?"

I shook my head. "I've never heard of Phil Dauger."

"No. The prosecution would have pounced on it immediately if the defense made the attempt. But I'm sure the name Emilio Maldade came up."

"The Beast," I said, immediately remembering the bizarre nickname.

"Associating Maldade to an animal is an insult to animals. He was an evil SOB. Cold-bloodedly killed at least twenty people."

"Sounds like Vinnie Giuda. The defense managed to mention that Maldade was Giuda's mentor," I offered.

"That he was," Bob said, nodding his head. "And the student followed his teacher's example, even admitting to the exact number of murders, and then getting a plea deal for offering incriminating information."

"Yeah, Giuda received the get-out-of-jail-free card, and let's not forget the $20,000 when he passed go."

Bob's look was inquisitive.

"The Department of Justice gave Giuda $20,000 upon his release from prison. They were obviously very pleased with his performance." I took a sip of wine. "So, who's Phil Dauger? Why was he in prison?"

"In 1965, Maldade and some of his thugs were involved in the murder of a man by the name of O'Hare. At that time, Maldade was being groomed as a witness by FBI Special Agent Andrew Ricardo."

"Ricardo? The same agent involved in the Walton murder in Kentucky?" I asked.

Bob nodded. "Same agent. Maldade pinned the O'Hare murder on four innocent men. The four men were indicted, tried, and convicted of first-degree murder. They went away for life with no chance of parole."

"That's awful."

"Oh, I promise it gets worse." Bob took a sip of wine. "It later came out that Ricardo and the FBI knew these men were innocent. From the day the murder occurred, Ricardo and his partner, Cordon, knew who killed O'Hare. They did nothing." Bob took another sip of wine. "One of the most heroic attorneys I ever had the privilege of knowing, Henry Carton, heard about Dauger's claim of innocence. Carton fought for thirty years to prove it. He never took a cent from the Dauger family."

"Thirty years?" I asked in awe.

Bob nodded, staring across the room, obviously deep in thought. "Two of the accused died in prison. Phil Dauger and another were released. Dauger had a wife and young family when he went in. His wife—their marriage—was testimony to committed love. She and the kids stuck by him through it all."

"And the FBI knew?" I was incredulous.

Bob nodded and slowly responded. "According to testimony in the hearing, the FBI knew about it all the way to the top." He paused, and then looked at me. "While in Congress, I pushed for stricter guidelines for the FBI informant program, and serious penalties for agents who violate them. Informants are given immunity for certain criminal behavior in order to gather intelligence—never for murder."

"Is there anyone in Congress who continues to carry that torch?" I asked.

"I hope so." He didn't sound too sure.

We went back to eating.

"Something else that might interest you. I want full disclosure here," Bob said, his plate now empty. He wiped his mouth, finished off the glass of wine, and leaned back in the chair. There was a curious, almost embarrassed grin on his face. I stopped eating, picked up my wineglass, and waited.

"Vinnie Giuda is my cousin."

I choked on the wine I had just sipped. "Seriously?" I managed to ask.

"We were pretty close through eighth grade. Went to the same parochial school. Even served together as altar boys—"

"Giuda was an altar boy?"

Bob raised his eyebrows as he nodded. "We went to different high schools, and went our separate ways."

"That's an understatement!"

Again, he nodded. "I ran into Vinnie a few times while DA. Once at a restaurant near the office. He was with Devaney and Diavolo. Vinnie came over, put his arm around me, kissed me on the cheek, and then commented about our different paths in life. I told him that he and his pals better stay clean while in my county." Bob paused. "Not long after, the owner of the restaurant came to my office. Said he was being extorted by the Old Harbor Gang. Wanted help."

"What did you do?"

"Put him in contact with the Boston FBI. They did nothing. I tried to help, but I couldn't do much without the FBI. But, yeah, I have pictures of me and Cousin Vinnie as kids. He was a good-looking kid.

Great athlete and a good student. He was offered athletic scholarships from a few colleges. Turned them down. Problem was, my aunt died when Vinnie was young. His dad got involved in organized crime. Had a bar in the Combat Zone. Vinnie was just a kid when he started working there."

I shook my head, imagining a child trying to survive unscathed in the Combat Zone, an area of Boston that was infamous for murder, rape, robbery, and prostitution.

"There always seems to be a reason for human depravity," I offered.

"A reason, but not an excuse," the former DA clarified. "I'll dig out those pictures for you," he promised, standing and pouring us both more wine. "Let's go into the living room. It's more comfortable." He pulled out my chair. We picked up our wineglasses, and I followed him.

I sat in a chair adjacent to his and looked around the room. There was a masculine feel to it, but at the same time it had a pleasant softness with the artful display of numerous pictures of his children and grandchildren. "Your grandchildren are beautiful."

He smiled and nodded as he glanced at the pictures. "How old is your grandson?"

"Just turned one. An absolute delight." I took a sip of wine. "I'm impressed with your place, Bob. Very tidy for a bachelor."

"Worked hard to get it to look like this."

"You mean your cleaning woman worked hard." I laughed.

He smiled and nodded. "And the guest room, where you'll be staying tonight, is just as clean."

"Staying?" I queried with a smile.

"You're in no condition to drive, Alex. Neither am I." He held up the wineglass.

"It's very kind of you to invite me to stay, but—"

"You're not driving home," Bob insisted.

"I don't intend to, but—"

"I have extra toothbrushes. You can wear one of my shirts," he offered, anticipating my objection.

"But—"

"But?" Bemused, he held me under his gaze, finally allowing me to finish the sentence.

"I'm being banished to the guest room? How insulting." The wine was giving me the courage to verbalize such thoughts.

Bob's eyes lit up.

"I was attracted to you from the first time we met," I boldly confessed.

"When the Hamel Leather Company was put on the National Register?"

"You remember?" I was astonished.

"Umm." Smiling, he nodded his head. "You approached me as though you'd known me for years, even calling me Bob."

I could feel my face burning. His memory was exact.

"As I recall, we discussed Charlie and his interest in West Point. He must have been about sixteen at the time." He smiled and slowly shook his head. "How time flies."

"You have amazing recall."

"The suggestive way you squeezed my elbow as you shook my hand got my full attention. It isn't the usual introduction I get from a woman who's a total stranger." He laughed.

"I did not!"

"Oh, yes you did." With a steady gaze, he reached over and took hold of my hand.

"You never—" I was too embarrassed to finish the sentence.

"Never what?" he prodded with a grin.

"Never seemed interested." Embarrassed, I looked down as I heard myself saying the words.

"Nor did you after that initial meeting. I surmised you were just a touchy-feely kind of person, a lioness seeking information that might advance her cub."

"Charlie?"

He nodded. "Are you telling me I got it wrong?"

"I did want info for Charlie." I looked straight at him. "But I was also hoping to get your attention."

"You succeeded." He smiled.

"Don and Nancy's wedding? What happened that night?"

"Realized I couldn't risk being alone with you. Knew it might cause grief that neither of us needed."

I stroked the back of his hand. "Such willpower!"

"Damn. It wasn't easy." He laughed, looking down at my hand. "You took it off."

"What?" I was confused.

"The wedding band. You had it on that night."

A memory flashed through my mind of Bob kissing my hand while on the dance floor. "Yeah," I said, looking at my left hand, "shortly after that wedding. It was time to move on."

He slowly ran his fingertips over the bare skin of my ring finger, and then suddenly looked at his watch. "I have to make a call," he announced, looking at me. "I may be a while. Sorry."

"Late."

"West Coast."

"Am I still banished to the guest room?"

"If you can't drive, you're in no condition to seduce. Guest room's over there." He gestured. "I'll get the shirt, toothbrush, and toothpaste. Need anything else?"

"Nope." I got my purse and went to the room, leaving the door open.

"They're on the bed," he called to me once I was in the bathroom.

"You can just hand them to me," I said, opening the door. "I'll jump in the shower while you're on the phone." Clad in a skimpy black bra and matching panties, I held out my hand for the items.

Bob didn't move.

"Is there a problem?" I asked, pulling the combs from my hair and tousling the dark shoulder-length locks as I walked toward him.

"Nooo." He slowly scanned my body.

Leaning in, I kissed his cheek, making certain to brush my lips against his. "You'd better get to your phone call," I said, taking the items from his hand. Turning, I walked into the bathroom, closing the door behind me—and listening. He didn't leave right away, I noted with a triumphant smile.

After showering, I slipped into the button-down shirt and rolled up the sleeves. The soft worn cotton felt good against my skin. Bob's scent lingered on the fabric. I took a small brush from my purse and pulled it through my damp hair. My bare hip became visible below the loose-fitting shirt. As I put down the brush, the shirt slipped off my shoulder, partially exposing my breast. The thin white cloth revealed my nipples beneath, still hardened at the thought of Bob's touch.

I searched through my purse, pulling out a deep-red lipstick. Carefully, I applied it to my lips. Then I took one more look in the mirror, quite satisfied with my reflection.

The office door was open and the conversation winding down when I stepped over the threshold with our two unfinished glasses of wine. Bob accepted the glass with a smile as he tried to end the call. Sitting on the leather sofa across from his desk, I curled my legs under my body, making certain that the shirt rode up past my hip.

He hung up the phone and held out the wineglass. "You trying to intoxicate me?"

"It would defeat my purpose." I shifted my position, deliberately offering him a teasing glimpse between my legs before unhurriedly pulling down the shirt.

His eyes followed my every move as he spoke. "You admit you have a purpose?"

"Absolutely," I said, standing and leisurely moving toward him. "I intend to have my way with you, Mr. Congressman."

"Do you?" he asked. Placing my wineglass beside his on the desk, I stepped between his legs. His hands were instinctively drawn to my breasts.

"I do. And I want you to remember every sizzling moment."

He unbuttoned the shirt, sighing as he began to fondle my breasts. Gently, he twisted the hardened nipples between his thumb and finger, before exploring them with his mouth.

My body yielded to his touch. My heart began to pound, my respirations became deep and rapid. Delighting in his secure hold of each breast and his tongue's enthralling caress, I desperately longed for more.

As though sensing my need, Bob stood, pulling me hard against his body. His kisses blanketed my bare shoulders and neck, moved up to my lips, and teasingly passed them by. I pushed my pelvis into his, causing his hands to settle on my buttocks, pulling me hard against his body. My hips began to move. I determinedly grinding my pelvis against his erection.

"Are you at all concerned that you might be taking advantage of me?" he teasingly asked between kisses.

"Oh, you're right. Shame on me." I laughed, pushing away.

He quickly grabbed me by the hand, drawing me into a tight embrace. His eager tongue slipped between my open lips, rousing me all the more.

Still holding my hand, he began moving away from the desk. "Come with me."

"Oh, but I intend to—"

He turned his head and smiled as he led me to his bedroom.

Chapter 13

It is not honorable to take mere legal advantage,
when it happens to be contrary to justice.
—Thomas Jefferson

TOM SMILED BACK AT THE PHOTO THAT HIS NIECE had sent of her two grandchildren. A young girl was kissing the cheek of a sleeping infant she held tight in her arms. The children resembled their grandmother, clearly of Irish descent.

Carefully placing the picture on the tarnished metal table, Tom moved slowly from the cold metal chair to the bed, lying down on the flimsy mattress. He closed his eyes and covered them with his arm against the constant glaring light.

His mind filled with memories of Sunday dinners years ago, from the laughter at the table of his parents when he and his siblings were young to the same laughter at the home of his brother Peter and wife, Theresa. Their brood of twelve lined both sides of the extended dining room table. Each face glowed with health and joy, reflecting the secure and loving home life provided.

"Tommy, as long as you leave your other life at the doorstep, you're always welcome. You're my brother, and I love you," Peter told him. Peter had been true to his word. He, Theresa, and the kids opened their home and hearts.

~

The airing of the CNN interview sent flocks of journalists and cameramen to my home. Satellite-dish-burdened vans lined the road as the journalists congregated at the front door. One knocked. The others lay in wait, ready to pounce on whoever responded.

Ilona, with little Paulie on her hip, opened the door. Before she could say a word, the barrage began in unison.

"NECN. I'd like to interview Alexandra Fischer."

"News Center 5. Is Ms. Fischer able to talk?"

"I'm here with Fox 25 News to speak with Alex Fischer."

"*Boston Times* to interview Alexandra Fischer."

"7 News is here."

"Reporter from the *Boston Post*."

Ilona took a step backward to avoid the microphones being shoved at her and Paulie. "Put down the microphones," she said respectfully but determinedly. "My mother isn't here."

This announcement set off another barrage of questions.

"Where is she?"

"When will she be back?"

"I have her cell. Will you verify the number?"

Ilona laughed. "You have her cell? Yeah, right. Why don't you give me the number and I'll tell you if it's right."

There was no reply. The journalist was lying.

"She's not here. We have some nice restaurants close by. Why don't you go have some lunch," Ilona said. Then she closed the door.

"They're unbelievable!" she exclaimed to her brother, who had just come from the bathroom. She put Paulie down.

"You'd better warn Ma. Where'd she go?" Charlie asked.

"You live here and you don't know where she is?"

"I got in late. Didn't see her."

"I'm sure she left a note."

Ilona walked to the bathroom and pulled off the note that was taped to the mirror. "You didn't see this?" She was laughing.

"Nope. I never see the notes. Don't know why she leaves them."

"Why don't you open your eyes? And you're being trained to protect the country?"

"*Being* is the key word." Charlie picked Paulie up and threw him in the air. "Where is she?"

"Boston. Having lunch with Sly Devaney's attorney."

Charlie's quizzical expression was his only response.

~

Ilona called and told me about the reporters. I instructed her to tell them what time I'd return, hoping this would get them out of the neighborhood for a few hours. After ending the call, I turned my attention back to Curt Jordan, who was sitting opposite me at the table.

"They don't like what you're saying. Doesn't fit with the story they've been telling for years. And because it's been told over and over, the public believes every word."

"That's why I wanted to talk to you, Curt. I realized from opening statements to closing arguments that much wasn't being told."

"Gag orders and numerous motions from the prosecution to keep information from the jury—as well as the testimony of many of our witnesses. Let me start by asking if you remember the name Joshua O'Toole coming up in testimony?"

"The federal attorney heading up the Strike Task Force? I wrote his name in my notebook, because every time he was mentioned, Chavere and Altier threw a fit."

"They certainly did," Curt agreed. "Joshua O'Toole gave Tom Devaney immunity."

"Because he was an informant? You said during the trial that he wasn't," I objected.

"No, he didn't give O'Toole information. Tom was given immunity in exchange for protecting O'Toole and his family," Curt said.

"Protecting them from what?"

"O'Toole was taking down La Costa Nostra."

"The Mafia?" I asked.

"Yes. They made threats against O'Toole. He took the threats seriously and made arrangements, through a priest, to meet with Tom in private. O'Toole promised Tom immunity in exchange for protection. Tom agreed."

"Why didn't O'Toole have the FBI protect him?" I asked.

"He couldn't trust the FBI."

"So, the prosecution didn't want this deal between O'Toole and Devaney to be brought up?" I asked.

"Exactly. We weren't allowed to present it."

"But what difference does it make? If the informant file on Devaney was real, shouldn't he already have immunity?" As I spoke the words, I realized I had never considered the obvious.

"That's how I thought the game was played," Curt responded. "But, then again, the Department of Justice created the game, and the rules can be changed on a whim."

"Why doesn't O'Toole come forward?" I asked.

Curt took a bite of food and swallowed before he continued. "He died in 2009. Reported to have had a massive heart attack when he was sixty-five."

"You doubt that?" I asked, noting his forlorn expression.

"There's a lot I doubt anymore. In 1998, O'Toole was supposed to testify about his relationship with Devaney in the US district court in Boston. He couldn't testify because he had suffered a series of strokes, which ended up putting him in a coma for over a month. At that time, he was only fifty-five and appeared to be in perfect health."

Curt paused as his words sank in. I felt like the wind had just been knocked out of me.

"Something else that will interest you: when Tom was arrested, he agreed to plead guilty to all charges and accept an expedited death sentence, sparing the court the cost of a trial. His only request was that they show leniency to Kathleen Mercer."

"The woman he was living with?"

"Yes. She has no prior record. If they'd been married, she wouldn't have been charged."

"But they did charge her?"

"Oh yes. The recommendation from the parole board of two years' confinement was totally ignored. Chavere and Altier convinced the federal judge to give her the maximum sentence—eight years—for harboring a fugitive. The first year was in solitary confinement. And when she is released, she cannot make money off her story."

"Giuda's girlfriend wasn't charged," I objected.

Curt shook his head slowly. "No. That was part of Giuda's proffer agreement."

"Giuda, Diavolo, James—all of them made money off their stories."

Curt nodded. "Yes, *their* stories." I noted that he emphasized the word *their*.

"They're afraid of Kathleen's story?" I asked.

He nodded again. "And Tom's and Skip Goot's."

"Goot? The FBI agent who threatened to expose the DOJ's corruption?" I queried.

"Yes. Devaney and Goot know too much. The strategy's been to control the so-called facts, prosecute Goot and Devaney, put them in jail, and throw away the keys. Out of sight, out of mind."

"And the cover-up continues," I added.

"Oh, not just the cover-up, Alex. The crimes continue. Individuals still have immunity from the government as they escape prosecution from heinous crimes and continue in their criminal activity," Curt said. He paused to take a bite of food. After swallowing, he continued. "Do you remember Alan Hand being mentioned?"

"You identified him as being an accomplice in the O'Leary and Monahan murders, and also the three murders at the house."

"Hand has never been charged with any of those crimes. In fact, after I announced Hand's involvement in the O'Leary and Monahan murders, Hand was brought before Judge Blake. His attorney invoked his Fifth Amendment right. That was the end of it."

Curt took another bite of food and a sip of his water before continuing. "When Rob and I got the case, we had less than two years to prepare for a trial that Chavere had been working on for twenty. The pile of government documents we had to review was insurmountable. We were forced to hire another attorney and a few more paralegals. We still have about five hundred pages that we never had time to look at. Yet the enormous cost of this trial could have easily been avoided."

"If the DOJ accepted Devaney's guilty plea?" I asked.

Curt nodded. "We presented it again to Dick Altier at the very beginning of the process. He said he needed to talk to US Attorney Yan and Chavere. The response was, 'No. We're going to trial.' And here we are—almost three million dollars of the taxpayers' money later, and still counting. But do you know who's going down for the excessive cost?"

"The defense team," I acknowledged.

"Exactly. We had a job to do, and we did it. In the process, Rob and I realized Devaney's crimes were no worse than those of the Department of Justice. In fact, given the intended purpose, duty, and obligation of the DOJ, its criminality is far worse."

We ate in silence for a moment. "Curt, what about the families of Giuda's victims? What about the people he damaged for life? What's been done to help them?"

"Nothing. The court has excused itself from obligation to these victims in determining that Giuda owes them no restitution."

"What about the teenage boy and girl?" The anger in my soul over their deaths ate at me.

"The teenagers were black," he responded with a steady gaze.

"I don't understand."

"Many claim that the reason few cared enough to cry foul when Giuda was released was because many of his victims were of African American descent."

"So, the lives of Giuda's victims were insignificant to the court?" I asked.

"And the news media. Little was said. There wasn't any money to be made in focusing on Giuda's early murders. The murders that got the attention of the public were the ones Giuda claimed he carried out with Tom Devaney. Boston's two newspapers were being fed information the readers craved by Giuda, Diavolo, James, and Arnold. Didn't matter if it was true; there was money to be made. The Boston journalists wrote the articles, and then went on to write their books. Each of them profited." Curt paused as the waitress handed him the bill.

"I'll take that. You were kind enough to meet," I offered.

"No." He smiled, placing a credit card into the slot on the bill pad. "During the trial, Rob and I were informed that a detective with the state police reported that Giuda and James were still involved in criminal activity. I went to Massachusetts State Police Headquarters to read the report. It was sealed. I sought out the detective. He refused to talk. I later found out that Carla Chavere had visited headquarters immediately after we were informed of the alleged criminal activity."

"She had the case sealed?" I asked.

"It seems she sought the order, and implemented it. My office hired a private detective to observe Giuda and James. It wasn't long before he reported that the information we received was correct. Our detective also discovered that the state police detective had been demoted and threatened with losing his job if he said any more about his findings. This guy had a young family to feed. He couldn't take the risk."

I was aghast. "Why wasn't this brought up in testimony?"

"Our detective pleaded with us not to make him testify. He received a phone call demanding that he stop the investigation or someone would get hurt. The caller then recited the detective's wife's car make, model, and plate number, her place of business, and her daily routine. When the call ended, he traced the number to a government office."

I sat back against the chair and stared at the wall beyond Curt, shocked by what I was hearing.

"Giuda and James continue in crime with no fear of arrest?" I asked.

"Giuda, James, Alan Hand. Alan Hand hosts a reality show about illegal gambling on one of the popular cable channels. And I have every reason to believe that Tony Diavolo is back on the streets doing whatever he wants, living a comfortable life with the tainted fortune returned to him."

"Out on the legal statute you mentioned?" I was frightened by the thought.

Curt nodded. "Rule 35 motion." He took the bill pad from the waitress, filled out the receipt, and signed it, handing it back to her. "Sentencing will take place in November. Rob will work on the appeal. I won't be part of it."

We stood, walked to the door, and stepped outside, instantly greeted by the humidity of the August day. The bustle and noise of the Boston sidewalk was a sharp contrast to the mellow atmosphere of the restaurant. Curt began to speak, but then he stopped as a fire truck whizzed by, siren blaring.

"I always keep one memento from my cases. Tom gave me an invitation he received to a reunion at Alcatraz. They're having a dinner for former inmates and prison personnel." Curt smiled. "I'll keep that."

We said our goodbyes. As I walked to my car, I listened to a voice message from Charlie.

"Ma, telling them that you weren't home didn't work. These people are pathetic. They set up camp out front. I went out and told them to leave or I'd call the police. They packed their vans and drove off. Not sure where they went."

As I drove down the street perpendicular to mine, I came upon the convoy of media vans. The occupants strained to get a look at me as I passed. When my blinker went on, the engines of six vans turned over. I laughed, imagining the cartoonish scene of them trying to be the first to get to the door. Images of smashed vans and fallen satellites filled my mind. Obviously, the drivers were masterful at maneuvering the burdensome vehicles. But their Three Stooges–like trek to be the first to the door didn't disappoint. I slipped in the back door. Ilona went to the front.

"Really? She walks in the door and you're expecting an immediate interview? Where's your sense of decency? Can the woman use the bathroom first?" Ilona looked at each face in silence, her dark eyes blazing. "My second-grade students have more patience and common sense than any of you."

The interviews were given one at a time. My comments were the same. The revelation of corruption within the DOJ was more alarming than the crimes of Thomas Devaney.

The Associated Press and Boston's local PBS station asked for interviews the following day. Both journalists, I noted, unlike those I'd met the day before, showed more professionalism in their attitude and conduct. For that, I was grateful.

Unfortunately for me, Nick Mudd somehow got access to my taped interview with the local Fox News station. He in turn lifted parts out of context. He aired them on his daily radio show and wrote things in his newspaper article inciting his loyal followers. I was referred to as a "moon bat." He charged me with being a liberal and a bad juror, because, he stated, good jurors should mind their own business and keep their mouths shut.

I was a bad juror. I should've attempted to nullify the law regarding the irrational guilt by association. If I'd had a better understanding of jury nullification at the time, I would have. Americans need to be fully educated on the rights of a juror.

My days were quickly filled with preparations to get Charlie back to the academy and to get myself back to the classroom. I went through the motions robotically, my mind pondering inconsistencies from the trial.

Bob proved to distract me on the rare evenings when business didn't take him out of town. He answered the questions I put to him about Devaney, but his knowledge of some of the topics that caused me concern and confusion was limited.

"I received a letter from a production company that will be airing a documentary about Devaney's trial on CNN," I told Bob in the calm after the storm of passion.

Lying on his back with his arm under my shoulders, he pulled my body closer to his. "What do they want?"

"An interview. They're questioning whether Devaney was ever an FBI informant."

"The FBI has a file. Goot and Arnold protected him."

"Devaney still denies it. Too many oddities about the file. I plan to write him."

"Who?" He was obviously nodding off.

"Devaney."

"Why?"

"To get the truth."

"You think Sly Devaney's gonna give you truth? Come on, Alex—" His voice drifted away.

I rolled over. *I'm not sure anyone will tell the truth, but Devaney's the only one with nothing to lose.*

The following morning, I stopped by the Hallmark store, hoping to find a card to send Sly Devaney to somehow break the ice. Nothing seemed appropriate. *Is it too much to ask for the perfect card for the killer you helped put in prison for life?* I quietly laughed at my bizarre situation. Giving up, I was prepared to leave empty-handed. As I walked down the aisle, a picture caught my attention. There were no words on the card, just a black-and-white photo of a little girl standing under a giant boulder. Her arms were stretched out to touch it, appearing as though she were keeping the boulder from crushing her. I bought the card.

"Dear Mr. Devaney," I began writing. "The picture on this card depicts what I'm feeling about the vast depth of government corruption revealed in your trial. My name is Alexandra Fisher. I was juror #12. I have many questions and am hoping you can help me with some of the answers ..."

A few days after mailing the letter, I met with the film crew and producer of the Devaney documentary. I sat down with the producer, Gary Dillinger, prior to going before the cameras.

"Alex, I watched your interviews, and read the op-ed pieces you sent to the *Salem Ledger*. Obviously, I'm impressed. This trial raised more questions than it answered, yet the Boston media barely reported a thing in regard to the corruption—not even new information revealed. I want to pose those questions to the nation with this documentary."

"Someone needs to," I agreed.

"Our focus is the informant file the FBI claims is Devaney's. I'll ask you questions about that. Also, I have questions about Devaney's claim that the federal attorney heading up the Strike Task Force offered him immunity."

"Joshua O'Toole?" I asked to clarify.

"Yes."

"Only his name was mentioned. Nothing was said about him giving Devaney immunity," I explained.

"Exactly. That's what I want you to say." Gary paused. "Have you had time to do any research on Devaney since the trial ended?"

"Some. But I don't trust most of the sources."

"I understand. You know that Devaney lived a few minutes away from FBI Headquarters in Washington, DC?"

I nodded.

"Did you know that shortly after O'Toole's death, the FBI arrested Devaney?"

"How long after?"

"He died just a little over a year before Devaney was suddenly discovered living right under the nose of the FBI."

"You think they were waiting for him to die?" I asked, remembering that Curt Jordan had said that in 1998, O'Toole suffered a series of strokes and a coma just before he was supposed to testify before a US district court.

"I don't know what to think. I certainly find it interesting. Without O'Toole's testimony, Devaney's claim of immunity is just that—a claim."

We were instructed to move to the chairs in front of the cameras. "Do you know about the government's mistreatment of the families of Devaney's victims?" Gary asked as we sat down.

"It was obvious the families have no affection for Chavere or Altier," I offered.

"No. They don't. I've already interviewed the families. The government's been jerking them around for years. Lawsuits against the FBI for its negligence, which played into the death of many of their loved ones, have been stalled again and again."

Our conversation ended when the cameras began to roll. The interview went well. And Gary's comments off camera left me with a lot to think about, and many more questions.

~

Bob suggested we plan a trip to his place in Maine with Don and Nancy to view the autumn foliage. The four-hour drive through the northern New England states was breathtaking.

"A cabin?" Nancy chided from the front seat. "Does it have electricity? running water?"

Bob pretended to be offended. "Cold water. But it's a nice little cabin. You girls can take the bunks. Don and I will sleep on the floor."

"Seriously?" Nancy strained her neck to glare at him in the backseat.

"Quite a romantic weekend!" I laughed.

Bob took hold of my hand. "What? We can snuggle by the fire."

"You guys obviously feel a need to rough it. Alex and I will stay at a hotel," Nancy announced.

"The nearest hotel is twenty miles from the cabin," Don interjected with a smile.

"If it has a restaurant and a hot tub, we're all set," I added.

"You'll be pleased with the cabin. I promise." Bob squeezed my hand.

"Alex, have you heard from Devaney?" Don asked, looking at me in the rearview mirror.

"Not yet."

"I hope she doesn't," Bob mumbled. I looked at him questioningly. "Can't imagine he has anything of value to share."

"Weren't you planning to meet a friend of his?" Don asked.

"I did."

"Why would you do that? Aren't they all criminals?" Nancy exclaimed.

"No. This guy grew up with Devaney. Has known him most of his life."

"Did he offer any insight?" Don asked.

"Yeah. He did."

"What?" Nancy asked.

Bob laughed. "Alex's become an amateur psychologist. This guy convinced her that Devaney had ADHD as a kid," he teased.

"I don't care what you say." I smiled at Bob. "It makes sense. He was the oldest child in a large family. The dad was disabled; his mom, overwhelmed. No one knew about ADHD then. Kids were labeled as bad and incorrigible. Most parents probably didn't know what to do with them."

"From everything I've heard, his parents cared about him," Nancy interjected.

"I'm sure they did. It seems he was just a restless, somewhat hyper kid. He left home when he was about fifteen. Jumped trains and hitch-hiked around the country. Fell in with a bad crowd."

"That's a bit harsh, Alex. I'm sure the bank robbers he took up with were just misunderstood ADHD kids too," Bob teased.

"They very well may have been," was my response.

"The chemicals in his brain made him do it." Bob scoffed.

"Chemicals in our brains are responsible for much of what we do or don't do. It's a blessing to have them balanced, and a nightmare if they're not," Nancy stated.

"Chemical imbalance or not, Devaney wasn't insane. He knew right from wrong." The former DA was determined.

"Is that all Devaney's friend had to say?" Don asked. I was grateful the conversation was redirected. Bob and I had scuffled about the ADHD theory a few times already.

"No. He told me that when Giuda, Diavolo, and James were arrested, they shared the same attorney. They also spent a lot of time together in prison."

"Is there a problem with that?" Nancy turned in the front seat and looked at Bob. He looked out the window, pretending not to notice.

"Given their matching testimonies, yeah, I'd say there's a huge problem with it," I answered.

"I don't understand," Nancy said.

"Before the three of them were together in prison, before they shared the same attorney, the state police officers who interrogated them said the accounts they gave were quite different from what they offered the US Attorney's Office in return for reduced sentences," I explained.

"So, you're implying they lied," Don stated.

"I'm not implying anything. They did lie."

Bob turned from the window and looked at me. His expression was harsh. "Alex, you have to be careful. Statements like that can bring trouble." He changed the subject. Now I was looking out the window in silence.

Finally arriving at the "cabin," Nancy and I were delighted to find that the large house had all the conveniences of home, and more. The view of Flagstaff Lake surrounded by splashes of red, yellow, orange, and green leaves was spectacular.

After taking a leisurely shower, I dressed and quietly began to descend the staircase—too quietly, it seemed, because I heard Bob's impassioned plea below.

"Please, no more talk of Devaney. I brought her here to get away from it. She's become obsessed and needs to get it out of her mind."

"What if he writes her back?" Nancy asked.

"He won't."

~

Regardless of Bob's concern, I continued my research. I'd given up on receiving a response from Devaney, but I realized there were others I could attempt to contact. Sitting at the dining room table with my laptop, I googled the three witnesses whose testimonies had impacted me the most: FBI ASAC Wallace, who stated that Devaney wasn't an informant; Stanley Onesta, who spent twenty-two years in prison for conspiracy to commit a robbery; and Tom Donovan, the tavern owner who, it seemed, was knowingly charged and imprisoned for a murder he didn't commit. Taking into consideration Bob's concern about my "obsession," I even sent a letter to Ben James and Carla Chavere, asking if they would be willing to answer a few questions.

I placed the letters in my mailbox and was pulling up the red flag when the mail truck turned the corner. I removed the envelopes from the box and waited. "Perfect timing." I handed the mail carrier my letters.

"And some for you." He smiled, handing me a pile of envelopes.

I began to thumb through the envelopes as I walked inside. "Junk mail and bills," I mumbled, tossing the envelopes on the kitchen table. I made myself a cup of tea, picked up the envelopes again, and went to the dining room table to sort out the mail and finish up a lesson plan for my students.

The last envelope in the pile was handwritten. The return address was the Plymouth County Correctional Facility. The sender's name, written in neat cursive, was Thomas Devaney. His prison number was listed under his name. Quickly, I opened the envelope and began to read.

> Dear Ms. Fischer,
>
> Meaningful card—thank you.

I remembered the picture with the girl seemingly holding back a boulder. Eagerly, I continued to read.

> No disrespect, but I don't trust prosecutors, judges, jurors, FBI agents, CIA, or complicit media. Somewhere I read that you made statements regarding me. Before I would answer your card, I was reaching out to see if anyone had any info on what you said.
>
> Tonight, I heard angry people calling into a radio show because the US government reported that the legal bill for the trial is $2,700,000 and counting. Reality, which prompted me to write you, is that the US taxpayers will pay for the cost of my trial and the cost of Kathleen's trial. Add to that our care in prison, Kathleen's eight-year sentence and mine, which will be life. The final bill for the taxpayers will amount to many millions of dollars.
>
> Had they accepted the offer I made upon my arrest and after, which was simple and to the point, millions of dollars would have been saved. I offered to plead guilty to all crimes I've been accused of. I offered to accept any sentence with no appeal, even execution—expedited.

In return, I asked for leniency for Kathleen. She has no criminal record. Had we been married, she wouldn't have been charged. Do you remember Vinnie Giuda's girlfriend Bobbie? She was with Vinnie when he was on the lam for sixteen years. She laundered money and lied to a grand jury. She was never charged.

I had Devaney's attention, and he was verifying information Curt Jordan had already shared. Was there already a level of trust?

"Guess it's not every day that a mob boss has a juror write seeking truth," I mumbled to myself. I grabbed a piece of stationery from the desk drawer and sat down, preparing to respond. "Don't push it, Alex. He said he doesn't trust jurors. Introduce him to who you are."

Dear Mr. Devaney,

Maybe I should tell you a little about myself—

We exchanged letters about twice a week, and quickly found commonality between our lives. Shared experiences, whether religion, ethnicity, family traditions or tragedies—from these we broadened our communication and began, over the weeks and months, to form a friendship. There was no doubt in my mind that Tom Devaney was a criminal, and he was certain to point that out to me frequently. He also made me aware that our every letter was being read, and probably copied, by the assistant US attorneys Carla Chavere and Dick Altier. And, though I knew he was a criminal, there was no distinct image seared in my mind of the monster others envisioned.

I likened my unconditional acceptance of him to that of my husband's grandfather of me. Prior to my meeting Paul, his grandfather had been a violent alcoholic. The family had vivid memories of the horror endured during Granddad's binges. I only knew him as a recovering alcoholic with an enormous love for his family.

Tom Devaney's letters revealed his frustration for Kathleen's plight, and his sincere affection for her. Theirs was a true love story.

Here was a man who literally offered his life to keep her from harm. "She accomplished for me what the penal system failed to do—she kept me crime-free for eighteen years," he wrote, and encouraged me to write to Kathleen. Perhaps the greatest punishment Tom had received from the court was not being able to communicate with her.

I did write Kathleen. Her letters back were rather timid. I sensed her concern that everything she said was being read, perhaps read into. Her affection for Tom was as apparent as his for her. Not being able to communicate with the one dearest to her heart was pure agony. Then, suddenly, I was informed by the prison that held Kathleen that she would no longer receive correspondence from me. I was perplexed. Of course, Tom, who had no correspondence with her, had no idea why this was.

I was honest with Tom, telling him that Bob Costa was a friend. Tom's response was fascinating. He didn't like Bob; that was clear. But other than a comment about a young man named Ed Marshall whom Bob had supposedly sent to prison—a man who Tom claimed was innocent—Tom offered nothing. My friendship with the former DA was my business, and Tom said he didn't believe in ratting on people, no matter who they are. I accepted that the statement was what one would expect from a criminal in regard to a DA who had been actively seeking to prosecute him. I left it at that. Tom never said anything about Bob, and Bob never asked—two men apparently comfortable with who they were and what they were about.

~

"Alex, come on and sit down," Bob called out as I passed through the living room.

"Yeah, Ma, you've been working all afternoon," Charlie added, looking away from the television. "I forgot to tell you—dinner was good."

"Thank you." I smiled.

"How's the food at the Point?" Bob asked.

"Decent. But nothing like Ma's."

"What are you watching?" I asked, looking at the television.

"The Patriots," Bob stated.

"She hates football," Charlie interjected.

Bob looked at Charlie. "What do ya mean, she hates football? I took her to a game." He turned an incredulous gaze on me. "You were carrying on like a cheerleader."

"Amazing how a couple of beers affect me." I smiled sheepishly. "Didn't understand anything. Cheered when you cheered, grumbled when you grumbled."

"Learn from this, Charlie. You can never really trust them." Bob smiled and reached out his hand for mine. "The game's almost over. We can watch a movie."

"Yeah, I think the latest Bourne film is on," Charlie offered. "*Bourne Legacy.*"

"Those are about the CIA, aren't they?" I asked, sitting next to Bob on the sofa.

Bob nodded. "Haven't seen this one."

"Is there any truth to MKULTRA?" I asked. Both of them looked at me.

"M-K-what?" Charlie asked.

"Yeah," Bob responded. "Happened in the mid-1950s to mid-60s. CIA conducted experiments with biological and chemical agents."

"On people," I added.

Bob nodded. "Why are you asking?"

"I recently heard something about it. The movie reminded me." I didn't tell him that it was Tom Devaney who had told me. Devaney had been involved in the experimentation.

~

It was apparent that the less Bob knew about my active research into the DOJ's corruption, the better. I convinced myself that what he didn't know couldn't hurt him—or *us.*

Former FBI agent Joseph Wallace responded to my letter. We talked on several occasions. I finally made arrangements to meet him and his wife for dinner. Joe and Linda were pleasant and easy to be with. Joe let me know that Simon Cole, an acquaintance of his who was writing a book on the government corruption in the Devaney case, wanted to connect with me. I told Joe to give Simon my number.

Joe and Linda went on to tell me about the shock of Joe's experience with the FBI during the last few years of his twenty-year career, and of the bureau's determination to keep him from asking questions about obvious corruption within. His career culminated in an early retirement, to distance himself from immoral activities. To Joe and Linda's horror, his record of service was altered, now presenting him as a troubled agent who had quit the FBI, abandoning all benefits in the process—including his pension.

"They attempted to destroy him," Linda stated after Joe excused himself to go to the men's room. "They failed. Joe was very ill when the trial took place. He'd just come out of the hospital. His doctors didn't want him to testify. Joe felt he must. He had hoped that his testimony for the defense would spur the media to investigate Devaney's obvious protection from Washington, and that Lucy's corroborating statement would further incite them."

With the mention of the name of the elderly woman who had served for decades as secretary to the special agents in charge at the Boston office of the FBI, I instantly remembered her damning testimony. She clearly corroborated Joe's statement that Devaney was not an informant and should be made a target. Lucy had even presented a copy of the report to the court.

"The media was mesmerized by Dick Altier's abuse of Joe. They reported Altier's lies against Joe's character and completely ignored the fact that two witnesses had revealed corruption within the FBI going all the way to Washington." Linda was shaking her head. Her expression clearly revealed the years of pain her family had suffered at the hands of the FBI and the controlled media.

I remembered Altier's treatment of Joe on the witness stand. His monstrous performance, allowed by the judge, was a true example of judicial abuse of power, as far as I was concerned, and an embarrassment to the federal court. Yet, as Linda indicated, the media said nothing.

"There've been threats over the years to keep him silent," Linda stated.

"The FBI?"

Linda shrugged. "He wouldn't want me to tell you this." She looked in the direction of the restrooms as though to make certain Joe was not approaching. "Odd things have occurred since he retired. For example, we had gone out to dinner. When we returned, the legal paperwork pertaining to Joe's appeal to receive his FBI pension was spread out on his desk. Each page had been neatly cut in half. Previously the package had been in a locked file cabinet. There was no sign of forced entry into the house or the file cabinet. Nothing else was disturbed. I asked Joe why they would do it. He said it was just to show him that they could." Linda stopped talking as Joe approached the table.

I also received a response to my letter from Stanley Onesta—the man imprisoned for more than twenty years for conspiracy to rob a bank. I thoroughly enjoyed his letters, which were always polite and filled with sound ideas to improve society. His reentry into a world he had been separated from for twenty-two long years was shocking. His ideas for reform were well thought out and sound. Among Joseph's suggestions were anger management classes starting in elementary school; a national holiday for first responders; and a return of the death penalty. I was fascinated by the fact that Stanley Onesta and Tom Devaney commented on the changes in the prison system, as both had been incarcerated as young men. The changes they witnessed offered no reformation. To the contrary, the changes only promised that hard criminals would leave more hardened.

Onesta stated to me, as he had during his testimony, that prior to the trial he had never laid eyes on Tom Devaney. Why the US Attorney's Office subpoenaed him to testify, he didn't have a clue.

The three who never responded to my letters were Tom Donovan, Ben James, and Assistant US Attorney Carla Chavere. The fact that Chavere forever had Donovan and James by the balls in their proffer agreements was more than enough reason for them not to respond.

The fact that Chavere didn't respond? Why would she? She had nothing of value to say.

~

"Alex, did you see the paper this morning?" Connor asked when he spotted me at the coffee machine in the teachers' lounge.

"No. Woke up late. Barely had time to brush my teeth." I added some sugar and cream to the coffee.

He handed me a newspaper, opened it, and folded it back to reveal an article he wanted me to see. It was a short piece by the Associated Press. It didn't take long to read.

Connor, the school psychologist, laughed at my expression as I finished the article. "Calm down, Alex. No judge would allow it."

"What's it about?" Marjorie, the assistant headmaster, asked.

"Sly Devaney's sentencing," Connor answered.

"Isn't it a few weeks off? What's happening?"

"The AP claims Assistant US Attorneys Chavere and Altier are asking Judge Blake to allow family members of victims of murders Devaney was acquitted of to give impact statements at sentencing," I explained. My astonishment was evident.

"He can't allow it," Connor said.

I looked at him and shook my head. "From what I've seen and discovered, things that shouldn't be allowed do happen all the time in federal court."

"So, what if he does allow them to speak? What's the big deal?" Marjorie asked.

I was relieved that Connor answered. "The jury acquitted Devaney of certain murders. The court's attitude should be that he is no longer accountable for them. Allowing family members to speak of their pain and loss implies Devaney is guilty of the murders, and mocks the jury's verdict. It would also have an emotional effect on the judge and could—would, in my professional opinion—affect his decision in sentencing."

"You may have acquitted him, Alex, but most believe he had a part in killing those people. Let the families have their say," Marjorie said.

"A jury of twelve acquitted him, not just me. If these people are allowed to give impact statements, why not put a sign outside the courthouse inviting anyone who thinks they were offended by Devaney to come in and have their say?"

"You're overreacting, Alex," Marjorie responded with a smile.

"Overreacting? Why should a jury deliberate and come in with a verdict if a judge can ignore it? Why were we forced to sit through that trial for ten weeks only to have our verdict thrown aside?"

"The trial's over, Alex. Time to let it go." Marjorie walked past me toward the door.

"If they can do it to Devaney, they can do it to any of us," I called out.

She turned to look at me. "As far as I'm concerned, they can do whatever they need to do to make that monster suffer." Again, she moved toward the door.

"Hard cases make bad law, Marjorie."

"You're a teacher, Alex—" She stopped speaking, her hand on the doorknob, and turned to face me. "How's your history book coming?"

"Just started the final edit."

"Good. Shouldn't be long now. How proud the academy will be to have a published author teaching. You're a teacher, Alex. Leave the law to the politicians, judges, and attorneys." With that, Marjorie left.

I threw Connor a blank stare.

"I can't imagine the judge will allow it, but if he does, there's nothing you can do. No sense getting worked up about it." Connor followed Marjorie out of the room.

Though Connor's words were meant to be reassuring, they incited me all the more. "Lousy counsel from a psychologist," I mumbled.

My teaching plan abruptly changed that day. All classes discussed the fundamental role of a jury, and considered, through debate, a hypothetical judge allowing impact statements in regard to acquitted crimes. I was not surprised to find that the students, removed from the emotion and bias of the case, understood the danger to the judicial system if a judge were to grant such a request. *Tomorrow, I determined, we'll study the history of jury nullification.*

Bob was out of the country on business. I attempted to contact him when I got home, with no success.

I wrote a letter to Judge Blake, respectfully requesting that he protect the sanctity of the jury's verdict and deny the motion of the assistant US attorneys. I then contacted those who had served on the jury with me to see if any wanted to add their name to the letter. Only Dan affixed his name alongside mine. The letter was sent via certified mail.

"You received confirmation that the letter was delivered?" Bob asked, after reviewing a copy of it once he'd returned. He placed it on the end table and gestured for me to sit next to him on the sofa.

"Yes," I said, sitting down and snuggling against him. His arm went around my shoulders and pulled me closer.

"Then it's on the judge's docket and will be taken under consideration when he reviews the request."

"What does that mean?"

He smiled at my ignorance as he leaned down and softly kissed my lips. "It's part of the public court record."

I leaned my head on his shoulder. "I got the day off to go to sentencing."

"Why?" Bob asked, seemingly annoyed by my announcement.

"I feel like I should be there—see it through."

"Nothing good can come of you being there."

"Are you serious?" I lifted my head and pulled away from him.

"Yeah, I'm serious. Devaney's hated. The victims and media will eat you alive if they think you're supporting him in any way."

"I'm not supporting him. I just want the truth."

"And for some reason you equate truth with purity. There's no purity here, Alex, whatever the truth may be. These people are unlike any you've ever encountered, from Devaney to his gang members to most of his victims and their families. They're not like you. Stay away from it, Alex."

"Come with me," I said, relaxing again and leaning my body against his.

"I can't. I'll be in Germany that week." Bob put his arm around my shoulders again. "Why don't you come with me? Get away from it all for a while. I think it'll do you good."

"I can't leave the classroom for that long. Wish I could."

"Then promise you won't leave the classroom the day of sentencing." He pulled me tight against him as though protecting me from what he feared might come.

"I guess there's no good reason to go," I said, finally realizing how desperate he was to protect me.

~

"I was thinking of coming down tomorrow with Paulie, unless you have plans with Bob," Ilona said. "The weather's supposed to be nice and Steve's working this weekend," she added, referring to her husband. "I'll bring Paulie's Halloween costume so you can see it."

"Don't think this weekend is good. My boiler isn't working. It was fine when I left for work this morning. The gas company put a pole in front of my meter today."

"What kind of pole?"

"It's gray, about three feet high, six inches in diameter. I called them when I realized the boiler was off. Gasman came by and said they put the poles in to protect the meters from getting hit in driveways."

"Did he check for leaks?" she asked.

"Yeah. Didn't find anything. Boiler guy can't get here for three days."

"Three days? Maybe you should come up here for the weekend."

"Maybe I will. Bob's in New York on business."

"Seems he's gone more often than he's there," Ilona commented.

"He is. He's in New York this week, Washington next, and Germany after that. We've become like two ships in the night. It'll be good to get away. I'll head up in the morning."

On Monday, the repairman came and fidgeted with the boiler, replacing a few parts. Still, it wouldn't work. He suggested I call an electrician. I did—my brother. He came by the next day and looked it over, saying something had shorted out. The following day he replaced whatever it was. The boiler came on. Two hours later it went out again. My brother instructed me to call the gas company again, thinking the heavy pole might be sitting on the gas line and causing the flow to fluctuate somehow.

"Still not running?" the gasman asked.

I explained all that had been done so far. "Could it have something to do with that pole? This started the day the pole went in."

"Only if it kinked the gas line, but I didn't detect a problem with the gas flow when I was here. I'll pull it out and make sure it's not pressing on the line."

"Thanks," I said, turning to go back into the house. I stopped and faced him again. "Why did they put the pole in without notifying me? No one on this street, or in the neighborhood, has a pole in front of their meter."

"You didn't ask for it?" He seemed surprised. I shook my head. He went to the van and pulled out a clipboard with papers attached. After scanning the pages, he looked up at me. "Strange, there's no record of it being put in."

"Then it wasn't put in by the gas company?" I asked.

"Must have been. It's one of our poles. Whoever put it in didn't document it."

After he told me that the line was fine, I asked the gasman to take the pole with him, hoping that the problem would vanish with it. It didn't.

Numerous repairmen came by. More parts were replaced. The bills were mounting, but the boiler was still off. I began questioning whether I should just get a new one, until I was told it would cost about $10,000 to replace.

Halloween passed, as did the first week of November. The temperature was getting cold. I temporarily moved in with Bob, happy to see him as much as I could between business trips.

Three days before Devaney's sentencing, Judge Blake had still not made a decision on the request made by the prosecution to let family members give impact statements. I considered how frustrating the judge's indecision must be for Curt Jordan and Rob Willis. I called Curt, left a short message of encouragement on his voice mail, and then headed to my house to meet the owner of a long-established boiler repair shop who was coming by to see why his employees couldn't resolve the problem. He was in the basement for about two hours and finally got the boiler running.

"Not surprised they couldn't figure it out. I've been in this business over fifty years and never saw a similar problem." He took me into the cellar and showed me a small plastic box, one of three on the upper left side of the boiler. "It was slightly twisted. Just enough to arc the electrical current and cause a short. The insulation on the wires was burnt off from the arcing."

I looked at the box. It was too high to accidentally bump and twist out of place. "How would it get twisted? Could a mouse do it?" Visions of mice running up and down my basement walls sent a shiver up my spine.

"Don't see how. Too small. Can't imagine how it happened."

As soon as I saw the repairman off, the phone rang. It was Curt Jordan.

"Thanks for the words of encouragement. Can't tell you how much I appreciate it."

"Figure you and Rob are pretty stressed."

"An understatement. Rob and I spent yesterday at the Plymouth prison with Tom. He'll be transferred to a federal penitentiary after sentencing. He asked us to mail one of his books to you, *The Collected Works of Oscar Wilde*."

"Why?" I asked.

"He said it's a favorite of his, especially the poem, *The Ballad of Reading Gaol*." He wants you to have it. He can only take one book with him. Someone had recently sent him a Bible. He's planning to take that. I'll get the book in the mail to you this week."

"Thanks."

"I'm happy to do it. Also, Kathleen's attorney wanted me to tell you that Kathleen was offered an incentive she couldn't turn down if her correspondence with you ended."

"An incentive?"

"Kathleen was told that if she stopped writing to you, she and Tom would be allowed to correspond."

"I'm happy they'll be able to correspond, but why can't she write to me?"

"You're an author, and an intelligent, compassionate person. They probably don't want to risk letting you develop a relationship with her. They don't want her story being told."

"Curt, who exactly are "They?" I asked.

"Tell me, how has your autumn been?" he asked, obviously not wanting to answer the question.

"I've had a problem with my boiler for the past two weeks. Just got it fixed today."

"A problem with your boiler?" he asked, cutting me off. "Tell me about it." His genuine interest took me by surprise.

When I finished my tale of woe, he said, "And do you think it's just a coincidence?"

"I'm not sure what you mean." I was confused.

"Alex, you've been outspoken on things the government doesn't want any focus on. And you sent a letter to Judge Blake, but he's not acknowledging it. It's not on the docket. Alex, you're an annoyance to them, and they've been known to make life difficult for those who get in their way."

I didn't know how to respond. The silence between us seemed to last an eternity. "Are you saying my boiler was tampered with?"

The timidity in my voice caused Curt to laugh. "I'm saying it's a possibility. And more aggravating situations may follow."

"Like what?"

"Tax audit, passport complications, anything the federal government can do to make you aware that you need to get back in line. I'm not trying to scare you, Alex, just making you aware. There's a price to pay for opposing the actions of the Department of Justice."

Curt's words disturbed me.

As I gathered my things at Bob's, I shared my thoughts about what Curt had said.

"They could have pretended to be the gas company. They put the pole in and then went into the cellar. I left the bulkhead door open that day. There was easy access."

"I think you're letting your imagination get away with you." He was preoccupied with packing his own bag as I packed mine. "And even if it were so, which it isn't, you're moving on. The trial and all your concerns about it are in the past. There's no need to worry about the Department of Justice seeking revenge." He looked at me, his expression stern. "It's over, Alex."

That night, finally in my own bed, I couldn't help but think about what Linda Wallace had told me about their house being entered and Joe's papers pertaining to his FBI pension being destroyed. "Why did they do it?" I had asked Linda. Her response echoed through my mind: "Just to show him that they could."

~

The following day, Bob surprised me with a call from the airport. "Did the flowers arrive?"

"Flowers? No."

"They should be there tomorrow, brighten your day."

"Missing you already."

"You can still join me. I'll have my secretary arrange a flight."

"You know I can't." I laughed. "Got a call from the foreman of the jury this morning."

He hesitated. "Why?"

"He's going to sentencing tomorrow and wondered if I planned to go. He said that more than half of the jurors will be there."

Bob was silent.

"It will be good to see them. We'll go out for lunch, catch up on things."

"You know how I feel about it, Alex."

"I do, and I understand. I'll stay with them. It'll be okay."

"I've gotta go. The flight's boarding," he responded with abruptness.

"Okay. Have a safe flight. Call when you can," I said. But I realized, as I looked down at the phone, that he had already hung up.

Chapter 14

*Justice is justly represented blind, because she sees no
difference in the parties concerned. She has but one
scale and weight, for rich and poor, great and small.*
—William Penn (1644–1718), English
philosopher, minister, founder of
the colony of Pennsylvania

"COLORADO?" CURT JORDAN ASKED. "SHOWS OFFICER
Simpson's ignorance. The correctional facility won't be determined
until after sentencing."

"Journalists recently toured the supermax and reported that it's
not underground," Rob Willis added.

Tom caught the questioning glance Curt threw at Rob. "You don't
believe the report, do you, Curt?" Tom stated.

"A lot of different reports about the supermax in Colorado. Don't
know what to believe."

"Don't suppose it matters. If I could communicate with Kathleen—"
Tom stopped speaking as his eyes scanned the room. "If we could
communicate, I think I could handle anything."

"Speaking of Kathleen …" Curt removed a sealed white envelope from his briefcase and pushed it across the table toward Tom.
"Kathleen's attorney wanted me to give this to you. Why don't you
look at it while Rob and I take a short break."

Tom picked up the envelope and opened it as the attorneys sig-
naled for the guard to let them out of the room. The neat cursive

writing on the page within was familiar: "My dearest, I think of you continuously." It was a letter from Kathleen.

~

I walked toward the door of the courtroom, where a security guard stood. "Name?" he asked as I approached.

"Alexandra Fisher. I was a juror."

"Go to courtroom ten." He didn't even look up from the list of names before him.

"Judge Blake said the jurors would be seated in the main courtroom."

"Seems he changed his mind. Go to courtroom ten." It was clear he meant business.

As I walked down the massive hall, I spotted Pam approaching. She was with Herman Pander and Mrs. Monahan. She glanced at me, and quickly looked down. There was no hesitation with the guard, I noted, as Pam entered the main courtroom alongside them.

Entering courtroom ten, I searched for an empty seat. The room itself was identical to the main courtroom where the trial had taken place. Sitting on the hard wooden bench, I found that memories of jury selection filled my mind. Though only six months prior, it felt like a lifetime; in fact, it felt like an alternate life. Someone placed their hand on my back, distracting my thoughts. I turned as Richard slid onto the bench next to me. We exchanged a warm smile.

"Great to see you," Richard said. "Are the others here?"

"Only saw Pam."

"Where is she?" Richard was looking around.

"She got in the main courtroom with Herman Pander and Mrs. Monahan."

Richard appeared confused. "What's she doing with them?"

There was no time to respond, as just then Judge Blake appeared on the monitor at the front of the courtroom. He stated the verdict against Thomas Devaney, and announced that despite the motion made by the defense attorneys to keep certain family members of victims from making impact statements, he was going to allow it.

I squirmed at the announcement, noting that he had chosen his words carefully. No mention was made that Thomas Devaney had been acquitted of the murders these individuals would address. No explanation was given as to why he was negating the jury's verdict on these murders. Chavere and Altier had won, though I suspected it wasn't really a contest. My gut feeling was that Judge Blake had always intended to give Chavere and Altier their way. One last kick at Devaney. The same sick feeling I'd so often experienced in Judge Blake's courtroom took me by surprise; truth didn't seem to be the object in this courtroom.

Richard and I watched on the monitor as family members went to the microphone in the main courtroom, voicing their anger at Thomas Devaney. The son of David Walton gave a stirring account of his dad's life, and then described the void still felt by his violent death.

The next testimony was from the woman I'd often seen on the train with her son. Her voice was strong, with no hint of fear. She introduced herself as Lorraine, and announced that she was the daughter of Buddy Bartlett. Lorraine briefly recounted how her dad was held captive for hours before Devaney and Diavolo killed him. She explained that he had requested a picture be taken from his wallet to view one last time before he died. I recalled Ben James's testimony about taking the picture of a little girl from Bartlett's wallet. Lorraine revealed that she was the child in the picture, Buddy Bartlett's only daughter. She then did something quite extraordinary. Lorraine asked Devaney to look at her. It wasn't an angry demand, but a polite request. Devaney only glanced, and then Lorraine continued.

"Mr. Devaney, I want you to know that I forgive you. My hope is that you can seek forgiveness and salvation from the Judge of all— Jesus the Christ." Quietly, Lorraine walked away from the microphone and sat down. There was no drama, no outburst. Though the pain of her loss was apparent, her message of forgiveness was sincere.

The impact statements continued, with grown children of those murdered offering statements. Some of these were heartrending. I was moved by the distraught words of one woman as she related her horror as a child when her classmates would comment about her father's murder. Some statements bordered on the ridiculous, as the adult children of men who were murderers themselves, bemoaning all the wonderful things they would have experienced with their dads had they not been killed.

Seriously? I thought. *Those guys probably would have abandoned their families or, if their wives had any sense, been tossed out. If these men had lived, these same adult children would be telling anyone who would listen how much they hated their fathers for all the heartache they'd caused. Strange how a premature and shocking death alters the reality of the deceased's character. One who would have been despised had their life played out becomes venerated.*

Some of the impact statements unfolded like scenes from the most tasteless of reality TV shows. At one point, a brother and sister argued over who had been more important to their dear dead daddy, a man whose criminal record was about equal to Devaney's. Some of the grieving "children" lashed out with foul mouths, even attacking Devaney's brother, a once popular politician and educator in the city of Boston. The accepted story throughout Massachusetts, I had discovered, was that the younger Devaney was guilty of all sorts of imagined crimes simply because of his blood tie to the infamous Sly Devaney. It didn't matter that every accusation thrown at him by the Boston US Attorney's Office and tabloidized by the Boston newspapers always hit a brick wall.

Perhaps the most disturbing statement made against Devaney within the courtroom of Judge Peter Blake was a vile comment about Tom Devaney's young son, who had died of a rare disease many years before.

The courtroom fell silent. The venomous hatred this man, the son of a murderous criminal himself, exhibited toward a guiltless child had crossed a line. Judge Blake said nothing, allowing the memory of this innocent to be victimized and placed into the court record.

When all the bizarre drama had ended, the judge finally spoke. He asked Curt Jordan and Rob Willis if their client would like to make a statement. They answered in the negative.

Judge Blake then announced that the impact statements made in regard to the murders Devaney had been acquitted of would have no influence on his decision in sentencing.

Have no influence? I screamed within, shaking my head in open disgust.

Judge Blake recessed for lunch. Richard surprised me when he announced that he had made plans to meet someone, whom he did not identify. On the phone the day before, he'd said we would all have lunch together. Pam would, no doubt, lunch with Pander and Mrs. Monahan. I realized I was on my own.

~

Judge Blake's sentence seemed to me to be a bit of overkill. The aged Devaney would get two life sentences plus five years.

It was done. I followed the crowd out of the courtroom and into the large foyer to which all the courtrooms emptied. Journalists, like male dogs on the scent of a bitch in heat, flocked to the dubbed "dream team" of Chavere and Altier. The radiance from their gloating faces was enough to illuminate the foyer.

I spotted Richard and Pam. Richard was moving toward Pam through the throng of about two hundred. I began to follow him, but was stopped dead in my tracks by the voice of a woman shouting from the crowd.

"There she is! The bitch that defends the murderin' Devaney! How could you let him get away with killing my father? Where's my closure? Where's my justice?" It was the daughter of Billy Manning. Chavere and Altier had given the jury no information in regard to his murder.

I hadn't even had time to look at her when I spotted Herman Pander approaching. He immediately joined her protest.

"You no good piece of shit! Get out of here!"

Richard moved out of the way so Pander could pass. I glimpsed Pam's disturbed expression as she watched Pander move toward me.

"You fuckin' piece of shit!" His face was crimson; he pointed at me as he approached.

I turned to leave, already exhausted by the drama. People moved away as Pander came near. He began to circle me, screaming the same thing over and over: "You fuckin' piece of shit!"

Everyone in the foyer heard him—the guards, bailiffs, journalists, and attorneys. It was impossible not to. I spotted the dream team out of the corner of my eye. Altier was laughing. A woman moved near to Pander and watched. I recognized her from the courtroom. She was the woman who'd related her horror as a child when her classmates harassed her about her father's murder. She looked upset. I expected her to join Pander in his ranting. I also spotted Gary Dillinger, the documentary producer who had interviewed me. His face was contorted as he observed Pander circling. I moved toward the elevators. Pander followed, continuing the verbal assault. No one attempted to stop him. Finally, Chavere and Altier decided to head outside. The crowd followed, including the journalists. Pander, seemingly enjoying the lens of the camera being pointed in his direction, was quick to follow.

Gary Dillinger passed near to me and said, "Meet me out front."

Before I could utter a response, he was gone. I hesitated, stunned by the sudden silence in the foyer. Only a few lingered.

"Ms. Fischer?"

A hand touched my arm as I turned in response to hearing my name. Lorraine Bartlett, the daughter of murder victim Buddy Bartlett, was looking at me. The younger man I'd often seen her with stood by her side. I braced myself for harsh words.

"Thank you for speaking out about the government corruption— about the revictimization of the families."

I was taken aback by her unexpected gratitude. "What you said today, offering forgiveness to the man who killed your dad—it was incredible. You're amazing."

She laughed. "No, not me. Christ within me. And I realize he gave you the courage to speak up." She looked at the young man to her side. "This is my son Adam."

Adam had a kind and gentle smile.

"It's good to meet you both."

The woman who had testified about the abuse of her childhood days, the one who'd observed Pander's verbal attack against me, began to approach. Needlessly, I braced myself.

"I can't believe Herman Pander did that. I wanted to stop him, but I figured he'd make more of a scene if I did. You'd think the guards would have done something."

"Freedom of speech, I guess. Thanks for staying close," I said.

"Thanks for speaking up. The Department of Justice has raked the families through the coals. It's reassuring to hear someone stand up to them."

I said goodbye and stopped at the ladies' room before heading outside. As I turned the corner, a woman was there, leaning against the wall. She had a small pad of paper in one hand and a pen in the other. She came to attention when she saw me.

"Ms. Fischer, I'm Vickie Walsh from the *Boston Times*. I have a few questions." Her in-your-face manner was offensive. Her many years in competitive journalism had given her a masculine air.

"Not interested, Ms. Walsh."

"Have you read my book?"

"Thumbed through it."

"I suggest you read it. You're way off base in your assumptions. You need to get better grounded in facts."

"Facts?" I laughed. "Whose facts? The scuttlebutt is that there may be some assistant US attorneys with a direct line to some Boston journalists. Or is it, perhaps, that some journalists have a direct line to them?"

"What are you implying?"

"Many wonder how it is that information from federal grand jury testimonies makes it into the *Boston Times* so quickly."

"How ridiculous!" She laughed a laugh that seemed more forced than ready.

"Is it?"

"I can't help it if grand jurors want to talk."

"Grand jurors? Doubtful. It's a violation of law for them to talk. I just don't see the average citizen willing to violate the law. It seems that the journalists in Boston are getting away with it because most Americans don't understand the rules of the grand jury, or the fact that only the prosecuting attorney is present. And, tragically, it seems that those within the legal system just don't want to be bothered to take on the improprieties of the questionable ethics of prosecutors and journalists."

"I'm doing my job, and I'm good at it." Walsh seethed, her tough-broad demeanor coming through loud and clear.

"Is it your job to slowly chisel away at the rights of individuals?"

"Fischer, you're an idealistic fool!"

I looked her in the eye, refusing to let her know that the remark stung like a slap in the face. Without another word, she turned and walked away.

I picked up my cell phone at the check-in station and then took my time heading out of the courthouse, hoping public statements and interviews would be over by the time I got out front. Unfortunately, they weren't. The dream team was gone—off celebrating, I surmised. Curt Jordan and Rob Willis were finishing up an interview. Herman Pander impatiently hovered close by, eager, it seemed, for his next opportunity to get before the camera. Mrs. Monahan and her oldest daughter, her face set in stone, waited with Pander. Pam was with them. She glanced at me, and then quickly turned away as though she wanted to avoid me. I walked past them, searching the crowd for Gary Dillinger.

"What are you doing out here, you piece of shit?"

Immediately, I recognized Pander's voice; even if I hadn't, his seeming limited vocabulary would have easily identified him. I continued to walk. He continued to follow.

He must have given up hope for another camera shot from the Boston TV news channels. He probably figures that hounding me will bring the attention he craves, I thought. Without acknowledging his presence, I positioned myself away from the crowd. Pander continued to bark the same refrain as he came closer. "You fuckin' piece of shit!" He was accomplishing what he wanted, as freelance cameramen and onlookers followed. The attention made him bold. He came right up to me and stuck his face directly in front of mine, spit spraying as he again yelled, "You piece of shit!"

Two Homeland Security police officers, standing guard outside the courthouse, came over and stood on each side of me. Pander backed off. But one of his cronies stepped in front of me. "You're one of those sickos that falls in love with criminals. You wanna be Devaney's woman? What, you think there'll be a movie? You want Julia Roberts playin' your role?"

"Julia Roberts?" I smiled at him. "That's quite a compliment. Thank you."

Glaring, he backed off. Behind him stood pathetic Herman Pander, mouthing the same words over and over: "You piece of shit!"

Finally, Gary appeared with a cameraman and escorted me over to the wall of the courthouse, carefully placing me beside an engraved quote by John Adams. I quickly read it: "The dignity and stability of government in all its branches, the morals of the people, and every blessing of society depend upon an upright and skillful administration of justice."

As I turned to face the camera, Herman was standing at my side.

"You piece of shit!" He reverted to the vocabulary he knew best. "No one wants to listen to you, you fuckin' moon bat!"

The term had been used to identify me in an article by Nick Mudd. Obviously, Herman was a fan of Mudd.

"What is a moon bat?" I asked Herman with a forced smile.

"You are! Why do you feel the need to be heard, you idiot?" Herman's tone was aggressive.

The camera was rolling, but I suddenly realized that Gary was no longer there. I looked at Herman and responded.

"Because the foundational principles of our judicial system have been threatened. This court's behavior throughout the trial, and now the judge's decision to nullify the jury's verdict by allowing impact statements in regard to acquitted crimes, has brought a dark cloud over the Constitution—over the blood sacrifice made to give it to us."

"What fuckin' blood sacrifice?"

"The blood freely given by those who fought to establish this country—for the blood that is still spilled for us to keep it!"

"You're fuckin' crazy!" Pander screamed.

"If I'm crazy, then so was John Adams!" I gestured toward the engraved quote on the wall.

"I don't fuckin' care about John Adams! What's he gotta do with what's goin' on here?"

For a brief moment, I felt sorry for Herman. Though everything I had observed, everything I had heard, indicated that he was a money-hungry attention seeker, I questioned whether my attitude was wrong. *Maybe he truly is still grieving the untimely death of his sister,* I allowed myself to think.

"Herman, I truly am sorry for your loss. Carol didn't deserve what happened—"

"You're damn right. She didn't deserve to be murdered by your boyfriend, you piece of shit! No one gives a damn about John Adams or the fuckin' Constitution! This is reality!"

The cameras shot around to film Herman as though he had revealed a profound truth. And at that moment, I realized he had. Few did give a damn, and of the few who did, only a small number dared to speak out. Of those who spoke, they were labeled "nuts" or "fanatical."

On the verge of tears, I pushed through the throng of the swarming vultures. One camera was literally shoved in my face, hitting my cheek. I reached up and pushed it away. Herman Pander, the victor, could be heard triumphantly yelling after me.

"Yeah! You're not welcome here! What's wrong with you anyway, you fuckin' piece of shit!"

Dejected and stunned, I headed toward the subway station, feeling as though I was caught in a sick dream. A man's voice called out my name. Hesitantly, I turned. The man—slim, dark-haired, and middle-aged—carried a large worn leather bag over his shoulder. He was accompanied by two companions. The male companion had a video camera. It wasn't on, but still I wanted to run.

"Alex! Are you all right?" the middle-aged man asked as he came to my side. "I've never seen a juror treated like that. ...My name is Simon Cole." He paused. "I'm a friend of Joe Wallace's," he quickly said, no doubt in response to my expression. My eyes were fixated on the video camera, which rested in the arms of the male companion. "Joe said he told you about me."

I nodded, recalling what Joe had said. Simon wrote books about organized crime. He wanted to cover the corruption of the Devaney case in the book he was currently working on.

"You can't get on the subway like this, Alex. You hungry? Want something to eat?" He asked with noted concern.

I shook my head and heard myself whisper, "No."

"How about a drink?" the woman standing beside Simon asked, with a thick Irish brogue. She placed her hand on my arm.

I leaned into her and began to cry. She put her arms around me. Then placing her hand behind my back, she guided me as we began to walk.

We all ordered a drink. Simon introduced his friends, both of whom were from Ireland. They were helping him with the research on his book. We talked about the trial, about the corruption throughout. Simon asked if I was willing to be interviewed.

Chapter 15

The dignity and stability of government in all
its branches, the morals of the people, and every
blessing of society depend upon an upright
and skillful administration of justice.
—John Adams, statesman, diplomat, first
vice president and second president of the
United States of America (1735–1826)

DEATH IS INEVITABLE AND ALWAYS BRINGS WITH IT
a degree of pain. Even so, the death of a young child is never accepted.
The consuming grief for a parent, for not having been able to protect
that child, is a lifelong torture. Memories merely increase the pain.
The only escape is to force the mind to shut off the remembrance; the
alternative is utter despair.

From birth, Danny filled Tom's life with delight. In his presence,
all negativity vanished. The fact that a child could bring such absolute joy took Tom by surprise. There was nothing he wouldn't do for
Danny, if only it were in his power. Reye syndrome, with its sudden onset, rapid progression, and fatal outcome, took everyone by
surprise—the medical community, the parents, and especially the
children.

Within the four walls of the cell, Tom Devaney tried unsuccess-
fully to drive the memory of his precious little boy back into an abyss
his mind had created for its keeping. Devastation gripped him with
the vivid recollection of Danny's small lifeless body; his ashen skin

against the white sheets of the hospital bed; his mother's weeping; and his own sobs. Tom squatted in the corner of the cell in a desperate attempt to escape the perpetual surveillance of the camera and the heartless scrutiny of the guard as he grieved his son anew.

~

"My God, Alex, you're all over the news!" Nancy informed me over the phone as I drove home from the train station. "It's not flattering. Don't even bother to watch."

"I won't."

"Is Bob back from Germany yet?"

"Tomorrow."

"How about Don and I come by? We'll bring pizza."

"Thanks. I have papers to correct and am still working on the editing changes on the book. I'm all right."

"You sure?"

"Yeah."

I had a sleepless night. Upon my arrival at work the next morning, the secretary ushered me into the headmaster's office.

"Alex, I understand your passion, but—" He hesitated, looking away for a brief moment. He redirected his attention. "I heard from teachers and parents last night. Many are concerned that your zeal will draw negative attention to the school."

"My concerns about the trial have nothing to do with the school."

"You're making public statements about your opinion of the trial that you claim are historically based. As a US history teacher here, your statements reflect on the school. Hopefully all of this will quickly fade into the background—" He gazed out the window. He didn't appear hopeful at all, I noted.

"May I go?" My tone was guarded.

"Yes."

I stood to leave.

"And, Alex, there'll be no talk of this trial or any comments on the judicial system to your students."

I only stared at him, unable to speak.

"You can leave."

I empathized with the more rambunctious students, now knowing what it felt like to be admonished by the headmaster.

~

Bob's anticipated call upon his arrival home never came. I called him twice, leaving a short message each time. He didn't return the calls. I was growing alarmed and called the office to get an update on his travel status.

"He got home early. Flew in last evening," the secretary said, laughing. "He doesn't travel as easily as he used to—"

"No, I suppose he feels his age after a long trip." I pretended to laugh, wondering why, if he'd arrived home almost twenty-four hours ago, he hadn't called.

"Let me get him for you."

"Thanks, Laura."

She was back on the phone quickly. "He's busy, Alex." She sounded unsure. "He said to tell you that he'll get back to you."

"Okay." It didn't feel okay.

Hate mail poured in, and both my Facebook and website took negative, even vulgar remarks. Cars drove by the house, hesitating in front, the people inside staring through the windows.

Bob never called.

"Come on, Alex. You need to confront him!" Nancy's attempt to comfort wasn't very comfortable.

"And say what, Nan? 'Oh, Bob, I happened to notice that you don't want anything to do with me. Is there a problem?'" I forced a laugh.

"So what? You pretend you didn't have a relationship? You two had something good."

Now my laugh was real, though pained. "Something good? Obviously not!" I stood up, gathered the empty coffee mugs from the table, and opened the dishwasher to load them. "It was my fault. He was fed up with hearing about Devaney. And then the media caught the best of me after sentencing; the pictures weren't flattering—"

"Listen to yourself, Alex! 'Oh, poor Bob. It's my fault. I have opinions he doesn't approve of. I didn't look like a Victoria's Secret model in front of the cameras. I dared to express intense emotion. Poor, poor Bobby! I embarrassed him.'"

I couldn't help but laugh at Nancy's imitation of me. "Never mind not looking like a Victoria's Secret model; I looked like the bride of Frankenstein—"

"What was the last thing you said to him on the phone?" she asked.

"Made a comment about the flowers he was sending."

"No. It must have had something to do with Devaney."

I thought about it for a moment. "Told him I was meeting some of the jurors at the courthouse."

"Had you promised him you wouldn't go?" Nancy asked.

"It wasn't a promise—"

"In his mind, he was trying to shield you and you rejected his protection. Fragile male pride. I bet that's all it is."

"And he won't talk to me? I'd like to think he's more mature than that. He developed pretty thick skin being a DA and a congressman. Certainly, he'd address it."

"Don't be so sure, Alex. Maybe you should show up and force the conversation."

"Yeah, maybe. … I'll think about it."

Nancy excused herself to use the bathroom. When she returned, I handed her a sealed envelope addressed to Ilona and Charlie. "What's this?" she asked.

"Would you keep it for me? In case something happens—"

"What the hell are you talking about?" Nancy was obviously alarmed.

"It's nothing. Nothing's gonna happen, but just in case something weird does happen."

"Alex!"

"Just give it to the kids, okay?"

"Alex— " Now she seemed angry.

"It's a simple request that you'll probably never fulfill, and when we're old and gray we can read the letter together and laugh at my paranoia." I smiled.

"You're making me crazy." Nancy placed the letter in her oversized purse.

~

No one attending the board meeting of the Wounded Soldiers' Trust would have suspected the rift between Bob and me. He was cordial, as was I. A few of us walked out to our cars together. As he attempted to slip away, I followed.

"Bob," I called after him. He stopped and slowly turned to face me. "Why not just get it over with? It's childish to avoid one another."

"I, um … I didn't want to hurt you. You're right, my behavior has been childish."

I nodded. "Your silence has hurt. Not sure anything you have to say can do more damage."

He hesitated and kept his distance. "I ran into a woman I had a serious relationship with years ago. We've been talking. She said she'd like to try again. I had a lot of time to think about it when I was away. I thought I was over her."

It was all I could do to keep from lashing out. It took every ounce of strength to hold back my emotions. My response was a blank stare. He looked away. I left.

~

"Hi, Joe. Just wanted to call and wish you and Linda a happy Thanksgiving."

"Thanks, Alex, and a happy Thanksgiving to you. Do you have plans?"

"I'll be with family. What about you?"

"All the kids will be here. Hey, did you get your tickets to the screening?"

"Screening?"

"Yeah. Gary Dillinger's documentary on the trial. Can't believe you haven't received them yet: one for you, one for a companion. The premiere is in two weeks. Give Gary a call and let him know the tickets never arrived. Linda and I will meet you there. Maybe we can have dinner afterward. Make sure to check out the promo online."

When I got off the phone with Joe, I sent an email to Gary. I was surprised by how quickly he replied.

> Hey, Alex. Sorry about the mix-up. I decided to end the documentary at the verdict, so your interview was cut. Didn't think to send you a ticket. I'll get one out to you tomorrow.

I was taken aback by the message. *Wonder why he didn't say anything before this?* I thought, as I googled the title of the documentary on the computer. It immediately became apparent. A picture of Gary Dillinger with his arm around the shoulders of a beaming Herman Pander was plastered on the website, with a caption announcing that Herman would be a main focus in telling the story throughout the documentary.

The lone ticket arrived a few days later. I debated whether or not to go, dreading the thought of Herman Pander's certain verbal attack. Joe and Linda would be there; I wanted to see them. I also wanted to see Joe's and Simon Cole's interviews. But still I was unsure. Simon had emailed that he'd be calling the night before the premiere. Perhaps a conversation with him would help me decide.

When the phone rang, with an unfamiliar area code, I was certain it was Simon. I quickly picked up the phone. "Hi."

The caller hesitated. "Is Alexandra Fischer there?" It wasn't Simon.

"This is Alexandra."

"Hi. I'm Ben James. You sent me a letter a few months ago."

I didn't respond.

"You wanted to talk to me?"

I don't remember. Perhaps I did. I was willing to talk to anyone to piece the facts together immediately after the trial. I think I sent him a letter. Yeah, I sent him a letter—

"Okay," I responded, considering what I might ask him, and how to word the questions.

Ben James didn't give me time to think. "Yeah, the jury did a great job. Tommy Devaney deserved everything he got, and then some. He'll die behind bars, as he should."

The fact that James was an accessory to five murders quickly came to mind. But there was no time to comment on that, or anything, as James continued with a monologue.

"Assistant US Attorneys Chavere and Altier are skilled prosecutors and two of the most decent people you'll ever meet—"

My thoughts came to high alert as James went on and on praising Chavere and Altier. *What the hell is going on?* I wondered. My heart was pounding. *Why did he wait so long to call? Why this sickening acclaim of the prosecutors who have his balls in a vice? Are they recording this conversation? I need to end this call before I'm tricked into saying something I might regret.*

I quickly realized there was little cause for concern. James offered no opportunity for comment. *Either he's nervous or he just likes hearing his own voice. I'm happy to listen!* I thought as the monologue continued.

More than an hour passed before he tired of talking.

"Can I call you at this number if I have any questions?" I asked, needing to digest all he'd said, not that I'd ever be able to get a question uttered.

"No. No. Don't call me. I'll call you." And with that, he hung up.

I stared at the phone for a moment. "Chavere and Altier think I'm attending the premiere. They're trying to convince me that they're the good guys!" I laughed at the realization, and made the decision to go. I then put Ben James's number and name in my phone contacts. I didn't want to be surprised by a call from him again.

I went over to the desk and grabbed a notebook. Most of what James had said was part of his testimony, so no surprise. But there were a few things of interest that weren't directly tied to Devaney.

Whether or not they were true, I couldn't say, but he had no reason to voice them to me—just part of his endless chatter. I jotted them down.

> **Nick Mudd:** James and Devaney intended to kill Mudd, and they let him know. Positioned themselves across from Mudd's house intending to fire on him when he came out to his car. Never could. Mudd always brought his kids out with him, regardless of the weather. Kids never went with him; just walked him to the car.

> Mudd reported in one of his books how he had to find a different way to go to work every day so Devaney and James couldn't find him. James laughed at this comment, stating, "He's such an idiot! It doesn't matter how you get from point A to point B. We wait at either point."

"That was pretty funny," I said to myself, remembering how the comment about Mudd's ridiculous statement made me laugh.

> **Vickie Walsh:** Her father was a friend of Tom Devaney's. Tom protected him and his business from some neighborhood thugs. Vickie was embarrassed by this fact.

> Skip Goot would brag to Devaney and James about his secret romance with the newspaper journalist. Goot was single; Walsh wasn't.

"Wonder if it's even true? Who knows?" I whispered.

> **Herman Pander:** As long as Diavolo gave Pander's mother gifts, she had no problem with him, even though she believed that Diavolo killed both her

husband and Carol. Though Carol is long dead, and Diavolo was incarcerated for life, Pander still tries to draw attention to her death, and in doing so, always seems to try to make light of Diavolo's involvement.

"Why doesn't Pander hate Diavolo as much as he does Devaney? No one disputes that Diavolo lured his sister to that house to die. His hatred toward Diavolo should be fierce, but it isn't. Why isn't it?"

~

I arrived at the theater before Joe and Linda. Standing by myself in the foyer, I waited for them to arrive. Gary Dillinger passed by and mumbled a barely audible hello. *Obviously, he's uncomfortable with me being here—* Before I had time to complete my thought, Herman Pander's gutter greeting came from behind.

"What the fuck are you doing here? You have no business being here." He swung around in front of me, much too close for comfort. "You're a fuckin' piece of shit."

Some things just never change, I realized.

Pander's face was suddenly up against mine; his spittle landing on my lips and cheeks. He placed his hands on my upper arms.

"If you don't let go of me and move back, I'll scream for the police." There was an officer across the lobby.

"I dare ya, ya fuckin' bitch," he bravely uttered as he immediately let go and backed away.

Dare me? I thought. *God, this man is an imbecile!* My body was trembling.

"I'm the one that needs to get the cop to throw you out!" he growled. Then he turned and actually motioned for the officer.

"Herman! Leave her alone!" It was Lorraine Bartlett, the daughter of murder victim Buddy Bartlett. She firmly took hold of my arm and directed me over by the police officer. He obviously hadn't seen Pander motion for him, or maybe he'd just ignored him.

"Let's stay clear of him. Are you alone?" she asked.

"Waiting for a couple of friends," I replied. "Are you alone?"

"Yes. Invited at the last minute, as most of the families were. I wasn't gonna come. Probably shouldn't have."

"Invited at the last minute? Aren't the families interviewed in the film?" I remembered that Dillinger told me that they would be.

"We were all interviewed, but they're only showing Herman, Mrs. Monahan, and one of her daughters."

When Joe and Linda arrived, I asked Lorraine to sit with us. She declined and said she would sit with other family members.

Joe sat between Linda and me in the theater. Shortly after we were seated, he told me that Chavere was threatening him with an indictment for perjury during his testimony in the trial.

"Perjury?" I was stunned.

"Yeah. Not in regard to anything I said about Devaney stating that he wasn't an informant, or about my trying to get headquarters to make him a target. Hell, it's not even about my stating that Ed O'Leary was basically draped in a bull's-eye when no one within the DOJ would grant him protection from Devaney. That's all true and can easily be proven. They'd never risk bringing it out in the open. So they needed to find another way to discredit me." It was evident that Joe was upset; Linda too.

"What are they saying you lied about?" I asked.

Joe didn't answer. Linda placed her hand on his and leaned toward me to talk.

"They're saying that he lied about his prior service in the FBI, saying he had no part in cases in which he claimed to be involved."

"How can they do that? It's documented, isn't it?" I asked.

"Yeah. It is," Joe said with what seemed to be a forced smile. He took hold of Linda's hand and squeezed it. "It's just a ploy to aggravate me."

"Is Chavere here?" I asked, looking around. I had seen Curt Jordan and Rob Willis in the lobby. They'd both acknowledged me with a nod.

"Chavere isn't, but I saw Altier. His last hurrah before leaving the US Attorney's Office," Joe stated with noted contempt, nodding toward Altier, who, for some reason was standing on the stage.

"Altier's leaving?"

"Yeah. Decided he wants to be a defense attorney. Expects to make big money with the Devaney trial under his belt."

"I wish Chavere would go with him," I stated, glaring at Altier.

"Chavere would never leave the DOJ. She's attained too much power. From what I've heard, although she doesn't hold the office of US attorney for Massachusetts, she tells him what to do. And it's rumored that she has profound influence over many of the state's federal judges as well."

The documentary began. We watched. Joe's and Simon's interviews were powerful. Dillinger brought up many questions about the government corruption surrounding and influencing Devaney's case, and the media bias in support of the government. I felt the questions would have had a greater impact if Herman Pander hadn't appeared. His every sentence, laced with vulgarities, seemed to contradict what Dillinger attempted to establish in regard to the corruption.

Immediately following the documentary, the audience was allowed to ask questions of a panel. Included on the panel was Assistant US Attorney Dick Altier. I got up from my seat and took my place in line.

"My question is for Attorney Altier," I said into the microphone. "Why didn't the US Attorney's Office accept Thomas Devaney's pleading of guilt to all charges and his willingness to accept any punishment given, including an expedited death sentence?"

Altier glared at me. "I will not answer to a juror!" he yelled.

"If not to a juror, who lost ten weeks of her life to sit on a trial you prosecuted, one that may not have been needed had the defendant's right to plead out been respected, then for whom will you answer the question?"

"I will not respond to her!" Altier shouted.

The microphone was taken from my hand, and I was guided out of the theater by an usher.

~

"Is Charlie already home?" Nancy asked, spotting the telltale laundry bag in front of the laundry room door.

"Yeah. This afternoon."

"It'll be good for you to have company. Don and I went to Ronald's Christmas party last night. The first of many. Let the madness begin."

I smiled, having experienced one of Ronald Deegan's soirees. As owner of the most prestigious public relations firm in New England, his social gatherings were over the top.

"Bob Costa was there." Nancy was waiting for my response. I disappointed her. "Aren't you curious?"

"No."

"He was alone."

I shrugged, though my heart began to race. "So?"

"Don said he's been alone at all the social functions he's attended." Nancy was annoyed by my seeming lack of interest. "Alex! Don't you think it's strange?"

"I'm trying not to think about it at all," I lied as my thoughts began racing. *He's always alone? Maybe he broke it off with the other woman. Maybe he's hoping I'll be at some of these functions. Maybe I should call—*

"No feelings?" Nancy asked, unaware of my struggle within.

I turned away from her gaze. "Too many feelings. That's the problem." I walked to the counter. "Want some coffee?"

She ignored my question. "I don't think he's seeing anyone. I think he made up that story."

I faced her. "And why would he?" I asked with a forced smile.

"Your communication with Devaney. Bob had to put some distance between you to protect his political reputation."

"He's out of politics."

"Once a politician, always a politician."

"So, he plunged a knife through my heart with his story of reuniting with his long-lost love to chase me off and save his political reputation?" I brought the two mugs of coffee to the table and sat down across from Nancy, holding her under a steady gaze. "Whatever it was between us—and obviously, it wasn't much—it's over."

She didn't respond. "What's this?" She thumbed through a pile of stapled pages on the table.

"I sent for the Senate hearing on the MKULTRA experiment. It came yesterday. Nan, you won't believe what they did."

"M-K what?" Nancy asked, as she pushed the papers toward me and took a sip of her coffee.

"The CIA's secret testing of LSD and other drugs."

She shook her head, indicating that she didn't know what I was talking about.

"They experimented on more than a thousand military personnel around the time of the Korean and the Vietnam Conflicts. The experimentation was done without the soldiers' full understanding. There were no records, so there was no way to prove it happened, and no recourse for physical and mental damage."

"I'm sure they had veterans' benefits," she said almost pitilessly.

"No proof the damage happened in the military. No proof, no coverage. Can you imagine how many families were destroyed by the effects of these drugs?"

Nancy shook her head, looking a bit more interested.

"It didn't end there. They tested their drugs in twelve American hospitals, at least three prisons, and at forty-four colleges."

"What was the reason?"

"Behavior modification."

"Why?"

"The CIA claimed that the Soviets and Chinese already had methods of altering human behavior, and that the United States needed to understand what they were," I said, then took a sip of coffee.

"So, they used people as guinea pigs?"

"Not the first time the U.S. government used its own citizens like lab rats. In the 1940's 60,000 military personnel were used to test the effects of lewisite and mustard gas. After World War II tens of thousands of military personnel were purposely exposed to radioactive fallout without their consent." I put the mug down on the table before me. "There's reference in the MKULTRA Senate hearing to the LSD and other drugs being used to develop homicidal tendencies."

"Homicidal tendencies? Making people murder?" Now I had her full attention.

"Yeah. Attempting to make killers out of unsuspecting human guinea pigs." I felt my cheeks burn as the blood raced to my face.

"They admitted that in the hearing?" she asked.

I pushed the stapled pages back toward her.

"Project MKULTRA, the CIA's Program of Research in Behavioral Modification." She looked up at me inquisitively after reading the title, and then looked back down and continued reading. "Wednesday, August 3, 1977, US Senate Select Committee on Intelligence and Subcommittee on Health and Scientific Research of the Committee on Human Resources, Washington, DC."

"Go to page thirty-four. I have it marked," I instructed.

Senator Huddleston: Was there any evidence or any indication that there were other motives that the [Central Intelligence] Agency might also be looking for drugs that could be applied for other purposes, such as debilitating an individual or even killing another person? Was this part of this kind of experimentation?

Admiral Turner: Yes; I think there is. I have not seen in this series of documentation evidence of desire to kill, but I think the project turned its character from a defensive to an offensive one as it went along, and there certainly was an intention here to develop drugs that could be of use.

Senator Huddleston: The project continued for some time after it was learned that, in fact, foreign powers did not have such a drug as was at first feared, didn't it?

Admiral Turner: That is my understanding. Yes, sir.

> **Senator Huddleston:** Is there any indication that knowledge gained as a result of these experiments has been useful or is being applied in any way to present operations?

> **Mr. Brody:** Senator, I am not sure if there is any body of knowledge. A great deal of what there was, I gather, was destroyed in 1973.

Nancy finished reading and let the stapled pages fall from her hand. She was silent as her eyes remained fixed on the papers.

"It seems to me that the first place they'd attempt that particular experiment would be in the prisons," I said.

Nancy looked up at me. "Devaney?"

"He was in prison for robbery, in his midtwenties at the time. Had never committed a murder."

She picked up the pages. Her eyes scanned the printed testimony.

"Another well-known murderer was also involved in MKULTRA," I offered.

Her eyes darted up questioningly.

"Ted Kaczynski, the Unabomber. He was exposed to it as an undergrad at Harvard."

"Harvard?"

I nodded. "The scientist conducting the experiments worked for the Office of Strategic Services. OSS became the Central Intelligence Agency."

"This was as bad as the Nazi experimentation on prisoners," Nancy said, perusing the entire Senate document. "Senator Ted Kennedy was on this committee."

I acknowledged her statements with a nod. "And the question is, if Devaney was given experimental drugs that altered his behavior, causing him to murder, is he responsible for those murders?"

"And the Unabomber?"

"Right."

"If the records were destroyed, you have no way to prove it," Nancy stated.

"A couple of sentences out of that hearing," I said, pointing to the booklet.

Nancy looked up at me, clearly upset. "Alex, Devaney and Kaczynski were the same age as Billy and Charlie when this was done to them," she said, referring respectively to her son and mine.

I nodded.

"The government robbed them of their lives."

I nodded again. "Them, and at least a thousand military personal, and who knows how many others that were used in the hospitals, universities, and prisons.

"Why didn't Devaney's attorneys use it as a defense?" she asked.

"Maybe they didn't know about the Senate hearing. I mailed a copy to them." I paused for a moment, not sure if I should continue. "Devaney sent me a couple of forms to apply for clearance to visit him. Would you be interested in going with me?"

"Are you serious, Alex? It's one thing to write him, quite another to visit."

"Every letter between us is probably read and copied. It would be much easier to speak face-to-face." I hesitated. "He doesn't think I should come alone."

"I'll talk to Don, see what he thinks," Nancy offered.

~

Being summoned to the headmaster's office was becoming a common occurrence. My lesson plans were scrutinized, my every word within the classroom seemingly known as soon as it was uttered. My growing paranoia about being called to the carpet hindered my creativity and joy of teaching. It was apparent that I was losing the interest of my students, and I was determined not to let that happen.

When immediately directed to the headmaster's office upon walking through the front door, I knew I was in trouble, and I knew why. What I didn't expect was to see the faces of five parents; Marjorie Peters, the assistant headmaster; and Connor Hale, the school psychologist. Their chairs formed a semicircle in front of the headmaster's desk. I stood awkwardly in the center; there was no chair for me.

"Mrs. Fischer, you know everyone present." The headmaster's tone was guarded.

I nodded. All eyes, except those of Connor, were fixed on my person. I suddenly felt exposed, like a slave being stripped for a lashing.

"We have received complaints from parents; only a few are now represented," the headmaster said. "Students have reported to their parents that you are fabricating stories about the CIA and FBI."

"Did the students actually say I was fabricating the stories?" I looked at the faces of each parent as I spoke.

"Whether or not they did, the fact is that you are!" one mother curtly responded.

"The stories are not fabricated. The information is documented in congressional records," I said directly to the headmaster.

"You were hired to teach American history," he began.

"The MKULTRA experimentation by the CIA, and the FBI's part in knowingly imprisoning four innocent men to protect their murderous informant, is, tragically, American history."

"That is highly debatable, Mrs. Fischer," Marjorie piped in angrily.

"It's documented in congressional records," I repeated with frustration. "I have them in my classroom. Let me get them."

"No. In fact, as of this moment, you are on medical leave—"

"Medical leave?" I felt certain I'd misheard.

"Yes. The stress of your husband's death, coupled with the gruesome trial you recently endured, has had an effect—"

"Have I been diagnosed without being examined?" I looked straight at Connor. He avoided my glare. "And now with this unethical practice of psychology, my diagnosis is being publicly declared. Isn't this a violation of HIPAA?"

"Enough, Mrs. Fischer!" the headmaster commanded. "You are on paid medical leave for twelve weeks. You will be expected to see an appointed psychologist during that time. Upon completion of your treatment, it will be determined whether or not you will continue teaching at the academy."

"Behavior modification," I murmured with a forced laugh.

"What are you talking about?" One of the parents scoffed.

"You don't approve of the way I'm behaving, and you want to modify that behavior."

"And there's nothing wrong with that," Marjorie interjected.

"I'm not a threat to myself or anyone else—"

"We disagree," another parent interrupted.

"The reality of how far our government has fallen from the foundational principles isn't a threat, but my teaching about it is?" I studied each face. No one responded. "I'll gather my things," I surrendered with utter disgust.

"No. I'll have your personal items sent to you. Please, let me escort you out," the headmaster said as he moved around his desk toward me.

"May I escort her, sir?" Connor spoke for the first time.

"Of course."

We walked in silence to my car.

"I had nothing to do with this, Alex," Connor finally uttered.

"Perhaps not, Connor. But did you do anything to stop it?"

"You know I did."

I turned to face him, desperately wanting to believe him. "Thanks, Connor."

He opened the car door. "I'll call you. We'll get together."

"Okay." Tears began to pool in my eyes as I climbed into the car. "I appreciate your friendship."

~

My correspondence with Tom Devaney continued. Whenever he seemed to settle into a prison, he'd suddenly be transferred. His health was deteriorating, and though his hip had been causing excruciating pain due to his frequent falls from the bed during MKULTRA-induced flashbacks, nothing was being done to determine if the hip was damaged, not even an x-ray. Instead, he was confined to a wheelchair. Though frustrated by his inability to walk, he explained that his poor health, in all likelihood, would keep him out of the Colorado supermax prison.

His sense of humor came through as he told me how he'd wheel himself out to the prison yard every day. Now imprisoned in Florida, he found that there was often an electrical storm after he managed to get outside.

"I can see the headline in the Boston papers," he wrote. "'Sly Devaney Killed by God When Lightning Struck His Metal Wheelchair!'"

I offered ideas of how to ground the wheelchair, and wondered why the ACLU wasn't protecting the basic rights to medical care for prisoners.

Tom's main concern was Kathleen's well-being. The US Attorney's Office in Boston had been making life as miserable for her as possible. I suspected it was Chavere's way of tormenting Devaney. It was working.

Kathleen's trial, which occurred months before Tom's, was, like his, a blatant mockery of justice. Her sentencing was even more so. Just as Judge Blake had shamelessly allowed impact statements in regard to murders of which Devaney had been acquitted by a jury, the judge in Kathleen's sentencing allowed impact statements in regard to all the murders Devaney had been accused of, but not tried for, at that time, murders that Kathleen had nothing to do with and was not charged with!

Her crime? Harboring the man she loved. Had they been husband and wife, there would not have been any charges. Her knowledge of his crimes? Limited at the time. The extent of Tom Devaney's criminal activity was not revealed until Chavere offered Giuda, James, and Diavolo a prison pass in exchange for their stories. Even at that, how much of it was true?

Kathleen had no prior charges whatsoever. She'd supported herself as a nurse, paid her taxes, cared for her family and friends, was kind to her neighbors, colleagues, and patients, and minded her own business. Given Kathleen's background, the probation department recommended two years in a low-security prison.

Chavere and Altier were livid, pressing the judge for eight years in maximum security, with the first year being in solitary confinement.

Part of Kathleen's sentencing was the stipulation that she sell her home as payment of the steep fines put upon her. Furthermore, she could never promote her story for financial gain. Giuda, Diavolo, and James could make hefty profits in the telling of their gruesome stories. Diavolo was even forgiven his fines and had millions of tainted dollars returned to him. But not Kathleen. It was determined by the court that she would have nothing when released from prison.

Chapter 16

Justice will not be served until those who are
unaffected are as outraged as those who are.
—Benjamin Franklin (1706–1790),
statesman, diplomat, author, scientist

A TROPICAL VACATION FOR MOST COUPLES INCLUDES partaking of the rich nightlife of the islands. Gambling, dancing, drinking, and the general frolicking that goes with it are part of the experience. Not so for Tom Devaney and Kathleen Mercer. Certainly, their need to be incognito was a good reason why. But it was more than that. They simply had no interest.

As the parties around them wore on into the wee hours of the morning, Tom and Kathleen would purchase large bags of cat food and seek out the many ferals, whose lineages went back to the abandoned cats of former tourists.

"It's time to head over to the hotel, Kathleen. You'll need to put the kitten down."

"It's so young, Tom. Not wild yet. Can't we take it back and see if someone wants it? The young girl who cleans our room—I bet she'd love to take it as a pet."

Tom smiled softly as he recalled the scene while lying on the bed in his prison cell. He could never say no to his Kathleen.

Thank God, she gets to spend time with the dogs, he thought. Kathleen had recently informed Tom that she'd been approved to take part in a prison program that trained dogs to serve as companions for individuals with disabilities.

~

"Hi. It's Alex. Got your message to call," I said when Simon answered the phone.

"Thanks, Alex. Moving forward on the book. Have a couple of things to clarify."

"Okay."

"Before we go there, did you hear that Joe Wallace was indicted today?"

"No. I can't believe this. Aren't there documented records of his service?"

"Joe claims that his records seem to get mysteriously altered, or just disappear altogether," Simon explained.

"Other agents can attest to his role," I argued.

"Let's hope they do, but don't forget the FBI's motto."

"'Fidelity, Bravery, Integrity'?" I had recently seen it on their website.

Simon laughed. "Hell no. *Don't Embarrass the Bureau.* Look it up. An interesting read."

~

"I had my first mandatory therapy session today," I told Nancy after the hostess seated us for lunch.

"And?" She looked apprehensive.

"And they didn't do a good job in shopping for the therapist." I picked up the menu.

"What do you mean?"

I continued to scan the menu. "Betsy is an older woman with many years' experience."

"Sounds to me like they put time into finding her," Nancy disagreed.

I put the menu down and looked at her. "She's from the Midwest. Her husband was a chaplain in the military, and recently passed on. She moved here to be closer to her daughter and grandkids."

"I don't get it. What does any of that matter?" Nancy asked.

"She and I have a lot of common ground, including the fact that she had no more knowledge of Tom Devaney before today than I had before the trial."

We shifted our attention to the waitress and gave her our order.

"Many outside of Massachusetts know little about Devaney. They haven't been pulled into the 'Old Harbor Gang cult' through the media frenzy and Nick Mudd's sick glamorization of Diavolo and Giuda in order to sell books. They haven't bought Ken Arnold's lies in *Devil's Town*, or Vickie Walsh's seemingly shared obsession with Chavere to dictate their version to the masses."

Nancy held me under a steady gaze without saying a word. She appeared confused by what I was saying.

"Nan, she said that what I'm experiencing is to be expected in light of who I was coming into the trial and what the trial revealed. She likened it to witnessing a violent crime and having no one believe that I saw what I did."

"So, will you keep seeing her?" Nancy asked.

"Yeah, she was a comfort. I need to work through the emotions of all this—I know that. But I'll be seeing her on my own, not through the academy."

"I thought they intended to cover sessions for three months?"

"They did. But, as Betsy pointed out, they expect me to return as though the trial experience never happened." I looked at Nancy as a tear spilled from my eye. "But it did happen." I wiped the tear. "And I'm forever changed. I'm not the same person. I'm not the same teacher. I can't teach US history and lie through omission. My students, our children, our grandchildren, they're the ones inheriting the corruption that our generation and the ones before us failed to keep in check. They need to be informed if there's any hope of them inheriting a free nation."

Nancy reached over and grabbed my hand, squeezing it tightly. "I came here planning to tell you that Don doesn't want me going with you to visit Tom Devaney. But I intend to be by the side of my best friend. Don can just deal with it."

~

Nancy offered to drive the rental car from the hotel to the prison. I was grateful. My stomach was in knots. While driving into the sparsely populated Florida countryside, occupied, so it seemed, only by roaming cattle, I became uncertain of what I was attempting to do. I couldn't make sense of what would drive me to this place. I was anxious. Certainly, Nancy guessed it from my frequent trips to the bathroom since we'd arrived in Florida.

I'm crazy. I've gotta be crazy. Devaney's a murderer. Whatever the government did wrong, the bottom line is that Devaney's a cold-blooded killer. I looked over at Nancy. She glanced back. I turned away, staring out the window.

Mom and the family have distanced themselves. Bob lied to get away from me. I lost my job, and Connor, a damned psychologist, won't even return my calls. What the hell am I doing here?

I looked back at Nancy. *What am I doing dragging her into this? Don doesn't want her here, and rightfully so.* A violent chill ran through my body.

Nancy appeared alarmed after glancing at me again. "Alex, you're white as a ghost."

"Pull over. I'm gonna be sick."

She jerked the car to the side of the road. I got out just in time. Nancy came to my side with a tissue and my phone in her hands.

"Let's head back," I said, doubled over. She handed me the tissue.

"Okay. We can do that," she agreed, leaning against the car. "Stand here for a few minutes. Let your stomach settle. Want some water?"

I shook my head as I moved next to her. The sun's warmth felt good against my skin.

"Here." She held the phone out toward me. "It buzzed. I think you have a text. Could be one of your kids."

My hand was trembling as I took the phone. The text wasn't from either of my children, but from Simon Cole. It was a picture of the front page of the *Boston Times*, with former FBI assistant special agent in charge Joseph Wallace in handcuffs. He was facing a trial on four counts of perjury. Chavere was the prosecuting attorney.

"Would you please read this to me?" I handed Nancy the phone.

When she finished the article, I took a deep breath and exhaled slowly. "I'm okay now. Let's keep going." The news of Joe's ordeal hit me like a hard slap to the face.

~

The exterior of the prison appeared sanitized with its whitewashed concrete walls and sparkling glass entry door. Even the reception area, to my surprise, was bright and lively. The guards who greeted us seemed genuinely friendly as they patiently assisted us in checking in. Not much needed to be done, as all our paperwork had already been sent and approved. Though the necessary precautions were taken of scanning our bodies and subjecting us to a general pat-down, they did it as quickly as possible.

There were about twelve visitors waiting to enter the complex. We were called forward one at a time to have our hands stamped with invisible ink. Before we could move into a holding room, our stamped hands were scanned. When it was time to leave the reception building, a massive metal door slowly clattered open and stopped with a harsh bang. We followed a guard through the door to the outside. This open area, about half the size of a football field, was enclosed by similar whitewashed concrete walls, about twelve feet high and two feet thick, with electrified barbed wire above. Massive rolls of thick razor wire were strategically placed near the base of the walls.

"Don't think anyone's getting out of here without permission," Nancy whispered.

"Don't they usually go underground?" I asked.

Nancy shrugged. Both of us were totally out of our element.

We were led across the courtyard to another building. The thick iron door struggled to slide open. We were instructed to enter a small rectangular room revealed behind the now open door. Once we were inside the room, the massive piece of iron clanged shut just as another one clattered open. Beyond the now open door was an immense room. We stepped into it as the door banged closed behind us, seeming to echo throughout the room. Nancy and I shared a glance as we simultaneously crossed our arms across our chests. It was an instinctive response to our discomfort when faced with both the situation and the cold.

"It's freezing in here," Nancy murmured. Goose bumps covered our skin. Each of us was dressed in cropped pants, a short-sleeve shirt, and sandals. "I don't think it's even sixty degrees," she added.

Rows of attached plastic chairs lined the room. Each row faced another, separated by about five feet. To the far wall were various vending machines and a microwave. To our left was the guards' desk. I counted seven guards present, noting that each of them had on a warm jacket. To the right was a door where prisoners came through into the visiting area. Each prisoner had to report to the desk before greeting his guests.

"These ladies are here to visit Thomas Devaney," the guard who brought us in told another guard at the desk, handing him paperwork.

"I'll call for someone to get him," the guard at the desk responded.

"Follow me," the first guard said. I was certain he would lead us to the secure visiting area, separating us from Devaney with a fiberglass barrier.

"It's probably best to sit here." He stopped at the end of a row of chairs. "Devaney's in a wheelchair. It'll be easier for him to be on the end." With that, he walked away.

Nancy and I looked at one another. "He's gonna be right here?" she asked. Now her face was white. "Jesus, Alex!"

"There are seven guards present," I pointed out.

"And you think that's enough?"

I couldn't help but laugh at her expression. "We're his friends."

"I can't believe you just said that. You may be his friend. I'm just here because ... oh my God, here he comes!" she softly squealed, slumping down a bit in her chair.

Tom wheeled himself to the desk and then looked in our direction. I stood to greet him. Nancy hesitantly followed my lead.

"Hi, Tom." I extended my hand to him. "This is my friend Nancy." Tom held his hand out to her.

"They keep it rather cold in here," I said, awkwardly starting the conversation.

"Cold throughout the prison. Fifty-eight degrees."

I glanced at Nancy. She was right on about the temperature. "The kids must be freezing." The three of us scanned the room. There were probably two dozen babies, toddlers, and preschoolers visiting their fathers. No older children were present, which I found odd.

"I hate to see them here," Tom said as he smiled and waved to a little boy near to us. "It's terrible that they can only have brief visits with their dads. These guys are in for quite a few years. Really tears the kids up when they have to say goodbye."

"So, Tom," Nancy began. I was shocked that she was addressing him so soon. "Do you think you'll be staying here until ...until ...you know what I mean." She became flustered and turned red in the face. I had no idea what she meant, but Tom did. He began to laugh.

"Do you mean am I gonna stay here 'til I croak?"

"I'm sorry, Tom! I didn't know how to say it."

Now I was laughing too.

"Yeah, I'll probably die here. Not a bad prison as far as prisons go."

"I shouldn't have asked." Nancy was still red.

"Ah, don't worry. One of the jurors said in an interview that I should die behind bars." He pointed at me and smiled.

I laughed. "And you still wrote to me."

From there, the conversation flowed. Reminiscing about our home state of Massachusetts led to local politics. Occasionally the conversation would ebb as Tom stopped to play peekaboo with a passing child.

We wandered onto a variety of subjects, including the trial and Tom's concern for Kathleen. He even shared disturbing stories of his criminality, and his former friendship with Giuda, Diavolo, and James. It was apparent that their betrayal wore heavily upon him. His experiences in prison were discussed, from the kindness of certain prison guards to the inhumanity of others, and the changes he'd observed since his incarceration sixty years prior.

"Back then, there was more structure. More discipline. We couldn't have radios or TVs blaring at all hours of the day and night. Anything we did watch was controlled. One movie a week. The old classics, with Walter Cronkite's news segment. Do you remember that?"

We both nodded. It was a memory from childhood.

"There was more solitude then, not the constant chaos of today's prisons. They can watch and listen to anything. Most of what I hear them listening to incites anger. Does nothing for rehabilitation."

He discussed other changes in the prison, including the opportunity to volunteer for medical studies.

"Years ago, you could volunteer. I remember volunteering for an experiment to find a cure for pertussis," he told us.

"Pertussis. That's whooping cough, right?" Nancy asked. "I remember my kids getting that vaccine. Made them pretty sick, as I recall."

"Made me pretty sick too," Tom said with a laugh. "It was awful. I'll never forget. It felt like they were injecting lava into my vein. My body was on fire for days."

"Why did you do it?" I asked.

"Quite a few of us did. We got a reduction in our sentences and were usually treated better by the guards for volunteering. But it was more than that for most of us. Strange as it may sound, there was a strong sense of patriotism among most of the prisoners then. We liked watching Walter Cronkite," he said with a laugh. "Wanted to feel like we were doing something to help America. Figured that volunteering for a way to prevent pertussis was helping the kids. Back then, a lot of kids died of whooping cough."

"So, with the pertussis experimentation you knew exactly what you were volunteering for?" I asked.

"Yeah, they told us up front what might happen. Even warned us we might die."

"And what about MKULTRA?" I questioned, already knowing the answer.

He shook his head and gazed beyond us. "No. We were lied to. Guys in suit coats—should've known something was off just because of that—told us they were looking for a cure for schizophrenia. Nineteen of us volunteered. We never had a clue of what they were really doing."

"Tom, did MKULTRA change you?" Nancy asked.

He nodded his head slowly. "Hallucinations. Insomnia."

"Beyond that. Did it change who you are?" I asked, leaning forward.

He nodded again, and continued to gaze beyond us. "Yeah. It changed me."

"Did you consider killing anyone before MKULTRA?" I queried further.

He considered the question, still staring at nothing in particular, as though trying to avoid the memories. After a moment, he looked at me. "When I was about fourteen, a South Boston cop gave me a brutal beating. I hadn't done anything; he just wanted to scare the neighborhood kids and used me to do it. I was enraged. Hated the guy." Tom paused for a moment. "At the time, I wanted him to die. Never fantasized about it or planned it. Forgot about him as time went on."

"You never seriously considered killing anyone before MKULTRA?" Nancy asked.

Tom shook his head. "No." He paused and looked over at the little boy and waved, a ready smile coming to his face. "Those are dark memories. There were two prisoners I was friendly with. Can't remember their names. They were involved in the experiment. Decent guys. Young guys. Not even twenty. One day they were in the room being injected with the drugs alongside me." He looked back at the toddler and smiled. It was a sad smile. "They were there, and then they were gone. I don't know if they died or went crazy. They just disappeared. It's always bothered me that I can't remember their names."

Nancy and I shared a sad glance. I noted that her eyes were moist.

"I'm gonna go back out and try to warm up," Nancy announced. We watched in silence as she walked toward the guard.

"Alex," Tom began, still watching Nancy, "how much do you know about Skip Goot?"

"Not much. FBI agent that you were able to corrupt."

Tom smiled as he perused the room. It made me uncomfortable. "I was a master at corrupting the incorruptible. And here's the secret, Alex. Money is more addicting than heroin. Once a person decides they want it, they must have more."

I chose to ignore Tom's statement and continued. "Goot stood trial in Arizona and was found guilty of being an accomplice in the murder of Paul Scalise. Goot is serving a fifty-year sentence, while Vinnie Giuda, the man who actually killed his best friend, Paul, served less than six months for his murder."

"Do you know what the Arizona jury actually got Goot on?" Tom asked.

"No."

"He was found guilty of carrying a firearm when the murder was committed."

"I don't understand. Was he in Arizona?"

"He was in Boston."

"Wasn't he an FBI agent at the time of Scalise's murder?"

Tom nodded, still scanning the room.

"Are you telling me that he was found guilty because he was carrying the firearm the FBI assigned him when Scalise was murdered more than two thousand miles away?"

"That's what I'm telling you."

"Was he involved in the murder?"

"No. Vinnie Giuda carried out the Walton and Scalise murders on his own. Think about it, Alex." He leaned forward in his wheelchair, his eyes fixed on mine. "I earned the reputation I had by being careful. Careful to a fault. The crimes I was involved in only involved the criminal element. I had no interest in going after honest businessmen like David Walton. And when Vinnie asked me if I'd take part in the murder, I said no way." He sat back in the wheelchair and watched with a smile as two small children ran toward the back of the room.

"For Walton's murder, Giuda had the guns shipped on a Greyhound bus, for Christ's sake," he began, still smiling as he watched the mother of the children try to rein them in. "Anyone who knows me knows I'd never be that sloppy. I would've driven to Kentucky with the weapons in a hidden compartment. I'd have taken them myself. Followed every traffic law so I wouldn't get stopped. Sending them on a Greyhound bus? Jesus!"

He looked at me again. "And then, Vinnie had to kill Scalise because he knew Scalise would spill his guts when the cops asked him about Walton's murder."

"So, how did a jury ever convict Skip Goot when he was more than two thousand miles away?"

"One word: Chavere."

"Wasn't it an Arizona trial? Chavere's a federal prosecutor. It was out of her jurisdiction."

"You know too much, Alex. That's why you're in this mess." He held me under a steady gaze. "Most Americans are ignorant. Most are content to be ignorant."

"Chavere wanted to silence Goot?"

Tom looked around the room again. "She certainly did. She managed to be part of the prosecution team, a federal attorney assisting in the trial of a state case. All the same circus clowns performed under her direction: Giuda, Diavolo, James, and Arnold. It was the dress rehearsal."

"Has Goot appealed?"

Tom nodded. "Denied. He'll keep appealing. He can't accept that he's gonna die in jail. If by some miracle he gets out—"he hesitated and looked at me again—"I believe Chavere will make certain he doesn't live long enough to be a threat."

"Do you correspond with Goot?"

Tom laughed. "Hell no! I detest the man."

Tom sensed my confusion.

"Goot knows I was never an informant. I bought information. I never sold it. Until the trial, I had no knowledge of Tony being an informant, or that there was an informant file associated with me. No idea." Tom looked away. His expression revealed a controlled anger. "They've used this lie to harm Kathleen and my family."

He was silent for a moment. "Alex, there are three things I long to see before I die. First, I want to see Kathleen released from prison. Second, I want to be exonerated for the murders of Carol Pander and Sandra Ford. And third, I want a public statement from Goot that the so-called informant file was created by him and Ken Arnold. With that, I'll die in relative peace. Then, I'll wait in hell for Chavere's arrival."

~

My introductory letter to Skip Goot contained an article I'd submitted to numerous Massachusetts newspapers concerning the upcoming Hollywood movie based on the book *Devil's Town*. In the article, I defended Goot's innocence of the Walton and Scalise murders.

The leading role in the movie was to be played by one of Hollywood's finest: Jonathan Height. He would take on the role of Tom Devaney. I read somewhere that Jonathan Height took his roles seriously, often meeting the character he was to portray in person and spending time with them. Yet he'd never attempted to visit Tom Devaney—never even wrote.

Goot responded to my letter, and our correspondence began. Our communications were short and to the point. I continuously urged him to tell the truth about the phony informant file. He never admitted the file was phony, but neither did he deny it. Instead, he would assure me that once he was released, he would "tell the entire, unvarnished truth."

Tom's right, I thought. *Goot won't accept that he'll die in prison.*

~

Kathleen was brought from a prison in Minnesota to Rhode Island, to appear before a grand jury. Chavere wanted to know where the remainder of Thomas Devaney's money was. Kathleen stated that she had no knowledge of any money other than the $800,000 confiscated when they were arrested. Chavere didn't believe her, and encouraged the federal court to attach eighteen more months to her already extreme sentence.

Tom's distress came through in his letters. "If I had more money, I'd gladly give it to Chavere so she'll stop going after Kathleen. Her freedom is more important than my life. Why would I hold money back and let them keep her in prison longer?"

But it seemed Chavere didn't care that Kathleen's prison sentence was beyond the pale. It appeared that she cared only about taking advantage of loopholes in the law and, seemingly, influencing the judge to further the torture of Devaney.

At times, the news of what occurred in the closed sessions of the grand jury hearings were regurgitated in the Boston newspapers. And no one asked how that could be. With all of the prestigious institutions of higher learning in Boston, not one law, history, or journalism professor asked how it was that information from a federal grand jury hearing was being published, sometimes within twenty-four hours of the hearing. No one within the legal system asked. No one said a thing. Chavere seemed unstoppable.

~

The summer breeze off Smith Cove in Gloucester's inner harbor was refreshing. The sun was gently setting, and the change in temperature was welcome. Nancy and I waited patiently for Don to arrive before we ordered dinner. Neither of us was bashful about asking for another glass of wine from the waitress. Just as it arrived, Don did—with Bob Costa at his side.

"Well, this is awkward," I said, turning a glare on Nancy.

She leaned toward me and whispered, "I didn't know."

"She's telling the truth," Bob began as he sat across from me. "Don and I attended a meeting here in Gloucester. He mentioned that he happened to be joining you and Nancy at the Rudder. It happens to be one of my favorite restaurants, and I'm hungry."

"Okay then," Nancy said, eagerly taking the drinks from the waitress and handing me mine. I took a gulp, as the men ordered theirs.

"You're looking good, Alex," Bob said rather awkwardly.

"As are you." I forced a smile.

"I understand you're not teaching anymore."

"School's out for the summer—"

"You're not teaching *anymore*." He emphasized the last word.

"Word gets around." I fixed a stern gaze on Don, who immediately looked away.

"How's the book coming?" Bob asked.

"The publication process takes forever."

"That's what I hear. How's your family?"

Small talk continued throughout dinner. By the time I had my third glass of wine, I was a bit more relaxed, but still not letting my guard down.

"Nancy, Don drove here with me. You willing to take him home?" Bob joked as we stood to leave. He had already paid the bill.

"I guess that would be okay," she replied with a smile.

"Alex, I'll drop you off. It's out of their way."

I wanted to object, but I knew it would be childish. "Thanks."

We drove in silence for a few minutes. "How's your lady friend?" I finally asked, trying to sound controlled when in truth I wanted to scream.

"I don't have a lady friend," he admitted, not taking his eyes off the road.

"Was it a lie?"

"Yes. And I'm sorry. I needed some distance, and I thought that was the best way. It was stupid. I am sorry."

When I didn't respond, he glanced at me. I still didn't respond.

"I'm sure you heard what happened with Kathleen Mercer yesterday."

I was aware. Kathleen, it was reported, had been threatened by a Massachusetts district federal judge with life imprisonment for pleading guilty to contempt of court for not answering yet another barrage of questions from a grand jury.

"Yeah, I know." I'm sure my sense of dejection came through. I looked at him. "I'm shocked that you would bring up the subject."

"I've done a lot of thinking. What's been happening to Kathleen Mercer is unscrupulous. Anyone with respect for the law realizes it."

I couldn't believe what I was hearing.

"I was invited to the premiere of *Devil's Town*."

"You were?"

He nodded. "Met a few old colleagues from the Devaney era there." He smiled. "We were reminiscing about concerns at the time. We were all targeting the Mafia. A few of us hired security to protect our families."

"Did you?"

"Yes. And my risk was much less than that of Joshua O'Toole. If he didn't feel that he could trust the FBI for protection, maybe he did ask Devaney."

I was aware that my mouth dropped open.

"After watching the movie, I remembered what you told me about Devaney claiming the informant file was contrived. I've come to wonder if it may have been."

He glanced at me. I met his glance with one of wide-eyed incredulity.

"Alex, what you don't know is that in 1979, Joshua O'Toole notified the assistant attorney general, by memo, that Devaney was being protected from prosecution. That memo still exists."

"And it was kept from being introduced in Devaney's trial?"

"It was sealed under executive order in early 2002."

"Two thousand two? George W. Bush was president—"

"Yes."

"Why?"

"Deemed to be a threat to national security."

"How do you know this?" I asked, staring at him.

"I remembered it coming up in the congressional hearings on the FBI back in 2004. It was quickly dismissed, and I gave it no further thought until this morning." He looked at me. I waited for him to continue.

He turned back to watching the road. "I ran into an old friend at the meeting today. I can't give you the details, but he viewed the memo before it was sealed." Bob glanced at me again. "According to this friend, O'Toole clearly stated in the memo that Devaney had immunity. That's all I know."

I sat in silence for a few minutes, digesting what he'd revealed.

"A threat to national security? Why? Because it might reveal dirty dealings of the DOJ at the time?"

He didn't respond.

"How do we get all of this before the Senate or House Judiciary Committees?" I finally asked.

"Not likely. They have an enormous amount on their plate." This was the reply from the former member of the House Judiciary Committee.

"What? Intellectual property rights? Antitrust laws? Or better yet, appointing new judges to the federal bench, where they risk being corrupted by certain powers already in place?"

He glanced at me, raising his eyebrows. "You're sounding like a conspiracy theorist."

"I don't mean to—" I hesitated, looking out the window. "It's all so overwhelming."

Bob pulled into my driveway and stopped the car. "Charlie's home," he stated, looking at Charlie's car.

"No, he went off for the weekend with friends. Are you avoiding my question about the judiciary committees?"

The outside light revealed his smile. He released his seat belt and turned his body to face mine. "Alex. It's not as simple as that. The judiciary committees cover a vast amount of legal oversight."

I gazed through the windshield at the garage. "They play a 'critical role in providing oversight of the Department of Justice and the agencies under the Department's jurisdiction, including the Federal Bureau of Investigation.'"

Bob laughed. "Did you memorize that?"

"Yes, it's under Committee Jurisdiction on the judiciary dot senate dot gov website. Would you like to hear more?"

"No." He smirked, and raised his hands, pretending to object. "I'm good."

I looked at him. "Let's face it, Bob; for at least fifty years, in certain areas, Congress has not done well in keeping the DOJ in check. Because of it, foundational principles are crumbling. Are you telling me that it's more important to build support for corporate and foreign law than to stabilize the foundation the US Constitution was built upon?"

"You know I'm not saying that. But like it or not, Alex, their plate is full."

"Fuck that," I murmured, looking away.

"What?" he asked with a laugh.

I turned to face him. "Seems to me that the judiciary committees need to wrap up what's on their goddamned plates and stick them in the freezer. If they don't take this unbridled power of the DOJ seriously, this country is going to collapse."

Bob's expression was somber as he held me under a steady gaze. "Alex," he finally said, turning his gaze away and then quickly turning back. Now there was a slight smile on his lips. "Why do you have to be so damned patriotic?"

I shrugged. "Why aren't all Americans, Mr. Congressman?"

"Come on. I'll walk you to the door." He stepped out and joined me on the other side of the car. We began to walk toward the house. "I'm still close to a few members on the judiciary committees. Let me run it by them."

We stopped at the door. "No promises, Alex." He held out his hand. "Friends?"

I placed my hand in his, surprised that the mere touch of his skin still affected me. "Friends," I said, shaking his hand and secretly longing for more.

"Good. Now get inside."

I retrieved the keys from my purse and opened the door.

"I'll call you in a couple of days to let you know what I find out." He turned and began to walk away. "Good night, kiddo."

~

With the release of Jonathan Height's movie *Devil's Town*, the contrived media account of Sly Devaney's story went nationwide. The devious retired FBI agent Ken Arnold's tale of Tom being an informant was now on the big screen, probably rewarding the murderous former agent with a substantial monetary recompense, and sanitizing the filthy deals of Carla Chavere and her Boston office of the US attorney.

Tom's letters were filled with despair. He was weary of the lies being verbalized under oath in courtrooms, written as fact by so-called journalists, presented in supposed nonfiction publication, and now mesmerizing the masses on the big screen. He was exasperated by the fact that Ken Arnold, an accessory to two murders, was never punished for his crimes, while Kathleen's torture continued.

"I'll never forget when Arnold asked me to kill his wife," he wrote. "The man had no conscience. He'd come to me with plans for robberies he wanted the gang to carry out. I told him, 'Sure, you put on a mask and come with us.' Of course, he never would. Neither did we.

"A lie unchallenged becomes the truth. I now realize that my silence has done nothing but bring harm to Kathleen and my family. I need to speak the truth to someone in the media who will take me seriously. Whom can I talk to?" I sensed Tom's inner conflict when reading the words. Throughout his life, he had lived by a code of silence.

Tom continued to send letters that clearly indicated his ongoing struggle in revealing information. "I remember Tony Diavolo telling me about a man he killed. He bragged of how he decapitated the body and wrapped the head in some newspaper, carrying it around the streets of Boston in broad daylight. I can tie Tony and the others to numerous cold cases.

"As for Goot, I always denied that I gave him money. Always protected him. I even tried to find a way to offer testimony in his defense during his trial. He had nothing to do with the Scalise murder.

"But still he won't tell the truth about the fake informant file. I'm done protecting him. After he divorced, I paid the rent on his luxury bachelor pad. I bought him a boat, a car, expensive jewelry and clothes, a summer place on the Cape. I always gave him a generous stipend for information. And I'll never forget the special Christmas gift he gave me. It was quite heavy and delivered a big bang. Why don't you ask him about it next time you write him?"

Tom's next letter stated that he had given a private interview to a noted cable news reporter. Everything was exposed: the extraordinary sums of money he had paid Goot and Arnold for information, Alan Hand's involvement with the IRA and his role in numerous murders, and the many unconfessed murders committed by Giuda and Diavolo. The questions now were, Would his interview be taken seriously? And would they have the courage to show it to the public?

~

Bob's request that I meet him for dinner that same evening took me by surprise. When I arrived at the Village Tavern in Salem, he was already seated. A glass of merlot was on the table.

"Let me get the chair for you," Bob said as he stood to greet me. I took the menu from the hostess.

We studied the menus for a moment and gave the waitress our orders.

"I called you from Washington. Just returned," he began. "I hope my abrupt request to meet didn't mess up any plans."

From his inquisitive expression, I knew that the statement had been made to obtain information.

"No plans. If I'm not with my kids or a girlfriend, I spend the weekend alone."

"Good." He smiled.

I offered him an empty smile, emotionally guarding myself, afraid of being hurt by him again.

"I spoke to the chairman of the Senate Judiciary Subcommittee on Crime and Terrorism."

"Crime and terrorism?"

"It's the subcommittee that has oversight of the DOJ."

"Oh?" I meekly hinted at my ignorance.

"I thought you memorized the website?"

"Just the vague opening description of what they do." I quickly picked up a glass of water and took a long sip.

He didn't need to respond with words. Over the rim of the glass I could see his smile as he shook his head.

"Of which is the DOJ guilty, crime or terrorism? Probably both?" I asked with a smile, trying to save face.

"And will you let the members of the subcommittee determine that?" Bob was still smiling.

"Will they hear it?" My astonishment was apparent.

"They'll consider it. There's a lot of work involved. A lot of documentation needed."

"Okay."

"But as soon as we submit the paperwork, I want to talk with Vinnie," he stated.

"Vinnie Giuda? Why?" I asked.

"Because, once the DOJ realizes they're being investigated, they'll start damage control. It may work to our advantage. The DOJ could make Chavere the scapegoat. Or Chavere may try to convince Vinnie and the other witnesses that congressional immunity won't apply to them and that their testimony might jeopardize their freedom."

"Will it?" I asked, suddenly aware that I knew nothing of how the Senate Judiciary Committee actually worked.

"No. Unfortunately, they are free men, regardless if they testify or not."

"Then why would they?"

"Because Chavere, a woman nonetheless, has them under her thumb. These guys like to be in control and be the ones to intimidate. I have no doubt that they hate Chavere. Given the chance to take her down, they will. I just need the opportunity to convince them that they can."

Chapter 17

We are not to simply bandage the wounds of
victims beneath the wheels of injustice, we
are to drive a spoke into the wheel itself.
—Dietrich Bonhoeffer (1906–1945),
German theologian, Nazi dissident,
sentenced to death by Adolf Hitler

"CALL THE INFIRMARY. TELL THEM HE MAY BE HAV-
ing a heart attack," one prison guard called to the other. "Try to relax,
Devaney. Help is on its way."

"No … don't want help. Let me die—"

"Can't do that, Devaney."

Tom closed his eyes and attempted to pray. The crushing pain
limited his concentration. "Let me go. Please let me go," he whispered.
"Chavere will stop torturing Kathleen if I'm not here for her to torment. Please, God! Let me help Kathleen! Take me now—"

~

Kathleen Mercer was scheduled to go before a federal judge in Boston
for sentencing. Her crime? Refusal to answer the questions of Chavere's
federal grand jury about who had offered support to Devaney when
he was on the lam.

"She has no answers to give them," Tom wrote in a letter. "The first
year we were on the run, I made the mistake of contacting a couple

of friends. They were arrested and tormented by the feds. Lost their jobs. Every member of my family was pulled in before one of Chavere's grand juries, even though they had no knowledge of where I was. I determined then that we could have no contact with anyone from our past. Kathleen has nothing to tell them, and she knows that Chavere won't accept that response. Chavere wants names, especially that of my brother, who served in public office. Kathleen has no names to give."

I didn't know what I could do to stop Chavere and try to bring sanity back to the judicial process. Finally, I decided to write a letter to the judge. It read as follows:

> I served as a juror in the trial of *US vs. Thomas D. Devaney*. That trial was alarming, but sadly, it was not the criminality of Devaney that was most disturbing. That was expected. Instead, it was the revelation of the depth of corruption within the Department of Justice in Boston, ongoing for at least fifty years. Almost equally disturbing was the lack of concern by the media, whose responsibility it is to keep the citizens of this country informed of such abuses of power.
>
> Sir, I am a student of the American Revolution. The respect I have for the courageous sacrifice made during that war by men and women of all walks of life inspired me to write about this central point of our history. The establishment of a just system of law, for all citizens, was fundamental. Those who fought in the American Revolution had experienced firsthand the abuses.
>
> I found the recent remarks you are reported to have made to Kathleen Mercer disturbing. It is my understanding from Devaney's trial that Mercer's initial sentence was significantly harsher than what the

probation department recommended. Now, according to the reports in the local papers, Your Honor has made it clear to Ms. Mercer that you can, and may, sentence her to life in prison.

May I respectfully remind Your Honor that Ms. Mercer has no criminal record beyond harboring Devaney; that she loves him as a wife loves a husband; and that her behavior in prison has been exemplary. May I also respectfully state that the statute of limitations is about to expire for the activity of any who may have aided Devaney while on the lam (if, in fact, anyone did; Ms. Mercer's refusal to speak does not mean that there are names to reveal). So, what does this display of power prove, except to make citizens realize how far the court has wandered from the intent of the founding fathers?

May I respectfully express my alarm, as a citizen, that heinous criminals like Vincent Giuda, Anthony Diavolo, and Benjamin James have been given far more lenient sentences in comparison to the horror of their crimes. May I respectfully express my incredulity, as a citizen, that Alan Hand, a man who has been identified as participating in numerous murders, has never been indicted for his willing role in taking the life of another; or that Ken Arnold, who swore an oath to protect the citizens of this country, received no punishment whatsoever for violating that oath, and participating in the death of two American citizens. In fact, sir, he was rewarded with promotions within the FBI, and full benefits upon his retirement, which American citizens are forced to pay. And may I respectfully express my confusion, as a citizen, over the fact that Roberta Little, who spent sixteen years with

Vincent Giuda while he was on the lam, who willingly participated in blatant acts of money laundering, and who lied to a grand jury, was never indicted for her crimes.

We were taught—as we continue to teach our children—that the blindfold on Justitia symbolizes that justice should be delivered without passion or prejudice. It has been my observation, and has become my opinion, that the US Attorney's Office in Boston and the Boston media have developed an obsessive, prejudiced passion in regard to Thomas Devaney (and anything associated with him).

Justitia's scales must cautiously weigh the claims of each side to render an informed judgment. Emotional impressions, or prejudicial attitudes of seemingly powerful and perhaps manipulative prosecutors, should never enter into the equation when considering the facts. Because Justitia's sword makes clear the reality that judgment can be swift and final, it is paramount that said judgment be just! Her garment is reminiscent of the attire of a sensible and learned civilization ruled by fairness and impartiality.

Do the federal judges in this country still hold to these beliefs? Can we continue to teach our children that their liberty is safe, because the federal courts are just and will not allow hard cases to render bad law? To be sure, sir, my faith in American jurisprudence has been shaken. I fear that the blood that was willingly poured out to obtain—and protect—the foundational right of our system of law was spilled in vain for our generation. Our children and grandchildren tragically shall suffer the oppression.

Please, sir, render a fair and just sentence to citizen
Kathleen Mercer.

The letter, released to the press a week before Kathleen's sentencing, had little impact on the judge, except for the fact that he publicly denied threatening Kathleen with life in prison. He also made a comment, which I had heard uttered verbatim by Chavere in her closing argument at the trial: "Sometimes when dealing with these crimes you have to put a clothespin on your nose and make deals with these criminals."

So that's it, I thought, *the clothespin keeps out the stench of the unvindicated decaying corpses piled up by these murderers whose lies got them out of prison.*

Kathleen Mercer had twenty-one months added to her sentence. She would remain in prison as long as Vinnie Giuda had for twenty cold-blooded murders.

God bless the United States of America, I thought with disgust.

~

After reading a section of the letter aloud to Bob, I folded it and placed it on my lap, and then looked at him. He was seated at his desk; the palms of his hands were together, and his forefingers rested on his lips. He appeared perplexed as he lowered his hands to his chin. "I can't believe that Devaney confides in you, knowing we're friends."

"He respects my honesty."

Bob raised his eyebrows in response. "Respect? I guess it's still hard for me to wrap my head around the possibility of Devaney being less than a monster."

"Chavere, the media, and Hollywood have told the lie for so long, it's become the truth in the minds of most. Hard to deprogram once you're brainwashed," I said with a smile.

"Though he may not be a monster, he's still a criminal, Alex."

"Yeah, but what's he truly guilty of?"

"Murder, extortion, money laundering. Nothing's changed. It's just that now we know he has a soul."

"Everything's changed. Yes, he did all those things, but would he have if the CIA hadn't modified his behavior?"

"We don't know for a fact that his behavior was modified."

I shook my head and leaned forward. "Please! You don't think that after having LSD and whatever else the CIA mixed into that concoction they shoved into his veins at least three times a week for eighteen months affected his brain?"

"He was in prison for robbing a bank before the CIA got hold of him."

"And if they didn't, he might have lived a normal life when released from prison."

"It's tragic. There's no denying that. We'll never know."

"It's something I want to discuss with him in detail when I visit."

"I'm not comfortable with you going." He raised a hand to silence my ready objection. "I know you want to ask him specific questions face-to-face, but we have enough documentation and written testimony to submit for a Senate hearing."

"Details of what he paid Goot, Arnold, and others in law enforcement, and information he has on cold cases, will be an asset," I objected.

"Alex, you don't even know if he'll tell you anything."

"Oh, he will," I said assuredly. "The lies of Chavere's puppets and those of Skip Goot have done such damage to Kathleen and his family. He wants the lies exposed to vindicate those he loves. You said yourself that the revelation of new crimes, or old murders yet to be uncovered, by those creeps Chavere and Altier gave free passes to will convince them to fess up to their dirty dealings with the Boston US Attorney's Office."

Bob held me under a steady gaze and then threw up his hands and smiled. "You never take my counsel. Why do I try?"

I laughed as I stood up and walked toward him. It was clear by his expression that he was confused by my steady advance. I reached the chair and easily rolled it away from the desk. "May I?" I patted his thighs, indicating that I intended to sit on his lap.

"By all means." He was still confused.

I sat upon his legs, wrapped my arms around his neck, and leaned in to kiss his lips. He was hesitant at first, but he quickly succumbed to the passion. It was a long, lustful kiss. My arms rested upon his shoulders when I pulled away.

Bob was hesitant to speak or move. I smiled and kissed his forehead.

"Have I passed the friendship test?" he asked timidly.

"You have." I laughed and kissed his cheek.

"Are we moving beyond friendship?" He was still cautious.

"That's entirely up to you, Mr. Costa."

Bob placed his hands behind my head and pulled me in for another sensual kiss.

~

Tom had received and responded to my letter about when I would fly to Florida to visit. He received few visitors given the distance between the prison and the places where his family lived. Such a rare visit was anticipated with pleasure as much for reuniting with those who cared as for outside contact. My paperwork had already been submitted and approved upon my first visit. The process to return was simple: show up, present your identification and his prison number, get scanned, patted down, and stamped, and then go into the visiting room.

The clanging metal doors didn't startle me this time, and I was prepared for the frigid temperature with layers of clothing.

I took the seat at the end of a row of connected chairs closest to the door from which the prisoners came. *It will be easier for him here,* I thought. *Less distance for him to maneuver the wheelchair, and plenty of room.*

I watched prisoners come through the door and walk to their families and friends. After thirty minutes, a guard approached.

"Ma'am, I need to ask you to move."

"Okay." I stood and followed him to a row of connected chairs in front of the guards' desk. The seat was between two aisles.

"Is Mr. Devaney still in a wheelchair?" I asked, realizing the space was not wide enough.

"Yeah, that's right," the guard agreed. Then he moved me to the other end of the row, right under the guards' desk.

Prisoners continued to come and go, yet there was no sign of Tom. After two hours of waiting, another prison guard came through the doorway. This man's uniform was different from the navy blue the others wore. He wore a white shirt with insignia. I assumed he was an officer. Between his hulk-like form and stern expression, he commanded respect within the room. His conversation with the young guard who had seated me caused both of them to look in my direction.

"Ms. Fischer," he stated in a deep, firm tone. "Follow me."

Before I had time to acknowledge my name, he had given his command, had turned, and began walking away.

Is Tom sick? I wondered as I followed. We stepped into the middle chamber between the foyer and visiting room. He pushed a button on the wall and the door behind us clamored shut. Finally, he turned to face me.

"You cannot visit the prisoner." The other door clattered open as he spoke.

"Why?" I asked, concerned that Tom must indeed be ill.

"You didn't know the prisoner prior to incarceration," he snapped as he moved past the open steel door into the foyer.

I was taken aback as much by his abrupt statement as by the fact that no one was in the foyer. "I was allowed to visit before—"

"You were a juror in his trial," he stated.

"I was."

"Information you withheld," he accused.

"I didn't withhold anything," I respectfully argued, keenly aware that this was his turf, there were no witnesses, and he had a gun.

He walked toward the front doors. I followed.

"Am I not allowed to see Mr. Devaney because I didn't know him prior to incarceration or because I served as a juror?"

"Jurors aren't allowed to visit."

"I am no longer a juror. The trial ended two years ago."

"Jurors aren't allowed." He held his upturned hand toward me and opened his palm to reveal my rental car keys. "Leave," he barked.

I barely noticed the boiling temperature and blinding sun as I walked toward the car. *What the hell just happened?* I questioned, taking a deep breath. *He had the keys taken from my locker. Did he clear out the foyer? Why did they let me in and then let me wait two hours?*

"Chavere!" I exclaimed, stopping in the middle of the parking lot and looking back at the prison. "I wonder if that bitch instructed them not to let me in!" Surprising myself, I began to laugh as I continued to walk toward the car.

She knows from the letters that I was planning to be here today. Probably ordered them to call if I actually showed up. It's a Sunday; they couldn't get her right away. Couldn't just leave me in the waiting area until Chavere decided to return their call, so they brought me into the visiting room while they awaited her instructions. Is she that frightened of me that she'll alter the rules of visitation?

I got into the car, turned on the air-conditioner, and called Bob.

~

"Good morning, Alex." Don acknowledged my presence without looking at me. "What sort of trouble do you intend to get my wife into today?" he asked as he thumbed through a magazine on the kitchen table. "Did you see this?" He tossed the magazine at me before I had the opportunity to respond to his question.

"Page five," he instructed, his back toward me as he grabbed a mug and began to pour coffee into it.

I flipped the pages, stopping on page five and an article entitled "Jury Foreman Tells All."

"That goddamned foreman threw you under the bus, sweetheart. Didn't you say he was a nice guy and a friend?"

I was reading the article as Don sat down across from me at the table.

"Darlin', I think you need to boot the bastard out of your circle of friends."

"Richard actually told the reporter that he was determined to become the foreman and bring in a guilty verdict before the trial even began?" I asked incredulously, not taking my eyes from the page.

"Oh yeah, sweetheart, and that he used you every step of the way. Let me read it to you." Don held out his hand for the magazine.

"Quoting Richard, 'Alex Fischer, juror twelve, had influence. She was the only threat of taking the position of foreman from me. In the end, she didn't want the responsibility. But I felt she might have enough influence to cause a hung jury. Her questions in deliberations were making the other jurors question if the witnesses for the prosecution were credible. She had convinced the jurors to acquit Devaney of the first three murders, and worked hard to acquit him of the murders of the women. Devaney was guilty, and I wasn't about to let a bleeding heart like Alex Fischer prevent him from rotting in prison. I subtly manipulated her emotions. It worked.'"

Don put the magazine down and gazed at me. His expression was sad. "Alex, most people suck."

~

"What was your reaction to the magazine article?" Betsy asked at the start of the therapy session.

"Anger. Betrayal. I remember thinking that I should've listened to my mother."

"What do you mean?"

"When I was called for the jury pool, she told me to lie."

"To get you out of the jury pool?"

"Yes."

"And you wished you had?" Betsy wore a soft accepting smile.

"I've wished it many times, and yes, I wished it when I saw the article. But the next day I read about Tom's correspondence with some local high school kids. He shared with them his regrets for the path he took.

"I often mull over the MKULTRA experiments and wonder what his life might have been if the CIA hadn't used him as a human guinea pig. Then I think of the young and innocent soldiers and sailors permanently damaged by a government they trusted—a thousand young men who blindly offered their service to the country. I consider all the abuses of power, all the lives damaged, and I realize that if I hadn't experienced the trial, I'd remain naïve. And if I remained naïve, I couldn't speak against it. And if people don't speak against such injustices and crimes, those crimes and injustices continue."

"And you feel you've made a change?"

"If the Senate Judiciary Committee takes our presentation under serious consideration, then yes. If reporters, like the young man at the *Huffington Post*, continue with articles about the cozy relationship the US Attorney's Office has with reputable newspapers, then yes."

"I read the article. They're challenging the relationship the Boston office has with the Boston journalists. You've shared your concern about this. You must be pleased that it's finally being exposed." Her warm smile remained.

I nodded and wiped a tear that threatened to escape from my eye.

"And you feel safe with Congressman Costa?"

I smiled at her. "Yeah. I do."

"I'm happy for you, Alex. It seems that the darkness you've experienced is passing."

~

"Alex. It's Joe Wallace. Give me a call when you get a chance." The edginess in Joe's voice came through in the voice mail. I immediately called.

"Hey, Joe. It's Alex. Everything okay?" I asked when he answered the phone.

"Far from okay. Wanted to tell you before the story hits the papers tomorrow—" He became silent.

Instantly, I was nervous. "Tell me what?"

"Due to my health, and the strain and expense a trial would bring to me and my family, I decided to plead out."

"What are you saying, Joe?"

"They've got this all tied up. FBI documents to back my testimony have disappeared. Former agents who can corroborate my stories have been warned off."

"What about Lucy, the secretary to the special agent in charge? She testified that she saw your report on Devaney, and showed it to three incoming SACs."

"Lucy has been diagnosed with Alzheimer's. They're claiming the disease probably affected her testimony."

"And the copy of the report?"

"Gone."

"How can it be gone? It was a court document."

"Alex, they won. They always do. I've decided that I'm not going to spend the last few years I have left in a jail cell. I want to be with Linda and the girls. Can you forgive me for that?" Joe's voice cracked.

"There's nothing to forgive, Joe." I began to cry.

"I've already said too much on the phone. I'll let you know when sentencing is scheduled."

The same federal judge who had recently added eighteen months to the sentence of Kathleen Mercer was to sentence former FBI assistant special agent in charge Joseph Wallace. The Boston newspapers were all over it like flies on a pile of dung. They failed to mention that Joe had attempted to save the life of Edward O'Leary. The biased media only stated what Chavere and Altier fed them—that former ASAC Wallace was a liar and was getting what he deserved.

I wrote another letter to the federal judge. I was appalled to discover that neither the family of Edward O'Leary nor Donald Monahan came to Joe's defense.

~

"And he's off!" Ilona exclaimed as Paulie raced toward the water. His father and uncle sprinted after him.

Ilona, Nancy, and I laughed as the toddler dashed effortlessly across the beach, with no regard for empty blankets or sprawled towels.

"I don't think they're gonna catch him!" I chuckled. The men avoided the blankets and towels, slowing their attempted retrieval.

"How embarrassing," Ilona moaned, pulling the sun visor down low in a feeble attempt to hide.

"Don't worry, sweetie. If you come to the beach, you have to expect sand." Nancy patted Ilona's leg.

"I'd get so annoyed when parents let their kids run on the beach," Ilona stated, still trying to hide.

"All part of the beach experience," I said.

"So is sex on the beach, but it doesn't make it right," Ilona said.

"What?"

"Well, I mean, the beach has to be empty."

"Ilona!" I scolded.

"Never, Mom? You and Dad never?"

I could feel my cheeks redden, and it wasn't from the sun.

"No. I suppose Dad led too many combat charges on beaches to ever consider the setting as romantic." Ilona laughed. "God, I miss him—"

I reached out and squeezed her arm. "And how do you think your dad would react to that question?" I asked her with a smile.

She pushed the visor back as she watched Charlie take hold of Paulie and toss him in the air. Paulie's squeal of delight was heard across the beach. "Dad would tell me that I was right, that he didn't stop to recognize a tender moment or see the beauty of nature. Then he'd tell me he was sorry and hug me."

Paul had come to discover this reality only after he'd left the army. A tear came to my eye as I envisioned the many tender moments between Paul and the kids in the year before he died.

"You seem to be spending a lot more time with Bob Costa these days. What's with that?" Ilona abruptly changed the subject.

Nancy winked at Ilona. "I've heard rumors through the grapevine that they almost may be an official couple," Nancy said, looking past me and directly at Ilona.

"Does this grapevine answer to the name Don?" I asked with a chuckle.

"I never reveal my sources."

"So, you're back with Bob, eh?" Ilona asked, giggling. I braced myself for some teasing. "You and Bob should have sex on the beach—"

"Ilona!"

"Come on, Mom. It's something everyone should experience."

"Yeah, Alex. Loads of fun with sand in your hair and up your rear. Fleabites in parts that never see the light of day. Loads of fun!" Nancy looked at Ilona. "Come on, sweetie, the two of them are too old to get down on the sand, never mind getting up again!"

The arrival of Charlie, and Paulie in his father Steve's arms, put an end to the sordid conversation between my best friend and my daughter.

"Charlie, since we're all together, let's talk about plans for graduation," I suggested as they plopped onto the blanket in front of our beach chairs.

"It's a year away," he protested.

"No, it's only nine months away, and now's the time to plan."

"Your mother's right, Charlie," Nancy interjected.

"I can't think about this on an empty stomach. Going over to Captain Dusty's. Anyone want anything?"

Everyone did. Charlie, Ilona, and Steve went to get the food, leaving Paulie on my lap. I pulled him close.

"I don't think either of us will be able to chase him across the beach," Nancy said.

"I don't think we'll have to. He's worn out." Paulie's little head bobbled as he dozed.

"Is Bob still intent on meeting with Vinnie Giuda?" Nancy asked. She and my therapist were the only ones I had confided in regarding the hoped-for Senate judiciary hearing.

"Yeah. The documentation is already under review in the Senate Committee. Word is that they will call a hearing. Bob's determined that Giuda needs to hear it from him before Chavere gets word."

"Why?" Nancy asked.

"Bob thinks Chavere will convince Giuda and the others that they'll lose their immunity if they change their testimony at the judiciary hearing. And if she does convince him, Giuda will stick to the stories Chavere and Altier created and rehearsed for twenty years. If Giuda and the others aren't willing to speak the truth, the cycle of corruption within the Boston US Attorney's Office continues."

Nancy looked out over the ocean for a moment. "If they talk, Chavere and Altier may go away for a long time."

"I hope so. And even if they put them in a special unit for imprisoned law enforcement, there's bound to be someone among them whom Chavere and Altier prosecuted. There'll be no escape."

We watched in silence as the waves crashed along the shoreline.

"We'll be meeting with Giuda at Limae's Restaurant next Tuesday."

"In Boston?" Nancy asked.

I nodded. "I'll be relieved when it's over."

~

"Hey, Ma. Ya might wanna see this. Something about a witness from the Devaney trial," Charlie called out.

Walking toward the living room, I could hear the newscast. "Stanley Onesta, who testified that Sly Devaney shot him nine times, has now been charged with murder in a thirty-year-old cold case."

A picture of Stanley in handcuffs was on the screen when I came into the room. His face was contorted with emotion.

"Though all witnesses to the murder are now deceased, the assistant DA has stated that evidence has come to light which clearly implicates Onesta," the reporter continued.

"Didn't you go visit that guy?" Charlie asked.

I nodded, unable to take my eyes off the screen to respond.

"Jesus, Ma! You're so naïve—"

"Naïve?" I heard myself shout back. "I'm naïve? You believe he's guilty after listening to a sixty-second segment, and I'm naïve?" I was furious. "They lied. Stanley never testified that Devaney shot him. Doesn't it seem strange that there are no living witnesses to this murder?"

"They said they have evidence," Charlie calmly stated.

"Evidence? They can throw people in jail for a long, long time without proper evidence," I protested.

"Why would they go after this old guy unless they were sure?"

"Because this old guy had the guts to reveal the deception of the Boston US Attorney's Office in his testimony. He didn't properly act out his part in their puppet show—didn't let Chavere and Altier pull his strings. He, like Joe Wallace, made Chavere and Altier look like fools. Now, like Joe, Stanley, it seems, is gonna pay."

Charlie didn't respond.

"The courts function under the golden rule, Charlie."

"The golden rule? From the Bible?"

"Oh, no. The attorney with the most gold wins. The US Attorney's Office has plenty of gold at their disposal."

~

"You don't seem the least bit concerned," I commented as Bob merged onto Route 1A heading toward Boston.

He glanced at me and chuckled. "We're just having a couple of drinks with Cousin Vinnie."

"He's a killer."

"So's Devaney, and you've spent time with him." He laughed.

"Under the watch of armed guards," I shot back. I folded my arms across my chest and stared blankly out the window. "Giuda's different. Killed two kids and his best friend."

"You don't need to go with me," he said, without taking his eyes off the road. "If it scares you, I'll take you home and meet him alone—"

I shot my head around to look at him. "Meet him alone? Absolutely not!"

"It's either that or we call if off completely. He's not gonna talk with anyone else present." Bob took his right hand off the steering wheel and reached toward me. "Give me your hand."

I abandoned my protective posture and continued to look out the window as I placed my hand in his.

"We'll have one drink, say what we have to say, and leave. I'll have you home within two hours. I promise." He glanced at me as he squeezed my hand.

My position remained the same.

"Alex," he began, looking back at the road. "Vinnie has immunity. We're not a threat."

"Have me home within ninety minutes," I said.

He laughed. "Okay. Ninety minutes. My home, my bed." Again, he reached out and squeezed my hand.

I looked at him and smiled. We rode in silence the rest of the way.

"There it is. One of the oldest restaurants in Boston." Bob pointed to an old brick building. We pulled into a small parking lot to the right of it. As we walked toward the restaurant, I spotted a burly man chatting with a woman on the sidewalk beyond the restaurant.

"Bobby! Hey, Bobby!" the burly figure called out, beginning to walk toward us as the woman watched. As he approached, I could see that it was Vinnie Giuda. Bob appeared relaxed. I wasn't.

Giuda greeted Bob with a wide grin and a bear hug. Bob's smile appeared genuine. *Years of playing the politician,* I considered.

"Christ, Bobby, it's been a few years! How are the kids? How many grandkids do ya have?"

"They're well. Four grandchildren."

"Uncle Dave, God rest his soul, would be proud that you passed on the Costa name," Giuda said, referring to Bob's father. "And my mother, God rest her soul, would be damned pleased as well."

For the first time, Vinnie glanced at me. His countenance instantly changed. "You're a tenacious little thing. Not surprised that Bobby's into you." Turning his attention back to Bob, he said, "You always had a thing for feisty bitches." He laughed as he jokingly slapped Bob on the back. "Come over here," Vinnie called out to the woman he had been talking to.

Slowly she walked toward us.

"Bobby, you remember Paul Hennessey? This is his daughter, Linda."

Bob greeted the woman as though he knew her.

"My son's picking me up. Vinnie insists on staying with me 'til he gets here," Linda told Bob.

"Just protecting the lady, Bobby. You and I know the streets aren't safe." Vinnie chuckled and slapped Bob on the back again. "Why don't the two of you go inside. I'll only be a few minutes. Order me a gin and tonic."

"But I want ya to meet Matt. He served in the navy," Linda said to Bob. She obviously knew he was a former naval officer.

Bob turned to me. "Why don't you go in," he said quietly.

"Okay." I was grateful to spend as little time in the presence of Vinnie Giuda as I could.

"Tell Joanie you're with me," Vinnie stated.

"Joanie?" I asked.

"The hostess. I told her to save us a table."

I nodded and said goodbye to Linda. After throwing a weak smile at Bob, I headed to the restaurant.

Joanie greeted me, shouting above the raucous crowd around the bar. "A twenty-first-birthday party. The night's young and they're already smashed." She laughed. Joanie didn't appear to be much older than twenty-one herself. She was a stunning young woman, as Irish as she could be, with hazel eyes and soft orange ringlets flowing to her midback. We walked past the ornate mahogany mirrored bar. Every stool and table in the room was occupied by reveling young adults.

"Big party," I commented.

"Yeah, they rented the restaurant for the night. Vinnie told me to take you to the back dining room."

I followed Joanie into a smaller room. There were four small dining tables cozily arranged, and an exit door on the far wall. *Good,* I thought.

"Can I get you a drink?" Joanie asked.

"A glass of merlot, and Vinnie asked for a gin and tonic." I couldn't believe I was ordering a drink for Giuda. My stomach began to churn. "Oh, and a Coors Light." I stood up. "Could you tell me where the ladies' room is?"

"Follow me." Joanie directed me back past the crowded bar and instructed me to go down a flight of stairs to the restroom.

I found my way back to the private dining area. *What's taking them so long?* I wondered, knowing full well that Bob was probably chatting it up with the young man about the navy.

Joanie entered the room with the drinks. As she left, I heard Vinnie's voice from across the restaurant bellowing out greetings. His bulky form soon appeared in the doorway.

"Where's Bob?" I asked.

"Men's room. Bob tells me your son's at West Point."

I nodded, feeling awkward under his steady gaze.

"When does he graduate?"

"He's going into his senior year."

"And then how long does the army own him?"

"Five years active, three reserve."

Footsteps approached the doorway. I anxiously anticipated Bob's appearance. It wasn't him.

"Want me to check on him?" Vinnie asked, obviously aware of my concern.

"No. He probably met someone he knows. He always does." I forced a smile and took a sip of the wine. *So much for having me home in ninety minutes,* was my agitated thought.

Vinnie smiled. "He always talked too much. He's good at spinning a tale too. Got us out of a few scrapes as kids."

There was an awkward silence—for me, anyway. Vinnie began to tap a beat on the table with his thumbs.

"Do you play the drums?" I asked, searching for something meaningless to talk about. *Bob! Where the hell are you?* I shouted within.

"Drums?" He seemed confused and was suddenly serious.

"The drummers I know have a habit of tapping a beat with their thumbs."

"You know a lot of drummers?" he asked.

"A few."

Vinnie pounded his palms on the table and then turned his body, looking toward the main dining area. "Maybe I should check on him." He turned back, facing me again. "We don't have all night."

"Thank you," I heard myself say.

"You're welcome." He snickered as he stood up. "Good jurors should do their job and then keep their fucking mouths shut," Vinnie said as he walked to the door. He turned to look at me. "You should've kept Bobby out of this." He walked out of the room and closed the door.

My heart was pounding, yet my chest felt hollow. I took a deep breath. With a shaking hand, I picked up the wineglass, took a gulp, and clumsily placed it back on the table.

I heard movement from behind.

Bob? Please be Bob! I hesitated, afraid to look.

Grabbed from behind, my neck jerked back as the assail-ant attempted to cover my mouth. Instinctively, I franticly bit the glove-covered hand that was over my mouth as my hands reached up in a desperate struggle to loosen the grip.

A deep sadistic snigger greeted my feeble attempt. The grip around my mouth tightened even more.

A second gloved hand appeared before me on the table, clenching an object that was dropped with a thud.

"You see it, darlin'? I want you to see it."

I could barely hear the words above the booming of my heart.

He bent down, putting his mouth against my ear as he pushed the object to the center of the table. "A necessary tool of the trade."

Heavy metal pliers came into view.

Diavolo! My God, Diavolo! My body was soaked in perspiration; I was shuddering violently.

His free hand tightly grasped my neck before he moved the other from my mouth.

The scream failed to emit against the pressure of his hands.

My body contorted to free itself from his grip. Grabbing, scratch-ing, kicking—desperation took control. His laughter, more beastly than human, filled the room.

~

Vinnie was greeted by the locals when he walked into the neighbor-hood sports tavern. He stopped to chat with a few as he made his way to the far side of the bar.

"Hey, Vinnie. The usual?" The bartender asked.

"Mark, ya know me too well," Vinnie responded with a chuckle, taking the only empty seat at the end of the bar.

"It's done," he quietly said after Mark walked away to make the drink. "If you try to implicate us in any of this, you're coming down too."

Vinnie pulled out some cash as Mark approached with his drink. "Thanks, pal." He handed Mark the cash, took the drink, and walked away.

~

"Mrs. Clark, Mr. Fischer, the senator will see you now."

Ilona and Charlie stood and followed the aide into the inner office.

A middle-aged woman in a black tailored business suit stood. She walked out from behind the large mahogany desk, her hand extended to greet them. "Mrs. Clark, Mr. Fischer, welcome. Your letter of introduction was intriguing. How may I help?"

Ilona pulled a white envelope from her purse and handed it to the senator.

"Ma'am, our mother left this letter before she disappeared," Charlie began. "We think you should read it."

Appendices

Note that appendices A through H present excepts of actual letters written to the author. At times, the spelling, punctuation, and capitalization has been edited for purposes of clarity. Also, dates, state names, and numbers have been spelled out, and ampersands have been replaced by the word *and*.

Appendix A

Excerpts from Letters Sent to the Author by James Bulger

September 12, 2013

Ms. Uhlar,

Beautiful card—thank you. No disrespect, but I don't trust prosecutors, judges, jurors, FBI agents, CIA, complicit media, brutal police, prison goon squads, etc., who follow orders (blindly). Somewhere I read statement you made. I'm not sure the context, but it regarded me. Before I would answer your card, I was searching out to see if anyone had any info on it.

Tonight I heard a radio "hate merchant" upset because, according to him, the US government had to pay a $2,7000,000 bill so far for "Whitey's legal bills," and counting. ... Had they accepted my offer on day one, and since I offered to plead guilty to all crimes I'm accused of [whether I'm] innocent or guilty, I will accept any sentence, no appeal, execution, life sentence—and if execution, will "fast track" it. In return, leniency for Catherine Greig. Their answer was, *"No!"*

[Author's Note: Catherine Greig has no prior criminal record. Had she been legally married to Jim Bulger, it is unlikely she would have been charged. She is now serving almost twelve years in prison for being with Bulger and refusing to answer questions. John Martorano's girlfriend, who was guilty of the same crime plus money laundering and lying to a grand jury, served no time whatsoever. John Martorano served less than twelve years for numerous federal crimes and twenty premeditated cold-blooded murders.]

November 17, 2013

Radio says Florida wants to try me. I'm rested up now and ready for the next trial. I won't go into detail because they copy all my mail for the government. I will say I'm innocent of both of the crimes [the Wheeler and Callahan murders] and can only hope that in a state trial, maybe I can get a fair hearing.

Won't be easy, because all the witnesses of [Assistant U.S. Attorney] Wyshak will be there all rehearsed, rewarded with money and freedom for their testimony. One lies; the other swears to it. A Barboza trial—repeat performance.

I really felt bad for the families. I don't read the papers—doubt they reported how survivors verbally attacked the corruption of the FBI, government, et al. When Wheeler's son started [Assistant U.S. Attorneys] Wyshak and Kelly both put their heads down and shuffled papers. ... Wheeler feels I'm part of his father's death. Hope I can convince them of the truth. Felt bad for his sister in court. The father was quite a guy. USN [United States Navy] invented system that benefits the United States and society. Had so much to live for, and [was] killed because of a scheme fueled with cocaine and to end the investigation of Rico and Callahan for stealing money from World Jai Lai. More to it, but will save things for court. I intend to fight, hoping the state trial will be honest, not like "Boston government trial and their propaganda machine." ... Will write a longer letter next time, Janet. Just wanted to let you know I'm thinking of you and when in Florida will write as long as I'm alive and as long as you care to hear from me. If the government has its way, they hope to silence me … who knows what's ahead. [Author's Note: As of March 1, 2018, the state of Florida has not tried James J. Bulger for the murder of John Callahan, a murder in which he states he was not involved. John Martorano confessed that he committed this cold-blooded murder of his "best friend." His punishment? Less than six months in prison. As of November 7, 2017, the state of Oklahoma has not tried James J. Bulger for the murder of Roger Wheeler, a murder in which he states he was not involved. John Martorano confessed that he committed this calculated cold-blooded murder of an innocent businessman and navy veteran. His punishment? Less than six months in prison.]

November 19, 2013

I was silent in Boston—recognized from first minutes. Jury [was] not in courtroom. Judge from bench discussing with assistant US attorney how important [it is] to streamline things. "Have to consider jurors are going to be inconvenienced, have families, etc., so want to move this through quickly"— just about verbatim. I felt like saying, "Hey, I'm here and have been waiting for two years and don't want to be 'streamlined.'" It was like [Defense Attorney] Carney, [Defense Attorney] Brennan, and I were invisible. In a way we were; we didn't count—and out of the loop.

… any witness that came forth, the government never tried to verify if their "story" was accurate and truthful. … Lindholm was best example—every word, location, dialogue, Russian roulette, sum of money, payments, barges full of marijuana, 135 tons! Two barges across open water from "Colombia" (I think he said), then towed up the Mississippi to rented farm in Illinois. And think he told contradictory story of renting farm in Ohio! Every word he uttered was a lie. Two days he entertained the court, rambling on and on. At that point I wished I could cross-examine him. I felt the guy's insane or on drugs.

He had a history right here in this jail [Plymouth County Correctional Facility]. He was put in cell with younger prisoner who [allegedly] made a bomb that was being removed from a motor vehicle by bomb squad. It exploded, killing police officer. This Lindholm was put in cell, [said he] got young guy to tell him the story (L.'s story) given to court as government witness and convicts bomber. L. rewarded with his freedom. This guy is a professional witness in US court; under oath holds everyone's attention—some spellbound! And all lies. In cross, he admits he is serving five branches of the government.

November 21, 2013

What I'd like to do is have a chance to talk to Wheeler son and daughter ... hate to die and not let them hear the *true story*, and they can decide after if they feel I'm guilty or innocent. Feel I can prove my innocence, and if they could guarantee that I be given a polygraph test by a neutral person for their peace, I'd do it. The son's testimony was electrifying, and I was impressed by the father's achievements and the good life he led and gave much to the country. Killed by Callahan, Rico, and their puppet J.M. [John Martorano], [whom] they dispatched to do what they didn't dare do. And John, to impress J.C. [John Callahan], and also for something to break the routine, enjoyed doing, and also Joe M. [McDonald], a different kind of person, a person who was always up for killing—long story.

If nothing else, I will write out my story and all the particulars and seal to be opened when I die, to be read to son and daughter of R. Wheeler. They both impressed me. They have placed all their faith in the judgment of [Detective] Huff. He has quite a reputation in Tulsa and has interviewed J.M. and Pat Nee, Nee in secret, Nee who had time to speak to J.M. here at this jail. All aboard are S.F. [Steve Flemmi], K.W. [Keven Weeks], Pat Nee, and J.M. A long tale of lies. One lies; next swears to it. Like K.W. said very truthfully, "Yes, I lie. I always lie. I lie to my wife, my girlfriends ..."

November 23, 2013

I'm on the run. They have these people as charged, heavy evidence and witnesses … I'm on the run. They have powerful case against me, yet they free these people, pay J.M. [John Martorano] $20,000 on release, $6,000 for canteen. Ordinarily they would have tried, convicted, and sentenced J.M. to death in Florida and Oklahoma, and life in Boston. Then, if I was captured, they could offer a little break for their testimony and they knew I'd confess to free Catherine. They knew because of [my] profile, plus my age. Conviction for one of those machine guns could be life—twenty-five years for each one. Same for silencers. … They didn't need any witnesses.

But they wanted the "Big Show." They wanted to cover up corruption. They accepted as gospel each and every sentence uttered against me. Guys offered freedom or death, freedom or life in prison, they jumped at it and knew what [Assistant U.S. Attorney] Wyshak wanted to hear. One lies; other swears it's the truth. It was a sham trial.

October 1, 2013

I'm innocent of Wheeler murder … hadn't seen or talked to J.M. [John Martorano] in years. He received hundreds of thousands [of dollars] every year [from us], lived better than me or Steve. He calls Steve and declares he's going to kill Wheeler and we will have $ coming out of World Jai Alai. Steve tells me. I said (word for word), "Is he crazy? Tell him [to] forget that. We send him $—plenty. Wheeler is a legit guy and legit business. Talk him out of that. If he does that, he will never survive. This isn't killing a criminal. Talk him out of it." Steve relays [that] J. [John] said, "Okay, if you're not in, I'm doing it any way." Quiet period passes and he kills Wheeler.

Later we hear J.C. [John Callahan] is going to be called to grand jury in Florida. I tell Steve, "We've got to get J.M. to move. Everyone down there knows who he is." I told Steve, "Have him meet us in New York City." You couldn't talk him out of Wheeler. "Better let me try to talk J. into getting out of Florida—relocate—and if nothing comes of grand jury, he can go back to Florida, and if anything goes wrong, he's off-scene and safe—new life." We meet in New York. I explain all to protect him. He agrees. J.C. is his best friend of twenty-five years—close. We shake hands, [say] goodbye. Figure he will pack, get new ID, and lay low. No. He goes down to Florida—lazy. Figures he'll [kill] Callahan. No grand jury—no problem for J.M.! Me and Steve shocked. This was his best friend. Proved to me how cold J.M. is. That's why we met in New York. He's trapped. Makes deal to give me up, but deal is more to get J.C. [John Connolly] and shut him up (hide corruption). Me—I'm on the run. They may never catch me. I could die. Reason [was] to stop J.C. [John Connolly].

I had nothing to do with Wheeler. Rico was person who ran that show and covered up his stealing $. … J.M. has been out and gone from Massachusetts for years. If I was involved, I'd have been there in Oklahoma and Florida. J.M. was a good friend. I'd have been there if I was with it. I was against and tried to prevent. I'm too smart for such a stupid move, and all the people [I] extorted were in criminal business.

July 28, 2014

After two years and eleven months, have been able to correspond with Catherine. We write each other every day. There's much to write about. … She's in Paws Program and trains a black lab to later be a service dog to handicapped person. She has [a] dog for [a] year and a half … amazing how fast they learn … and great system. Worthwhile project. I used to think of such a project like this back in 1956 when I saw all the wasted man hours in Atlanta Penitentiary. Then I thought of training black labs as seeing-eye dogs.

[Author's Note: The following is the response I received after I'd shared that my father served in the Merchant Marines during World War II. The vital role and courage of the Merchant Marines was not recognized for decades.] Enclosing page about the Merchant Marines in WWII and facts of high casualties in that war—higher than US Navy. When they were torpedoed, they were left to die by navy and other merchant ships. If attempted rescue, that ship would be sunk easily by German subs that hunted in packs. They sank lots of ships. All hands died in the cold water of the North Atlantic. The ships, most, were delivering war material: tanks, trucks, planes, food, gasoline, ammo …

August 22, 2014

Hoping you get away for a deserved vacation and rest from all the intrigue of Boston. I call [it] the "Boston gang." The government and media marriage—a marriage made in hell.

October 14, 2014

Dear Janet,

Forgive me for not writing you and others. Have been in and out of isolation, moving by bus and plane, and on stopovers kept in isolation. Goes with high-profile!

Florida weather hot, humid, and too much rain, which keeps us off the yard. Lightning is an issue and me in a metal wheelchair—not a bad way to go. Mother Nature could turn my wheelchair into quite an electric chair. Across the network, "God got Whitey."

This place physically like last place—"pod system." Solid doors, TV sets hang from ceiling … I prefer the old system of bars on cell doors, no TV. It's silent, but the viewers [in prison] heavily addicted [to TV] scream all through any sports game as if they can affect the outcome of any game. They stand up and yell and scream like a pack of wild animals. I stay in my cell and read and think these fools worship their TV screens. It's their religion, their escape from thinking, introspection, retrospection. Empty words in this environment. TV is the opiate of the majority. Positive or negative? Negative—negates the lesson that may have come when each is forced by degrees of isolation to review, self-examine, and search for the answer to "How did I get here?" TV is their anodyne. Is this all by design? If so, it controls them in here, but one day if released, what is being unleashed? Someone who is years older and has had years of being desensitized to violence by years of TV violence hours every day.

On Alcatraz, on some holidays, like Christmas Eve, the warden would leave the radio on and lights on until midnight or so. Those times the convicts would talk over things and [share] memories of past things, and it would lead to "movies." The most popular with all of us were crime movies. Favorite actors were Jimmy Cagney, John Garfield, George Raft, Alan Lass, Bogart, Lawrence Tierney (played Dillinger), Edward G. Robinson—all of these plus others played gangster roles. They were our heroes! Says something for the power of suggestion and Hollywood portraying the bad guys in such a way [that] they were heroes. We were all bank robbers, rebels, risk takers, etc. Always think of the younger generation—hours of it every day, music conditioning them through their earplugs and violent music, rap, gangster, etc. No wonder the prison population has become huge—ten times what it was when I first got started in prison in 1950s. I see all of the TV, pills, etc., as something to control things and people while they are in here. But that does not help society ...

February 1, 2016

No man can say they had a better wife—sixteen years on the run. I can't remember a hard word or argument. This woman [Catherine

Greig] was there for me and kept me from committing any crimes. The longest period in my life. Made me human; felt emotions I didn't think I possessed. I'd shut down feelings in prison to deal with family separation, loneliness.

Maybe MKULTRA unleashed demons. I don't know, but disappointment and rejection, etc., helped me to quit trying and [turn] back to crime. I felt like ice most of the time.

Met women I cared a lot for but lived for the moment. Marriage was out; always felt the reward over my head and thought my life … could end in a flash. Didn't want anyone to cry over me—wanted them to forget and go on with their lives. Tried never to be serious with those I loved; figured it made it easier to deal with my end. Never expected to live this long. I mention this to explain not getting married—one of my biggest regrets. Plus, there was another woman in my life for years. Had I gotten married to Catherine, I felt, would hurt this good woman—my reason. By the time I would have … it was impossible. We were top fugitives …

February 7, 2016

As a teenager [I] received many beatings by police. No civil rights back then for people in the projects or poor people. One beating in basement of project by out-of-control drunken cop and other one … I felt fear and thought I was going to die. He fractured my arm with club. I put arm up. I was lying on the ground. He beat me across legs with club and said he would put my nose all over my face as he swung at my face, fracturing my arm. Took out his .38 pistol revolver, shoved it in my mouth, and pulled back hammer with his thumb, screaming, "I'll kill you." Could smell the booze. Spit at me. I thought I would be killed. … Other cop screamed, "Stop, you will kill him." … Beating continued. I was dragged out, forced to feet, and kicked and punched as I was forced to move away out of project to [the] boulevard. When in light they left me. I wound up in [Boston] City Hospital, driven there by motorist. I passed out in street. Woke up to cop in [Boston] City Hospital with clipboard. "What happened to you?" Told him, "I was jumped by gang of kids and hit with club." I never would tell anyone, even that cop. Worst beating of my life. I always looked for that cop … never saw him again. Figured the other cop may have told to get him transferred. … I was a young teenager …

May 19, 2016

When arrested, I dealt with it by thinking, *This is for the best. Will make a deal*—a deal the government wins, wins, and wins. I personally asked for nothing for me, just leniency for Catherine. Selfishly thought I'd get executed and escape years of prison; also intended to help J.C. [John Connolly], a fellow South Bostonian from the projects.

I'd seen on TV how all the cooperating killers put him in prison for forty years, and on TV K.W. [Kevin Weeks] saying he delivered envelopes full of cash to him from me. Felt betrayal of anyone who lived up to their end of the bargain was wrong, regardless if he was law or criminal.

June 22, 2016

Received treatment not usually meted out. I was isolated for three and a half years. Special treatment, a form of torture taught by CIA in School of America [Fort Benning, Georgia] to the police and military from Mexico, Central [America], and South America. Special treatment designed to break the will of prisoner by sleep deprivation: degrade and dehumanize. Enter your cell in force at all hours, day and night, "search," tear up bed, check papers, photos, etc. Strip you naked. Examine you like an animal; "degrade and dehumanize" produces hate. In my case [I felt hatred] to [the point of] rage to want to kill, but [I had] no weapons. Three or four in goon squad, [they] spied on regular guards and did dirty work in my case. I'd ask, "Why?" Never saw the likes of it in my fourteen years of prison. To my "Why?" they would reply, "Following orders of the US government." I had four months of this torture of sleep deprivation, five times a day, at all hours. Designed to keep me awake and wear me down! Four months of the strip searches, one hundred and fifty a month—and six hundred times over four months. Never heard of any American prisoner subjected to this. Decent guards told me in history of Plymouth Jail, "No man had this treatment … not even John Read, British Muslim terrorist who tried to blow up airliner over the Atlantic full of passengers." … This treatment was successful in breaking down my health. Stress kills, and this was rough—thought I'd go insane. Watched twenty-four hours a day by guard through open slot in door and glass panel, plus camera in ceiling …

As I see it now, I feel they [the government] bought their [John Martorano's, Kevin Weeks's, Steve Flemmi's, and John Morris's] freedom with money and cooperation, lies, etc., to prove J.C. [John Connolly] and Morris were corrupt and [that] not in any way was the corruption higher up in the US Attorney's Office. How I wish you could have seen on TV the congressional investigation on corruption in Boston. Live on TV—I saw it while on the run in Santa Monica. Any person who saw it and viewed US Attorney Jerimiah O'Sullivan being questioned, "Why wasn't Bulger ever indicted?" and watched him testify and answer questions and knew what you know—have heard from me. Saw in court how my defense regarding J.O'S. [Jerimiah O'Sullivan] was denied! And my attorneys [were] threatened if they dared to say his name … [Assistant U.S. Attorney] Wyshak wanted conviction of J.C. and felt it stopped there and ensured the integrity of the US Attorney's Office. Reason why they were in state of panic. Once Wyshak hollered, "He's [Bulger's attorney] trying to say that name." Feared the name J. O'Sullivan. Did a good job of shutting down all reference.

If I had any money when they rejected my offer to plead guilty in return for freedom for Catherine, when rejected, I'd have offered $ if I had it. There is no more.

November 2, 2016

I gave him [John Connolly] years, more than two years, before my trial to admit the truth about the file he branded me with. He probably felt I'd die by now ... but no way will I die until I set the record straight. I will submit to a lie detector test. ... When I fight back with the truth, he's gone. I have good memory for past. His is an old *tale*. My story will be the truth and I'm forced to name times, names. What happened to names? Names bought from ... once this starts, "Pandora's box." ... I'll fire all guns and win this contest. ...

Cleaning lady testified J.C. [John Connolly] had stack of paychecks not cashed in his desk drawer ... tells he's cash-rich. FBI not paid in cash by the government. But some employers pay employees in police department—state police—and FBI cash, but usually make no record to cover themselves, and expect corrupted to do the same. Usually the known criminal would be the one setting [the] other up or making record or tape of transactions in case of double cross. John has suffered for his violation of the rules, provided [Assistant U.S. Attorney] Wyshak with weapon to destroy him. Now John thinks that weapon is valued and can back up his absurd claim of innocence. ... Please make him aware I will fight this with the cold, brutal truth. I've been silent, hoping he would set the record straight. ... He lies. I'll combat it with the truth and will let the court of public opinion decide ...

March 13, 2017

When I was real young, a friend and I had a pack of cigarettes and [were] trying to smoke in a project hallway. ... Older guy caught us, forced us to smoke and eat cigarettes. Sick. Never smoked all my life.

When young, fourteen or fifteen, had bottle of whiskey, drank it, and got violently sick. ... Never drank whiskey again.

MKULTRA! Horrible. Every week, twenty-four hours locked in big room. ... Frightening for a year; wanted to quit ... would fight to the death to prevent anyone ever putting that needle and syringe full of it [LSD] into me. Had no desire to try anything on the street, and regarding meth—angel dust, put death penalty on anyone who brought it into South Boston to sell or use. Do you remember my attorney on cross-exam asking extortion witnesses who sold marijuana and some cocaine, "Did you sell angel dust or heroin in South Boston?" All answered no. "Why?" [my attorney asked]. Because he would kill you. ...

Regret now that instead of running crack house operations out of town, maybe should have shot them ...

Appendix B

Excerpts of Letters from James Bulger regarding Morris and Connolly

May 4, 2014

Black Mass portrays me as an informant, as Morris got them to print in the [Boston] *Globe* … if I was what John Morris says, then why would I have paid them over half [a] million dollars, all tax-free? No way. Now they force me to say something. … A real uphill battle for me, but I'm not lying down for this.

As I told John Morris when I called him in Quantico, Virginia, "John, you're the one who put that story on me [*Boston Globe* story stating Bulger was an FBI informant]. You tried to get me killed to silence me." He said, "I'm sorry, I made a mistake." … Question for Morris: "John, when you sold information, what did you think was going to happen? Did you care?"—my words to him in that phone call. Told him, "You were my paid FBI informant." [I] cursed him, told him, "When I go down, you go with me—and that request I refused will be revealed." That caused him to have nonfatal heart attack. Line went dead. I sent over $500,000 that way in his and others' direction. Bought information; never sold it nor gave any. … They created file for alibi in case any question of why they were talking to me.

June 17, 2015

Bottom line, Janet, I'm not long for this world, and *if anyone lies about me, I'll fight it with the truth.* I have found out the hard way—"A lie unanswered becomes the truth!" All these years I've kept quiet and would have lied for John Connolly, until I saw and found out about a file in 2011 upon my arrest. ... Will answer all lies with the truth. ...

November 6, 2015

You saw it ... how casual J. Morris was about terrifying a woman and her children as bomb squad removed bomb that Morris manufactured and attached to her husband's (target of Morris) car. When asked by my lawyer, "Did you ever tell the wife not to live in fear as she was, and every time she started her car fearing it would explode in ball of fire and kill her—"

Morris answered no to the question of did he tell her truth, so she wasn't forced to live in terror. Morris answered, "No." He didn't tell her. My lawyer: "Why?" Morris's arrogant answer: "Because I didn't have to." That was the real John Morris talking, who asked me to kill his wife because she was going to take the house and bank account and sue for his pension ...

December 23, 2015

Regarding my mentioning J.C. [John Connolly] to Howie [Winter] and Johnnie [Martorano]—purpose was to discuss my meeting with J.C. and that I felt uncomfortable, feeling feds were dangerous and uncertain. Cops were one thing.

Mentioned meeting on strength of fact as we're both from Southie and he offered to tip me off if [it] would help me to avoid arrest. Considered it may be a trap. Had never heard of any FBI agent who would help any person on far side of the law.

I wanted them to decide is it worth the risk that he's on the level. I wasn't eager for this, but would if they felt the risk worth it? They thought, *Yes. You're too clever to walk into a trap.* And see if you can give him something $ or expensive watch for openers. That was the way it started. I felt uneasy but would not close door on what would be a valuable asset—beyond Boston Police or state police sources of info.

Later I tested John. Took a big chance, but was concerned that he was deceptive—litmus test. Serious incident took place. … I told John C., "I did that." If he was playing double agent, I'd be arrested, and if he was on the job, I'd be in trouble. He wouldn't let that pass by. If he didn't report it, chances were he was on the level with me. Risky, but only way I could test him …

August 1, 2016

Back to Morris. His story he told J.C. [John Connolly] about Brian [Halloran] out on $10,000 bail and making deal to get off the hook, blaming me for Louis L.'s murder. Boston Police drove Brian to spot he said he saw me kill L.L.—shoot him and stab him and put him in trunk of car. Boston Police had Brian in van parked at spot he described where he was and saw all of this. Detective said, "Brian, you're lying—impossible to have seen." Feds accepted his story, [which was] rejected by Boston Police. Feds didn't check. Morris said he heard story and told John [Connolly], and John told me and Brian [and Donovan] gunned down. Morris bought his freedom with this story that helped destroy J.C. Morris and John, very clever, think like criminals; in fact, they were criminals and spent time discussing armed robberies that could be lucrative, and other things. My interest was how the feds operated, built cases—new equipment, hi-tech surveillance, etc. Paid well for any and all information on cases working that involved our gang. Bought info; didn't sell or give info.

August 9, 2016

J.C. [John Connolly] lied. I won't. When you write him, you can tell him I'm angry about his saying the file is true and I will fight to get truth out. Steve said we paid him $242,000. … I feel it's too low— the ring for his wife, his apartment, Christmas, thousands; trips, thousands; holidays, thousands; jewelry, solid gold watch, condo, thousands. Ask J.C. what was the 45 lb. Xmas present wrapped in Christmas paper that K.W. [Kevin Weeks] picked up from him on Thomas Park—*"Very explosive!"* Ask him to explain …

November 11, 2016

J. Morris was the boss of the Organized Crime Squad. J.C. [John Connolly] under him. Morris got one year probation and kept his job. Went on to be in charge of LA FBI office, about as high up as he could possibly rise! And pled guilty to being corrupted by me. For Morris to get a deal, he took immunity and lied about J.C., *his best friend.* I can't pinpoint it, but J.M. publicly stated once that I was not aware of any file on me. He didn't know J.C. had done this! I didn't. I was shocked to find out about this file put together with information J.C. stole from fellow agents' files. My lawyers had retired FBI agents from Boston office at my trial. Lawyer asked these retired agents, "What was the general opinion of J.C. by the agents in the office?" Their shocking answer: *"Dirty."* Told how he would go into secure room and steal info out of their "sensitive files" protected and identities protected.

My attorney read from file J.C. had put together to save himself if things went bad. Ex–FBI agents identified files that they had written reports into—confidential—word for word that J.C. had stolen and put into *his file*, a file he used to enhance his career, get bonuses, and upgraded. Put my name on it ...

Here I am paying both of them, J. Morris and J. Connolly, many thousands, hundreds of thousands, of dollars, gifts, jewelry—all expensive. To me it was money well spent. I knew what the Hunters were up to, and by [my] being generous with steady flow of cash and gifts, they get to point of addiction and I recognized early that $ is more addictive than heroin ...

While I paid Morris and J.C. and many others unnamed by me, they plotted how to survive investigation by Washington about leaks in the office. Witnesses against organized crime people were being killed to silence them. There was a parade of survivors, relations of the dead witnesses. They sued the government for selling the names and information. ... They were killed and the government paid millions to the families.

Steve Flemmi cooperated with the government—stated when the names of the cooperators were sold they wound up dead. Are the people who gave or sold the names going to say they didn't know what was going to happen to them?

Why would the government pay six million to R. Castucci's wife? He was killed. ... Why did government pay three and a half million to McIntyre family, and others? Reason given, because Morris and J.C. sold the names to the killers—pretty serious charge. I've been accused and found guilty of some of these murders.

Won't go on with list of names. Such things are purchased from corrupt officials, and there's no statute of limitation on murder, and people who sold names knew what the sale meant! ...

J.C. tried to brand me (through the file he created) to hide his role as *my* paid FBI informant. ...

J.M.'s attempt to get me killed was because I refused a favor. His wife had caught him in five-year affair with his secretary (new wife). First wife threatened to sue for house, money in the bank, and his pension. John M. asks me, after swearing me to secrecy, "Get rid of my wife. Silence her. Solve the problem for me. Make her disappear and you don't have to ever give me any money."

Told him, "Sorry, John. No way. And forget about it—later your children will hate you. It's out of the question. I'll give you extra money. Buy her off!"

"No, I hate her." Told him, "No way." He got silent and cold. Knew he regretted asking me because of my *no!*

Appendix C

Excerpts of Letters from James Bulger regarding John Martorano

July 5, 2016

"Touch," [the] young black male J.M. [John Martorano] admitted he stabbed "a few times." He had Touch in car with him. He saw him and said, "Hop in." Proceeded to stab him in chest, etc. "A few times." My lawyer said autopsy says thirty-two times, plus throat cut.

August 1, 2016

You heard the testimony of J.M. [John Martorano], killer of twenty, when he told how he murdered the two black teens and their adult friend who was driving them home. Driver thought he was being a friend and giving John a lift to another club.

"Why did you shoot and kill the two teenagers?"

"I thought they were going to kill me!"

"A girl, nineteen years old. A boy, seventeen years old. Driver thought you were a friend? A girl?"

"Thought she was a male. Had a hood on!"

"When you shot her on the right side of her head, the hood was not on her head—no bullet hole."

J. [John] shrugged as if to say, "So what?" ...

John is ex-member of Barboza Gang. He, [along] with Paul Rico, FBI agent killer, and US Attorney [Edward] Harrington, conspired and framed four Italian Americans sentenced to life [with] no parole in Massachusetts State Prison. Joe Barboza for this is freed to walk. He said in court, "Yes, I killed Eddie Deegan, but those four men told me to do it." They were found guilty. Barboza walks free to kill some more. In San Francisco he kills innocent man. Arrested. Calls Boston and tells FBI Rico, "Come here and get me out!" Rico says, "We can't." Joe said, "You, your partner Dennis Condon, and US Attorney Harrington be on the next plane west or I'll recant my confession and tell how we framed four innocent men." On the next plane west was Rico, Condon, and US Attorney Harrington. They talk to judge; charge reduced and Barboza freed. Rico leaks info to underworld of Joe's location, etc.—leads to his being gunned down. Lesson here: Johnnie's ex-member of Barboza Gang and he knows the power he has. ...

Rico in jail for other charge in Florida murder. When asked how he felt after framing the four innocent men, Rico said, "What do you want, tears? They can write a book." Rico was in jail awaiting trial for murder of his boss Roger Wheeler and John Callahan. He died in jail before trial.

During the thirty-two years in prison, the innocent men were kept there by each succeeding US attorney, including US Attorney Jerimiah O'Sullivan.

September 8, 2016

US Attorney Harrington, Paul Rico, killer FBI agent, and prolific killer Joe Barboza—these three conspired and sent four innocent men to prison for life in Massachusetts State Prison. For this Barboza walked free. He said what they wanted: "Yes, I killed Edward Deegan, but those four men told me to do it." He walks free to kill some more. The four innocent men go to prison—two to die there, two for thirty-two years on killer's (confessed) word. Goes like this: "Yes, I killed Roger Wheeler, shot him between the eyes." [John Martorano's] exact words. "Yes, I killed John Callahan. But Whitey told me to do it." Killer walks free after six months for each killing—$20,000 gift from prosecutor, $6,000 for snacks [while in prison]. Sounds weird. Justice?

Appendix D

Excerpts of Letters from James Bulger regarding Steve Flemmi

May 4, 2014

[Steve Flemmi] killed so many people, had to chuckle when he asked for list. "I can't remember them all." What a scene the trial was, John [Martorano] was the "Equal Opportunity Killer," and Stevie the "Forgetful Killer." Kevin [Weeks], "Low Man on the Numbers Game," and all forced by [Assistant U.S. Attorney] Wyshak to have his moment on stage. Wyshak denied my request to plead guilty to all charges if he freed Catherine, who never hurt anyone. No, he wanted her to play a role in his "Big Burlesque Show," and now his puppets are free. What next? He prays they never get caught in new crimes. Only time will tell.

October 10, 2015

[John Connolly] knew Steve's relation with Rico—with the FBI since 1960. Met with him in secret time after time, un[be]known to me. ... If Steve had any idea that I was aware of his other life, he would have killed me to ensure I would not discuss it with others; John M. [Martorano], or J.R. in Mafia. I can't say how I would have dealt with it. Would have been hard for me to believe it.

August 1, 2016

Steve, one of my closest friends, un[be]known to me was giving info on the Mafia since 1960. I met Steve in 1970 or so after he returned from five years on the run in Canada. We became close friends. None of us had any hint that he was working for the feds. Found that out when I was on the run when he confessed to this. Shocked everyone.

He and J.C. [John Connolly] met many times, un[be]known to me, to work on bugging the induction ceremony. Sonny Mercurio was part of that also. Sonny M. was Jerry's (Mafia) liaison man between us and the Boston Mafia. Found out him and Steve helped set up other traps, and all came out at Steve's trial …

August 9, 2016

They [Joe Barboza, US Attorney Ed Harrington, FBI Agent Paul Rico] lied, but so did J.C. [John Connolly] when he created that fraudulent file to cover himself and enhance his career—bonus $. And never did I suspect him. I knew Morris tried to get me killed, [but] not Stevie, because Stevie was working for them since 1960! What an actor. … I was his best friend (I thought) since 1970, for twenty-five years.

January 7, 2017

When asked, "How many people did you kill?" [Steve] answered, "I can't remember all of them. Give me a list." … One killing was Benjamin from D Street projects, in a bar on Dudley Street in Roxbury. They tied Benjamin to a pole, slapped him around. He's cursing. Off-duty cop standing there. Steve reached over, pulled his gun out of holster, and shot Benjamin between the eyes. Cop said, "Damn, the bullet's in his head. Ballistics will tell it came from my gun." Steve solved it—cut Benjamin's head off. Used knife, but had to use hacksaw to cut spinal cord to brain. Wrapped it in newspaper under his arm, walked down Dudley Street—daylight. Buried it in a vacant lot …

Appendix E

Excerpts of Letter from James Bulger regarding Kevin Weeks

October 11, 2013

Kevin Weeks knew I was never an informant. That's his justification for his giving up after two weeks in a cell! Often, he delivered envelopes full of $ to J.C. [John Connolly]. I made it obvious I met with J.C., had K.W. [Kevin Weeks] drop me off [and] then pick me up. He delivered $ many times. Once I told him I was upset because Steve, off to side, answered a question from John C., a question J.C., I felt, had a nerve to ask, and dumb of S. [Steve] to answer. End of meeting, I called K.W. on walkie-talkie to pick us up. I was berating S. for answering J.C. Told him, "We pay; we don't say! We buy; we don't sell!" K.W. heard part of conversation. We dropped S. at his car. I remember saying how sometimes S. reminds me of Ritchie F., same mannerisms, and R.F. "No good." Then I got past it. Never in wildest dreams knew or figured out that Steve since 1960 was giving Paul Rico and Condon information. I never caught on. He, J.C., and Morris met different times. Steve set up bugs, other things, like "secret Mafia induction ceremony" with another informant in the Mafia, Sonny Mercurio. I was never aware of it. Those years S. and I were together night and day. He fooled everyone ...

Appendix F

Excerpts of Letters from James Bulger regarding Jeremiah O'Sullivan

February 5, 2016

At the trial Steve [Flemmi] tells of leaving New York City. Goes to Florida, stays at Rico's [home], and then he goes to Montreal. Hides there for five years. Can see picture [of] J.C. [John Connolly] in New York City seeing Frank Salemme, Steve's partner in bombing of Fitzgerald. [Fitzgerald was] Joe Barboza's lawyer. [Bombing done] on orders of Larry Z., a.k.a. Larry Baione, same person years later recorded on FBI tapes as wanting to hurt Jerry O'Sullivan, the US attorney in Boston, [a] person who has to be concerned. And on tape Larry is saying, "We can get Whitey to kill anyone. He's with us 100 percent," etc., etc. Jerry O'Sullivan reaches me through a friend, an elderly priest from St. Augustine's. We, J.O. and I, meet in Public Garden by Beacon and Charles Streets on a bench. My friend asks me to please help this person, [saying], "He's a good Catholic Irishman. Do what you can for him."

September 8, 2016

Larry B., consigliere of Mafia, ... on illegal wiretap talking: "We aren't going to take it. We've got to fight back and hurt someone." (They know the four Italian Americans innocent, were framed ... that Irish Jeremiah O'Sullivan talked how he left his office and would walk down to North Station to catch commuter train. O'Sullivan feared for his life.) Also heard them say, "We can get Whitey and Steve to kill anyone for us." Jerry said about the same. O'Sullivan knew historically the Mafia would get non-Italian in high-profile hits so there would be no blowback if anything went wrong. Reason O'Sullivan reached out for me via a Catholic priest—Irish—and he asked me to please help the man. "He's a good family man." I explained my meeting with O'Sullivan—long conversation. My best friend, Billy O'Sullivan, was gunned down in front of wife and six children. J.O. mentioned it, etc. He felt I would be asked to kill him. He knew we did work for Mafia boss, etc. I agreed to keep him alive. He died a natural death years later. We parted from the meeting in the Public Garden. I would protect him at all costs. No spy. He had to rely on my judgment and methods. He said, "I feel much better." He was very concerned—now felt much better. Told, "I'm under your umbrella of safety. You're under mine for past and present while I'm in office. Do whatever it takes to keep me vertical." We shook hands. I made contact with Larry and started my campaign to change his mind, and him thinking it was his idea. Long story. I knew Larry for years way back when he was driver for Mafia boss, etc. Long story. Plus, he came to me for "favors" ...

Appendix G

Excerpts of Letters from James Bulger regarding MKULTRA

November 8, 2013

I will write soon and discuss MKULTRA and answer your questions. I will say this, under the drug and insane period they put machine on me, said it was polygraph. I was under power of heavy dose and real bad. Machine operator asked me, "Did you ever kill anyone? Would you kill anyone? Would you *kill?*" *Repeated; never forgot that; and the operator was not a medical person.*

January 16, 2015

I'm forwarding some papers on the MKULTRA project to my attorney. My name is mentioned: "Gangster Bulger volunteered for the project while in prison." Truth is, I was recruited to join a project seeking a cure to schizophrenia conducted by Emory University of Atlanta, Georgia. No mention of CIA. MKULTRA [was] illegal experiment against Nuremberg Code written by nine American jurists! Unabomber reported on same project at Harvard College.

August 7, 2016

My only drug experience was on MKULTRA, and that was a pro-longed nightmare. When shipped to the Rock [Alcatraz], felt one good thing: free of medical experiments. Was on two: MKULTRA, and pertussis research for vaccine—whooping cough, no. 1 killer of infants. Project painful—injected with raw whooping cough germs. Felt like molten lava! But vaccine has solved whooping cough problem in infants.

I'm for medical experimentation in prisons. But volunteer has to be given facts, not lied to, as I was by CIA. … [MKULTRA] project damaged all of us in different ways. Two men, Benoit and Jennings, went stark raving mad—failed Babinski test. Put in cell and vanished! We never could find out where they were. Strange! Still a mystery.

CIA used us, then walked away [with] no effort to help us. I didn't know, and on the Rock at times felt I was going insane—auditory and visual hallucinations and violent nightmares. Still have them. Always slept with lights on. Helps when I was up about every hour from nightmares since 1957. Had to sleep alone. Even my little poodles would jump out of the bed and run into Catherine's room when I'd be having nightmares—every-night routine.

November 18, 2016

Don't know if I ever gave you these pages on MKULTRA. … This project was a life changer for me. Still have nightmares and never slept past two hours. It's wake up every hour or so [from] nightmare, lay awake, doze off, then bad dreams, awake, and doze—

Neglected to mention, but Dr. Carl Pfeiffer of Emory University, front man for CIA, asked me to drink a fluid every a.m. for long time—months. Told me this was a psychic energizer he perfected and wanted me to write reports on any effects. Told me, "You're my best subject. Faithfully write your weekly report." On the twenty-four-hour lockdown in big room we were locked into—"eight volunteers." Lied to, appealed to our sense of "doing something worthwhile for society." Some believed (me for one), and others in for the "ride and good time." Three days off your sentence for each month. ... When on MKULTRA, injected with massive dosages of LSD and other hallucinogenic drugs—many LSD25, most powerful. Drove two men into psychotic state. Failed "Babinski test." Two, Jennings and Benoit, taken out, one foaming at the mouth, growling like a wild animal; other stiffened out, had to pry fingers loose. Stiff; could be picked up under head and heels and moved!

Appendix H

Excerpt from Letter Sent to the Author by John Connolly

March 18, 2015

Janet, God willing, this Florida ordeal will end when the courts concede my conviction is unlawful and I was wrongfully convicted. I'm hoping that will be soon.

Be secure in the fact that when I am set free, *the whole, unvarnished truth will come out._*[Author's Note: Connolly was charged with "second-degree murder with a firearm" of John Callahan. At the time this murder was committed in Florida—confessed to by John Martorano—Connolly was serving as an FBI agent in Boston. Yes, he did have a firearm on his person: the gun assigned to him by the FBI. The same assistant US attorney who tried both John Connolly (2002) and James Bulger (2013) in Boston was involved in the bogus and reprehensible trial (this author's strong belief) in Florida of Connolly. James Bulger has stated numerous times that neither he nor Connolly had any part in the murder of John Callahan. Although Connolly was fifteen hundred miles away at the time of this murder, it seems *God was not willing* to end his ordeal. The courts in Florida denied his release. Connolly has now served twenty years for this outrageous conviction (again, this author's strong belief). In July of 2017,

Florida's parole commission ruled, during a brief hearing, that John Connolly's parole will not be considered until the year 2039, at which time Connolly will be ninety-eight years old. Though this author does not believe that Connolly was involved in any way in this particular murder, this author does believe that Connolly is guilty of corruption while serving in the FBI. Why? I hope the reader asks, is it seemingly so vital to keep this man in prison? Perhaps he can reveal things about the DOJ's involvement in the top-echelon informant program and so much more that the citizens of the United States should be made aware of. Again, let this author remind the reader that John Martorano confessed to have calculatedly and cold-bloodedly murdered his "best friend" John Callahan, yet the Boston US Attorney's Office and the federal court required that he serve less than six months for this crime.

Why is it that the combined crimes (including fifty murders and counting) of Flemmi, Martorano, Weeks, Morris, and more have been considered less reprehensible than the crimes of Bulger and Connolly? And what if Bulger had never been found? Martorano, Weeks, and Morris were gifted their freedom long before Bulger's capture. Pat Nee has never been indicted for the murders.]

Appendix I

Letter to Presiding Judge

The following letter was sent to the presiding judge of the *USA vs. James J. Bulger* trial in response to an Associated Press article stating that the prosecution had requested that this judge allow impact statements before sentencing from family members of murder victims, crimes of which James Bulger had been acquitted by the jury. Even though the author received verification from the US Postal Service that the following letter was received by the court, the letter, to this author's knowledge, was never put on the court docket or made public.

The Honorable Denise J. Casper
c/o Timothy Maynard, Docket Clerk
John Joseph Moakley United States Courthouse
One Courthouse Way, Suite 2300
Boston, MA 02210

Janet Uhlar and [redacted]
c/o 64 Dory Lane
Eastham, MA 02642

October 15, 2013

Re: *United States vs. James J. Bulger*

Dear Honorable Denise J. Casper:

We, Janet Uhlar and [redacted], served on the jury of the above-named trial. It has come to our attention that the prosecutors in this case have requested that the court allow family members of eight murder victims, which the jury determined were not proven (seven), or could not come to a decision on (one), to offer impact statements at Mr. Bulger's sentencing. The prosecution's reason for this surprising request, as reported in an Associated Press article on Saturday, October 12, 2013, is that "Bulger was convicted of two racketeering charges that required the jury to find that he was part of a criminal enterprise responsible for the murders of all victims, regardless of whether he was the actual killer."

This was not the understanding of the jury. Our deliberations on these specific matters included questions as to whether Mr. Bulger and the criminal enterprise with which he was associated had any part whatsoever in these particular crimes. We, Janet Uhlar and [redacted], are concerned the prosecution is seeking a unilateral approach to the court and introducing evidence at sentencing contrary to the facts we found to be true or not true in support of our verdict.

As impartial jurors, we fulfilled our duty as citizens of the United States of America to weigh the evidence admitted during the trial to find the true facts with respect to the charges. We the jury concluded, through an arduous deliberative process, that those charges were not established and no sentence should follow on them.

The prosecution's proffer to the court of victim statements by family members relating to charges that were not proven makes a mockery of the jury's painstaking deliberation and resulting verdict. If these proffered victim statements are not given weight by the court for sentencing, then they only serve to goad the press to make sport of our verdict. A jury verdict wrought through such a sacrifice deserves more.

We, Janet Uhlar and [redacted], object to the prosecution's proposal, as it appears to be a waste of our time. It diminishes the sanctity of this jury's service and sacrifice, and our deliberations and attention to our oath.

Respectfully,

Janet Uhlar and [redacted]

Appendix J

Response to the Book and Movie *Black Mass*

Black Mass, the best-selling book by *Globe* reporters Dick Lehr and Gerard O'Neill, became a movie produced by Warner Brothers. The *Black Mass* story has been heavily marketed as nonfiction and accepted as the "gospel truth," virtually without question. As a juror who sat through ten grueling weeks of testimony in the trial of James "Whitey" Bulger, the trial evidence raised substantial questions, in my opinion, about the accuracy of the *Black Mass* story. The trial proved two points beyond my personal doubt. There appeared from evidence an epic and systemic failure in crime-fighting strategy by federal law enforcement for decades, and that failure directly caused many people and their families to suffer. Their suffering was exponentially compounded by the apparent stonewalling of the Department of Justice (DOJ) as it attempted to contain the damage to its reputation and avoid paying monetary damages. Unfortunately, *Black Mass* represents only the DOJ's damage-control story. It does nothing to bring to the attention of movie viewers the government's systemic failures, such as the top-echelon informant program. It gives no deference or respect to the victims who have been shamefully revictimized by the government's process. It appears as a narrow, seemingly myopic spin that blames all law enforcement misconduct that came to light on one FBI agent and all criminality and mayhem on Bulger. In that regard, *Black Mass* is very effective. Few in the media or government have apparently broken their focus away from Connolly and Bulger to investigate the prevalence of such evidence suggesting institutionalized corruption throughout the country; those who have attempted haven't gotten very far. Unfortunately, the *Black Mass* story is more of a defense of federal law enforcement than an accurate portrayal of historical events. The evidence at trial showed a very different story.

The apparent outcome, from my perspective, of the reason why *Black Mass* appears as skewed to favor federal law enforcement is that the authors were likely satisfied with their government sources for much of their story as provided to them by the feds. Specifically, the authors relied heavily on information provided directly to them by retired FBI supervisor John Morris. The trial evidence established, at least for me, that Morris was the least credible person in this entire saga. He was repeatedly caught lying throughout his career to everyone, colleagues, supervisors, judges, and juries. There was evidence to persuade me, and most any fair and open-minded person, that John Morris is as corrupt as corrupt can be: accessory to two murders, complicit in others, accepting cash bribes and gifts from at least three individuals involved in organized crime. Despite his history of credibility, Morris was the prosecution's centerpiece in the trial of Bulger. Not surprisingly, Morris is seemingly also the centerpiece in *Black Mass*. Perhaps it is Morris's questionable virtue to spin the truth in *a way that can sell* that the feds and the *Black Mass* authors found so appealing. Morris admitted at trial that he illegally leaked secret information to "his friend" Gerard O'Neill for many years. He willingly yielded to others who suggested he use his position to obtain confidential documents for them. One of these instances appears insidious and unscrupulous in the extreme. After Morris had repeatedly taken bribes and been totally compromised by Bulger, he hatched a plan to have Bulger murdered. Morris went to *Boston Globe* reporters and helped them to publish a news report claiming that Bulger was an informant against the Mafia and other organized crime competitors so that the Boston Mafia would seek its vengeance and do the dirty work for him. The presiding judge later found that Morris employed the willing *Boston Globe* reporters/authors to help him destroy Bulger. (Note that Steve Flemmi was not a target here, because Flemmi had, in fact, been an informant for the FBI since 1960. It was Flemmi who had knowledge of Mafia dealings and shared it with the FBI.)

The *Globe* reporters also used Morris. They convinced him to open an FBI investigation into William Bulger, then an elected official, over the 75 State Street project. The FBI and US attorneys investigated the case but found no evidence of a crime "on the merits," so the investigation was closed. O'Neill then convinced Morris to reopen the FBI investigation to interview William Bulger and then illegally "leak" the interview process reports to his friends at the *Globe* for a smear. Morris did leak the information to the *Globe* reporters/authors, but the investigations still found that there was no evidence of a crime. Assistant US Attorney Ralph Gants also interviewed William Bulger and concluded there was no crime.

Strange thing is, Morris never spent a day in jail. In fact, he was rewarded by the DOJ for his conduct. When asked by his DOJ superiors if he leaked the above-mentioned information to the authors, Morris at first perjured himself and denied the report. After he was caught in the false statement, he was lightly disciplined by the DOJ for "lack of candor." Soon after that, he was rewarded with a promotion to lead the FBI's Los Angeles office, and ultimately promoted to train new FBI agents at Quantico. He is retired now and living comfortably on his inflated pension. Stranger thing: Morris—there is evidence that I believe is credible—played a leading role in helping the assistant US attorneys in Boston make certain that his subordinate John Connolly go to jail. Why? Some might say because John Morris was a link in the chain of knowledge to his DOJ superiors in Washington and his incriminating information needed protection. If Connolly, in my opinion a lesser player, was neutralized through conviction and sentencing, he was no longer a threat. The DOJ usually "rolls up" criminal organizations by indicting the lower guys and immunizing them as they seek information and cooperation to go up to get the leaders. When it came to investigating their own organization, it seems the DOJ did the opposite. Notably they immunized Morris and rolled down to Connolly. It seems that the authors of *Black Mass* were content in their storytelling for profit to fail to investigate up the DOJ chain or look at any other FBI offices in the country for facts on the whole story.

Other testimony on the outcome of Connolly's conviction: John Martorano, the man who murdered *at least* twenty people, and injured many more, testified against Connolly. His sentence? Less than six months for each murder, and awarded $20,000 upon his release from prison. My understanding is that the DOJ even returned his illegal assets from a life of violent crime. He never faced trial in Florida, though he was the one who committed the murder Connolly was charged with and then sentenced. More testimony, from similarly questionable witnesses, presents similar stories. Each one, though known to be guilty of horrendous crimes, received the equivalent of a slap on the wrist from the same assistant US attorneys for "telling the truth." Really?

Although the Boston FBI agents clearly played a role in corruption and cover-up of Boston's organized crime, perhaps more attention needs now to be focused on the US Attorney's Office. The US Attorney's Office's strategy successfully avoided all blame by shifting focus to the FBI and its scapegoat John Connolly. This cover-up appears to go back at least fifty years to Joe "the Animal" Barboza, and likely continues today with Mark Rosetti. It's not a local Boston matter either. Federal law enforcement informants are being protected from prosecution routinely, and all across the country while they commit crimes without consequences. Isn't it time to look into the practices of the Department of Justice as a whole, for the security of our citizens and the future of our children? It's time to get answers. The United States has a free press for this very reason. Reporters are protected so they can carry out their solemn constitutional duty to protect the citizens from the government by criticizing the government, investigating it, and asking difficult questions. The authors of *Black Mass*, in my opinion, have ignored their constitutional privilege by hopping into bed with corrupt law enforcement officials and then selling us, for their own profit, bogus stories. Glorifying the DOJ cover-up in a movie only rewards the wicked by concealing the whole truth. What I witnessed as a juror in the trial of James "Whitey" Bulger, and the evidence I see in researching that trial and those of John Connolly, is not a black mass. It is testimony to a massive and systemic institutional law enforcement failure; it is racketeering with racketeers with hideous consequences. Shame on those who avoid their duty in order to get rich from others' suffering. That's lower than John Morris.

Janet Uhlar
May 31, 2014

Suggested Reading

"American Nuclear Guinea Pigs: Three Decades of Radiation Experiments on U.S. Citizens," report prepared by the staff of Massachusetts Representative Edward J. Markey, Chairman of the Subcommittee on Energy Conservation and Power of the Committee on Energy and Commerce, U.S. House of Representatives (Washington: U.S. Government Printing Office, November 1986).

George Andrews, *MKULTRA: The CIA's Top Secret Program in Human Experimentation & Behavior Modification* (Winston-Salem: Healthnet Press, 2001). This book includes "Project MKULTRA, the CIA's Program of Research in Behavioral Modification," Wednesday, August 3, 1977, U.S. Senate Select Committee on Intelligence and Subcommittee on Health and Scientific Research of the Committee on Human Resources, Washington, DC.

"The FBI'S Controversial Handling of Organized Crime Investigations in Boston: The Case of Joseph Salvati," hearing before the Committee on Government Reform, House of Representatives, 107th Congress, First Session, May 3, 2001, serial no. 107-25, Washington, DC.

Stephen Kinzer, *The Brothers: John Foster Dulles, Allen Dulles, and Their Secret World War* (New York: Times Books, 2013).

Daniel Marans and Ryan Grim, "This Federal Prosecutor Is Building a Career Indicting the Good Guys: But Is US Attorney Carmen Ortiz the One Gone Wrong?" *Huffington Post* (July 5, 2016).

John Marks, *The Search for the "Manchurian Candidate": The CIA and Mind Control: The Secret History of the Behavioral Sciences* (New York: W.W. Norton & Company, August 17, 1991).

Sidney Powell, *Licensed to Lie: Exposing Corruption in the Department of Justice* (Dallas: Brown Books Publishing, 2014).

Harvey A. Silverglate, *Three Felonies a Day: How the Feds Target the Innocent* (New York: Encounter Books, 2011).

Adrian Walker, "Deal with Killer Dishonors Dead," *Boston Globe* (September 9, 1999).

CPSIA information can be obtained
at www.ICGtesting.com
Printed in the USA
LVOW11*1614120418
573252LV00006B/66/P